A PRICE TO BE PAID

Dan Kesler spotted the note immediately, tucked beneath the windshield wiper on the driver's side. Lost in thought, he wandered back toward the house, note in his hand.

"What is it, Dani?" Aya asked.

He handed the note to her.

FORGET NAHALAT SHIM'ON. NO WARNING NEXT TIME.

She searched his eyes for an explanation. "Nahalat Shim'on?"

"It's where they found the tomb."

She froze. "Dani, I tell you, I don't like it. Where did this come from? The colonel?"

"Not him personally. He'd have got someone else to do it. It's standard technique."

She caught his arm. "Dani, you will be careful, won't you? Don't underestimate the authorities—not on something like this."

He gave a hollow laugh.

She was suddenly serious. "Dani, I know that if it weren't for me you wouldn't be a freelancer now. You'd be a big-shot bureau chief somewhere. I know what you gave up for me and Beni, and I know what it cost you. If you were now paying another price, I would never forgive myself."

He kissed her lightly on the forehead. "I know why I love you," he said, and left.

As he closed the iron gate behind him, he wondered how much more he should have told her when he had gone freelance, about the other price he had paid. It was too late now.

On the Third Day

Michael Delahaye

BANTAM BOOKS
TORONTO · NEW YORK · LONDON · SYDNEY · AUCKLAND

For Rosemary

*This low-priced Bantam Book
has been completely reset in a type face
designed for easy reading, and was printed
from new plates. It contains the complete
text of the original hard-cover edition.*
NOT ONE WORD HAS BEEN OMITTED.

ON THE THIRD DAY

*A Bantam Book / published by arrangement with
Macmillan Publishing Company*

PRINTING HISTORY
Macmillan edition published July 1984
Bantam edition / October 1986

*Bantam Books are published by Bantam Books, Inc. Its trademark,
consisting of the words "Bantam Books" and the portrayal of a
rooster, is Registered in U.S. Patent and Trademark Office and in
other countries. Marca Registrada. Bantam Books, Inc., 666 Fifth
Avenue, New York, New York 10103.*

PRINTED IN THE UNITED STATES OF AMERICA

KR   0 9 8 7 6 5 4 3 2 1

It is 1989 and Israel faces the most serious threat to its survival since the creation of the State. Not a war but an ultimatum from its staunchest ally: Negotiate the surrender of the Arab lands taken in 1967 or face the consequences.

But the Americans have not reckoned on the Israelis' ability to respond in kind and, when a first-century tomb is discovered in East Jerusalem, it is the Roman Catholic Church and the nations of the West who have to face the consequences.

"If Christ has not been raised, then our preaching is in vain and your faith is in vain." St. Paul, I Corinthians

Burial Vault of a Nazirite

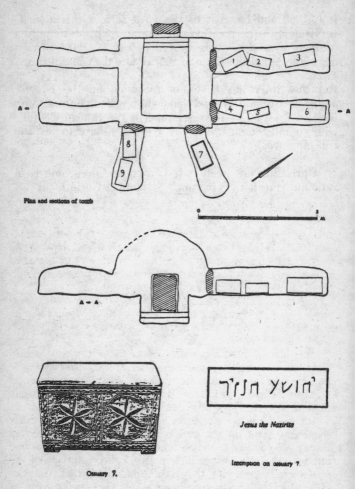

Plan and sections of tomb

A — A

Ossuary 7.

יהושע הנזיר'

Jesus the Nazirite

Inscription on ossuary 7.

ANTHROPOLOGICAL RÉSUMÉ

Male (30–35 years old). Long-headed (cranial index 73). Fair but robust facial skeleton. All teeth present; no caries; no attrition. Death caused by crucifixion. *Stature*: 162–170 cm.

Prologue

THE shaft of natural light through the hole in the roof had lost its midday brilliance and was now supplemented by a naked bulb run off the building workers' generator above.

The two men stood in the well of the tomb, the pink and white Jerusalem stone a foot above their heads. Ranged around them at waist level were half a dozen small tunnels leading off the central chamber. The pair on the right were empty and, although cut, had apparently never been used. Those on the left had been sealed by stone slabs which now lay on one of the broad shelves of rock where the bodies would have been laid out to decompose at the time of interment. The ossuaries—the stone caskets into which the bones would have been packed for eternal storage about a year later—had been removed from the tunnels during the morning and lined up on the opposite shelf.

The senior of the two regarded the slab blocking the third tunnel and, with the gesture more of a surgeon than an archaeologist, held out his hand without turning. An implement resembling a tire iron was placed in it.

The slab tumbled forward, was caught, and was carefully transferred to the shelf alongside. The archaeologist swapped the tire iron for the lamp and directed it into the tunnel.

"Only the one, by the look of it," he remarked, indicating to his colleague to hold the light.

Attempting to peer over his superior's shoulder, the other shone the light on the end of the ossuary. There was an inscription crudely scratched into the smooth white limestone but his view was obscured. What little he could see of the square-character script, though, suggested a hybrid Aramaic-Hebrew of the sort used during the first century.

The lamp started to feel heavy.

"Anything interesting?" he asked at length.

The other turned and made a clumsy attempt to block the tunnel with his body.

"Just more of the same," he replied. But his expression betrayed him.

REVELATIONS

IT HAD BEEN raining throughout the night and showed no signs of letting up, although "rain" was a barely adequate term for the great gusts of smoky moisture that in early spring wrap themselves in cotton-candy wreaths around Jerusalem's tallest buildings. Seventeen years earlier, colleagues back in the Baltimore head office had laughed when Dan Kesler had announced that he was taking an umbrella to Israel and, to show he was serious, had screwed the money out of the expenses department. But Kesler had been proved correct, and within weeks of his taking up his appointment as the *Post*'s Jerusalem correspondent it had become the in-joke for him to sign off every cable with a weather update.

By the time he reached the Government Press Office in the Beit Agron, his trousers were soaked to the knees and the elevator that took him up to the 9:00 AM press conference on the second floor was awash with the drippings of those more conscientious colleagues who had arrived on time.

It was a full house. After scanning the packed rows, Kesler eased himself into a seat at the back next to the *Newsweek* correspondent.

"Anything I've missed?" he whispered, extracting a pen and pad.

"Not much. Just a few more flying Palestinians."

"Uh?"

"West Bank Arabs wounded by our Israeli friends firing into the air."

Kesler grunted and, resting a foot on the chair in front of him, settled back to listen to the Israel Defense Forces' lieutenant colonel go through the usual spokesmanspeak. As always, the vocabulary was more revealing than the content, "Judea and Samaria" totally supplanting "the so-called West Bank" and indicating to some at least a calculated defiance in

3

the face of the American President's demands for Arab autonomy.

A spokesman from the Foreign Ministry took the IDF man's place at the lectern to the accompaniment of seventy-odd reporters' notepads turning in unison. Mechanically, Kesler scribbled on the top line, *Israeli fears of Camp David*, hoping, as was his regular delusion, that the act of inscribing the title of a commissioned article might help it become fact. Occasionally it worked; more often it ended up the center-piece for an elaborate doodle extending over half the page. He looked around. How many other poor bastards, he wondered, had been saddled with the same five-hundred-word scene-setter? At least in the days when he had been on the *Baltimore Post's* payroll he had been able to kill a story at the source before some overzealous duty editor had wished it into existence; nobody ever questioned the judgement of a staff correspondent. But as a freelance it was different. You were obliged to deliver what your commissioning editors wanted, and if that was only to fill a hole in their papers or give their readers the impression they had their own man on the spot, then that was what you gave them. Or you starved. Hence the collection of pseudonyms. Whatever the ethics of writing essentially the same article for different papers under different bylines, you weren't telling lies in the actual reporting and at the end of the day everybody was happy. More to the point, there were two—sometimes three—paychecks. Dog lick dog.

In obsessive detail the Foreign Ministry spokesman was working through a description of the Israeli Prime Minister's flight, landing, and formal greeting by the President of the United States—a scene which he knew full well tens of millions of American newspaper readers would already have seen for themselves live on their television screens. A woman reporter interrupted at one point to ask if the hug accorded the Israeli Prime Minister had not been markedly shorter than those given the Arab leaders who had arrived earlier. The spokesman's only response was a deadpan apology for not having run his stopwatch. As the laughter died, the *Newsweek* man next to Kesler made a valiant attempt to elicit the Israelis' "negotiating stance" by enumerating every possible concession ever floated in the hope that just one might get a flicker of reaction. The ploy failed. The spokesman smiled wearily, confirming what everyone in the room already suspected—that he had no more idea how his country was going to get itself off the hook than did they or, for that matter, probably Prime Minister Avraham Rubinger himself.

There were no more questions and the spokesman concluded the conference with the politely sardonic observation that he trusted he had, as usual, given satisfaction. At the barrage of sarcastic rejoinders, he smiled and left.

Ahead of the crowd, Kesler made for a table in the far corner of the bar on the floor below and within twenty minutes had knocked off a 550-word piece that bristled with references to "usually reliable sources" and "highly-placed government contacts" but which in all honesty amounted to nothing more than speculation—and hardly "informed" at that. He read it through, added a couple of journalistic disclaimers—an "arguably" here, an "allegedly" there—and vowed not for the first time that he would give serious thought to a change of profession before it was too late.

He turned his attention to the view through the window and immediately felt better. The rain had stopped and, although the top floors of the Plaza on the far side of Independence Garden were still cocooned in mist, somewhere up above the sun was trying to break through. By the time he had dropped off his humble offering at the telex office in Jaffa Road and got back to the house in Bnei Brit, the sky would be blue, the veranda dry, and the air heavy with the smell of lemon blossom and percolating coffee. Camp David would have to start without him.

★

Beni greeted him with the *really* important news of the day—the new school he had been to see. "Fantastic," he declared unreservedly. There had been lots of projects and in the half hour he had spent in the class he had made three new friends among the other eight-year-olds.

Aya stood in the doorway smiling. It was a smile that, within weeks of his arrival in Israel, Kesler had come to recognize on the face of many an Israeli mother as she watched an infant son laugh, chat, or play—a smile that always had a trace of sadness in it, informed by the realization that the Middle East's periodic bouts of bloodletting denied any guarantee of survival beyond seventeen, the age of conscription.

"I don't think we need have any worries about his settling in," she said slipping her arm through Kesler's. "As nice a bunch of middle-class Jewish kids as you'll find anywhere outside New York." She paused and with an impish grin added, "I dare say that, given a week or two, he could slip into Brooklyn unnoticed."

"With *his* Yiddish?." rejoined Kesler. "Not a hope!"

For several seconds they said nothing but looked at each other in recognition of old battles and old wounds, long healed. Had it not been for Aya and the irresistible combination of black hair, olive skin, and ludicrously incongruous dark blue eyes—the product of a Sephardi grandmother and Danish grandfather—Kesler would have returned to the States fifteen years earlier at the end of his term as the *Post*'s "man in Jerusalem." As a place, Israel had held few attractions for him and, despite a German Jewish immigrant grandfather in his own genealogy, which by Hitler's definition at least made him a Jew, he had felt no ideological or emotional commitment to the country. The emotional commitment, when it had come, had been of a different order. He had been doing a story about the plight of amputee victims of the Yom Kippur War and the attempts being made to rehabilitate them. Within an hour of setting eyes on the petite physiotherapist in the special unit at Tel Hashomer Hospital he had sensed that this was the woman he was going to marry. In the months of courtship that followed he had also sensed, although it was never articulated, that a condition of their marriage would be his preparedness to make a permanent home in Israel. Within a year of the wedding, therefore, he had had no choice but to resign his staff post and go freelance, it being against company policy to let correspondents stay indefinitely in one place. In the process—although he had never told Aya—he had turned down the offer of becoming the *Post*'s Far East bureau chief, working out of Hong Kong.

At the time, he had rationalized the decision by arguing that the absence of a staff meal ticket would keep him on his toes. But, for years after, he had continued to nurture the hope that as soon as Beni reached school age they might all move to the States—to Baltimore or Boston perhaps. With that in mind, he had retained contact with his former employers and made a point of looking up his old editor on his occasional trips back to see his parents. Eventually, on the pretext of showing Beni to his grandparents, he had persuaded Aya to agree to a family holiday in the States. It had been a disaster. She had seen through the stratagem within hours of arrival and had reacted with an emotional outburst that Kesler would never forget. How, she had yelled resentfully, could he possibly have imagined that she could ever become one of those *yordim* who took the soft option and cleared their consciences with a twice-yearly donation to the United Jewish Appeal? And Beni, what about Beni? Was he to grow up in America, while the country of his birth—the land for which generations of his ancestors had yearned, fought, and died—faded into a picturesque folk memory? Never! Israel was his birthright. Thwarted and angry, Kesler had retorted in kind. What about *his* birthright, *his* family, *his* land? But even as he had uttered the words, he had known they were hollow. Since when had he ever regarded America as home?—he who had spent the best part of his working life abroad; he who had always been the first to deride apple-pie patriotism; he who, despite his Waspish pretensions, had more than once declared himself more in tune with Judaism than Christianity.

After that there had been no more argument. Just a state of stony, palpable nonargument that had gone on for weeks. Life back in Israel had continued, but only as a mechanical interaction between physical objects devoid of emotion, spontaneity, or humor.

Mercifully, a single rekindling spark of humor somehow survived. One morning a letter had appeared in the *Jerusalem Post* from a Joseph Appelbaum in Scarsdale, New York, lamenting the loss of real friendship, honesty, and intellectual vigor that the writer claimed to have found only in Israel. Tossing the paper across the breakfast table, Aya had remarked, "I know penance is a Christian virtue, but did you have to resort to one of your journalistic aliases?" They had laughed, embraced, and, in the bedroom upstairs with the long windows open onto the veranda, made love with an intensity of which neither knew the other capable.

In tacit acknowledgement of the unalloyed happiness of the last three years, Kesler rested his hands lightly on his wife's hips and kissed her on the mouth. Nuzzling into her hair, he asked, "Anyone call?"

"Not in the twenty minutes or so since we've been back from the school, but I haven't checked upstairs."

Upstairs in his office, Kesler found the red light glowing on the telephone answering machine. He ran the tape back, wondering who it could be at this time of the morning. America, by his calculation, would be asleep for at least another hour.

The voice was that of Zvi Matzliah, a reporter on the Jewish daily, *Ha'aretz*. He had to see Kesler on a matter of some urgency at the Hilton that evening. He would meet him in the lobby at eight and Kesler wasn't to bother about confirming it as he, Matzliah, would be out all day on a story up north. Just be there.

"*Jawohl, mein Herr!*" muttered Kesler with a click of the heels, amused by the Israeli's peremptory tone but less so by his choice of venue. Of all the places to choose, why the Hilton?

★

Joe McCrae sat on the flagstoned terrace at the back of Aspen Lodge, nursing a glass of freshly squeezed orange juice in the early morning sunshine. He was alone, his expression a study in grim introspection—what his aides referred to as his Mount Rushmore pose. In his left hand were a dozen pages of stapled typescript.

A young Navy guard wearing a Camp David parka and deck cap appeared fleetingly through the undergrowth fifty yards away beyond the figure-eight swimming pool and one-hole golf course, and—suddenly mindful of the order to maintain a patrol unobtrusive to the point of invisibility—darted back out of sight like a startled fawn. If McCrae saw the incident, he didn't register it, although normally he would have permitted himself at least a smile. Surprising the guards was one of the harmless pleasures of Camp David, and there were any number of young enlisted men who could tell incredulous parents of the latenight chats they had had in the Catoctin Woods with the President of the United States.

A door opened behind the President to reveal the lanky, shambling form of Carl Romford, McCrae's Secretary of State. Dispensing with any greetings, Romford waved his own copy of the document and remarked simply, "I suppose it was to be expected."

"Like death and old age are to be expected, you mean?" grunted the President.

Romford drew up one of the wicker chairs.

"Joe, it's just tactics—an opening gambit, nothing more. We forget that not losing face is as important to the Israelis as to the Arabs. Remember too that Rubinger is going to have to sell a pretty unpalatable package to his electorate when he gets back. In the end we'll probably have to bring out the big guns, but in the meantime—for the opening session at least—we should allow him a little posturing."

"A little posturing!" retorted McCrae. "Is that what you call this? We ask for a position paper and we get a rehash of the Zionist Charter that reads like the Ten fucking Commandments!" Thumbing wetly through the pages, he read aloud, "No curtailment of Jewish settlement rights . . . *No* restriction on movement of the Israeli military . . . *No* Palestinian power of legislation . . . *No* outside Arab military personnel or advisers . . . Jesus, Carl, we're meant to be discussing an autonomous Arab entity on the West Bank and Gaza; Rubinger and his people make it sound more like . . . like a fucking game reserve! Well, I tell you, Carl, I am personally going to get great satisfaction in screwing that son of a Yiddish bitch and all his congressional friends in the 'Kosher Nostra.' "

Romford couldn't suppress a smile. One thing Joe McCrae could never be accused of was discrimination; he hated all Jews equally. Not that he didn't have reason. The Jewish lobby in Congress had done its damnedest to prevent his election after he had publicly pledged that under a McCrae presidency America's foreign policy would be neither manipulated nor undermined by "externally directed special interest groups." McCrae wasn't the first to say it, of course, but he was the first presidential candidate to have the courage to say it across the ballot box—and win. The result, however, was the deepest low in Israeli-U.S. relations since Yitzhak Rabin had declined newly elected President Jimmy Carter's invitation to "just go up and say goodnight to Amy."

"I tell you, Carl," McCrae was declaring, "Rubinger is going to give, and if he tries to play the lobby card, I'll make every one of those Jewish bastards in Congress take the oath of allegiance and declare publicly where their loyalties lie— here or there. Because, make no mistake, that's what it comes down to. If they're for Israel on this, they're against America—and they can make their reservations with El Al right now. And you know what, Carl? There won't be a loyal American who won't be at the airport to see them off!"

The Secretary of State pulled his ear in embarrassment. He could only pray that by getting the venom out of his system now, the President might display more diplomacy later when it really mattered.

"And that'll be only the beginning, Carl," continued McCrae. "With Congress on our side, we'll hit Rubinger with a list of *No*'s he never imagined: *No* military hardware; *no* grants; *no* loans; *no* tax concessions on Jewish Appeal donations; *no* favored nation status. Jesus, Carl, there's not a country in the world that gets more from us and gives us more shit in return. Well, Avram baby, the reckoning has come. The days of the indulgent parent and the spoiled brat are over. This week we're going to teach you some goddam table manners!"

The taxi pulled up beneath the Hilton's stylized concrete palms. It was nearly quarter past eight, but journalists never expect other journalists to be on time. As arranged, Zvi Matzliah was waiting in the lobby, half-concealed behind the ridiculous bronze ball that the hotel's inspired architects had deemed the perfect centerpiece.

"Welcome to the World Center of Traveling Jewryatrical!" quipped the Israeli cheerfully.

"It was *your* choice," responded Kesler. "I'd have been quite happy with La Belle."

"Ah, there's a reason, my friend," said the Israeli, leading him off to the hotel's Judea Bar. "For one thing, the Hilton is probably the only meeting place in Jerusalem that isn't bugged—old Conrad frowned on that sort of thing, you know— and for another, it's one of the few places where you can sit and talk in public and yet be totally unobserved."

Kesler saw what he meant. Apart from being decorated throughout in black leather and black fabric, the bar was illuminated solely by single candles on each table, giving the impression of a subterranean cave inhabited by a colony of glowworms. Matzliah was evidently at home.

"Jack!" he cried at a form on the other side of the bar,

distinguishable only by its white shirt. "A bourbon on the rocks. What'll you have, Dan?"

"Same."

"Twice!"

The shirt registered the order and underwent a partial eclipse behind the bar. Turning back to Kesler, the Israeli began in a tone that defied indifference, "Dan, I need your help, but I think it's the sort of help that may in turn help you. A story has come our way—by which I mean myself and a couple of other Israeli reporters—which the Government is doing its damnedest to suppress. No, suppress is the wrong word; they won't even let us get at it. The Censor's Office has gone totally over the top and for no apparent . . ."

"To do with Camp David?"

"No, that's what is so strange. Correction. That's what they're arguing—that, because of Camp David, this is a diplomatically sensitive time—but it just doesn't figure."

"Go on."

"Well, you know that great triangular patch of wasteland north of where the old Mandelbaum Gate used to be—before '67?"

"Behind the UN observation post—Nahalat Shim'on?"

"Exactly, Nahalat Shim'on. And you know they started building there about a month ago—damned great apartment blocks . . ."

"I remember the protests."

"Well, about a fortnight ago . . ."

Matzliah paused for the waiter to place the drinks and a bowl of peanuts.

"About a fortnight ago they stopped, threw a double barbed wire fence around the site, and posted armed guards on it. Then, when as a matter of routine we asked the municipality the reason, they referred us directly to the Censor's Office."

"And?"

"Oh, the usual—national security at stake and all the rest, together with vague—strictly off the record, old boy—hints about the need to avoid provocative acts while Camp David is on, the implication being that the Government has only now recognized the unsubtlety of erecting seven-story tank traps on what, nominally at least, is still neutral territory."

"Doesn't sound entirely implausible," remarked Kesler. "Didn't they start doing something similar on that site just after the Yom Kippur War, and then stopped, again for no apparent reason?"

"That was different, just a bit of muscle-flexing after being forced to accept a stalemate by the Big Boys. A token gesture of defiance, if you like. But this time there's the barbed wire and armed guards. Ask yourself, Dan, who do they think is going to make off with a couple of fifty-ton earthmovers and a workmen's latrine? What's the price of human excrement on the commodity market these days?"

Kesler smiled, recalling countless previous occasions when the Israeli had used the same reductio ad absurdum to point up the nonsense of some earnest government spokesman.

"Besides, there's something else," added Matzliah, demonstrating what it was that made him one of the country's more readable commentators—never give away the story in the first paragraph. "The buzz is that they've dug up a tomb—jewish, first century."

"Why should that be politically sensitive?" asked Kesler, for the first time conceding a journalistic curiosity, "unless it's the usual business of the Rabbinate and the Religious Party kicking up about desecration."

The Israeli grunted.

"Hardly a question of national security, Dan. Anyway, the whole area north and east of the city is one big graveyard; it was *the* Jewish burial ground up to the fall of the Second Temple. They must have dug up dozens of tombs over the years—most of them, like this one, when putting in building footings. But never before a reaction like this. No, Dan, this one is special, really special."

"So what's your guess?"

"It's more than a guess. The last time anyone in our office can remember anything remotely like this sort of fuss was back in '68—before both our times—when they found the body of that crucified man up at Giv'at ha-Mivtar. It was the first one they'd ever found—the first, that is, that they could say for sure had been crucified, because of the nail still embedded in the ankle bones. You know the one I'm talking about?"

"Dimly."

"Well, according to those in our office who were around at the time, it caused no small flap in certain quarters not a million miles from the Apostolic Delegation on the Mount of

Olives. Apparently the relief was almost palpable when examination of the skeleton revealed that, whoever the poor bastard was, he had had a cleft palate and a deformed head, as well as being no more than twenty-eight when he died." He paused. "You see what I'm getting at, don't you?"

"That this time it could be the real thing."

"Exactly, and all that goes with it. Christian theology was never my strong subject—our schools are rather remiss in that area—but I know enough to guess at the sort of impact this could have if it ever got out. It would certainly be the end of the Catholic Church, if not Christianity itself. You might as well tear up the whole of the New Testament . . ."

The two of them lapsed into silence as Kesler followed through the implications for himself. He repeated the drinks order, and then asked, "So where do I fit into the scheme of things? I hate to admit and professional pride forbid, but if *you*'ve failed, why should I succeed?"

A knowing look came into the Israeli's eyes.

"Come off it, Dan. Don't play innocent with me. It's been done dozens of times before and, for all I know, by you. As a foreign national writing for foreign publications, you can beat the censor any time you want. You surely don't want me to insult you by teaching you your craft?"

Kesler slumped back in his chair. When the barman was again out of earshot, he leaned forward.

"I could get away with it once, I suppose—send the copy out by 'carrier pigeon' on a scheduled flight, or some such thing—but, sure as hell, I'd be rumbled as soon as the story appeared in print. And then what? Is your editor going to offer me a job as a reward for my fearless services to journalism? Or will it be just another nomination for the Woodward-Bernstein Brown Trouser Trophy?"

Matzliah grinned.

"And why should you be rumbled, Dan Kesler? Or should I be addressing myself to Steve Harman or—who's the other one?—Morgan Lunz?"

He held back to judge the effect of his remarks. Kesler, despite his alarm at having his aliases bandied around in public, pretended to be unfazed.

"Just tell me one thing. Why are you so eager that I should have the story?"

"Eager I'm not!" snorted Matzliah. "And in any other

circumstances I'd be doing my damnedest to keep it from you. It's just that the only way we good, law-abiding, security-conscious, God-fearing Israeli newshounds can get at this story is for some dumb irresponsible goy like yourself to break it outside the country. Then the censor can go whistle; he'll be powerless to stop it. As I see it, you could be our savior, Dan Kesler. Doesn't that give you a warm and wonderful feeling deep down inside?"

"You're right," murmured Kesler, "Christian theology *isn't* your strong subject, or you'd remember what happened to the last savior you were sent."

★

"The Holy Father must be told," ventured Archbishop Ramone.

"On the contrary, the Holy Father is the one person who must be kept in ignorance!" countered the Cardinal Secretary of State, "particularly at this time when he already has so much on his mind with our brothers in Holland."

The archbishop demurred. The workings of the Vatican had always been beyond him. As the Apostolic Delegate in Jerusalem and Palestine for the last two years, Archbishop Francesco Ramone had been too exclusively preoccupied with treading the diplomatic tightrope required of the representative of the Catholic Church in the land of the Jews. Nor had his job been made any easier by the fact that, forty years after its creation, the State of Israel was still not recognized by the Holy See.

Ramone's unheralded return to Rome had been entirely on his own initiative, the news he bore being too important to be entrusted to the normal channels of diplomatic communication. His overwhelming feeling now was one of relief at having unburdened himself to a superior.

"And you are quite sure of the reliability of your source?" queried the Secretary of State from the other side of his desk.

"I have no reason to doubt it," hedged Ramone. "As I say, Eminence, it came to me direct from my brother archbishop, the Patriarch of the Greek Catholic Church in Jerusalem— and he was told of it by a member of his church, an Arab employed at the Hebrew University." Looking down at the desk, he added, "And of course you have the copy of the report that this man photocopied in the Department of Archaeology."

"But you haven't spoken to this Arab yourself?" pressed the cardinal. The reply, however, was forestalled by a knock at the door and the appearance of the florid-faced young monsignor who served the Secretary of State as his secretary.

"Eminence," he announced, "the Holy Father wishes to talk to you in confidence on your direct line in quarter of an hour's time. I've taken the liberty of assuring the switchboard in Holland that you will be here in your office to receive it." Suddenly appreciating the delicate nature of the conversation he was interrupting, he added uncertainly, "I assumed it would be convenient . . ."

"You did correctly, Giovanni," said the Secretary of State. "I will expect the call in a quarter of an hour."

With an effort he got up from the desk and walked over to the window. The archbishop was shocked at the evident deterioration in the arthritic joints of his superior since their last meeting only months previously.

Staring out over the courtyard of the Belvedere, the Secretary of State declared, "These are difficult times for the Church, Francesco, and what is going on in Holland—this absurd Declaration of Utrecht—is only part of it. In my view, the Holy Father's decision to confront the Dutch bishops on their own territory has great inherent risks. It's no secret, I think, that I advised strongly against it." He turned to face Ramone. "And now this news that you bring me. At any other time I would have felt confident of the Church's ability to ride it. But now . . . now I am deeply fearful. It is as though the forces of evil had conspired to strike at precisely the time when they knew our defenses would be at their weakest. Pray God that we may find the strength to resist!"

The archbishop intoned an instinctive "Amen," and added, "It is as you say, Eminence. The timing is most inopportune. The only comfort we may draw is that, despite the report, the Israelis as yet show no sign of publicizing the find. By my calculation, it must be at least . . ."

"There is no time to lose, Francesco," cut in the Secretary of State. "I shall call a meeting of the Curia Segreta for nine o'clock tomorrow morning. And I shall require your presence, so that you may repeat what you have told me this afternoon. If you come here at ten to, Giovanni will bring you along.' He moved painfully back to the desk and picked up the single sheet of paper. "In the meantime, I shall hold on to this."

A red light winked on the telephone console. Spotting it at the same time as the cardinal, Ramone rose and with a respectful bow headed for the door.

"*A domani, Eminenza,*" he concluded.

"No, Francesco, *ad Dominum!*" corrected the Secretary of State without humor.

★

It was after eleven when the taxi dropped Kesler off at the intersection of Shemu'el Ha-navi and St. George's, just up from the UN observation post. The only sign of life in the building was a single light on the second floor.

Crossing onto the edge of the wasteland, he looked north over the rocky ground that sloped gently down towards "the New Walls of Jerusalem," the ring of apartment blocks which, half a mile away, now encircled the city on three sides. It was cold, blustery, and dark, but the building site, illuminated by a pair of arcs, stood out like a nocturnal mirage. Getting at it for a closer look wasn't going to be easy; its right-hand boundary ran alongside the road, which meant the only detection-free approach would have to be across the hundred yards of rock- and rubble-strewn terrain from the other side.

He hesitated. As a journalist, he had never been cast in the derring-do mold and felt no great admiration for those who were. Strangers who learned what he did for a living generally first expressed surprise, then embarrassment, and finally tried to make amends by explaining that they simply imagined journalists to be rather more self-assertive and pushy—not quite so, well, gentlemanly. Now for possibly the first time in a decade, Kesler was prompted by the challenge of how a truly go-getting foreign correspondent would act in the same situation. It was quite out of character, and in a saner moment he would describe his response as a form of inverted cowardice—a fear of not measuring up to other people's expectations. In a sadder moment he would also be forced to acknowledge that in this single impetuous act were planted seeds of the destruction which, in a matter of days, was to overtake his life.

Using the twin arcs as his bearings, he moved cautiously

across the darkened wasteland, feeling rather than threading his way through an obstacle course of boulders and hunks of jagged, rusting metal. The soft earth was still awash with the morning's downpour and with every step his feet grew heavier as the mud caked the bottoms of his shoes.

Matzliah had been right. The entire site was fenced off with coils of barbed wire, and posted conspicuously by the main entrance was a soldier in full combat gear. But the most prominent feature of this extraordinary nightscape was a large mechanical digger in the northernmost corner of the site, its arm reared up and bent at the wrist in a peculiarly predatory gesture. If a tomb had indeed been discovered, then this, he reasoned, was most likely to have been the instrument responsible.

The problem was that he was at least six feet too low to get a look at the area directly beneath the digger's claw. The guard, he again noted, was at the other end of the site and, although there was always the chance that he made occasional patrols, it was a risk that had to be taken, now that he had come this far.

Moving into the light, he reached up, wrapped his fingers carefully round a strand of the barbed wire so as to avoid the barbs, and tugged. It hardly gave, suggesting that it was firmly staked into the ground. Reassured, he took a strand in each hand and, working on the escarpment with his mud-caked feet, hauled himself up onto the level.

"Amod! Mi sham?"

The hoarse cry was the more startling for coming from a totally unexpected direction. In an instant he realized that in his concern for what the entrance guard might be up to, he had overlooked the possibility of there being a second guard patrolling the perimeter. There was nothing he could do. It briefly crossed his mind to leap back, but a twisted ankle at best and a bullet in the back at worst would have made escape impossible anyway. Instead, feeling faintly ridiculous, he clung to the wire, as helpless as a fly in a spider's web.

The second guard was not inside the fence but, like himself, outside. The shaft of a flashlight indicated the direction in which he was required to move, and after a dozen shuffled steps to the right he found himself a few feet from a human figure silhouetted against one of the arcs. The voice addressed him again in Hebrew:

"Ma ata osay sham?"

In the thirty seconds or so he had had to move along the wire, the germ of an idea had already formulated in his mind. It wasn't new, but from experience he knew it was usually effective: Act dumb and act American.

"Hey, I'm sorry, pal, but I don't understand your language too well," he declared, hamming the accent and affecting a naive jauntiness.

"What are you doing?" asked the voice in a slow, over-articulated English.

"Well, hell, I'm trying to figure out the way back to my hotel. That's what I'm doing, but, damn me, if I don't seem to have gotten lost."

"What hotel?"

Kesler had anticipated the question.

"Well, it's called the American Colony. You must know it. It's the old Turkish pasha's palace. It's right by here some-place. You happen to know whereabouts?"

The voice didn't reply and, with the light still in his eyes, Kesler had no way of knowing how his act was going down. Instinctively, though, he felt the next line had to come from the other player.

"Tourist?" asked the voice at length.

"Sure, tourist," confirmed Kesler with relief, and for a moment the flashlight seemed to waver.

"Your passport."

Kesler fumbled in his pocket, his thoughts running ahead. He had already taken one risk; the guard had only to check with the American Colony to find that he wasn't booked in there. His request for the passport, though, suggested he might be more easily satisfied. And there was no mention of journalist in it—just a nicely ambiguous "writer." As he handed it over, the light dropped from his face.

Slinging his semiautomatic over one shoulder, the guard flipped to the front page and turned the document sideways. Briefly the light flashed back onto Kesler's face as he checked it against the photograph.

"You arrive in Israel when?"

"Oh, just over a week ago, ten days maybe . . ."

Suddenly Kesler's teeth turned to chalk as he realized the reason for the question and saw the soldier start thumbing back through the visa pages in search of the entry stamp that would confirm his answer. He wouldn't find one, it being an unwritten agreement that Israeli immigration officers didn't stamp the passports of foreign journalists lest this deny them entry to Arab countries. In the soldier's eyes, however, the absence of an entry stamp would mean only one thing—that the man before him was an illegal infiltrator and, as like as not, a terrorist or a spy.

Kesler froze. Like a ball of twine, the sequence of events was starting to unravel and, once started, would be impossible to stop—arrest, interrogation, explanation, reprimand, withdrawal of accreditation. He watched, mesmerized, as with difficulty the soldier worked his way through pages that were dense with stamps in a dozen different languages indicating entry, exit, visa, renewal, and—that journalistic campaign ribbon—*persona non grata*. Partly out of nerves, partly out of genuine fatigue, he yawned. He felt a sudden desire to put an end to the whole charade.

"Look, I reckon you should know something . . ." he started, but was cut short by a shout from the other end of the site. It was the guard at the entrance; the relief shift had arrived and was impatient to be signed in. Kesler quickly bundled his thoughts into order. The flashlight was still playing on his opened passport but the soldier's attention was now elsewhere. The distraction had to be exploited.

"Hey, look," he blurted out as the soldier turned round again, "this hotel, the American Colony, it must be pretty close by. Why don't you just come with me, and that way you can check my story with the deskclerk and *show* me the way. Then we'll both be happy."

If the possibility of a psychological bluff occurred to the soldier, it was overtaken by more immediate thoughts of home. Without a word, he indicated by a sweep of the flashlight the circuitous route around the perimeter fence by which Kesler could reach the hotel. Kesler was already on his way when he realized the passport was back in his hand.

"What time is it?" Aya blinked.

"Nearly one," he answered, edging in beside her. She rolled over and snuggled into his chest, throwing a leg over his with the innocent abandon of a sleeping child.

"What was it all about then, Mr. Hemingway?"

Kesler wished he knew. There was so much that he himself couldn't understand, let alone explain to others. At the back of his mind, though, was the thought that he was being set up by Matzliah and his reporter friends. Even by Matzliah's standards, the whole performance at the Hilton had been too slick by half. And yet all the evidence of his subsequent nocturnal ramblings suggested that there *was* a story and that it could well be along lines Matzliah had indicated. The Israeli's worries about the censor were equally plausible and in the circumstances it was true that Kesler probably was their "savior." But it was hard to see Matzliah and his friends rushing to his defense when he was summoned to the Censor's Office; he'd be lucky to get a character reference out of that bunch. He had no illusions; he was just the patsy.

"They think they've found the tomb of Christ," he said, marveling in the dark at the inadequacy of everyday language to convey matters of such cosmic import. There was several seconds' silence before she asked, "Empty?"

"Don't know, but it seems not."

"Hmm," she mused. "The Pope isn't going to like that."

★

"Above all, we promise to maintain secret all matters pertaining to our deliberations and decisions in this room today . . ."

With these words Egidio Cardinal Pellegrini, Vatican Secretary of State and second in importance to the Holy Father, passed the small white Bible to his brother cardinal. Clearing his throat, the other affirmed, "I so vow and swear," adding with his right hand on the book, "So help me God and these Holy Gospels which I touch with my hand"—and in turn passed it to his neighbor.

At a far end of the horseshoe configuration of tables, Archbishop Ramone, the Holy See's Apostolic Delegate in Jerusalem, watched in awe as the procedure continued around the room. He was witnessing, he knew, something that officially didn't exist: the Curia Segreta, the governing body of the Roman Catholic Church. So far as the outside world was aware, it was the Pope, the Church's "administrative, judicial, and executive head," who ultimately formulated policy, albeit usually in consultation with his three thousand bishops through synods and councils. As for the Curia, that was merely the Vatican bureaucracy, the implementing machinery. To ever admit publicly that the Holy Father was not the supreme and final formulator of Church policy would be to deny the guiding role of the Holy Spirit in working through the heart and mind of the latest successor of St. Peter. To admit that "the Holy Spirit" was in fact a committee of a dozen aged cardinals normally meeting on the first Wednesday of every month in what had once been a repository for broken statuary would be nothing short of blasphemy.

Most pontiffs naturally resisted so blatant an infringement of the Petrine prerogative, which relegated them in effect to the position of constitutional monarchs, but they very soon realized that nothing was possible without the cooperation of the Curia—and capitulated. Those who fought on had to be *made* to realize, and accordingly found their decrees and initiatives passed from one bureau to another, referred, deferred, delayed by "translation problems," or simply lost in the vast and complex curial machine. Even those decrees that finally got through could still be undermined by being made subjects for line-by-line interpretation or debate over the precise degree of authority they should be accorded by the faithful. In recent times, only one pope had beaten the system: John XXIII, ironically the man credited with the remark, "Don't ask me; I'm only the pope round here"—and then only by summoning a full Vatican Council over the heads of the Curia. Even so, the curial cardinals had swiftly reasserted their control by frustrating every attempt of John's successor, Paul VI, to get the decrees of the Second Vatican Council implemented. On the death of Pope Paul in 1978, the world's bishops were still awaiting the new guidelines for seminarians that had been mandated by Vatican II and fed into the curial machine thirteen years earlier.

Such was the Curia Segreta's formidable reputation that in some circles it was even credited with the assassination of the thirty-three-day pontiff Papa Luciani, known to the world as John Paul I. The curial caucus—so the theory went—after contriving the election of the papal candidate they deemed most malleable, had been horrified to discover that Luciani was bent on the democratization of the Church to the extent of allowing priests and parishioners to elect their own bishops. Since an extreme threat called for extreme measures, they had allegedly resorted to the ultimate remedy.

Now, it was rumored, the caucus was engaged in yet another power struggle with a headstrong pontiff determined to be his own man—or at least the Holy Spirit's. But this time there were few bets on the outcome, for the challenger, apart from never having been a curial cardinal himself, was not even an Italian.

It was with these thoughts in mind that Ramone studied the faces before him. Extraordinary faces and yet quite expressionless. Faces that from an early age had *learned* to be expressionless, to mask real feelings and counterfeit unreal ones. Joy, hope, disappointment, despair—all were resolved into the same marmoreal set about the eyes and mouth. Most of all disappointment. Despite the power they enjoyed collectively, there wasn't one of the dozen who wouldn't gladly have traded his seat in the Hall of the Broken Heads for the papal throne, the reality of power for the superficial glitter of its ceremonial reflection. Most had tried; several had actually been tipped as *papabile*; all had been ultimately disappointed—*bruciati*, to use another, less flattering Italian term denoting that their aspirations, no less than the voting slips upon which their names had been written, had been incinerated in the conclave stove. Nor were any of them likely to get a second chance; barring another attempt on his life, the present keeper of the keys of Saint Peter looked like holding on to them at least until the year 2000.

Last in line at the end of the table, Ramone took hold of the Bible and self-consciously repeated the oath. His words were followed by a shrill scraping of wood on marble as, at the Cardinal Secretary of State's bidding, the members of the council sat down. It was then that for the first time the archibishop noticed the single sheets of paper, face down on the table, before each chair. Turning over his own, he was taken aback to find that they were copies of the photostat he had brought with him from Jerusalem and given to the cardinal the day before. This, he inferred, had to be Pellegrini's way of apprising his brother cardinals of the reason for their emergency session without having to spell it out. As a shock tactic, it seemed to have the desired effect. Pupils that hadn't dilated in decades slid back as the implication of what they now beheld sank in.

Within seconds the storm was rising all around Ramone as first one cardinal, then another, and finally all in unison clamored to know the meaning of this heretical scrap of paper that threatened to destroy two thousand years of confidence and complacency.

Calm at the other end of the hall, Secretary of State Pellegrini waited for the chorus of questions to peak before calling for order. Then, requesting his brother cardinals' indulgence to be allowed to remain seated on account of his arthritis, he said softly, "Most eminent brothers, the document you have before you was handed to me yesterday by our representative in Jerusalem, Archbishop Francesco Ramone," nodding in Ramone's direction, "whom I have asked to join us this morning and whom I think some of you know already." Ramone blushed; he certainly knew all of *them* but, with the exception of the Secretary of State, he doubted whether any of them would have owned to even a nodding acquaintance with *him*.

"The document speaks for itself," continued Pellegrini. "So, all I will say by way of introduction is that the original emanates, as you can see, from the Hebrew University of Jerusalem's Institute of Archaeology, where it was photocopied by an Arab employed there as a technical assistant, who also happens to be a member of the Greek Catholic Church in Jerusalem. By such circuitous means it has come into our possession. As for the tomb it refers to, we have reason to believe it was discovered on a building site to the north of the city about a fortnight ago." He paused for a sip of water and, looking slowly round, added, "Decisions at the highest level must clearly be made concerning the reaction of the Church, official or unofficial."

"Reaction? There can be only one reaction!" bellowed the eighty-two-year-old Cardinal Sirelli with the lungpower of a man half his years. "We ignore it! It is patently a fabrication devised by the Zionists for the specific purpose of discrediting the Holy Catholic Church. To accord it even a moment's attention is to give credence to a self-evident tissue of lies!"

The Secretary of State held up his hand in an attitude akin to that of blessing. Sirelli's outburst had been totally predictable. With good reason was the head of the Congregation for the Doctrine of the Faith—formerly the dreaded Holy Office of the Inquisition and still referred to simply as the Holy

Office—known as *Il Carabiniere di Dio*—God's Policeman. Over the years, though, the old man's spleen had increased in direct relation to the whittling away by successive pontiffs of his department's importance. Gone were the days when the Holy Office could claim to be "the supreme congregation" and, having now passed eighty, Sirelli himself wasn't even eligible to sit in a conclave. The Curia Segreta was his last real power base, but even here his contributions were increasingly regarded as owing more to indigestion than inspiration.

"Brother Sirelli," responded Secretary of State Pellegrini in the same reasonable tones of his opening remarks, "nobody here doubts the Holy Office's vigilance in protecting our Mother Church from the attempts of the Devil to spread false doctrine; your efforts over the years have won the respect and admiration of all of us around this table. However, what we have before us today is not solely a matter of theology—not even principally, if you will permit me to say so. It is a matter of politics and, to a lesser extent, of archaeology. Personally, I am convinced that human remains have been discovered which in most relevant details accord with those of our beloved savior, the Lord Jesus Christ. In this, I should add, there is nothing particularly remarkable, for this discovery is of a sort that we have long anticipated with the acceleration of building work by the Israeli authorities around Jerusalem. Psychologically, therefore, my brothers, we should not feel unprepared." Turning again to the head of the Holy Office, he continued, "That this is *not* the body of Our Lord—*cannot* be—I need hardly emphasize. We must not, however, on that account blind ourselves to the unprecedented opportunity for mischief that this discovery may offer our many enemies. God himself, I am persuaded, has delivered this document into our hands at this time precisely so that we may frustrate those attempts by our own efforts."

As he spoke, Pellegrini noted the scarlet skullcap of Cardinal Della Sera—not normally one of his curial allies—bob vigorously in agreement. Such support was not to be ignored.

"Perhaps we might hear the views of our brother, the Cardinal Prefect of the Congregation for Evangelization of Peoples," he ventured.

"They are much in accordance with your own, Eminence," replied Della Sera, "and I would respectfully ask our brother, the Cardinal Prefect of the Holy Office, who felt this matter unworthy of our further attention, to consider the social and economic state in which most of the Church's eight hundred million faithful are obliged to live. The majority of the flock, I have to remind him, are not the educated populations of Europe, the United States, and Canada, but the oppressed, impoverished masses of Central and South America, whose faith is daily tried by hunger and hardship mercifully beyond our imaginings. We are talking about simple people—people for whom, in the absence of literacy and intellectual sophistication, their God-given faith is the only bulwark against an unholy Communist ideology that daily tempts them with false promises of a better tomorrow. I urge you, Brother Sirelli, to consider how much more sorely this faith will be tried if, in addition to their present deprivations, they are required to endure the taunts and jests engendered by the public display of these . . . these remains." Brandishing the photostat, he concluded, "For my part, Secretary of State, I have no hesitation in averring that we must take every opportunity God grants us to destroy this canker before it spreads. If not . . ."

The sentence hung unfinished in the air. In the silence that followed, the only sound was that of Sirelli sucking in his long, leathery cheeks. The Secretary of State turned to Ramone.

"Archbiship, there are, I think, one or two points on which you wish to elaborate, regarding the circumstances of the discovery."

Ramone stood up, the center of such attention as he had never in his life imagined possible.

"My most eminent and most reverend Lord Cardinals, I would not presume to talk on these matters if it were not for the fact that over the years I have cultivated a personal interest—although strictly amateur—in the subject of archaeology and particularly, since my good fortune to be appointed Apostolic Delegate in Jerusalem and Palestine, in the archaeological history of the Holy Land at the time of Our Lord. In this connection, there are certain factual observations that it is my duty to bring to Your Eminences' attention. First, you will observe in the document before you that the burial vault is referred to as that of a Nazirite. This could be misleading, since the tomb itself seems to have been built primarily for communal purposes. Of the nine ossuaries, only number seven apparently makes reference to its contents being the remains of a Nazirite—*Jesus* the Nazirite, as the inscription . . ."

"In God's name, since when was Our Lord ever a Nazirite?" exploded Sirelli, cheeks quivering. "Do you know nothing of the Gospels, man? Our Lord was a Nazarene, a resident of the town of Nazareth, since it seems necessary to spell it out. The Naz*irites* were a group of sectarians who abstained from drink and followed a totally segregated way of life. You surely don't need me to tell you that Our Lord not only turned water into wine but associated freely with all manner of people, prostitutes and publicans included! Well, do you?"

Ramone's worst fears were being realized. How was he to teach Bible study to the Church's principal theologian—a man who furthermore regarded modern biblical scholarship as a form of sacrilege? Yet he had to try.

"With the greatest respect, Your Eminence, it is no more my contention than it is the Secretary of State's that these remains could possibly be those of Our Lord; I am concerning myself solely with the facts as they are related in this document. I am indeed aware of what is known as 'the Nazirite heresy,' although it was my belief that contemporary opinion on the subject was less than unanimous . . ."

"Contemporary what?" barked Sirelli.

The Secretary of State intervened.

"My Lord Cardinals, I must insist that our brother, the archbishop, be allowed to speak without interruption—or intimidation.'"

Sirelli glared at Pellegrini, but fell silent with a petulant snort. Ramone resumed.

"We do find that even in the minds of the gospel writers themselves there is a degree of ambivalence. Saint Matthew, for example, in his version of the Nativity talks of Joseph coming to dwell in Nazareth in order to fulfil what was spoken by the prophets: that he, Our Lord, should be called a Nazarene. But the *actual* prophecy, as we have it in the Old Testament Book of Judges, where it is quoted in reference to the birth of Samson, quite clearly specifies that the Messiah will be 'a Naz*irite* unto God from the womb.' "

The head of the Holy Office gazed heavenward, as though to indicate that all his misgivings about modern biblical scholarship were being demonstrably borne out.

"It is now also widely accepted, I believe," continued the archbishop, "that the family into which Our Lord was born was steeped in the old ascetic Nazirite tradition of Galilee, and, whether or not Our Lord personally remained faithful to that tradition, it is at least probable that in the eyes of the Judeans and Jerusalemites he would have been regarded as much as a Nazirite as a Nazarene—arguably the more so, for being a religious leader. In short, Eminences, I think it would be a mistake to draw comfort from what at first sight may appear to be an obvious discrepancy. Far from attempting to excuse or explain the Nazirite reference, our enemies will, I fear, seize upon it and point to it as being in line with one of the strongest currents of contemporary biblical scholarship. Apart from this, there are other details of which Your Eminences should, I feel, be apprised." He looked across the hall to Pellegrini and, getting a discreet nod, drew breath, "Our Arab informant at the Hebrew University claims that what we have here—this single sheet—is no more than a précis of a fuller report which he was unable to copy. What he was able to see of it, though, indicated that the body was unquestionably nailed to the cross, instead of being tied as was the more common practice, and that the victim was spared the customary *crurifragium*, the breaking of the shinbones to hasten death by asphyxiation resulting from his inability to support his own weight."

He paused to see how many of his audience had appreciated the significance of his last statement. There was little sign of enlightenment; only the smoldering resentment accorded most bearers of bad news.

"I am sure I don't need to remind Your Eminences," he added, "that Our Lord was spared this final cruelty on account of his being already dead by sunset. So, in conclusion, Eminences, I fear it is likely to be argued by our enemies that, although many thousands of Jews and Gentiles are known to have been crucified by the Romans during the first half of the first century, although nailing the victim to the cross was not a unique variant of this form of execution, although many would have died before requiring the coup de grace, although Jesus or Yeshua was a common enough name in those times, and although many of those so named and so executed would have been in their early thirties—the coincidence of *all* these factors coming together in the case we have before

us leads to only one conclusion . . . That at least would be
their argument."

Silence. The inscrutable marble façades around the table
had regained control, although, hidden from view, many an
eminent toe was curled within its scarlet stocking.

"Brothers," said the Secretary of State in a voice barely
above a whisper, "having heard the worst, are we now agreed
on action?"

Every head nodded except Sirelli's.

"In which case, I have to tell you that we may have little
time. As the archbishop has already mentioned, the document we have here is merely a summary of a fuller, more
detailed report. For what purpose, we must ask ourselves,
would such a summary be compiled and printed, if not for
wider distribution? Although the Israeli authorities have given
no indication of an impending public statement or—God
forbid!—a press conference, we cannot discount these possibilities. I propose therefore that the archbishop, as our representative in Israel, return there as soon as possible and that he
seek an urgent meeting with the Israeli Foreign Minister, at
which to express the wish of the Holy See that steps be taken
forthwith to suppress all information relating to his discovery
until such time as we can come to a mutually acceptable
accommodation. May I take it that I have your support?"

The only dissenter—abstainer perhaps—was again Sirelli,
who stared fixedly ahead.

Relieved, Pellegrini added casually, "The Holy Father has
not been informed of this matter. I am sure we are all of one
mind that it would be inconsiderate to concern him at a time
when other business so manifestly requires his undivided
attention. It is also preferable, I feel, that he at least should
be personally insulated from any embarrassment that may
later be occasioned by this regrettable affair."

"Insulated by ignorance, Eminence?" queried Sirelli
mischievously.

"Put that way, if you must, Brother Sirelli," replied Pellegrini, "then yes, insulated by ignorance."

★

"Now you know how the early Christians felt in the Colos-
seum," observed the Secretary of State as he poured two
glasses of an amber aperitif and passed one to Ramone.

The archbishop wasn't sure how to react. It was the first even mildly humorous remark he had ever heard the cardinal make—assuming it to be humorous. But it was also the first time he had ever been invited to Pellegrini's private apartment and he realized he was now seeing a side to the man he had never suspected. No longer the austere administrator, the cardinal was relaxed and urbane.

"You did well this morning, Francesco, well indeed," continued Pellegrini, closing the door on the two white-clothed sisters who were setting the table for lunch in the next room, "and don't be misled by Their Eminences' reaction. They were doing no more than demonstrating that human penchant for executing the messenger instead of the malefactor. I know them—and they were impressed."

Ramone sank deeper into the red damask sofa, warmed by the unaccustomed praise and already mildly intoxicated by the aromatic liquor. The next remark had a more sobering effect, however.

"You didn't tell the whole story this morning, Francesco."

"Eminence?"

"Perhaps I should say, then, the full implications of the story. Sirelli cut you short with that diversion about Nazarenes and Nazirites. As usual, he missed the more important point."

The archbishop suspected what he was referring to and tried to avoid his gaze.

"Before Sirelli sidetracked you, Francesco, you mentioned that the tomb in which the ossuary was found was not the tomb of a Nazirite but an ordinary communal tomb. Correct me if I am wrong, but the implication was that for some reason this Nazirite's bones had been placed in a tomb that was 'unworthy' of them—a hollowed out hole in the rock rather than a perhaps somewhat grander resting place. The question to be asked I would have thought is, Why? Why do *you* think, Francesco?"

Ramone could feel his color rising. He was unwilling to be drawn for fear of being suspected of heresy. It was illogical perhaps, but it was one thing to argue before a formal council of cardinals that "this is how our enemies will put the case; forewarned is forearmed," and quite another to pursue the same line in a private, personal conversation with a superior who, after all, was second only to the Holy Father in the Church's hierarchy.

The archbishop's embarrassment communicated itself to his superior.

"Then let *me* play the devil's advocate on this occasion," said the Secretary of State, "bearing in mind that my knowledge of archaeological matters is far inferior to yours. According to the Gospels, Our Lord's body was placed in the tomb of Joseph of Arimathea, who we are told was a wealthy man. Well, clearly the tomb we have here is even less likely to be that of a wealthy man than that of a Nazirite. So it would seem we can rule out that possibility. There is, however, a school of thought—undoubtedly heretical in Brother Sirelli's eyes—that seeks to explain the phenomenon of the Resurrection by arguing that, although Our Lord's body was initially placed in Joseph of Arimathea's tomb, this was never intended as anything more than a temporary resting place to comply with the Jewish law enjoining burial of a crucified prisoner before sunset. Sometime within the next couple of days, it is suggested, the body would have been transferred to another, permanent resting place. Who transferred it and where to are matters of speculation. It could have been the Jewish authorities themselves, anxious to prevent the tomb becoming an object of veneration as Christ himself had been in life—and certainly by this reading it would have made sense for them to choose a nondescript communal tomb. Admittedly, you then have to explain why they would have put an inscription on the ossuary, but there is a powerful superstition in Judaism no less than in most other religions about unmarked graves and anyway, according to the diagram, the ossuary was pushed out of sight into one of the tunnels, on its own and with a stone blocking the entrance. Even more heretically, the disciples themselves might have been responsible for removing and reburying the body, with the intention of perpetrating a deliberate fraud to persuade others that Our Lord had indeed risen from the dead. . . . You look shocked, Francesco, but, believe me, I am not the first to raise such possibilities."

Ramone was shocked, but less by what the cardinal said—he too had read the books on the subject—than by the way he said it. His Eminence's tone suggested that he gave these wild theories at least as much credence as the orthodox version. And yet this was the same man who, less than an hour earlier, had gone out of his way to assure the cantankerous old Sirelli that of course this could not be the body of Our Lord.

"All this too, I fear, our enemies will make much of," responded Ramone.

Pellegrini looked down into his glass.

"You haven't understood, Francesco, or perhaps you simply fear the consequences of your understanding. I am saying that such possibilities are frankly no less unlikely than the Resurrection itself and that, taken together with all the other circumstantial details that you so admirably listed earlier, I see no reason for doubting that this could indeed be Our Lord's body."

Ramone could no longer disbelieve the evidence of his own ears.

"But what about faith?" he stammered. "The Creed, what about the Apostles' Creed—' . . . the third day He arose again from the dead, ascended into Heaven, and sits at the right hand of . . . ' "

Pellegrini shook his head.

"Francesco, Francesco, don't let an old cynic deflect you from your faith—for I sincerely envy you it—but if we are in the confessional, I have to tell you that despite any evidence to the contrary I haven't 'believed' in twenty years. Nor, I suspect, have most of those sitting round that table this morning. Believing in the existence of a God, a Supreme Being—that is not so difficult; it's believing that God is good . . . Oh, I have heard the arguments to explain His seeming indifference to suffering and to the evil that men do to each other. But, Francesco, putting to one side the wars, murders, and tortures, how does one explain the famines, floods, earthquakes, and all those other human catastrophes that we all too aptly call 'acts of God'? Frankly, it is more comforting to conclude that God doesn't exist than that such a God who allows these things *does*. If, however, one is determined to believe, then it is at least more intellectually honest to take the Jewish view that His will is unknowable and inexplicable and that the only hope for man is to submit himself to it."

Ramone was horrified. Here was the most senior prince of the Holy Catholic Church talking like a crypto-Jew and, as though that weren't enough, suggesting that the Church itself was run by a band of like-minded infidels. He had not been so shattered since, as an adolescent, he had discovered his father had a mistress. The childhood memory prompted a question he hardly dared ask:

"And the Holy Father—he feels this way too?"

Pellegrini looked across to a large silver-framed photograph of himself on his knees before the Holy Father, skullcap in hand, tendering his congratulations during the ceremony marking the new pope's installation.

"No, he believes . . . All Holy Fathers believe, at least in my experience. More often than not, that is why they're chosen. I've seen it happen. It's not that we all go into the conclave with the intention of choosing the best and holiest amongst us. Far from it—saints make terrible popes. But it is a fact that the men who genuinely believe that the Holy Spirit makes the selection do seem to radiate an extraordinary self-confidence, a sublime indifference, and for that reason one of them invariably emerges as the most appealing candidate. To that extent I suppose it could be argued that the Holy Spirit really does guide the judgement of the conclave."

He looked for a response from Ramone but the archbishop was still too shocked to articulate his thoughts.

"You think I'm a hypocrite, Francesco. Yes? Well, insofar as I think one thing and act another, I am. But don't think I am proud of it. Believe me, I despise myself for the pretense to which I have condemned myself. I ask you only to look at it this way: A man who has devoted his life to the Church—*sacrificed* his life in terms of what he has forgone—wakes up one morning to find he no longer believes. Because that is how it happens. The process of erosion may take years but the realization is as sudden as anything on the road to Damascus. So what does he do? He still believes in one respect; he still believes the Church to be the greatest force for good in an evil world, and it follows that he wishes to continue serving it. What he no longer believes is—and I don't use the word lightly—the mythology. If you like, he believes in Christianity but not in Christ. There are then . . ."

"B-But if he believes in Christianity he can still believe in a Christian God, even if he rejects the person of Christ—can he not?"

"Not easily, Francesco, not when you have been taught throughout a lifetime to use the one as the path to the other.

If there is a God, I no longer know how to find him. For that I would have to be reborn as a Muslim or a Hindu. But, to return to 'our man,' there are only two options open to him: to leave the Church, in which case the loss will be both the Church's and his—as well as the loss of those the Church serves—or to take a personal vow of silence on his true beliefs, while continuing in his daily life to use the vocabulary of the believer. He becomes in effect a Catholic humanist. And, Francesco, I am not alone in having arrived at this point. At every level in the Church, from the humblest parish priest to the highest echelons of the Sacred College, *you* will find us. Only on the rarest occasions would we ever admit to it, but it is easy enough to recognize in others when one has experienced it in oneself."

He paused, and in response to the unasked question said:

"So why am I telling you this—and why now? I'll tell you . . . Partly to persuade you of the paramount importance of the task that we have this morning laid upon your shoulders, for if we who have little or no faith feel so keenly that the welfare of mankind is dependent upon your success, how much more keenly should you, a believer, feel it? But more specifically, Francesco, to impress upon you that you are engaged on a mission for the Church, not on a personal crusade against forces that threaten only your own religious beliefs. Confuse the two, and you risk not just your own sanity but the very survival of the Church, because, believe me, the man who has your sort of faith is as vulnerable in a case like this as he is strong."

He placed his empty glass on the table beside his chair and glanced towards the dining room.

"But come. We must eat, and there is much else we must talk about in the little time left us before your departure."

★

"My secretary said you wanted to see me, Mr. Kesler, but she omitted to say what it was about."

Extending a pudgy hand, the little man stood up behind the desk in the tiny second-floor room that he used as his private study in preference to his office on the floor below. The only furniture was a desk, two chairs, and a tall metal filing cabinet that prevented the door opening beyond ninety degrees. Apart from the lavatories, it was joked, it was the

only room in the Institute of Archaeology without a telephone—on the professor's specific orders.

As Kesler squeezed his lanky six-foot-two frame into the
chair facing the desk, he again wondered how wise he had
been to come, for the man's obvious unease confirmed that
he had already guessed what it was about. On the other
hand, if the story was to be smuggled out of the country, it
would have to be at least nominally substantiated before any
reputable agency or publication would touch it—particularly
with a false byline. And except for the government itself,
there was no other point of contact that was sufficiently
authoritative. Besides, the professor knew him and, even if
he wouldn't confirm the story, he could be relied on to give
a broad enough hint. Ben Ami was a master of the art of the
loaded negative, as he had demonstrated during the battle
with the religious authorities over the 1981 City of David
excavations.

"I know you're a busy man," Kesler began, "so I won't
waste your time. There are rumors that a first century tomb
has been found in Nahalat Shim'on."

Kesler read the man's expression—the inner debate over
which was preferable, the outright denial or the guarded
affirmation. The latter won.

"I don't know about any rumors, Mr. Kesler, but yes, a
tomb has been found. I don't need to tell you, though, that
there's nothing remarkable in that. From what I recall of our
previous meetings, you are not entirely ignorant of the archaeology of Jerusalem."

Kesler tested the ground further, mindful of giving them
both a way out, should one be needed.

"It's just that, well, the security on this occasion seems
rather excessive."

"I wouldn't say so."

"Barbed wire, armed guards?"

He stopped before citing Matzliah's experience of being
referred to the Censor's Office; there was no point in giving
away more than was necessary at this stage. The emotional
atmosphere in the room had already become as claustrophobic as the physical. Wedged behind his desk, the professor
gave the impression of being verbally cornered as he glanced
from side to side. Kesler leaned back a little to allow him
breathing space.

"The area where this tomb has been discovered, Mr. Kesler, is a sensitive one. Up to 1967 . . . ."

"It is my understanding, Professor," Kesler cut in, "that the contents are more sensitive than the area—that they could even be the remains of Jesus Christ."

The game was over. The little man slumped in his chair and, removing his glasses, sighed.

"Mr. Kesler, I must tell you that you are playing with fire. I do not wish to insult your intelligence, but these are matters that you cannot be expected to understand. The implication of the questions you are . . ."

"I'm just trying to establish the truth," put in Kesler, instantly regretting the most banal and hypocritical of all journalistic justifications. It was too late; the professor saw his chance and took it.

"And the truth, Mr. Kesler—as you will no doubt have heard before—is like the onion; it has many skins!" Replacing his glasses, he leaned forward, indicating a sudden switch to the offensive. "Mr. Kesler, it may be inexcusable chutzpah for a Jew to teach a Christian Christianity, but do you really appreciate the theological implications if the body of Jesus Christ *were* found?"

"It would give the lie to the Resurrection," answered Kesler in an assertive tone to mask his profound ignorance on the subject. He was annoyed with himself for having so stupidly lost the initiative. It was his turn to slump in his chair.

"Far more than that, Mr. Kesler, far, far more," responded the professor with evident Socratic delight. "It would give the lie to Christianity itself! 'If Christ has not been raised, then our preaching is in vain and your faith is in vain.' Do you know who said that?' "

Kesler shook his head.

"Saint Paul, Mr. Kesler, First Epistle to the Corinthians, chapter fifteen, verse fourteen. But let me give you another quote—one you *will* know: 'You are Peter, and on this rock I will build My church, and . . . I will give you the keys of the kingdom of heaven.' That one you have heard, yes? And if you've ever been to St. Peter's in Rome, you may even have seen it written on the frieze that runs under the drum of the cupola. Yes?"

Kesler remained silent.

"But you probably don't know why it is so important, at

least to the Catholics. So I will explain. It is one of the so-called Petrine texts, which in layman's language means it establishes the authority first of St. Peter and secondly of his successors—that is, every pope right up to the present one—to act as the representative of Jesus Christ on earth. From which it follows, of course, that the Roman Catholic Church is the only true Church of Christ. But that quote is only one of *three* Petrine texts, and it was spoken while Jesus was alive. The one which in many Catholic eyes carries even more weight is the one he spoke after his death or, put another way, the one he came back from the dead specifically to speak. It comes at the end of St. John's Gospel where, after the crucifixion and Resurrection, Jesus appears to Peter on the shore of Lake Galilee and says to him: 'Feed my lambs . . . Tend my sheep . . . Feed my sheep.' What could be clearer than that? The trouble is that the Catholic Church has always insisted on a *physical* Resurrection. Whereas most other Christian denominations would probably accept some sort of otherworldly manifestation, Catholics are insistent that it was no spirit, no mere ghost, who conferred this authority on Peter, but Jesus himself in the very body that was crucified—the body which, in that same passage from St. John, is even shown eating bread and fish. So, if that body were now to turn up in a tomb, you can well imagine how it would discredit the Catholic Church's claim to be the sole authoritative voice of Christendom."

Kesler gave a peevish shrug.

"I don't see how discrediting a claim to preeminence discredits Catholicism itself."

"I'm coming to that," rejoined the professor, "but first you have to realize that the Catholic Church is unlike any other church, any other denomination, in the way it has developed its structure of doctrines over the last two thousand years, insofar as *its* doctrines have mostly grown out of each other through a process of logical necessity. So, if Jesus was God as well as Man, it follows that he must have been born of a pure vessel untainted by any suggestion of carnal procreation— hence the Virgin Birth. But the Virgin herself, to be that pure vessel, had to be free of original sin; so her birth too had to be special—hence the Immaculate Conception. And of course, since her son rose bodily from the dead and ascended into Heaven, it would be fitting if she did something similar—

hence the Assumption of the Virgin. And so on. You see what I mean about this 'logical necessity'? In its way, in its appeal to a sort of reason, it is very satisfying, I think, but it has the very great inherent danger, Mr. Kesler, that, if you take away a key premise, all the rest will come tumbling to the ground.

"And Resurrection is *the* key premise. It's far more than just the Christian's personal guarantee of life after death— God the Father did it for his Son; ergo, He'll do it for the rest of us—it is the bedrock proof of Jesus' claim to be Son of God, for who but the Son of God could triumph over death? But if the Resurrection never happened, then Jesus is no longer the Messiah, but just the exceptionally gifted teacher that we Jews have always believed him to be. And where then is the justification for the Virgin Birth, the Immaculate Conception, and the rest? You need go no further; you have already destroyed the two most fundamental tenets of Catholicism—Christ not God and Mary not a virgin! And that, Mr. Kesler, is why I ask you to forget all this business about Nahalat Shim'on. A 'seeker after truth' you may be, but you should know that the truth can be dangerous. The poet Kipling warned about the way it can be twisted by knaves to make a trap for fools—and he was right."

Kesler couldn't suppress a grunt of impatience; he'd had more than enough quotes for one morning. Ben Ami, however, seemed not to notice.

"But you're no doubt wondering why I, as a Jew, should appear so worried about the collapse of the Catholic Church, yes? So, to explain, let me tell you a true story." Kesler glanced at his watch. " . . . and a short one. Many years ago, before you were even born—1930, to be exact—Professor Sukenik, one of my predecessors here at the Institute of Archaeology, made an interesting discovery in the Rockefeller Museum here in Jerusalem. You have heard of Professor Sukenik, yes?"

"The man who identified the Dead Sea Scrolls—the father of Yigael Yadin."

"Correct. Well, he was making a study of inscriptions on first century Jewish sarcophagi and ossuaries, and in those days the Rockefeller had dozens of them stored in its basement. Anyway, one of the inscriptions that the professor deciphered read, *Yeshua bar Yosef* . . ." He paused to gauge

Kesler's grasp of basic Aramaic. "That's right, 'Jesus, son of Joseph'. Now, that—as the professor knew better than anybody—was actually of little significance. Yeshua and Yosef were among the commonest names in current usage during the first century—far commoner, for example, than your name, Daniel, is today. But it was at least worthy of note. And so, when a little later the professor was invited to Berlin to give a lecture on his work, he included a passing reference to this inscription—purely as a matter of interest. It was, I am afraid, a most unfortunate decision, given the political climate in Germany at the time and what we now know was to happen later under Hitler. The poor man was pilloried, Mr. Kesler, and his casual remark was exploited for the purposes of the crudest propaganda. He was accused, along with the rest of his race, of attempting to subvert the Christian religion! Times do not change as much as we think, Mr. Kesler; anti-Semitism may not be as overt as it was in the 1930s but it still exists and needs sadly little to reawaken it. That is why I implore you, Mr. Kesler, don't give the world yet another excuse to make the Jew its whipping boy."

Kesler emerged from the Institute building bewildered. It was a common enough experience in his job to have someone give conflicting signals during the course of an interview, but never to this extent. Why, at the same time as "imploring" him to leave the story alone, had the old man gone out of his way to deliver a lecture on the very implications that made it journalistically irresistible? There was no explanation and Kesler felt much the same confusion as he had the night before, after his meeting with Matzliah in the Hilton. And again it was a reawakening of his latent professionalism that triumphed; intellectual sparring with academics, he decided, was no substitute for a bit of old-fashioned foot-slogging.

The sun was at its height, but there was a cooling breeze and the two-mile walk from Mount Scopus down to the Old City took barely half an hour. At the Damascus Gate he turned left and followed the walls round to the old Arab bus station, where the ancient Mercedes behemoths with their high radiators and ornate, cow-catching fenders bore destinations that read like an index of biblical placenames. Sidestepping the number 22 to Bethlehem, he entered the station bar and, conspicuously American in his tailored trousers and button-down shirt, took a seat beneath the fading photograph of King Abdullah.

Halid, one of the joint proprietors, was nowhere to be seen, but the boy who brought Kesler his iced tea assured him he would be back in ten minutes.

An old Arab in brown ankle-length thob and white keffiyeh stared at him from the other side of the room, sucking all the while on a glass hookah stowed beneath the table. There was no hostility in his gaze, nor even curiosity; it was as though he regarded the American merely as a more interesting subject for contemplation than any of the other furniture. Kesler attempted to acknowledge the interest but, getting no response, swung his chair round to look through the large dirty windows onto the triangle of pavement outside, where the more masochistic customers yelled at each other above the blare of Arabic music from the nearby tape and record shop.

The boy was right. On seeing Kesler, Halid grinned broadly, swung a welcoming hand and drew up a chair opposite, conveniently obscuring the old Arab's view.

"You been busy, my friend, eh?" he enquired with a conspiratorial wink.

"What makes you say that?" replied Kesler guiltily.

"Just haven't seen you for a long time—thought maybe you were getting your tip-offs at some other bar these days."

"Not at all. I just like to keep you in reserve for the really important stuff."

"Ah, that's it. You want my views on Camp David," joshed the Arab.

"Sure, but not immediately. Something a little less—global. Do you still get a lot of building workers through here?"

"For sure! From Ramallah, Hebron, Jericho—from all around by the busload."

"To help build nice big Israeli apartment blocks, eh?" Kesler couldn't help remarking.

Halid gave a pragmatic shrug.

"Work is work, my friend. When we have our own state, things will be different."

Kesler resisted the temptation to pursue the point. Yes, things would be different. For one thing, Halid and all the rest of the West Bank Palestinians who had grown fat and prosperous under Israeli rule would be regarded as collaborators, Vichy Arabs. What had *they* done for the liberation? they would be asked and, in the absence of an answer, would once again become the second-class citizens in their own country that they had been when the West Bank had been part of Jordan.

"So what do you have in mind?" asked Halid.

Kesler checked on the old man with the hookah and was gratified to see he was now looking through the window. He was becoming paranoid, he told himself; the professor's little talk had perhaps had a greater effect on him than he cared to acknowledge.

"There's a building site just up the road, at Nahalat Shim'on, the old no-man's-land. Up to a couple of weeks ago they were putting in footings for new apartment blocks. Then, literally overnight, they stopped. All the laborers, including the watchman, were laid off without notice. What I want to know, Halid, is why?"

The Arab stroked his moustache, forefinger and thumb tracing the creases down the sides of his mouth.

"I can't tell you anything immediately. This is the first time that I hear about it."

"I didn't expect anything immediately—but someone must know, and, as likely as not, one of your customers. There must have been at least two dozen men working on that site."

"You have any suspicions?" asked Halid.

Kesler squeezed the lemon into his tea. The old Arab still had his back turned.

"It's possible they found something. What I don't know. It might have been nothing more than an unexploded mortar from '67. Let's just say that I'm curious. Know what I mean?"

The Arab grinned, displaying enough gold to fill a jeweler's window.

"Ever thought of becoming a journalist, Mr. Kesler?"

"Every morning when I wake up, Halid, but I don't know; by midday I just seem to lose interest . . . Now, will you do some asking around for me—discreetly?"

"When did I ever let my American friend down? But you make sure that that President of yours doesn't let *us* down in the next couple of days. Then the Israelis will have to build their own apartment blocks—on their own land!"

★

"Dan, there's someone to see you."

She only called him Dan when she was angry with him or was telling him something she didn't think he'd want to hear. It seemed to be a case of the latter; whoever the visitor was, he wasn't welcome. A second later he caught sight of the olive-drab shirt and twin oak leaves through the half-open door to the living room.

"Mr. Kesler, I regret not being able to notify you of my visit in advance," said the Israeli lieutenant colonel, "but I needed to be sure of talking to you in privacy—more so than my office unfortunately allows . . ."

He cast a glance in Aya's direction. Taking the hint, she announced that she would get Beni's meal ready and feed him separately. The door closed. Noting the glass already in the colonel's hand, Kesler fixed himself a drink.

"It must be something important to require the attention of the Defense Forces' spokesman in person. I'm honored."

The colonel said nothing until Kesler had seated himself in the easy chair opposite.

"Mr. Kesler, I had a call from Professor Ben Ami this afternoon—at half past one, to be precise."

Kesler was tempted to smile but checked himself. So the prof had shopped him; so much for his journalistic conceit in thinking he knew his man.

"And?"

"Mr. Kesler," sighed the colonel, "it's been a bad day and I'm too tired to play games. The professor tells me that you were asking about the Nahalat Shim'on site. I will say only that my reason for coming in person is to avoid any possibility of a misunderstanding; to tell you that the Nahalat Shim'on site and the suspension of building work there are matters of political sensitivity which have been deemed by the Government Censor to concern the security of the state. I do not ask you where your information came from; I know all about journalists protecting their sources. I am telling you simply and unequivocally that this matter is not to be reported, communicated to others, or in any way whatsoever published. Do I make myself clear?"

"You make yourself clear, Colonel," Kesler replied. "Am I permitted to ask why the suspension of work on a building site should be a matter of state security?"

"Don't you read your own newspapers, Mr. Kesler? Not even the front page?"

Kesler gave a sarcastic laugh.

"You're not going to persuade me surely that shenanigans on a municipal building site are related to what is going on at Camp David?"

"You're right, Mr. Kesler, I'm not going to persuade you. I'm telling you. Persuasion is more your line. On this occasion I'm just the uniformed messenger."

"In which case," snapped Kesler angrily, "it's little wonder the country is going bankrupt when it uses its military spokesmen as bellhops."

A smile played about the colonel's lips, but only briefly.

"I must also tell you," he resumed with an attempt at official *gravitas*, "that we are not unaware of the means by which the censor can be bypassed by a journalist who is prepared to breach the trust which his favored status allows him, and you should be aware that, if we find you attempting to pass this story to any publication anywhere in the world, we shall view the renewal of your credentials in a light commensurate with the future trust we feel we can place in you."

The man had become a speaking machine. But the implications were clear. The colonel was too subtle to spell out his knowledge of the false byline trick. In all likelihood, he knew every one of Kesler's pseudonyms and had them written down in his card index, most probably cross-referenced with the newspapers in which they had appeared. The threat alone was enough. At worst, Kesler's press credentials would not be renewed at the end of the year; at best, his access to information would be limited to government handouts and on-the-record briefings. Either way, professionally he would be dead.

The colonel was on his feet.

"I won't take up any more of your time, Mr. Kesler. I trust that my visit has not inconvenienced your wife. Please convey my apologies."

"About the tomb?" she enquired, as he walked into the kitchen after showing the colonel out.

He nodded. "Right the first time," and gave the evening meal an approving sniff.

She reached out to take him lightly by the wrist. Kesler recognized the gesture; she had something serious to say.

"Dani, this Nahalat Shim'on business—it worries me."

"Why?"

"Military spokesmen don't pay journalists courtesy calls, Dani. I'm not asking you to tell me what he said, but if it was about the tomb I've a good enough idea. It's just that, well, very few men have taken on the Israeli Government and gotten away with it, and I imagine even fewer have taken on the Vatican and gotten away with it. Now you're taking on both. You could hardly have chosen a more formidable pair of opponents. That's why I'm worried—that and the fact that you are living in the land of the one and threatening the existence of the other."

Kesler was about to respond but was prevented by Beni bursting through the door.

"*Abba*," he panted excitedly, "can I go to Rivka's party on Thursday? It's after school. Everybody else is going!"

Kesler looked at Aya and laughed.

"I don't see why not. We don't want you to feel discriminated against at your age, do we?"

The child's face took on a quizzical look.

"What's de-skiminated?"

Those who had known Defense Minister Gideon Berman before his injury had reckoned him quite handsome, although the IDF colonel found it hard to credit, as he sat in the minister's office half an hour later, looking at the grotesque mask opposite. It was as though a pair of scissors had been taken to a portrait photo and the two halves taped together but not properly lined up.

"You've been to see him?" Berman asked.

"Just came from his house."

"And his reaction?"

"Mainly surprise that we knew about his meeting with Ben Ami."

"But he got the message this time."

"I couldn't have spelled it out more clearly."

The diagonal scar grew suddenly more prominent as the minister's expression tautened.

"That's not what I'm asking. Look, I've got a cabinet meeting in half an hour and I need to be sure about Kesler. We can't afford a second miscalculation. Ben Ami's talk had no effect at all. This time I have to be sure. Now, in your judgement can Kesler be counted on?"

The colonel bit his lip.

"Yes," he heard himself say and, sensing that he was now superfluous, was glad to excuse himself on the pretext of having to write up the report for Military Intelligence. The newspapers regularly described the minister as a cold fish but in the colonel's opinion that was a rare example of journalistic understatement.

The few who knew Gideon Berman better attributed his coldness more to background than nature. Just as insanity can be seen as a sane reaction to an insane world, so—it was argued—could Berman's often automaton-like behavior be seen as a human reaction to the inhumanity he had experienced in early life.

Born in the Polish textile center of Lodz, he had been just five when the Germans entered the city on September 8, 1939. Within months, he, his mother, father, grandfather, elder sister, and baby brother had been evicted from their spacious house in the city center and herded, together with the rest of the Jewish population, into a sealed-off ghetto. His first childhood memory was of the savage winter of 1941, when he and sister Hannah, directed by their mother, had scrambled on hands and knees over the ghetto rubbish dump for potato peelings. Their father, who for weeks had deprived himself of nourishment to enable his family to eat, had already succumbed to typhus and death—along with five thousand other Jews in the Lodz ghetto who that winter died of starvation, disease, cold, or a slowly debilitating combination of all three.

Then in the spring and summer of 1942, the Nazis made the first moves to implement their final solution of "the Jewish problem." From the Lodz ghetto the very young and very old were the first to be dispatched to the newly built extermination camp at Chelmno, sixty miles to the north. Among them were Gideon's grandfather and three-year-old brother. One morning, a German soldier came to the door and led the toddler off by the hand, like a kindly uncle taking him for a picnic in the country. After that, Gideon's mother was never to be entirely sane, and the only other surviving member of the family, Gideon's sixteen-year-old sister Hannah, took over as head of the household.

But later in the same year, rumors of German reverses on the battlefield started to circulate—the Allied landings in North Africa, the Russians' massive counterattack at Stalingrad, and in June 1944 the Normandy landings. Despite the continuing privations, spirits in the ghetto rose; liberation, whether by the British and Americans driving east or by the Russians pushing west, couldn't be long delayed.

The anticipation of liberty was cruelly premature. In August 1944, with the Allied forces sweeping across northern Europe and only days from Paris, the Jews of Lodz were persuaded to move "for their own protection"; their labor, they were told, was required in the munitions factories of the Reich. Gideon's sister came to an agonizing decision. She and their mother would go as ordered, but he must hide in the house to await their return as soon as the war was over. So, to the familiar cries of *Los, los! Schneller!*, the last members of Gideon Berman's family had left—not for the promised munitions factory but for a three-hour train journey south to the gas chambers of Auschwitz.

When the Russians entered Lodz on January 19, 1945, the sole survivors of the former ghetto population of 164,000 were fewer than a thousand wraith-thin scavengers who, like Gideon, had managed to hide themselves during the Germans' final roundup. At the age of eleven and weighing fifty pounds, the future Defense Minister had already acquired more experience of cruelty and horror than most people would get in a dozen lifetimes. And something else—a conviction that, in the world into which he had been born, to be a Jew meant to be on one's own.

The wound—the diagonal slash across his face—had come decades later, during the Yom Kippur War of October 1973. A major general in command of a tank brigade, Berman had crossed the Suez Canal with Arik Sharon in pursuit of the fleeing Egyptian Third Army and, in the fashion of Israeli tank commanders, had been standing erect in the turret of his Centurion when an Arab rocket-propelled grenade had exploded at the base of the turret. The canvas masking around the breech had immediately burst into flames and this in turn had ignited the ammunition belt of the turret machine gun. It was never ascertained which had done the damage, but either a piece of the grenade shrapnel or one of the ricocheting machine gun rounds had bisected Berman's face as neatly as a comb parting hair. A hundred and twenty stitches applied in a field hospital had joined the flaps of skin together again, in the expectation that plastic surgery would be applied later to make good the provisional repair. When the time came, however, Berman had refused any such "cosmetics," arguing that the surgeons' time and skill were better spent on men more in need of their attention—and ironically giving ammunition to his political opponents who would later ascribe the gesture to an inverted vanity and a desire to preserve his battle scars. Neither on nor off the battlefield had Gideon Berman ever lacked enemies.

Acting Prime Minister Reuven Shavit sat at the head of the Cabinet table before the Menorah emblem of the State of Israel with the self-assurance of one who knew the seat would soon be his by right. It was no secret that Prime Minister Rubinger had terminal lung cancer and at most six months to live—even if the cynics were constantly noting that Golda Meir had similarly had six months to live for the last ten years of her life. Camp David was Rubinger's last venue in a starring role, his last chance to assure himself of a place in the pantheon of Israeli history alongside Weizmann, Ben-Gurion, Meir, and Dayan. He already dominated party and Cabinet alike, and no decision in either had ever been taken that wasn't in line with his known wishes. Such was the reward for a man who had been called out of retirement to bring the party back into power after its years in the political doldrums.

That Reuven Shavit was Rubinger's chosen successor there now seemed no doubt. Among the "young" men in the Cabinet—those in their early fifties—there was only one other possible: Defense Minister Gideon Berman. But Berman's reputation for being a loner contrasted uncomfortably with Shavit's Hollywood good looks, glamorous wife, and obvious appeal as the Kennedy-style candidate heralding a new era of youth and dynamism. Nor did the Defense Minister's Holocaust childhood elicit especial sympathy in a country where concentration camp tattoos were as common as freckles.

Alone in the Cabinet, Foreign Minister Ya'acov Rosenstein continued to believe that the battle between "Beauty and the Beast," as it had inevitably been dubbed, was still an open contest. Of the same generation as Rubinger, he was closer to the old man than any of the others and, despite Rubinger's appointment of Shavit as his stand-in, suspected that both candidates were being put to the test in the present situation. Rosenstein had never made any secret of his own preference: Reuven Shavit was undeniably a whiz kid, a product of the party machine, a polished performer, and consummate politician, but at bottom he lacked a soul, and in the Foreign Minister's view such a man would likely as not be the country's last Prime Minister if he were ever to assume the position of ultimate power. Nonetheless, watching him now call the Cabinet to order, he had to admit that his own worst fears looked like being realized.

"Gentlemen," Shavit announced, "it is late and I have no intention of keeping you longer than necessary. We have only two items on the agenda, both concerned with Operation Ezekiel." He looked across to Foreign Minister Rosenstein. "First, Ya'acov has some news."

"Only," shrugged Rosenstein, "that the Apostolic Delegate, Archbishop Ramone, has requested an urgent appointment for first thing tomorrow morning, but I don't foresee any problems there."

Shavit nodded and switched to Berman.

"And you, Gideon. Any problems with our journalist friend, Kesler?"

"No problems as such, although it's taking rather longer than we calculated. However, further pressure has been put on him within the last hour and I remain confident of his response."

Shavit feigned alarm.

"Let us hope that confidence is justified! If Ya'acov is seeing the Apostolic Delegate first thing tomorrow morning, we have no more than twenty-four hours after that, which means . . ."

"I know what it means," cut in Berman, "and I repeat, I remain confident."

★

Meetings between the Foreign Minister and the Apostolic Delegate were characterized by an excess of protocol that made an audience with the Pope seem like a casual chat—the phone call via personal assistants to fix the time; the elaborate parking arrangements to accommodate the Vatican car; and the stiff formality of the meeting itself, with Minister Rosenstein invariably guiding the archbishop to the pair of uncomfortable high-backed chairs at the far end of the room. For a people who prided themselves on informality in official life, the Israelis always struck Ramone as strangely adept at exploiting every ounce of diplomatic intimidation when they wished to convey a frosty displeasure. What, in Ramone's case, made it doubly ironic was that the post of Apostolic Delegate was not in the strictest sense a diplomatic one anyway, such diplomatic privileges as he was accorded being a matter of courtesy and custom only. In fact, Ramone's own feelings about the Vatican's refusal to recognize the State of Israel were highly ambivalent. The official line, which was as deeply etched in his memory as the Magnificat from the number of times he had been required to quote it, was that the Holy See did not recognize countries whose borders were a matter of dispute—as Israel's had been ever since the founding of the state. But, as the Israelis pointed out, that hadn't stopped a dozen other countries according them recognition, and in his own conscience Ramone couldn't deny that the truth was more starkly simple: There were more Arabs in the Catholic Church than Jews.

"You have come to see me on a matter of politics or religion, Archbishop?" asked the Foreign Minister.

"Both, I suspect," Ramone replied.

The minister cocked an eyebrow.

"Please tell me how I can help you, Archbishop."

Ramone wondered how much the Israeli already knew. Was it really possible that the absence of any public statement on the Nahalat Shim'on discovery was because the archaeologists hadn't seen the political implications?

"It is a matter that my superiors in Rome fear could become a source of unnecessary embarrassment to both our states," he said, choosing the last word with particular care. He looked to the minister for a sign of approval, but was disappointed. "It is not an entirely new situation. We had a very similar incident which you may recall back in 1968 with the discovery of the tomb at Giv'at ha-Mivtar." Still no reaction. "The Holy See was most appreciative of the tact and sensitivity shown by the Israeli Government of the time."

The archbishop felt more than usually conscious of the tightness of the silk sash around his midriff; the man opposite either didn't know what he was talking about or, more ominously, was pretending he didn't. And yet Ya'acov Rosenstein was no political ingenue. He was most often described as a *yekke*, a kindly term for those German Jews who had fled Hitler's regime during the 1930s but who in this land of the open-necked shirt still clung to their jackets and ties and a corresponding formality of behavior. A committed Zionist, he had been a company commander in the Seventh Palmach Brigade during the fight against the Arabs in 1948, and still carried the marks of battle on a left leg that with each passing year gave more pain and lately obliged him to use a stick. Already in his seventies, with two heart attacks behind him and a pacemaker within, he owed his present position in the Government to his proven political abilities and his lifelong friendship with the Prime Minister, in almost equal measures. Ramone watched him straighten his injured leg and was reminded of the arthritic cripple back in Rome from whom he had taken his orders only twenty-four hours earlier. The world was old, governed by old men who could no longer even stand on their feet. What the Jews termed "the End of Days" had suddenly never seemed closer. With an effort, he wrenched himself back to the more immediate issue.

"I will come to the point, Minister," he said, reconciled to the inevitability of having to make a specific request which he had hoped to avoid. "It has been rumored that the body of another crucifixion victim has been discovered in a first century tomb to the north of the Old City. In my capacity as representative of the Holy See, I am here to convey to you the earnest hope that, if true, this matter will be handled with the degree of discretion that we have come to expect and appreciate from your Government."

"You mean you'd rather we kept quiet about it," responded Rosenstein with a bluntness that caught the archbishop off balance.

"Well, that, Minister, must be up to you. We obviously

have no desire to interfere in the internal affairs of the State of Israel."

Rosenstein gave an unexpected smile.

"The what, Archbishop?"

Ramone was alarmed. This time the word had slipped out unintentionally. It was one thing to talk casually about "both our states," but quite another to refer specifically to "the State of Israel." He recalled the furor when poor John Paul I, during one of his lamentably few days in office, had written a letter to the Mayor of Jerusalem, addressing the envelope in his own hand to the "State of Israel"—thereby, it was argued by the Vatican purists, conferring the diplomatic recognition that the Holy See had so long withheld.

"I said, Minister, that we have no desire to interfere in your internal affairs."

Rosenstein brought his hands together.

"Given then that the Holy See has no desire to interfere, what—if the State of Israel were responsive to your wishes—would you like us to do?"

It wasn't going well. Already at a disadvantage, Ramone could see that he was now being asked to expose a vulnerable flank. Cautiously he answered, "Our fear, Minister, is that the public revelation of this discovery could be exploited by the enemies of the Church. I don't have to tell you that there are many in this world who would see this as an opportunity to deride and even destroy the Catholic Church—and I trust I am right in believing that you would not wish to see this happen." He was tempted to cite the common link that bound the people of the Old Testament with those of the New, but judged it inappropriate in the circumstances. "We would therefore . . ."

"Do you know exactly where these archaeological remains have been found, Archbishop?" broke in Rosenstein.

Again, Ramone was caught off balance.

"A-As I say, we understand from what we have heard—the rumors, that is—that they have been found somewhere to the north of the Old City. In the area of Nahalat Shim'on, we are given to believe."

The Minister's gaze wandered up to the ceiling.

"And do you know to whom the area of Nahalat Shim'on is deemed to belong by the rest of the world, the Holy See included?"

"I am not a politician, Minister."

"Of course not, Archbishop, of course not. Then let me inform you that Nahalat Shim'on is known in military parlance as no-man's-land. It was so declared in 1948 and, technically at least, has remained so ever since in the absence of a comprehensive Middle East agreement. Now, according to international law, this means that it belongs either literally to 'no man' or, more realistically, to the United Nations, who still have an active observation post there. It does not—by this interpretation—belong to Israel, despite our de facto possession of it since the Six Day War of 1967. You said a few minutes ago, Archbishop, that you were here in your capacity as representative of the Holy See. Regrettably, I have to inform you that the Holy See should be addressing any requests regarding this controversial piece of land to the United Nations in New York, where, if I remember correctly, you have a full-time observer."

Ramone was stunned into silence. The minister, however, became suddenly genial.

"In one respect, though, Archbishop, I may be able to help you. If you will excuse me, I will put a call through to our Minister of Education and Culture, Mr. Kaufman, who—within *our* jurisdiction, of course—has responsibility for archaeological matters. He may be able to cast some light on the subject."

Rosenstein hobbled to the other end of the room and picked up the telephone. Being ignorant of all but the most rudimentary Hebrew, the archbishop understood nothing of the conversation that followed. At length, the minister returned to his seat.

"It seems, Archbishop, that the matter is out of both our hands. The Minister of Education informs me that a press conference is to be announced within the next twenty-four hours concerning the Nahalat Shim'on discovery. They're just waiting for the Department of Archaeology at the Hebrew University to complete its paperwork."

★

Kesler spotted the note immediately, tucked beneath the windshield wiper on the driver's side. His first thought was that it would be a terse reminder from a neighbor to park closer to the wall to allow others to get through the narrow one-way street. Wrong.

He swung round in the crazy expectation of seeing the author, whoever he was, just disappearing round a corner. But the paper was damp, suggesting it had been planted hours before—the previous evening most likely, although he hadn't noticed it when seeing off the colonel.

Lost in thought, he wandered back toward the house, note still in hand.

"What is it, Dani?" Aya asked.

There was no point in playacting. He handed it to her to read for herself.

FORGET NAHALAT SHIM'ON. NO WARNING NEXT TIME.

She looked up, searching his eyes for an explanation.

"Nahalat Shim'on?"

"It's where they found the tomb."

She froze.

"Dani, I tell you, I don't like it. Where did this come from?"

"It was on the car. Probably our visitor last night."

"The colonel?"

"Not him personally. He'd have got someone else to do it. But it fits. The official warning first, followed by the crude backup supposedly from another source. It's standard technique."

"What are you going to do about it?"

"Do about it? Ignore it."

"Not even report it to the authorities?"

"What! And give them the satisfaction of knowing that their bullyboy tactics have paid off? No, sirree. I must be off."

She caught his arm.

"Dani, I know it sounds melodramatic, but you will be careful, won't you? Just don't underestimate the authorities—not on something like this."

He gave a hollow laugh.

"You mean they might have second thoughts about bumping off the Jerusalem correspondent of the *Baltimore Post*, but they'd swat a troublesome freelance without giving it a second thought. That it?"

She was suddenly serious.

"Dani, I know that if it weren't for me you wouldn't be a freelancer now. You'd be a big-shot bureau chief somewhere exotic or even back in the Baltimore head office. What I'm saying is that I know what you gave up for me and Beni, and I know what it cost you—in every way. If, on top of that, you were now to pay another price, I would never forgive myself. That's all. If you like, I'm just being selfish because I don't want to be made to feel doubly guilty."

He looked down at her—his "Canaanite concubine," as he often called her, after an exquisitely modeled statuette he had once been shown by Moshe Dayan. How such an outwardly delicate creature could within be made of such steel was still a mystery to him after fifteen years together. He was reminded of one of Halid's less scurrilous quips about marriage being like a melon because by the time you had found out whether it was good or bad it was too late to change it. He had no complaints on that score and, bending low, he kissed her lightly on the forehead.

"I know why I love you," he said, and left.

As he closed the iron gate behind him, he wondered how much more he should have told her when he had gone freelance, about the other price he had paid. As with the melon, it was too late now.

"So what's the news from Ramallah, Hebron, and Jericho?" he enquired as Halid laid down the glass of tea.

"You're still interested?" asked the Arab with apparent surprise.

Kesler stared at him.

"Why shouldn't I be?"

"I just didn't think it was that important."

"You mean you haven't asked anybody about the site?"

"Not yet, no."

"But, what the . . ."

Then he understood. Halid too had received a visitor.

"It's all right," he said with a tired smile. "I see it all. What were they going to do? Slap on a hygiene order? Investigate your tax returns? Or stop you visiting your brother in Amman?"

"Sorry?"

"Halid, you don't have to explain. And don't worry about the site. Forget it, in fact—the whole business. It was unfair of me to involve you in the first place. I'll do my own dirty work."

The Arab was suddenly perturbed. "Dan, take some of

your own advice: Forget this whole business. It's not worth it, believe me. Besides . . ."

He stopped.

"Besides what, Halid?"

In the absence of a reply, Kesler filled the silence.

"Besides, they're out to screw me as well. It's alright. I know. I had my warning last night—double-barreled. And don't worry; I won't embarrass you by being seen in here—not for a week or two at least."

He finished the tea and slapped a bank note down on the table.

Halid watched him walk out and carry on along the walls until he was out of sight. A minute later, closeted in the small booth behind the bar, he picked up the old-fashioned black telephone and dialed. Another Arab voice answered.

In his subconscious Kesler had made the decision the night before, after the colonel's visit. Such an overreaction on the part of the authorities was proof enough that the story had more than journalistic significance. And the journalistic avenue was now blocked anyway.

The Agency was bound to find out from some source and, since he had already had two warnings from McKenzie about the quality of recent material, it was preferable that he be the first to file. The only question was how to make the drop without being detected. The episode with Halid had left him in no doubt that he was being shadowed, but that was no great problem; there was no place in the world where it was easier to throw off a tail.

He stepped into the glass-fronted Umayyah Restaurant opposite Herod's Gate, a hundred yards along from the old Arab bus station, and ordered a plate of humus, a Caesar salad, and the baked lamb. From his seat in a corner next to the window he could see everything that happened, inside and out. No obvious tail had followed him in, but then tails weren't meant to be obvious. He remembered an Israeli intelligence officer once confiding that tails dreaded bars and restaurants because such places invariably had at least two exits. So if your mark went to the lavatory, you had to decide whether to stick with him and perhaps be drawn into ball

banter at the urinal, which would blow your cover, or let him
go and risk losing him through a back alley.

Three-quarters of an hour later and after an unaccom-
panied inspection of the restaurant's graffiti gallery, Kesler
settled the bill and left. The only person to follow him out
was a young German hitchhiker who set off in the opposite
direction. His tail, it seemed, had been dedicated enough to
forgo lunch and maintain his watch from outside.

At a brisk pace, looking over his shoulder only to cross the
double lanes of traffic, he headed back west along the walls
and this time past the Arab bus station. Arriving at the
Damascus Gate, he pushed his way through the honey-cake
vendors and money changers into the Old City proper. The
rest was easy. Taking the right fork into the Suq Khan Ez-
Zait, he turned into the Via Dolorosa and, sucked and fun-
neled through the warren of vaulted streets to the sound of
hollering, chanting, and retching, was soon caught up in the
tide of tourists and traders around the Church of the Holy
Sepulchre. To add to the usual confusion, dozens of Dutch
pilgrims, led by a cross-carrying pastor, were diligently
retracing the traditional footsteps of Christ on His way to
Calvary, attempting to persuade themselves—despite the gui-
tar accompaniment—that the Jerusalem of His time must
have been much the same.

The smell of the spice stalls still in his nostrils, Kesler
emerged from the Old City through the Jaffa Gate and headed
northwest up the Jaffa Road. At the small municipal garden
near the new post office, he sat on a bench and drew a crisp
new bank note from his wallet. Along one of the edges he
neatly wrote a single sentence prefixed by his Agency cryptonym, simply stating the facts as he believed them to be; if
McKenzie wanted more, he knew how to get in touch.

The kiosk—an insubstantial structure of fluted aluminum
seemingly held together by Marlboro and Camel advertise-
ments—was on the left just past the Davidka Memorial in
Herut Square. He recognized the hunched figure inside,
with the black beret pulled down over one ear, from previous
occasions, and asked for a pack of Rothman's king-size.

"Don't stock Rothman's. Only Dunhill," the man responded,
adding without a flicker. "You'll have to go to Ben Yehuda
Street if you want Rothman's."

"I'll take the Dunhill," Kesler said, flipping open his wallet and handing over the folded bank note.

The message was on its way.

The feeling afterward was always the same—not treason, but adultery. In betraying Israel he betrayed Aya. In the early days he had tried to argue that passing on the information of one country to that country's closest ally and staunchest defender could only help strengthen the bonds that joined them by removing the secrecy that might otherwise divide. But that, he now recognized, was specious, self-serving bullshit.

It hadn't started as a conscious act. It was after he had gone freelance, shortly after he and Aya had married. Their finances were strapped. Jerusalem wasn't the sort of forgotten corner of the world where a freelance could set himself up as the local wire king and string for a dozen international dailies that couldn't justify keeping their own man on the spot for the one story that might break only every six months. To be a freelance in Jerusalem was to grub and scratch for every half-chewed morsel from the staff boys' table. As a result, his earnings dropped by more than half in the months following his resignation from the *Post*. But that wasn't the real reason. They could have managed on a quarter of his staff salary, and still have been happy. The real reason had more to do with self-esteem. With vanity.

He had been flattered when, despite his reduced journalistic status, he had received the usual invitation from the U.S. Consulate to join the traditional cocktail party on Thanksgiving Day. It had coincided with a particular low in his morale—a realization of just how much clout the opening line, "This is Dan Kesler of the *Baltimore Post*" carried compared with "This is Dan Kesler; I'm a freelance journalist and I was wondering if . . ." Worse still, he recently had even found himself saying, "This is Dan Kesler; I think we last talked when I was with the *Baltimore Post*." He was on his own, and after years of working for an infuriatingly paternalistic but internationally prestigious concern like the *Post*, he had never felt more naked.

So he had gone to the consulate cocktail party; had put on a good show of self-sufficiency before colleagues who marveled at his courage in throwing up a staff meal ticket; had forced himself to be pleasant to the patronizing upstart who had been sent out as his replacement and who wondered aloud why it was that "nobody" before him had appreciated the newsworthiness of the story he was currently working on; and had ended up, his faculties only marginally impaired by alcohol, in a huddle with the consulate's second secretary, a good-looking immaculately tailored black man named George Livingstone.

He had had dealings with George before and remembered his nice line in self-deprecating humor—how the State Department's only answer to staffing a consulate in a place as racially divided as Jerusalem was to fill it with blacks. Which was hardly true; apart from a secretary, George was the only black man in the building.

In retrospect, George had been all too plausible. The ambassador in Tel Aviv, he said, was anxious to establish a more effective briefing service. They wanted someone to do what was basically a collating job—to compile a weekly digest, for the ambassador's exclusive use, of the most relevant articles and features that had appeared in the Israeli papers. That required, though, a rather special sort of animal—someone who could understand and translate Hebrew and yet had the editorial flair to separate the wheat from the chaff. According to George, they had cast around within the Tel Aviv Embassy and the two Jerusalem consulates, East and West, and had drawn a blank. Dan, however, could be just the man for the job—assuming of course that he was interested and had the time to fit it in. It was just a long shot.

It had all been done in a way that was charming, subtle—and seductive. At no point, Kesler was to recall, had George mentioned money or implied that his changed status might make such an offer more attractive than previously.

In fact, it had been Kesler himself who had introduced the subject of remuneration, in a roundabout way. How many pages, he had asked, did the ambassador want this digest to run to? Oh, replied George, not more than a dozen—enough for a half-hour read at the end of each week to give the ambassador a grasp of what was going on beneath the surface of Israeli politics and society; of the sort of currents that might one day without warning turn into a tide. Kesler thought: A dozen pages, most requiring translation, worked out at about six hours' work a week. He certainly had the time and, despite himself, rather liked the idea of "working directly for the ambassador"—to use George's phrase. A sort of adviser, in fact. Yes, he had replied, he'd be prepared to give it a go, so long of course as the terms were acceptable. Well, said George, they were thinking in the region of eighty dollars a week but, in view of Kesler's credentials, he had no hesitation in rounding it up to a hundred. Kesler had masked his surprise with difficulty; a hundred dollars a week in those days accounted for a quarter of his former salary as a *Post* correspondent—easy money for a man whose job it was to read all the newspapers anyway.

Too easy. Which was why he hadn't told Aya. But, he reassured himself, he would always know where and when to draw the line.

It was three months later—around February—when he was told by George that the ambassador was so pleased with his work that he wanted to thank him personally. Accordingly he had gone to Tel Aviv for an hour-long stroking session during which His Excellency—"Call me Murray"—had suggested it would be of immense help if Kesler could occasionally tack an extra page onto his weekly digests giving his own analysis of the week's reporting. But only if he had the time. Kesler had the time, and a few weeks later noticed his remuneration had gone up by a half.

A year later to the day—Thanksgiving—Kesler had finally been forced to admit to himself what he had for some time half-suspected: that he was a paid United States Government informant. The remark wasn't accidental, he knew. He and George had been discussing the digest, and George had mentioned that top staffers in the two Jerusalem consulates were now ordering regular copies for themselves before the primary copy went off to the ambassador in Tel Aviv. Kesler expressed concern that what had started out as a purely private digest for the ambassador's eyes only was now apparently going into circulation—together, he assumed, with his interpretive addenda. The last thing he wanted was to be fingered by the Israelis as a U.S. Government stooge and lose whatever journalistic credibility he might have.

George was blandly reassuring. Kesler wasn't to lose a second's sleep on that count. As his case officer, he could personally guarantee the confidentiality of Kesler's material.

The words hit him with the force of a sledgehammer. *Case*

officer? What the fuck was he talking about? George put on a show of surprise at his naivete. How long had he been a journalist? He must have guessed that his salary was being paid by the Agency. Anyway, like it or not, his name was on the Agency payroll and, as one of their employees, naturally he had a case officer. "You mean I'm a fucking spy!" Kesler blurted out. George had laughed and put a comforting arm round him. Not quite; that required a little more training. Then what was he in Agency terminology? Kesler demanded. George thought. A company casual. Did that sound so bad?

That evening Kesler returned home devastated. It was as though he had been flattered into allowing someone to paint his portrait, only to find that the result was a grotesque caricature. He felt angry, conned, and physically ill. Somewhere in Washington his name was there on the record as a CIA employee. He was branded—and this at a time, the mid 1970s, when the image of the Agency was at its lowest following the revelations of its part in the downfall of Allende in Chile.

The next morning he went to see George in his office. He wanted out, he told him. George was all sympathy. Of course he understood why he was reacting this way, but "out" at this stage was neither easy nor advisable. If he came off the payroll, the Agency was under no obligation to protect him from exposure, and in the wake of Philip Agee's kiss-and-tell excursion into the literary field every present and former member of the Agency had reason to worry. Washington was in the grip of a Salem-like hysteria; there was no telling how far the madness might spread; it was known that at least two other books were already being written by ex-agents.

Kesler didn't know what to think. He was pinned like a butterfly to a board, with all possible movement revolving round the same central axis. He couldn't be sure, but there was reason enough to believe that George was blackmailing him: continued cooperation or exposure. It would be no good trying to assure the Israelis that he was now an ex-employee of the Agency, and yet for how long could he carry on without being exposed anyway? His confusion was all too evident to George.

"Dan," said George smoothly, "I think I see a way out here. There's nothing I can do about your name on the payroll and I think we're both agreed that it's better it stays there where at least it's protected by Langley's double-ledger system. So what I . . ."

Kesler frowned.

"Every Agency operative," George explained, "has what's known as a 201 File—just as the *Post* no doubt still has a file on you back in Baltimore. The Langley file, though, is divided into two parts and these are stored separately to ensure maximum security. One part gives your real name and identity and the other your Agency call-in code name. It means that even if one part is blown, there's no way a tie-up can be made between the two. So, anyway, what I suggest is this: We take you off the digest—that way none of your work will crop up in U.S. diplomatic channels here in Israel—and then we distance you from the consulate here in Jerusalem by means of this call-in code I've just mentioned."

"I'm not as fucking naive as you think I am," erupted Kesler suddenly. "Why don't you give this 'call-in code' its real name? 'Cryptonym' is the word you're so studiously avoiding. Right, George? Well, you can stuff it, because I'm not going to be an agent, spy, paid informant, or whatever other euphemism you care to dream up. Is that clear?"

George gave an indulgent smile.

"Dan, you've got it all wrong. In your case a cryptonym—if that's what you want to call it—is nothing more than a distancing device—for your own benefit and protection. But if you really want it with the bark off, then OK, I'll give it to you. We've got a central problem here and it's this: If you want your name to remain on the Agency payroll, where your identity will continue to be protected, then you've got to do something in return for the money. Now, I swear, I'm not asking you to inform on anybody. In fact, I'm not asking you to do anything that you wouldn't normally do in the course of your everyday journalistic activity. What I have in mind is simply that you put us on your list of subscribers."

"Why don't you just read the papers I write for?" remarked Kesler tersely.

"Oh, come off it, Dan," retorted George with a show of impatience. "Let's cut the crap. We both know that there's a bundle of stuff that never gets into print for any number of reasons."

"Censored material, you mean?"

"Perhaps. But you know that so-called censored material

isn't always what it seems. Censorship can be a pretty handy device on occasions for suppressing what the government may find politically embarrassing—like, say, the infringement of Palestinian civil rights." He paused as though catching up with his own thought processes. "Look, I'll tell you what, Dan. You just file whatever your conscience allows you to file. Now, there's nothing unethical about that—neither journalistically nor morally. Just the opposite, in fact. It gives you an outlet for material that you may think the Israelis have no good reason to sit on but that no newspaper would touch for fear of offending them. How about it?"

When Kesler seemed to waver, George was ready with the clincher.

"You will of course have to accept a cut in salary. Pretty substantial, I'm afraid. Probably as much as fifty per cent."

Fifty per cent of Kesler's guilt evaporated on the instant. Fifteen pieces of silver had to be better than thirty. Besides, for all his show of wanting out, he had already made the calculation that his personal finances would be crippled by the sudden cutoff of what now amounted to a sizeable hunk of his income. What George was proposing sounded like a realistic compromise.

"OK," he sighed at last. "But I want to be clear on the ground rules."

Yet for all his insistence on ground rules, Kesler had left George's office in the full knowledge that he had sold out. He hadn't even considered whether this time he would tell Aya—for it was her reaction, he now realized, that he feared just as much as any public humiliation. As for his qualms of conscience, they were resolved rather than settled by an event a few weeks later. On the twenty-third of December, 1975, Richard S. Welch, the CIA station chief in Greece, was killed by terrorists just outside Athens; three days before, his CIA identity had been revealed in a local newspaper. It just went to show, said George, how careful one had to be.

★

The meeting of the Curia Segreta was the shortest on record.

"There will of course be no stopping the Israelis, now that they know that we know," opined the Cardinal Prefect of the Holy Office. "As I warned at the time, we have played into

their hands, right into their hands. . . . Only a diplomatic
intervention at the highest level by the Holy Father can
possibly save the situation, and frankly even then . . ."

His voice tailed off as he realized that every other face
around the horseshoe table was resolutely turned toward the
slight figure at the center.

For a long time the Secretary of State said nothing. The
decoded cable from Archbishop Ramone in Jerusalem, which
he had read out at the start of the meeting, lay before him on
the blotter. A press conference in twenty-four hours! And
already four of those hours had gone just in the time it had
taken to relay the message to Rome and reconvene the secret
council in emergency session. Even now as he pondered
what best to do, time was slipping by. An institution that was
credited with thinking in centuries was being required to
think in minutes and act in hours, in order to avert nothing
less than its own extinction. Never before had a man felt
more in need of the guidance of a God whose existence he
denied. He pulled the mozzetta more tightly about his shoulders and, eyes still on the blotter, said:

"That a diplomatic intervention at the highest level is now
essential, I agree—but neither by the Holy Father nor with
the Israelis. With the Holy Father in Holland and Prime
Minister Rubinger at Camp David, logistics are plainly against
it. And if it were to fail like the last one, what time would
then be left to attempt another initiative?" He gave a delicate
cough and in a lower voice added: "Besides, any participation
by the Holy Father would require that he first be . . . briefed."
He looked up and, taking in both arms of the horseshoe,
declared: "No, we must take a leaf out of the Israelis' book.
Thinking one step ahead is not enough; we must act it.
Without delay we must contact Cardinal DeWohl in New
York."

By the time the Secretary of State had finished outlining
his proposal five minutes later, he sensed there would be no
need for a vote, nor even for discussion. Not that he was
under any illusions about his powers of persuasion. Looking
at the gallery of profiles before him, he knew that what Their
Eminences were registering was less a tacit vote of confidence than an expression of relief that one of their number
was prepared to take the full responsibility for so momentous
a decision upon his own shoulders.

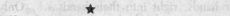

"The Spirit of Camp David"—coined after the successful 1959 summit between President Eisenhower and Nikita Khrushchev—had never been less in evidence. With one exception, there wasn't a person around the conference table in Laurel Lodge who didn't recognize the signs of presidential irritation and imminent eruption—the head sunk into the shoulders, the muscles flexed at the corners of the mouth, and the absolute motionlessness of a wild animal about to spring. The exception was the Israeli Prime Minister, Avraham (Avram to friends and colleagues) Rubinger. He alone appeared to be as oblivious as a bird on a bough of the cat below. Secretary of State Romford attempted to head off the inevitable.

"What I think the President finds hard to comprehend, Mr. Prime Minister, if you will permit me to speak frankly on his behalf, is your apparent inability to match the Palestinian position even part of the way. Not only have the PLO recognized the right of Israel to exist—without which these talks would never have gotten off the ground—but, if I read the signs correctly, they might now be prepared to drop their demand for a Palestinian state and settle instead for a homeland in return for your dismantling the Jewish settlements on the West Bank."

With a sad, sardonic smile the Israeli Prime Minister gazed at the American in a manner which, taken together with his long hair, putty nose, and walrus moustache, would have guaranteed him first prize in any Albert Einstein look-alike contest.

"And if you will permit me to speak frankly on behalf of the people of Israel, Mr. Secretary, you still have a long way to go in your understanding of the Palestinians. They are dealing in semantics, don't you see. Words like 'homeland' are nothing more than semantic devices to mask an unacceptable reality."

"With respect, Mr. Prime Minister," Romford countered, "it's hardly semantics if they're prepared to go along with an arms-free zone throughout the West Bank and allow the Israeli Army control of the borders. As for the question of the Jewish settlements, both the President and myself have indicated to you more than once in our closed sessions over the last three days that, in the interests of a comprehensive Middle East agreement, we would willingly recommend to Congress the establishment of a fund to compensate displaced Jewish settlers. You know you have only to name your price on that one." With an attempt at levity, he added, "Since most of them come from Brooklyn anyway, I can't see Congress objecting."

But the Israeli's mood had changed.

"Mr. Secretary," he said icily, "it grieves me to have to tell a man in your position that you have once again failed to understand. The Jews you refer to in Judea and Samaria—it is not they who are the settlers. This area you are talking so glibly about as 'a Palestinian homeland' is our *heart*land. It was there in Judea and Samaria that our nation was born; there that our prophets prophesied; there that our ancient culture was developed. The settlers, Mr. Secretary, are the Palestinians! They are guests in our land, and if they are not prepared to live side by side with their hosts, then it is *they* who should leave—they who should be bought off by your boundless generosity. Go offer Mr. Hamiya your dollars. See how *he* reacts!"

"What's your goddam fucking game, Rubinger?" boomed a voice from the other end of the table. The only surprise was that it had been so long in coming. The President was on his feet. He leaned across the table and shook the butt-filled ashtray at the Israeli Prime Minister.

"For three days now, Rubinger, we have sat here listening to you deliver your pious platitudes about Jewish rights, rattling the ashes of your six million dead in response to any and every request for even a gesture of flexibility. 'You don't understand what it is to be a Jew . . . You don't know what it's like never to feel safe—to be surrounded by a hundred million hostile Arabs . . .' Well, let me tell you, Rubinger, I've had just so goddam much, and . . ."

"Joe, Joe," cut in Secretary Romford, placing a restraining hand on McCrae's shoulder and lowering the ashtray gently but forcibly, "it's already late and we're all tired. Let's leave it for tonight."

The Israeli gave a polite smile, as to a parent attempting to excuse the behavior of an obstreperous child.

"I am sure you are right, Mr. Secretary," he said. "To-

morrow, with the benefit of a good night's sleep, we may all
see things differently. Who knows, we may . . ."

But the President was gone.

Back in the presidential quarters in Aspen Lodge, Secretary Romford handed McCrae a generous whisky.

"If it's any comfort, I share your puzzlement, Joe," he
volunteered. "I've never seen Rubinger like that, and I must
have met the man on more than twenty occasions now.
There's an . . . an insolence about him that I don't get. The
man is impervious to pleas and threats alike. He sure as hell
has a game plan of some sort, but I'm jiggered if I can see
what it is. Can't be the Jewish lobby. He must realize that
they couldn't back him without at least a token concession on
his part. But nothing . . . not a goddam thing."

"And it was you who said that Zionist declaration on the
opening day was just an opening gambit. Right?" remarked
the President flatly.

"Right, Joe. You don't have to rub it in. And it's still a
gambit. It *has* to be. It can't be in Rubinger's interests to
have the talks break down because of his intransigence; it
would be like inviting us to impose a settlement and that's
the last thing he wants."

McCrae grunted.

"What's the atmosphere like in the Arab camp?"

"Not good, Joe, not good. The Saudis and Jordanians are
OK, but the Palestinians and Egyptians are coming heavy. I
give them till tomorrow lunchtime before they start packing.
It's not just the frustration; it's the humiliation . . . the loss
of face. That and the claustrophobia of being cooped up in
their cabins for three days."

"Yea, I know the feeling," sympathized McCrae and belched.
"What was that phrase Begin once used? 'A deluxe concentration camp.' Never said a truer word. We give the bastards till
tomorrow then." He glanced at his watch. "Correction, today."

★

"My name is DeWohl, Cardinal John D. DeWohl, and I
repeat that I am here to see Secretary Romford on a matter of
considerable urgency."

The Marine sergeant looked again at the man, the car, and the driver. The car was large and black like any one of a million others; the driver was wearing a plain gray suit with no identifying insignia; and, as for the man, he may have claimed to be the Pope himself but in his working black garb with cutaway collar he could have as easily been a parish priest. He was certainly unlike any cardinals the sergeant had ever seen—admittedly only on television—who always wore scarlet robes and box-shaped hats. Besides, it was a quarter past one in the morning.

"Do you have any identification, Cardinal . . . sir?" he asked, aware that there had to be a more proper form of address.

"No, I do not, young man. It is rare in the extreme that I am required to prove I am who I say I am, and I wouldn't be here in person at this hour of the night if it wasn't for the seeming impossibility of getting any sense out of the White House switchboard. To believe them, you'd have to believe that there was no such place as Camp David! Now, sergeant, will you just . . ."

He stopped.

"I tell you what. We can resolve this matter very easily. If you are not prepared to take me at my word, I assume you will agree to take a note to Secretary Romford if I now write one in my own hand. He can then be the judge of my honesty."

The sergeant was about to protest that this wasn't the normal way of doing things and that, anyway, it was more than likely that the Secretary of State was fast asleep, but the cardinal's menacing look, combined with the fact that he was already scribbling, stopped the words in his throat. He took the piece of paper and promised to do what he could, but with no guarantee of success.

Twenty minutes later, a Secret Service man arrived at the gatehouse to escort His Eminence to Secretary Romford's quarters.

★

"Good to see you, John!" said Romford with the lopsided grin that invariably masked a state of extreme fatigue. "But what in heaven's name brings you up here at this hour?" He waved the note. "And what's all this about appealing to my faith? You don't have to threaten me with excommunication to get an appointment, you know!"

Impatiently, DeWohl beckoned him to sit down and, his face even paler than usual, fixed him with a sobering stare.

"Carl, as you are a good Catholic, you must believe me when I say that every minute could make the difference between the Church's survival and its . . . extinction. What you have been discussing here today fades into insignificance by comparison with what I have to tell you." He paused, his eyes closed as though in prayer, and announced, "The Israelis have discovered a tomb containing bones which they have every intention of exhibiting as the mortal remains of our Lord Jesus Christ. Not just that, but they are planning an imminent press conference—tomorrow, or rather today as it already is there—to publicize their diabolical find to the world. I hardly need to tell you that the consequences of . . ."

"When exactly? You have a time?" interrupted Romford, reaching for the telephone.

DeWohl shook his head.

"We don't know, but certainly within hours. Carl, the President must be told. Only *he* can persuade Rubinger to stop that press conference."

Romford raised a restraining hand.

"John, just hold it there. I'm sorry but there's a call I have to make before we go any further. It's not that I don't believe what you're saying, but I must check with our own people to see what they've got. They could even have a time."

He picked up the ivory telephone on the table.

"Maureen, will you patch me through to the duty officer at Langley, please—priority."

As he waited, drumming his fingers on the edge of the table, he glanced up at DeWohl.

"This could just explain one helluva lot, John. One helluva lot."

A voice came on the line:

"Duty Officer. Can I help you?"

"This is Secretary of State Romford on secure line 404, calling from Camp David. You want voiceprint verification?"

"If you would, sir."

Self-consciously Romford recited the first two lines of a nursery rhyme and waited. Five seconds later the duty officer's voice responded:

"Thank you, Mr. Secretary. Who would you like to speak to, sir?"

"Whoever is on duty in the Israeli Branch," replied Romford.

He looked at his watch. It was getting on to two o'clock, and after a thirty-second wait it was evident that nobody was on duty in the Israeli Branch. The flustered duty officer suggested he page the canteen, but Romford had been taken up that path too many times before.

"I'll tell you what," he said. "You just contact Stan Harding, the Director's Special Assistant for the Middle East, at home; tell him where I am, and tell him I want anything he's got on an archaeological discovery in Jerusalem which the Israeli government allegedly intends making the subject of a press conference. Tell him I want it *now*. Right?"

The duty officer was impressed; here was a politician who knew his way round the Agency. The message would be relayed immediately, he promised.

Romford loosened his collar and went over to the drinks tray. He held up the whisky bottle. His guest hesitated, and then nodded.

It was another twenty-five minutes before the phone buzzed into life.

"Romford here."

"Sir, I have Mr. Harding on the line for you."

The Secretary of State attempted to check his irritation. It didn't take nearly half an hour to track down a tape. At least it shouldn't.

"What have you got, Harding?" he asked tersely.

"Not a great deal, I'm afraid, sir," came the reply. "There's a report just in from Jerusalem. One of our stringers there—a freelance journalist—reported the discovery of some bones at a place called Nahalat Shim'on north of the Old City. He says there's speculation that they could be those of Jesus Christ but makes no mention of any press conference. We sent back a request for an update but we're still waiting. We didn't want to bother the President—or yourself, sir—until we got that update back."

Romford drew his hand down over his face in exasperation and, covering the mouthpiece, muttered "bullshit!" He sensed a cleanup job. "Just in" in Langley's terminology could mean anything from five minutes ago to five goddam days ago. He was tempted to press Harding on the exact timing but knew that, if it came to a showdown, the director was quite capable of cooking the tapes to bear out the Agency version of the story. Even so, he wasn't going to let that fat, incompetent slug Spender think he had gotten away with it.

"It's something, I suppose," he said, "but I can tell you the President is pretty wild about this. Most of all, he wants to know how come we get this story first from the Vatican and not from our own people. Now, it's not my position to tell your director that his story had better be a good one, but I reckon it's only fair he should be warned what sort of flak he's likely to run into first thing in the morning."

DeWohl looked shocked, but Romford just grinned. Putting the phone down, he observed, "The Church doesn't have a monopoly on penances, John. By my calculation, Mr. Director has exactly five hours to ironclad his backside. And talking about ironcladding . . ."

He picked up the phone again.

"Maureen, I'm afraid you're going to have to wake the President."

★

Although the middle of the night at Camp David, six thousand miles away in Jerusalem it was already dawn. Just before seven, Dan Kesler was awakened by the insistent purr of the telephone in the room that he used as his office next door. Cursing himself, he remembered that he had forgotten to plug it through to the bedroom the night before, and stumbled towards the door.

He picked up the receiver.

"Mr. Kesler?"

"Speaking."

"Mr. Kesler, this is Professor Ben Ami's secretary—the Institute of Archaeology?"

Kesler shook himself awake.

"Yes, yes, I know the professor."

"Good. The professor apologizes for bothering you this early in the morning," continued the light female voice. "He intended phoning you himself last night, but the clearance didn't come through till very late. Are you still there?"

"Yes, I'm still here. Go on."

"Well, the professor was wondering—he appreciates that

it's very short notice—but he was wondering if you could possibly meet him at the site within the hour?"

"The site?" queried Kesler with a calculated display of ignorance.

"The building site at Nahalat Shim'on. The professor said you knew about it."

"I know about it. You said within the hour?"

"About eight o'clock, if that's possible."

A dozen different thoughts crowded in on Kesler's mind, but it was hopeless even to attempt to work through them in his still-dazed state.

"Tell the professor I'll see him at the site at eight," he confirmed.

Only when he had put the phone down did he think to ask why it was the professor himself hadn't made this morning's call. Perhaps, though, the old man was justifiably embarrassed about having passed on the details of their last meeting to the authorities and wanted to explain in person.

"There's an intriguing turnabout," Kesler announced, returning to the bedroom.

"Surprise me," responded a voice from beneath the sheet, heavy with indifference.

"My old friend the professor wants to see me at Nahalat Shim'on—eight o'clock sharp. The wraps are off!"

The sheet snapped back.

"Dani! I forgot to tell you. We've got to see the headmaster and Beni's teacher at half-past nine. They particularly asked to see us both. I said I was sure it would be alright, and then it just slipped my mind."

Kesler made a face.

"Why both of us?"

"It's just their way of doing things. You know the thinking: To understand the child, you have to know the parents. If you see only one parent, you understand only half the child."

"Hmm, just as I thought," murmured Kesler with a grin, "a foreskin inspection, right?"

"Oh, Dani, don't be silly. It's nothing of the sort. They couldn't care if you were a practicing sun worshiper. They're simply concerned with gauging the kind of intellectual stimulus the child is likely to get at home."

"You mean you want me to go in humming Brahms and Bruckner and spike my conversation with quotes from Proust?"

"Well, if you can hum Brahms and Bruckner at the same time, I have no doubt they'll be greatly impressed."

Kesler pinned her down on the bed and took a mock bite out of her neck.

"A massive, festering love bite on the mother's neck should tell them something about the sort of intellectual stimulus Beni gets at home!"

"What are you saying about me?" a small voice piped from the landing. A second later, Beni appeared in his pajamas.

"Just that your school seems more worried about your environment than your genes, old son," Kesler answered.

"What's wrong with my jeans?" asked Beni cautiously, aware that he was the butt of an adult joke he couldn't hope to understand.

"Nothing, darling, nothing," said Aya. "*Abba* just wants to show that he can be the intellectual equal of an eight-year-old. Now, run along and get dressed."

In a subconscious attempt to put his thoughts in order, Kesler ran his fingers through his tousled hair.

"We can get around this," he declared at last. "I'll drive to the site, meet the professor as arranged, and with any luck I'll be through with him by nine. Let's say just after. You take a taxi and meet me at the site, and then we'll all three go on together to the school. We'll make nine-thirty easily. How does that sound?"

"We meet you at the site just after nine?"

"Exactly. If you don't see me around, wait in the car. You've got your keys?"

"Yes."

"Then there's no problem."

He stopped the car some distance from the site entrance and, taking care to avoid the worst of the debris, pulled well off the road onto the wasteland. The only sign of life was an Arab crouched on his haunches, keeping his eye on a flock of long-eared goats that were busily foraging among the rocks for what scant vegetation there was. The site itself appeared deserted.

Since it wasn't yet eight, Kesler decided to wait in the car. But when Professor Ben Ami still hadn't appeared at ten past, he got out, locked up, and strolled over to the main entrance.

To his surprise, there appeared to be no one on guard. He wondered whether this might indicate that the professor was already on the site waiting for him so he ventured forward in the direction of the digger with its still uplifted claw at the far end.

"*Amod! Mi sham?*"

He spun round. The cry was a familiar one, although it was the first time he had seen the young, unshaven face.

But it was the guard who was the more disconcerted of the two, when the man he had taken to be a disoriented American tourist only three nights earlier broke into fluent Hebrew. He quickly regained his composure, however. What was Kesler doing here again? More to the point, who exactly *was* he if he wasn't what he had pretended to be previously?

Savoring the younger man's bewilderment, Kesler revealed the truth about his journalistic status and his onsite appointment with the Professor of Archaeology from the Hebrew University. The soldier refused to be impressed. What about his deception of the other night, then? Kesler smiled apologetically—just one of those ruses that journalists have to resort to occasionally. The soldier's eyes narrowed. If Kesler was this time telling him the truth, where was this professor he was meant to be meeting? Kesler wished he knew. In fact why didn't they telephone the university to find out? Presumably there was an army telephone on the site, and there would be no difficulty in getting the military operator to connect them to an outside line. This time the soldier decided to call the American's bluff, remembering how just such a trick had been played on him during their previous encounter when Kesler had brazenly proposed that the two of them go to his hotel to check out his story. Well, it wasn't going to work a second time.

The call was put through to the professor's office. The girl who answered took immediate offense at the soldier's brusque manner of asking her straight off who she was. She was the professor's secretary—his *personal* secretary. In which case, asked the soldier, perhaps she could tell him where her boss was. On his way to the office, she assumed; he normally arrived about half past eight, and it was now twenty-five past.

Listening to the conversation, Kesler interrupted to make another suggestion: Why didn't the guard simply ask her about the phone call she had made to his house at seven o'clock to set up the meeting? Grudgingly, the soldier complied. Phone call? responded the girl, what phone call? She hadn't made any phone call to anyone at seven—and yes, she was the professor's *only* secretary. In frustration, Kesler grabbed the phone to talk to the girl directly. The voice, however, told him immediately that it wasn't the same girl, and she could offer no explanation except that he had imagined the whole episode.

The guard, too, Kesler could see, was thinking along similar lines, although attributing a more sinister motive. Without saying a word but keeping his eye fixed on Kesler, he picked up the receiver again and asked the operator to put him through to Security. As he did so, his free hand slipped round his M16, the index finger within reach of the trigger. Kesler looked at his watch and sighed in acknowledgement of what would now be several hours' delay before the whole mess was sorted out.

At ten past nine, and with still no sign of anybody from Security, Kesler made two requests: first, that they try the University again to see if the professor was in his office yet and, second, that he be allowed to explain to his wife and son waiting outside that there was no point in them hanging on. But the soldier was adamant. All that, he remarked, could be dealt with when the officer arrived from Security. From the tone of voice, Kesler could tell there was no point in pressing further.

★

Their departure from the house had been delayed by Beni's inability to find the present they had bought the previous evening for Rivka's party. Beni was distraught; the party was straight after school, and he would be the only one turning up without a present. Well, consoled Aya, if it wasn't anywhere in the house, it was either lost or in the car, in which case they would very soon know. And if it wasn't in the car, they could always stop off on the way to school and buy another present for Rivka.

They picked up a taxi on Ha-nevi'im without difficulty but, because of Aya's uncertainty about the exact location of the site, they found themselves dropped on the wrong side of the Nahalat Shim'on triangle, on Shemu'el Hanavi instead of St. George's.

Looking round, Aya spotted the car on the far side of the wasteland. It looked empty, but at that distance it was impossible to tell. Beni tugged at his mother's hand. Why didn't they cut straight across instead of walking all the way around by road? After all, the Arab and his goats proved that the ground must have dried out since the rain earlier in the week. Aya smiled. The scaled-down landscape of boulders, crags, and outcrops was an irresistible temptation for any boy of Beni's age.

"OK, commando," she said, "show me your true Sabra spirit. But your fashion-conscious mother is going to stick to the road to preserve her expensive Italian shoe-leather. If *Abba* is in the car, tell him I'm bringing up the rear!"

Beni frowned at the literal absurdity of the expression, committed it to memory, and charged off. Aya watched him, lamenting the same independence of which only a second earlier she had felt so proud. The child was a baby no more, and in no time at all he wouldn't be a child.

A few minutes later, as she rounded the side of the UN command post, she saw both the car and Beni. He was no more than twenty yards from it, clambering up the last incline before his final assault on the summit, his imaginary Uzi blazing away. In that same instant her mind registered an anomaly in the scene. The car wasn't right. Facing her straight on, it was lifted up at an angle by the rough ground, and silhouetted against the light that shone through clear beneath it was a package fixed to the underside. Wires hung from it.

She started to run and shout at the same time. Beni turned but, thinking it was part of the game, plunged forward again. She kept running, but the air wrapped itself round her legs like heavy, viscous liquid. Again she screamed—a silent, underwater scream—as with all his child's might Beni tugged at the door handle.

★

Archbishop Ramone stood before the two-story building that was both his residence and workplace, the Apostolic Delegation high on the slope of the Mount of Olives. It was one of the little rituals of his working day to come out onto the terrace at this time of the morning after putting in a full hour behind his desk. In its way it was also an act of worship—a spiritual preparation for the day ahead. Inhaling the aroma of pine and cypress, Ramone would trace in his mind's eye the passage of a white-robed figure being led by soldiers from the Garden of Gethsemane below, across the Valley of Kidron, and up the steep slope into the walled city opposite. To his death. No matter that the present walls were sixteenth century or that the skyline was dominated by the Plaza and Hilton hotels; it was the place that mattered. This was holy ground, and only by excavating a great wedge to the core of the earth could the proximity which at such moments Ramone felt with his Lord ever be destroyed. There were even mornings when he had to dab away a tear.

But not this one. This morning his mind was elsewhere, absorbed by the events of the previous night.

The dream had started unexceptionally with a flight of steps leading to a high door—a conventional enough symbol first put into his head, he suspected, some forty-five years earlier by a Genovese grandmother who had told him that dying was merely the passage from one life to another, as painless as passing from one room to the next. "*La morte, Francesco, è solamente una porta!*" was how she had put it, although when the time came, nobody had shown more reluctance to go through the door.

In his dream Ramone had gone through quite willingly, but had found not the ethereal paradise of his grandmother's promise, but a vast rain-swept open grave—an abyss piled deep with the bones of every being that had ever lived and died. Millions upon millions of them. The rain had lashed his face but, reducing his eyes to slits, he had made out a cross on the far side planted on a hillock. Hanging from it had been a skeleton. In the shock of realization his eyes closed in on the scene, reducing the hundreds of feet across the chasm to a mere dozen so that, inexplicably, he had found himself kneeling at the foot of the cross, hands across his chest like a figure in a fresco, staring up at the flapping, clanking limbs and the loose-jawed skull.

In the bright light of morning it required no Joseph, still less a Freud, to interpret the phenomenon, so clearly rooted as it seemed to be in his waking experience. The Nahalat Shim'on discovery had consumed his every thought for the past week and determined most of his actions. And he was still in a state of shock from the "confessional" with Cardinal Pellegrini in the Secretary of State's apartment. The whole

dream smacked of fear fulfillment, and he wondered how far
his treacherous subconscious was articulating what his conscious preferred to ignore—that the Nahalat Shim'on find
might indeed be what circumstantial evidence suggested, and
the promise of Christianity no more than a jangling skeleton
on a tree.

He sighed. How hard it was to be truly honest with oneself
in such a situation. Had he the blind faith of a Sirelli, he
could have dismissed the bones as the work of the Devil. But
for a man with his absorbing interest in archaeology the
question of faith was infinitely more complex. He smiled
bitterly as he recalled the words of his teacher at the Pontifical Ecclesiastical Academy where he had received his early
training in diplomacy: "Those whom the Devil wishes to
destroy, he first interests in science." "Not so, Father," he
had replied with the arrogance of youth, "for science can be
the tool of faith, helping to build platforms in the air from
which those capable of only limited flight may make the final
leap to glory!" It had been prettily put, but his rhetorical
triumph seemed singularly hollow now, and when he considered . . .

His meditation was broken by a reverberating blast that
shunted the air and seemed to come from beyond the Rockefeller Museum. At first he paid no more attention to it than to
the sounds made a dozen times a day by Israeli fighters
bursting the sound barrier above the city, but a few minutes
later the wail of sirens emerging from the Hadassah Hospital
drifted across from Mount Scopus. He turned to see one of
the delegation sisters cross herself and, belatedly, did the
same.

A single image dominated Kesler's intermittent consciousness: a metallic blue Ford lying on its side, hood yawn-
ing and roof punched out. No smoke and no movement, all
the activity was centered on a knot of people off to the right,
while above and beyond, a blue and white United Nations
flag fluttered incongruously. The rest was a blur, as though
the film of which his mind was an observer had jumped its
sprockets. The last half hour seemed to have been a ludicrous
succession of sitting—or rather being made to sit by others:
first, in the army jeep that had whisked him behind the

ambulance to the hospital; then, flanked by military guards, in the hospital foyer; and now in a clinically bare room somewhere on the third floor. Definitely the third floor. The clearest fragment of his mosaic memory was of the guard's finger pushing the third button and his own attempt to remember whether the Israelis followed the American practice of calling the ground floor the first floor, as though nothing in the world was more important at that moment. He had even asked the guard about it but had forgotten the answer.

At some point, a medical orderly had come into the room to apply a plaster to the gash on his left temple where the rifle butt had caught him. But no words. The guards too seemed inhibited, and relieved when he broke the silence and asked for a cigarette, adding that it would be his first in fifteen years.

"When will I hear someth-thing," his lips faltered.

"Almost now," replied the guard and lit his cigarette.

Much later the lieutenant colonel—the Defense Forces' spokesman—entered and, dismissing the guards, sat at the table opposite him. He examined the plaster on his head.

"I'm sorry," he said, "but the man wasn't to know the car was yours. As far as he was concerned, he was restraining an unauthorized intruder who was attempting to escape. If you'd managed to get away, he could have shot you. In one respect . . ."

He stopped and, screwing his hands into a ball, put them to his lips.

"It's not good."

"Tell me."

"Your son died in the blast. Instantly."

He studied Kesler's reaction. In his experience, bad news—and he had delivered more than enough of it in his time—was best taken at a single draft.

"Your wife is still in the operating room down the corridor. She could be there another couple of hours. The surgeon gives her a fifty-fifty chance. It seems she took the impact at about thirty feet."

"Bastards," whispered Kesler, his gaze locked on the corner of the table. "Murdering bastards!"

The colonel reached across and helped himself to one of the cigarettes.

"Kesler, our only chance of finding them is if you tell me your exact movements between the time I left your house . . ."

Kesler's head jerked up. With a strength he didn't know he possessed he rammed the table into the colonel's stomach and sent him sprawling, cigarette in hand, across the floor. The commotion brought in the guards before he was physically able to get his hands on the man. As the two of them held Kesler down in the chair, he started shouting and weeping:

"Bastards! You kill my son, maim my wife, and now . . . now you expect me to perform like a star witness to protect the incompetent bastard who bungled the operation. Well, fuck you and everything your perverted mind stands for. Weren't there other ways you could have devised to get me out of the way?"

Still shaken by the unexpected outburst, the colonel waited for the hysteria to subside and then again indicated to the guards to leave. Uncertainly they eased their grip and then loosened it altogether as Kesler slumped and succumbed to deep, racking sobs.

"You've got it wrong, Kesler," said the colonel when they were alone again. He pulled a plastic bag from his pocket and emptied the contents onto the table. From the pieces of charred metal he singled out what looked like a small pendulum about four inches long.

"Know what this is?" he asked.

Kesler neither knew nor cared. His only thoughts were of Beni's pathetic body being hurled into the air like a rag doll, and of Aya, obscenely gutted like a fish on a slab, fighting for life down the corridor. The man opposite was an irrelevance, except insofar as he was responsible for the carnage that in a fraction of a second had shattered his world.

The colonel picked up the pendulum, allowing it to dangle for several seconds between his fingers. Eventually Kesler's hands dropped from his face.

"I will tell you," said the colonel. "It's a cheap form of car alarm—an antitheft device. You can pick one up at any automobile accessory shop for a couple of hundred shekels." With his other hand he extracted a short length of tubing from the pile of debris. "Simple but effective. The pendulum is wired to the positive terminal of the car battery and hangs inside this tube which is connected through the bodywork to the negative earth. If the car is moved, the pendulum will touch the wall of the tube, make a circuit and set off the alarm—only in this case it was five kilos of gelignite." He paused and then added with a sigh, "The point I'm making, Kesler, is that only the most irresponsible idiot would have wired up a car like this if his intention were to get you out of the way. It could have been set off by a passing truck, a sheep rubbing against the car, or even the very act of installing it. It's not our style, Kesler; it's arbitrary and incompetent. Frankly, if we'd wanted to blow you up, we'd have used a radio-controlled servo or a mercury tilt-switch. But there are plenty of other ways we could have got you out of the way without resorting to such extremes."

"But none," Kesler retorted, "that would have looked so convincingly like the work of Palestinians."

The colonel was going to say something, but stopped. Instead, he got up and crossed to the phone on the windowsill. There followed a rapid flow of Hebrew, from which Kesler dimly gathered that either the Ministry of Defense or Military Intelligence was on the other end. There was talk of Kesler's reluctance to cooperate, of a file, and of the necessity of now showing it to him. To Kesler's mind, as confused as it was, the conversation bore all the hallmarks of an elaborate ploy. The sort of thing that veteran interrogation officers pass on to new recruits.

Returning to the table, the colonel dug into his briefcase and produced a blue folder with two red stripes across one corner to indicate its contents were classified. Ceremoniously, he placed it before Kesler.

"I had hoped it wasn't going to be necessary to show you this. Since, however, there seems no other way of persuading you that we were not responsible for what happened this morning . . ."

When Kesler remained immobile, refusing even to look at the object, he opened it himself, withdrew a pair of stapled pages and started to read aloud:

"December '76: Israeli moderates led by General Mati Peled hold secret meeting with Palestinians to discuss West Bank . . . January '77: Hondurans believed to have bought eight ex-IAF Mystères with U.S. engines in contravention of U.S. ban on resale . . . May '77: Moshe Dayan reliably reckoned to be joining Likud Government as Foreign Minister . . ." He laid down the paper. "Do you want me to go on—right up to the entry for two days ago sent from the kiosk near Herut Square?"

Kesler closed his eyes in an instinctive effort to black out the unbearable reality of what he had just heard.

"How?" he asked faintly.

"It wasn't difficult. As a foreign journalist, you were under immediate suspicion the moment you landed in Israel. But when you left the *Post* to go freelance you became doubly suspect. So we did all the usual things like random tails and intercepting your telexes, but—as often happens—what finally gave you away was an apparently insignificant anomaly in your behavior. One of the tails we put on you noticed that you didn't smoke."

"I gave it up."

"But you still bought cigarettes. We knew your wife didn't smoke. The rest was straightforward. The only question then was whether to haul you in, but it was decided that you were more use to us on the run—admittedly for largely negative reasons. If we'd picked you up, your masters would only have gotten someone else to take your place and we'd then have had to start all over again. And you were relatively harmless; if you'd ever passed on any really high-grade material, we could always have intercepted it. On the positive side, we were in a position to feed you information that we wanted relayed back—information, disinformation. It's hardly a new trick."

Kesler's brain reeled. A wave of nausea swept over him as the full implications of what he had just learned crystalized into splinters of truth and ripped into the soft fiber of his consciousness. He sat, condemned by his own stupidity.

"The appointment at the Hilton was a setup, then."

"If you mean, was Zvi Matzliah acting as an Israeli Government agent—yes. But you weren't the only one; the Vatican representative here was fed the same story by a more circuitous route. Both of you, we reckoned, could be relied on to report back to your respective masters. Coming from apparently independent sources, this would strengthen the story, as well as give the impression that we were trying to suppress it. The one thing we underestimated was the extent of your journalistic zeal. I anticipated your contacting the professor, knowing that you'd had dealings with him before.

He agreed to cooperate, and I figured that you'd be sufficiently intrigued—as much by what he didn't say as what he did—to make your Agency drop that afternoon. When by six o'clock that evening it was obvious that I had miscalculated, I had to force your hand."

"The house call?"

The colonel nodded.

"But, Kesler, we need to know who you talked to before then—that afternoon after you left the professor's office."

"Why not just ask whoever was meant to be tailing me?" retorted Kesler contemptuously.

"Because he was told to withdraw in case you became suspicious and delayed the drop. Anyway, it wasn't necessary; since we knew all your regular drops, we had only to post a man on each of them to keep watch." He looked at the clock. "Kesler, we need to know."

Physically and emotionally drained, Kesler reached into his pocket, pulled out his wallet, and handed to the colonel the crumpled note that had been stuck to his windshield. Although neither of them knew it, this was only the first—and the easiest—act of cooperation with the Israeli Government that Kesler would be called upon to make in the succeeding days.

★

Dimly, Bob Spender was aware of a noise in the room—an insistent pulse from the direction of the chair over which he had draped his clothes the night before.

Suddenly he was awake and, with little regard for the sleeping form by his side, threw back the covers, felt his way across the room, and seized the beeper in his vest pocket.

He twitched the curtains. It wasn't even dawn! Nobody at Langley would call him at this hour unless it was of the utmost urgency. Since being appointed Director of Central Intelligence eight months previously, he had never been beeped later than one or earlier than six-thirty. And here he now was, not even in his own home and not a secure phone within a mile.

His head teemed with conflicting thoughts. The rule book was quite specific: In the absence of a secure line, an ordinary public phone booth should be used. Never a private line. But, hell, who was going to bug Yvonne's phone? Not even his closest friends knew she existed. Particularly not his closest friends. A predecessor had once joked that if the West's chief spymaster couldn't get away with a little infidelity, who could?

Fighting back the accumulated sex- and alcohol-induced drowsiness, he tiptoed to the phone downstairs. The sleeping form slept on.

The Langley Operations Center picked up on the second ring. In polite terms the duty officer indicated that they'd been trying to get hold of him for the past four hours. Or rather, Mr. Harding, his Middle East adviser, had. Harding's voice came on the line.

"Chief?"

"Stan," replied Spender with an attempt at calm and composure, "what's this all about?"

There was a pause. Then:

"Chief, are you on a secure line?"

"It's alright. I'm calling from a public booth," he lied, taking the chance that Harding wouldn't check back with the duty officer.

"It's about the Jerusalem cable—the one I put on your desk yesterday afternoon. Secretary Romford called from the Woods at two this morning. He wanted to know why the President hadn't been told about it. I tried to get hold of you, but when . . ."

"You tried my home?"

"Well, yes, only when there was no response from your beeper."

"Shit," blurted Spender before he could check himself. It would be the second undercover appointment he would have to invent in a month. There had to be a limit to his wife's credulity.

"The point is," Harding continued, "the President has called an emergency session of the National Security Council for seven o'clock in the White House Cabinet Room. That's seven sharp. The President and Secretary Romford have to be back at Camp David in time for the start of the morning session at ten. Otherwise, the Israelis will start asking questions. According to Secretary Romford, the President is, well, none too happy that the news about the Jerusalem discovery came to them from the Vatican instead of . . ."

"But you covered."

"As best I could. I've ordered an update from Jerusalem and in the meantime I'm compiling a dossier for you to skim before the NSC meeting. I can have it sent round to you as soon as it's ready."

"No, it's alright, Stan," responded Spender hastily, "I'm on my way in." Glancing at his watch, he did a quick calculation. "I'll see you on the seventh floor in half an hour . . . and, Stan, perhaps you'd ring my wife and tell her . . . tell her you tracked me down up at the Woods with Secretary Romford."

"Right," responded Harding without a trace of surprise.

He was the last to arrive—conspicuously so. The Secretary of State, the Secretary of Defense, the Vice President, the President's Adviser on National Security, the Chairman of the Joint Chiefs of Staff, along with a few other figures he didn't recognize, were spread out around the huge mahogany table. In the middle, flanked by flags, sat Joe McCrae with the purposeful scowl that Spender had come to recognize as a sure storm warning.

He took a seat, blinked at the brightness of the early morning sun streaming through the Rose Garden colonnade, and only then noticed a large map propped on the easel next to the fireplace at the far end of the room. On it he could make out the words *World Catholic Population Distribution*. The President was talking:

"I won't go over the reasons we're here again, gentlemen. The Director of Central Intelligence is no doubt aware of the developments that have necessitated this meeting." The Director assumed an expression of confirmation, which the President ignored. "Suffice it to say, the Camp David talks seem to have gotten into a new dimension with the discovery of this pile of bones. We can only surmise that the Israelis are looking for a trade-off—their silence over the bones in return for our support of them against the Arabs at the conference table. In other words, blackmail. They want us to enable them to get away from Camp David with minimum concessions and maximum guarantees. It's obvious that they've already scared the shit out of the Vatican and I guess they reckon they can now do the same with us. We need to know whether they are right—which is why I've brought in Dave Hamersham here."

A close-cropped character squinting through gold-rimmed spectacles looked up from his seat next to the map and smiled modestly.

"Dave, as some of you will know," continued McCrae, "is one of the State Department's most experienced foreign analysts. He was one of Henry Kissinger's top aides in the early seventies, and has served under four consecutive presidents—now a fifth. Most importantly to us, Dave has been engaged in a long-term study of the influence of the Catholic Church on U.S. political interests around the globe. Dave, put us in the picture."

The man was suddenly familiar to Spender. He was living testimony to the old Washington adage that Presidents might not be able to fool all the people all the time, but there were those around town who could carry on fooling all the Presidents. Had he been a tad more honest with himself, Spender might also have admitted that his dislike for Hamersham extended as much to his age—to the fact that he had made it young, in his thirties, and a decade and a half later was still on top and comparatively youthful, whereas it had taken Spender himself sixty-two years to reach his present position. But the Director of Central Intelligence was not blessed with such insight.

"It is my considered opinion, Mr. President, gentlemen," began Hamersham, "that what we have here is pretty damned worrisome." He pulled a telescopic pointer from his top pocket and turned to the map. "It is part of the Catholic Church's uniqueness that it transcends not just national borders but global hemispheres—East, West, North, South. See what I mean: The predominantly Roman Catholic countries on this map are marked in red—or should I say scarlet?" he added with an easy smile.

Spender strained his eyes. As far as he could make out, all Latin America, most of Western Europe and much of Communist Eastern Europe were in red. There was even a sizeable blob in the middle of Southeast Asia.

"Now, I don't want to baffle you gentlemen with figures," Hamersham said, brandishing the pointer, "but of the eight hundred million Roman Catholics in the world you can readily see that the highest concentrations are in those areas that we would identify as having the greatest flash potential—those parts of the globe where we consider stability as crucial to American interests and, by extension, the interests of the Free World." He proceeded to swat the map as though putting down a virulent plague of mosquitos. "South and Central America, right here on our doorstep, alone account for nearly three hundred and fifty million Catholics. Across the Atlantic in Europe we have France, Italy, Spain, Portugal; weaken, say, the Christian Democrats in Italy, and you might as well send the Communist Party there a gold-embossed invitation card. Then, on the other side of the Iron Curtain, we've got Poland, Hungary, Czechoslovakia—all nominally good, godless, Communist states, but beneath the surface still solidly Roman Catholic. Moving still further east, we come to the Philippines down here—not just the only predominantly Catholic country in Asia but currently one of our most vital bases and listening posts in the whole area. And finally, full circle, we're back in your own back yard, Mr. President. Forty-five million Catholics may not make the United States a Catholic country, but you can't ignore one in five of the population. Personally—and whether we're talking domestically or globally, Mr. President—I wouldn't like to predict the effect of letting this cat out of the bag."

Spender watched McCrae suck in his lips and wondered cynically whether his mind was more on the dangers worldwide or the political implications for his own reelection nearer home. Hamersham was slick, he had to concede. Punchy and to the point, eschewing qualifications and exceptions, he delivered judgements that were packaged as neatly as a supermarket salad. The cartoonist who had depicted McCrae wheeling his trolley round a store selling plans, policies, and programs had come closer to the mark than he knew. And, in Spender's eyes, it was the cartoon caricature rather than the man who now asked:

"Anybody any questions?"

Tom Curran, the Secretary of Defense, pushed back his chair.

"There's one thing I don't follow. I can see the potential danger to us in a place like Poland where it can be argued that the influence of the Church is the most effective single antidote to Communism, and I can appreciate the political ramifications of a Communist takeover in a country like Italy, as well as the strategic threat in, say, the Philippines, but when we come to Latin America I lose you. It's always been my reading of the situation that the Catholic Church in the Latin American countries has lined itself up alongside the left-wingers, in often revolutionary opposition to right-wing and essentially pro-United States governments. It seems to me, therefore, that if the influence of the Church were taken out of the equation these regimes would be strengthened, not weakened. In short, it would be to our advantage."

Hamersham was on his feet again to reply.

"With respect, Tom, it doesn't work that way. In these Latin American countries, we're talking about very delicate balances of power, in which the Catholic Church is a sizeable chip. You suddenly take it away and, instead of tilting the balance in favor of the other side, you'd merely topple the scales—and create precisely the chaos, disorder, and political vacuum that the Communists thrive on. And you've got to remember one other thing, Tom. In the countries we're dealing with—countries where there is widespread poverty and hence the greatest potential for Communist exploitation—it is most often the Church that is the guarantor of social stability. I don't want to go into the realms of psychology but, wherever else I may part company with him, old Karl was right about religion being the opiate of the people. It takes the edge off reality; it makes the unbearable bearable; it gives hope in the midst of deprivation; it promises better things to come; but, above all, it preaches passivity—love thy enemy, turn the other cheek, and all the rest. Hell, why do you think the Commies have tried so hard to destroy it? No, Tom, I tell you, the Pope is doing a great job for Uncle Sam, and this bag of bones is real bad news for us. The destabilizing and demoralizing effect worldwide would be incalculable. One brushfire here, another there, like we've seen over the last couple of decades, and OK, we could cope. But half a dozen of them breaking out all at once, each in an area vital to our security—and Jesus, you'd need a hydrant the size of Niagara Falls!"

Impatient for an end to the meeting, the President cleared his throat.

"As I see it, gentlemen, Dave's arguments are pretty persuasive. It seems we have little choice but to take the Israelis' threat seriously and act accordingly. Anyone anything to add?"

Spender watched Hal Davidson, the President's Adviser on National Security, expecting him to put in his usual gibe at the expense of the intelligence community. It was embarrassing enough having a smart-ass from the State Department brought in to give what was essentially an intelligence analysis. Accordingly, when Davidson showed no sign of speaking, Spender decided to take the initiative—if only to recoup some of his lost turf by an entry in the minutes.

"It strikes me, Mr. President," he observed, "that there's a danger of our being forced into an overreaction on this. I wouldn't take issue with Dave Hamersham's reading of the situation or his conclusions, which in fact are borne out by the Agency's own assessment . . ." He tapped Stan Harding's black loose-leaf briefing folder on the table before him, impressively bulked out by triple-spaced typing. "But it's the premises that worry me. He is assuming that this is the body of Christ whereas our information is only that it *could* be. Now, I'm not saying that the Israelis are necessarily trying to put one over on us, but I reckon it is at least reasonable to . . ."

Davidson was in before he could finish.

"You're missing the point, Bob—if you'll excuse me, Mr. President. The concern of the Catholic Church—and I had a long talk with Cardinal DeWohl less than an hour ago—is not over the authenticity of the body but over the political use it could be put to, authenticated or not, in discrediting the Church. According to DeWohl, it accords with what would be expected of Christ's body in every salient respect—victim's age, date of death, type of injuries. There's even an inscription on the sarcophagus or whatever they call the box they put the bones in."

"Ossuary," remarked Spender quietly, but loud enough for all to hear.

"Right, the ossuary. Now DeWohl says none of this constitutes proof positive, but it still adds up to one helluva powerful package, propaganda-wise. You try teaching the gospel of the risen Christ and the life hereafter to several hundred million illiterates around the world with that can of worms sitting on a velvet cushion in an Israeli museum!"

Spender was furious with himself. By volunteering his views, he had given Davidson the opportunity to parade *his* homework, and thereby had unwittingly enabled the man to point up the uncomfortable truth that, instead of being behind his desk or parleying with a cardinal, the Director of Central Intelligence had been unavailable for most of the night. His instinct was to even the score by retaliating with some of the material in Harding's briefing file, but on reflection he decided to keep it for later when it might pass for something weightier than mere pointscoring. The meeting was already breaking up, anyway.

"Carl, Hal, Bob," said the President, "I want you to join me in the Oval Office straightway to thrash this thing through."

★

"As I see it, the yids have us by the balls," declared Joe McCrae, lining up his heels along the scuff marks on the presidential desktop, "and it might have helped, Bob, if you'd gotten your butt off that Jerusalem cable. For one thing we wouldn't now be sitting here with our trousers round our fucking ankles. Bureaucratic ass-covering seems to be about the only thing you guys at Langley are capable of doing right!"

"I'm sorry about that, Mr. President," mumbled Spender, trying to sound apologetic without giving Hal Davidson the satisfaction of seeing him eat dirt. "We had an interpretive problem in that the cable's relevance to Camp David wasn't immediately apparent."

"That figures, I guess," drawled McCrae sarcastically. "It only originated in the Middle East . . ."

Not for the first time, Spender found himself staring at the Remington bronze to the right of the President's desk. The rather tasteless statuette of a broncobuster whipping his victim into submission had become a singularly apposite symbol of his relationship with the President over the last few months. Carl Romford came to his rescue with a change of subject.

"Joe, there could be a way out that we haven't considered."

The President swung his legs off the desk to look in his Secretary of State's direction.

"What's that, Carl?"

"Steal it."

"Steal what, for Christ's sake?"

"The body, Joe . . . the bones . . . then, don't you see, the Israelis won't have anything to bargain with."

For several seconds McCrae, fingertips to his lips, was lost in contemplation of the fire crackling in the grate at the other end of the room.

"Possible, I suppose," he pronounced. "Do we know where it is though?"

Spender saw his opening and was suddenly glad he had kept back his ammunition during his earlier spat with Davidson in the Cabinet Room.

"We have, er, a fair idea, Mr. President," he said, recalling Harding's briefing document. "Our information is that the Israelis are keeping it in a textile factory."

"A what?"

"A textile factory. We don't know which, but the biggest complex is at Qiryat Gat, called Polgat Woollen Industries. It was founded by a Rumanian Jew in the early sixties."

A snort of laughter drowned his words.

"I'm sorry, Bob, you must forgive me," spluttered Hal Davidson. "It's just that, well—hey, I'm sure you must know this yourself, Bob—it's just that 'the textile factories' is the kinda jokey name the Israelis give to their atomic research establishment at Dimona down in the Negev Desert. I think Ben-Gurion himself first coined the phrase. And hell, if you think about it, nothing could be more logical than to keep the bones there. There's no place in the whole of the Middle East that is better guarded. Jesus, during the Six Day War, they even shot down one of their own Mirages when it strayed too close!"

Not even the Remington was capable of anchoring Spender's feelings this time and, looking past it through the south windows, he focused on the Washington Monument three-quarters of a mile away and wished he could put the same distance between himself and this latest scene of his humiliation. The ambient sound was deafening.

"Well, at least time is on our side, Joe," Romford remarked. "Today is Thursday. As I said last night, I calculate patience in the Arab camp will snap by lunchtime if there's nothing forthcoming from the other side—which, let's face it, there won't be, for reasons we now know. But if you can give the Arabs reason to believe that w're on the brink of a breakthrough with the Israelis—and that means staking your personal prestige on it—then I reckon they could be persuaded to hold on. If so, it'll give us three clear days to act—Friday, Saturday, Sunday, the three respective holy days. We had them penciled in as rest days from the start, barring exceptional progress." Biting the end of his pencil, he added, "Not that that is going to help us get into Dimona."

"You'll need three *years* to crack that one," Davidson said chuckling. "It's not just their own planes they shoot down, nor even the military ones. Don't you remember that Libyan airliner they downed just because it wandered within sighting distance of the place?"

Silence descended, and the longer it lasted, the more Bob Spender sensed danger. It'd be only a matter of time before someone came up with the good old standby: in the absence of the Cavalry and the Marines, get the Agency to mount a covert action! And Hal Davidson, the scent of blood already in his nostrils, was just the man to suggest it.

But it seemed he was wrong—although the voice was certainly Davidson's.

"It's only a rough idea, Mr. President, but how's this for size? We tell Rubinger we're willing to talk turkey, right, but say we're not prepared to buy blind. We've got to have some of our scientific boys take a look at the merchandise. A real close look. Get me?"

McCrae frowned.

"You're not seriously suggesting we send in a team of commandos gussied up in white coats? The Israelis would never . . ."

"No, no, you can rest easy on that one, Mr. President," reassured Davidson. "The object of the exercise is solely to get the Israelis to bring the bones out into the open, where we can take a crack at them. To make sure, we include in the inspection team someone who's well known on the nuclear circuit—someone like Wolf Schumacher." He laughed. "I tell you, Rubinger would convert to Catholicism before letting Schumacher within sniffing distance of Dimona."

"And then what?"

"Then, depending where they take it, we intercept it either on the way there or on the way back."

McCrae looked to his Secretary of State.

"What do you think, Carl?"

"Could just work, Joe. In the absence of anything else, I'd say it's worth a try."

Spender kept quiet. Significantly, his opinion hadn't been solicited and he was happy to stay on the periphery. His own feelings were that it was a harebrained scheme with insupera-ble follow-up problems—the sort of thing a Langley recruit might put up in a first-year training session. None of the others seemed to display the slightest perception of the cali-ber of the opposition. Those they were so nonchalantly plan-ning to hoodwink weren't a bunch of untrained amateurs, but in all probability included men who had pulled off the En-tebbe raid. So far at least, though, there had been no men-tion of Agency involvement.

"You don't think you could be underestimating our Israeli friends?" asked McCrae, coincidentally voicing Spender's own unspoken reservations. "Assuming they take the bait, we've still got to know where they're going to take the thing to be able to intercept it."

"No trouble, Mr. President," Davidson shot back. "Who-ever we get to do the inspection—and they'll have to be genuine to convince the Israelis—they're going to need a whole crateful of sophisticated hardware for carbon dating, X-rays, and the like. We'll insist on the most exhaustive tests possible—and of course with our equipment. All we do then is plant a signal generator in the middle of all the spaghetti, and wherever it goes, we'll be tracking it. It's the sort of thing that Bob's boys in the Technical Services Division are doing all the time. Right, Bob?"

Warily, Spender confirmed. It had all the makings of a setup.

"Who's going to pick up the signal?" he asked. "The Agency hasn't got a single listening post in the area."

Davidson gave a patronizing smile.

"A minor detail that needn't bother you, Bob. We'll get the NSA to send one of their boats on a little fishing expedition around the eastern Med."

As little as Spender liked the idea of supporting Davidson, Spender was prepared to be almost enthusiastic about any plan that involved the National Security Agency sharing in the dirty work and taking a few risks in the field for a change. The CIA had done enough flakcatching for the NSA in recent years.

The President stood up and, spinning the globe as he passed it, announced:

"OK, gentlemen, it sounds like a good one to me. After last night, I'm wiped out. Hal, I'll leave you to get the scientific team together then and liaise with the boys at the NSA. Carl and I'll go back to the Woods to spell out our terms to Rubinger and his kosher coterie."

"Joe," Romford added, "we haven't discussed the pickup details—how we're going to snatch the bones and get them out of the country."

"Hell, that's Bob's department," retorted McCrae, picking up the telephone on his call director to order the Marine helicopter for a takeoff from the South Lawn.

Spender gagged. He should have seen it coming; it was a typical sneaky McCrae tactic to deliver the knockout blow on his way out of the ring. And Davidson was part of it. It was all too neat. The whole playact had been gotten up, he would swear, by the two of them in advance.

"I'm sorry, Mr. President," he ventured as McCrae replaced the receiver, "but I'm not sure I get the drift. If we're talking about any sort of covert operation involving Agency personnel in a country with which we're supposedly friendly, then it has to be sanctioned by the appropriate congressional commit . . ."

"What the hell are you spouting about?" bawled McCrae. "You don't need any sanction; we've all agreed on the plan— you along with the rest of us. You're the boss in your own outfit, aren't you? Give yourself the goddam sanction!"

"Mr. President," uttered Spender in a voice he barely recognized as his own, "the law is quite clear on this: Any covert action by the Agency has to have the prior sanction of the appropriate congressional oversight committee, as laid . . ."

McCrae silenced him with a glance.

"Don't quote the fucking law at me, Spender. Congressional oversight committees! Jesus, where have you been these last years? The Jewish lobby would have the news back to Jerusalem before you'd got back to your office. Now, I'm telling you, Spender, and you'd better take this on board: If you don't get those bones out, I'll personally kick your fat ass the length of Pennsylvania Avenue."

★

The colonel was apprehensive. "I'm sorry about the file, but it was the only way of convincing him."

The Defense Minister's only reply was a grunt. Finally, he asked:

"Do we know who was responsible?"

"Everything points to Palestinian involvement," replied the colonel. "The only person Kesler remembers seeing near the site when he parked was an Arab goat herder. Also, the afternoon after he talked to Ben Ami at the University he says he sounded out one of his regular Arab contacts at the old bus station bar. The man is one of the joint proprietors and a known PLO sympathizer. Anyway, the next morning Kesler found this note stuck to his car." He handed over the piece of crumpled paper. "He thought it had come from us—a sort of follow-up to my visit to his house."

"With *this* handwriting?"

"Because of it. He reasoned that it was so obviously an Arab hand that it had to be the work of an Israeli—just as he was convinced that the crudeness of the bomb was proof of our attempt to put the blame on the Palestinians. There are times when I think we are victims of our own reputation."

Gideon Berman didn't smile.

"Do we assume then that the Palestinians know about Nahalat Shim'on?"

"I . . . I think we have to, although whether their motives for wanting to silence Kesler were religious or political is impossible to say. Politically, they'd have good enough reason, knowing how we could use the discovery to frustrate their demands at Camp David. If Kesler or any other journalist were to spill the beans, McCrae could be expected to come under virtually irresistible pressure to accede to whatever we asked. But there could equally well be a religious dimension. There are Christian Arabs among the Palestinian leadership and they would be as anxious as the Vatican to have the matter hushed up."

Berman swung round to face him.

"And the police, what are they up to?"

"Taking statements at the moment."

"Right. As soon as they've done that, pull them off. Tell them it's an intelligence matter. There's to be no investigation—at least, not until after Camp David. Understand?"

The colonel was shocked.

"But I told Kesler we had to know about his movements because . . ."

"There was a lot you told Kesler that would have been better untold. The last thing we want right now is somebody stirring up the Palestinians. If they *were* responsible for blowing up his car—and it's hard to see who else could be—they might just decide that if they're going to be brought in anyway they've got nothing to lose by going public. We can't risk it. Already it appears that one of the professor's loquacious assistants has accidentally given away the present location of the bones. The next thing we know, *Time* will be featuring them on its cover. And keep Kesler under surveillance from now on; I don't want him indulging in any freelance investigation of his son's murder."

"That's not likely while his wife is on the critical list," observed the colonel, hoping to awaken a more compassionate side of the minister's nature.

"It is if she dies—doubly likely. What do the doctors say?"

"Too early. But it doesn't look good—blast burns, internal hemorrhaging . . ."

"And Kesler can be relied on to stay by her bedside?"

The colonel was tempted to answer, "Wouldn't you?" but checked himself.

"I imagine so."

"Imagine nothing," retorted Berman and turned to some paperwork on his desk.

★

Bob Spender stood in his seventh-floor penthouse office at the CIA's Langley Headquarters high above the Potomac River, looking out on the stately trees that lined the George Washington Parkway. He felt sick. In the folds of fat at the back of his neck he could feel the sweat collecting, cool and clammy. Time weighed on his frame like an iron bell, as he calculated that he had precisely twelve hours in which to come up with a workable operation for getting the bones out of Israel. Painfully, his mind turned to the congressional ratification committees of not so many months earlier when he had been given hypothetical situations and asked how, as Director of Central Intelligence, he would react. The picture he had painted of himself then had been one of calm in crisis and leadership in chaos. Now, faced with the reality, his greatest desire was that his "too too solid flesh would melt,

thaw, and resolve itself into a dew." More realistically, that
he might be incapacitated by some freak accident.

The intercom buzzed and the arrival of his Middle East
adviser was announced. Spender was relieved and, in his
most positive gesture of the morning, shucked off his jacket
and tugged at his suspenders. Stan Harding had the coolly
analytical brain that he lacked at that moment; if anybody
could save the situation, Harding could.

"Mary," said Spender over the intercom, "send in a large
pot of coffee for us, will you, and have Services set up a desk
and telephone for Mr. Harding here in my office without
delay."

The large, bearded Harding lowered himself into one of
the easy chairs, adjusted his pebble-lensed glasses, and placed
a yellow pad and a map on the coffee table before him.

"Can it be done?" asked Spender, checking the tone of
anxiety in his voice.

Harding threaded a pencil meditatively through his beard.

"Possible, although it's not the plan I'd have chosen. Too
many if's—*if* the Israelis bring the bones out of Dimona; *if*
the area they take them to is both isolated and accessible; *if*
they agree to us using our own equipment . . . if, if, if."

"Well?"

"Well, assuming they do bring them out, my bet is that
they won't want to take them further from Dimona than they
have to. They're in a bind. Too close to Dimona and they risk
their nuclear secrets being compromised, but the further
away they take the bones, the longer the traveling time and
the greater their vulnerability to attack. If I were in their
shoes, I'd settle for an inspection somewhere within a thirty-
mile radius . . ." He inscribed a circle freehand on the map.
"The most obvious location in that area is the new Central
Negev air base down here at Ramon."

"Right!" put in Spender.

"That is why they won't choose it. Apart from being obvious, it was also built by the United States Army Corps of
Engineers in return for Begin agreeing to give up the Sinai.
Much of the reason for the Israelis' success at Entebbe was
that they themselves had constructed the airport buildings
and still had a copy of the plans. They're too smart to fall into
the same trap now the tables are turned."

"So we'll have to rely on the signal generator to give us a fix."

"I reckon so—which will require the ultimate flexibility of movement on our part and probably no more than an hour in which to deploy our snatch squad. The question then is how they're going to transport the bones. They could take them by road with a heavily armed escort, but that would be easily spotted and would necessitate an inspection site close to a highway. It would also take time. Alternatively . . ."

A pair of brown coats entered with a desk and telephone and set up a desk at right angles to Spender's own. But for the best part of the next hour Harding remained hunched over the coffee table carrying on the same one-man show, alternately putting up and shooting down his own arguments, while his boss snatched furtive glances at the clock and paced the length of the picture window. Three coffees later, the pencil dropped to the table and the beard looked up.

"Chief, there's just no way that we can get our own men in there to do a snatch. And even if we could, we'd still have the problem of getting them *and the bones* out. I tell you," he added jokingly, "it would make life a darned sight easier if we could just blow the goddam things up!"

Spender was suddenly galvanized.

"Stan, that's it!" he almost yelled. "Better even. That way we'd be one hundred percent sure the Israelis could never use them as a bargaining chip."

As he spoke, he punched the intercom.

"Mary, get me Secretary Romford right away. . . no, not at the State Department . . . up at the Woods—Camp David."

Five minutes later the Secretary of State's lazy drawl came on the line.

"Yea, Bob, you wanted to speak to me?"

Adopting a deliberately low-key tone, Spender answered:

"Carl, yes—and thanks for calling back so soon. We're pretty close to cracking it, we reckon, but it just occurred to us that a straightforward demolition job on these bones might be preferable to a snatch. It would seem to make better sense all around."

There was an agonizingly long delay before Romford responded:

"Bob, I'll be honest, I don't know. I'll have to check back with the President on this one, although personally I admit I can see the advantages. I'll be back with you just as soon as I can."

Spender laid down the phone and breathed a long, theatrical sigh of relief. It was a relief that Harding didn't seem to share—perhaps out of the knowledge that, snatch or destroy, he would still be expected to come up with a way of getting men in to do it. The only difference would be that, once they had disposed of the bones, they too could be disposed of.

Spender looked at the clock. Nearly midday. Buoyed by his new exuberance, he ordered a couple of club sandwiches and two glasses of milk. He was tempted to take something stronger but, recalling his excesses of the previous night, refrained—privately congratulating himself on his ability to beat the bottle fatigue to which he was so prone.

It was more than an hour later when Romford finally called back.

"Bob? Bad news, I'm afraid. The President wants you to stand by the plan that was agreed on in the Oval Office. There are good reasons. First, it's not beyond the Israelis to plant a dummy or a decoy, which could end up with us blowing up the wrong bones; second, even if we got the right bones, a bungled attempt at destroying them would be more damaging than outright failure; third—and this, let me admit, was Hal Davidson's argument—the carbon dating equipment will give a provisional readout in a matter of hours but a couple of days, it seems, are needed for confirmation. Hal's reasoning is that if that final figure proves to be decades out, then we've nothing to worry about anyway; so why risk a diplomatic incident when the whole thing may be a damp firecracker? I'm sorry, Bob, but, well, you know how meticulous Hal can be in his marshaling of facts and figures."

Spender gritted his teeth. Fuck Hal Davidson. He could just see McCrae's smart-assed Adviser on National Security Agency up in Aspen Lodge, quoting the experts he had "just" talked to and regurgitating a load of gobbledygook to impress McCrae.

He laid down the phone and with an intensity born of true feeling pronounced:

"Shit."

★

"We have had news from Camp David within the last hour," announced Israel's Acting Prime Minister, Reuven Shavit, to his Cabinet colleagues, "and it would appear that the Foreign Minister's meeting with the Apostolic Delegate has had the desired effect. With the agreement of all parties, the talks have been suspended for three days—to be resumed at ten o'clock U.S. Eastern Time on Monday. Meanwhile, though, the Americans are demanding an inspection of the bones by their own people using their own equipment."

"On their own territory?" queried the Interior Minister.

"Emphatically not, and they haven't even suggested it. Their idea—demand, rather—is that a four-man team with a container-load of equipment should fly here and examine the bones on the spot."

"At Dimona?" exclaimed a chorus of anxious voices.

Shavit passed a hand through his prematurely silvered hair and looked down at his papers.

"That is what we have to decide. I have here the names of those who'll be in the team: Professor George McVaney, an archaeologist for whom Professor Ben Ami claims to have the highest regard; Dr. James Lindorff, an anthropologist; Richard Klinger, described simply as an expert in X-ray and ultraviolet photography; and, finally, Dr. Wolf Schumacher, best known as the . . ."

" . . . as the 'father' of the neutron bomb," cut in Defense Minister Berman.

"Precisely," confirmed Shavit testily. "On the face of it, the choice of a top nuclear physicist whose discipline is arms rather than archaeology would seem an unlikely one. I'm told by the Weizmann Institute at Rehovot, however, that radiocarbon dating is a branch of nuclear physics, although concerned with low-level not high-level radiation. According to them, there's no doubt that Schumacher would understand the principle and would be able to operate the equipment with little instruction. They agree, though, that he remains an extraordinary choice for a team like this—given that America has at least half a dozen world-renowned specialists in carbon dating. We can only assume that his inclusion has a sinister intent."

"A snooping operation?" queried the Foreign Minister.

Shavit pursed his lips.

"It could be. I'd rate it as just a coincidence if we didn't have reason to believe that the Americans know where the bones are being held." In response to the raised eyebrows round the table, he expanded, "Someone claiming to be a photographer for the *National Geographic* phoned the Institute of Archaeology yesterday afternoon asking permission to see 'the Nahalat Shim'on find.' One of Ben Ami's assistants told him it was impossible and anyway it was no longer at the Institute but at Dimona. When we checked back, the *National Geographic* disclaimed any knowledge of any such request. In the light of that, we have now to decide whether to let Schumacher in and take the risk, or move the inspection—and the bones—to some other place."

"What's the feeling at Dimona?" asked the Minister of the Interior.

"That to let the man anywhere near the place is like inviting a mosquito into a malaria clinic. Someone with Schumacher's knowledge, they argue, could tell what's going on behind a door just by the color of its paint—and since we've never allowed international inspection of the site, it would be madness to let him in. Obviously they're exaggerating, but paranoia is a necessary part of their discipline and we'd be wrong to ignore their fears, however irrational. Besides, there is another consideration: If the Americans have it in mind to attempt to neutralize the bones in any way, their plans will be based on the assumption that the inspection will be held at Dimona—which is the best reason of all for holding it anywhere *but* Dimona." He paused and, confident of the effect, added, "For what it's worth, Avram's feelings are that we should consider an alternative inspection site—although naturally we agree that it should be a Cabinet decision."

Gideon Berman permitted himself a rare smile. Who was it said the present Cabinet had all the courage of their Prime Minister's convictions?

"So the question is: If not Dimona, where?" resumed Shavit, taking Cabinet compliance with Rubinger's wishes as a forgone conclusion.

"As close as possible and as far away as necessary, would seem the logical answer," remarked the Minister of the Interior.

"Agreed," Shavit said, nodding. "Personally, though, I'd suggest not one site but half a dozen possibles, with the final choice being left to the last minute. What do you think, Gideon?" he asked, looking in the Defense Minister's direction, "as the one who'll be responsible for operational arrangements."

Berman didn't answer immediately. He saw the trap: If he disagreed, he'd have to put up a better plan, but if he agreed, Shavit would afterward take credit for both the conception *and* its execution. Also, it was a good plan.

"It seems to make sense," he conceded, "but if you give me a few hours, the ministry will prepare some alternatives for the Cabinet's consideration and . . ."

"That won't be possible, I'm afraid," broke in Shavit. "There just isn't the time. We have to decide now. Avram was most insistent on the need for speed. Seventy-two hours is all we have—for everything. It might help your people choose the sites, though, if we can decide on the maximum flying time we have in mind."

Berman and Rosenstein exchanged glances.

"Flying time?" repeated the Foreign Minister. "What sort of aircraft are you thinking of?"

"A helicopter, of course."

The Defense Minister was taken aback.

"You're seriously suggesting putting the most valuable object that has come our way in two thousand years in a machine that can be popped out of the sky by a kid with a hunting rifle?"

"Do you have a better suggestion?"

"Yes, that we take what seems to me the lesser risk and leave the bones where they are—hold the inspection at Dimona."

"We've been through all that."

"You may have; *we* haven't."

Shavit sighed.

"Gideon, we can't afford the luxury of this bickering. If your reservations about this operation are so great, then . . ." sweeping his eyes round the other seventeen Cabinet members, "I'm sure we will understand if you wish to transfer operational command to someone else. On the other hand, I see no reason why a helicopter flight should entail the risks you envisage if adequate security measures are implemented on the ground. It's surely not beyond the IDF's resources to seal off the area for an hour or two?"

The diagonal scar across Gideon Berman's face stood out white against his rising color.

"Shavit, you are mad!" he exclaimed. "This area that you are talking about, assuming that you are still in favor of the six-site plan, will have to encompass the whole of the Negev. How in God's name are you going to seal that off? Barbed wire fences? Road blocks? With forty-five thousand Bedouin Arabs roaming around, who don't even use roads, never mind observe road blocks! I tell you, it cannot be done."

"With a little imagination the risks could be greatly minimized," responded the Acting Prime Minister acidly. "Before the helicopter takes off, for example, we could organize the departure of an armed convoy to act as a decoy, heading of course in the opposite direction."

"And you think that will fool them?" asked Berman contemptuously. "An armed convoy proceeding at a snail's pace out of Dimona directly beneath the cameras of their overhead satellites. You have a dangerously low opinion of their opinion of us, Shavit. This whole discussion is an exercise in folly." He paused and, looking in Foreign Minister Rosenstein's direction, added, "Since it is my ministry that will have to take responsibility for the operational arrangements of this folly, I demand a vote on it."

"That is your prerogative," said Shavit. "If you care then to give us the wording of your motion."

Berman addressed himself to the stenographer behind and to the right of Shavit's chair.

"That in view of the Defense Minister's grave reservations about the advisability of moving the Nahalat Shim'on bones from their present location, any inspection be held at the nuclear research establishment at Dimona."

It was a futile gesture. In the knowledge of both their present and their future leaders' feelings, the Cabinet united against Berman in a barricade of raised arms. His only supporter was Ya'acov Rosenstein.

"I'm not sure you should have done that, my friend," said Rosenstein to Berman, as they shared an official car back into the center of Jerusalem. "It was not wise to put yourself in such open opposition to Shavit at this time. It makes it easier for him to isolate you—politically, that is."

"Hang politics!" Berman replied. "Anyway, you voted with me, didn't you?"

"I was the only one who could afford to. When Avram goes, I will go." He tapped his heart. "Assuming technology

can keep me going that long. But you, Gideon, you're young.
You've still got a part to play if only you will . . ."

"Play the game. Yes?" Berman asked.

"If that's what you want to call it. But take the advice of an
older man, Gideon. It's more a matter of waiting your time
and spotting your opportunities. Shavit is too clever for his
own survival. Given the chance, he will destroy himself—but
not if you put yourself up as his political scapegoat."

★

For an hour and a half, Spender sat at his desk, impotently
switching his gaze between the clock and his Middle East
adviser ten feet away, partially hidden behind piles of folders
of press cuttings. Although it struck him as a strange way to
go about planning an operation, he had personally ordered
entire filing cabinets from the Agency's newspaper library on
Harding's behalf—together, inexplicably, with a copy of the
1989 *Catholic Year Book*. When a member of the library staff
had pointed out that, instead of the mountain being obliged
to come to Mohammed, it might be easier if Mr. Harding
used the computer search and microfiche services on the first
floor, Harding's terse response, relayed via the director, had
been that his eyesight had enough trouble coping with the
originals. There was a truculent familiarity about the man
that Spender didn't like, but he kept telling himself that
Harding had never let him down.

It was past two o'clock when Harding finally removed his
spectacles and skimmed half a dozen selected cuttings across
Spender's desk.

"I think we've cracked it, Chief," he declared with a plural-
ity which made up for much of his earlier disrespect. "Take a
look at these."

There were two lots. The cuttings in the first were all
recent and chronicled the activity of Palestinian infiltrators
within Israel—bombings in Tel Aviv, rocket attacks on West
Bank settlements, even an ambush on an Israeli Army patrol
south of Beersheva. None of them was more than six weeks
old. The others, though, went right back to 1974—and the
arrest of one Ilarion Capucci, Archbishop of the Melchite
Catholic Church, a branch of Roman Catholicism independent of, but allied to, the Vatican. Capucci had been given a
twelve-year jail sentence for gunrunning after Israeli border

police had discovered a cache of weapons and explosives destined for Palestinian guerrillas in the trunk of his official car. A later cutting, dated November 1977, carried a picture of the smiling patriarch giving a two-fingered victory sign and reported that, following a personal appeal from Pope Paul VI, he had in fact been released from prison.

"Yea, well . . ." said Spender, none the wiser.

Harding referred to his yellow pad.

"It's a two-stage operation, Chief, and the beauty of it is that at no point do we have to commit our own operatives. For the snatch we recruit the Palestinians. From these cuttings it's obvious that some of them are working in and around the Negev, and that they're well armed with handguns, AK 47s, and, most important of all, rocket launchers. And they're there *now*; this attack on the patrol south of Beersheva was only two days ago. The whole thing has clearly been orchestrated, like the West Bank riots, to coincide with Camp David—a less than subtle reminder for the Israelis of the enemy within and its ability to hit hard. By my reckoning, there has to be a hardcore cell working out of someplace like Hebron, where they could be sure of cover and backup. And they're not amateurs; amateurs don't provoke firefights with army patrols *and* get clean away. Our only problem is going to be one of communication."

"I was wondering about that," lied Spender.

"But a word to our old friend the Palestinian observer at the United Nations will soon fix it. His lines of communication with the boys back home are pretty impressive when they need to be—and you can bet they are right now, given the amount of orchestration that has gone into this latest campaign." He peered at the clock. "If we contact him in his office this afternoon, that'll give him time to alert his operations people in the field as to what is required for snatching the bones, in terms of men and machinery. We can then leave it to them to work out a means whereby we can notify them of the exact location of the inspection site as soon as we get our fix from the signal generator. That way they can be standing by and ready to go without any waste of time. All they'll have to do is draw a straight line between the inspection site and Dimona, and plant their sweet asses somewhere along it."

"But we've no idea how the Israelis will be transporting the bones."

"Wrong, Chief, we've an excellent idea. Whatever it is, it's got to be quick, untrackable by satellite surveillance, and unrestricted by geography. There's only one thing it can be—an aircraft. And, since there's no runway at Dimona, it's got to be a chopper." There was the suggestion of a smile somewhere beneath the mass of beard. "Wonderfully versatile little machines, choppers . . . wonderfully *vulnerable* little machines."

Spender looked skeptical.

"And what then? Even if they grab them, *we've* still got to get the bones out of the country."

"Correction, Chief," smiled the beard. "We haven't, but the Vatican has. Since they're the ones who are most anxious to get hold of them, they should take their share of the action—and the risk. You've read the cuttings on the good Archbishop Capucci and his fully equipped official limo. Well, there you have it. It's what the instructors at Camp Peary call the Tonto principle."

"The what?"

"It's an old trick, but it might just work."

"Like last time?"

"*Because* of it, Chief. Having been caught once, with all the political and diplomatic fallout that followed, it is inconceivable that the Vatican should try the same thing again. Which is why it'll work. And this time our man is going to be the Apostolic Delegate himself." Replacing his glasses, he referred to the 1989 *Catholic Year Book*, " 'His Excellency Francesco Silvio Ramone, born the fourteenth of March 1930 in Cortona, Italy.' Of course, we'll have to lay on a couple of diversions, a couple of false trails, but by the time the Israelis have figured them out, the good archbishop will be over the border and into Jordan—with the bones in his car. It's just a matter of timing."

Spender shook his head and ran a finger round the inside of his sweat-dampened collar.

"Jesus, Stan, I don't know. The whole thing sounds pretty slapdash to me. I don't like the fact that we have so little control—and then having to rely on Palestinian guerrillas and an archbishop, for Christ's sake! Anyway, why should a bunch of Muslim Arabs risk their necks for Christianity?"

"They're not," Harding replied. "That's incidental. Any risks they'll be taking will be to guarantee themselves a homeland. So long as the Israelis have those bones in their possession, they haven't a chance of getting it—neither at Camp David nor at any other time. And if they don't understand that already, we'll make them understand. I promise you, Chief, motivation will be the least of our headaches."

Spender threw himself down in his chair.

"Can't we get just *one* of our own people in—just to keep an eye on things?"

"Chief, it's not possible. And anyway, you know the rules better than anyone. Even one man would constitute a covert action. Congress would blow its cork and, if you'll excuse me saying so, it'd be your head on the block." Assuming a more aggressive tone, he continued, "If we can get the timing right on this one, it'll work. Just half an hour ahead of the Israelis at every stage, that's all we'll need."

"And if for some reason we don't get the timing right?"

"At least our hands will be clean. There'll be no confessions, no displays of Agency equipment, and no questions in Congress." He tapped his pencil on the desk. "Chief, we've got to set up these sideshows. We're going to need to talk to the Saudis and then the commander of the Sixth Fleet."

It was already dark in Jerusalem when the coach—property of the Mount of Olives Bus Company—lumbered up the steep incline out of the Valley of Kidron and, with only minimum slippage, made its scheduled stop opposite the gates of the Apostolic Delegation. The florid, perspiring prelate who got off then puffed his way up the further incline of the drive to the delegation building itself. As he came closer, the illuminated letters, *DOMUS DEI, PORTA COELI*— House of God, Gate of Heaven—hovered before him in the darkness, until he at last stood directly beneath them. He dropped his oversized briefcase and pushed the bell. Three times—each burst longer than the last. Even St. Peter, it seemed, was allowed a night off.

By venturing around the side of the building, he eventually managed to attract the attention of one of the resident sisters, who let him in the back way and showed him up the stairs to Archbishop Ramone's private quarters on the second floor.

The slight, ascetic figure stared at him in amazement.

"Giovanni . . . It is, isn't it? Cardinal Pellegrini's secretary?"

"It is, Excellency," answered the young monsignor, noting the dark crescents beneath the archbishop's eyes. Since their meeting in Rome a couple of days earlier, the man seemed to have aged ten years; even his hair seemed sparser and greyer.

"B-But why here? And why didn't His Eminence let me know you were coming? At least we could have had a car at the airport to meet you. The Secretary of State's private secretary deserves . . ."

"Excellency," interrupted the monsignor in a voice betokening urgency, "I will explain everything, but first—if you will allow—there are matters with which I must acquaint you . . ."

Half an hour later, Monsignor Giovanni concluded:

"And that, Excellency, is why my arrival had to be unannounced. Officially I am here to conduct a party of nuns on a visit to the Holy Land. I am booked into a hotel on the other side of the city under an assumed name." He smiled. "It's just as well the Vatican is able to issue its own passports."

But Ramone's mind was elsewhere.

"This plan that you speak of," he said, "this smuggling operation—it has been agreed by the Curia Segreta? I am not thinking of the dangers to myself, you understand; only the possible risks to the Church."

Relishing the privilege of knowing more than a superior, for whom he already had little regard, Monsignor Giovanni assumed an omniscient expression.

"My instructions from His Eminence were to convey to you only the message as we have received it from the Americans via Cardinal DeWohl in New York. However, I don't think it would be far outside my remit if I were to tell you that the Curia Segreta did indeed discuss the matter at some length and, like yourself, certain of Their Eminences expressed concern at the Church's involvement in such an enterprise. They were nonetheless persuaded by His Eminence the Secretary of State that a mightier hand was directing events and that it was God's will that the council should take whatever steps were necessary to prevent the public revelation of this outrage."

Recalling all too vividly the Secretary of State's affirmation of his Catholic humanism, the archbishop couldn't believe he was capable of spouting such a flow of hypocrisy. He doubted that the young man had been anywhere near the meeting—a doubt confirmed by his next statement.

"I might add, Excellency, that His Eminence also laid great stress on your abilities and expressed his personal conviction that, with the Almighty's guiding hand, you would discharge the task with complete competence."

"I am flattered," responded the archbishop with an irony that was lost on the monsignor, "that His Eminence has so much faith in us *both*. But, tell me, the Holy Father, is *he* aware of our intended cooperation with our Palestinian brethren?"

The monsignor flushed. Having implied his intimacy with the Curia Segreta's deliberations, he had no alternative but to answer.

"I am not aware that His Holiness is unaware," he replied with a convolution that even he found hard to follow. Flustered, he looked at his watch and added hastily, "In half an hour, Excellency, you will be receiving a phone call from Monsignor Cereti in Amman. For the purposes of credibility —in case the Israelis are monitoring your calls—he has been instructed to inform you of a diocesan matter over the border requiring your urgent personal attention. You will plead pressure of commitments here but, being pressed, will reluctantly agree to cross tomorrow evening—immediately after your visit to the International Ecumenical Institute."

That night Archbishop Ramone was to dream again. He had said his prayers but, before falling asleep, had been thinking of his original dream and the rain-lashed chasm of bones. He knew now where the idea had come from: the Old Testament Book of Ezekiel, where the hand of the Lord took the prophet and "set me down in the midst of the valley which was full of bones, and caused me to pass by them round about; and, behold, there were very many in the open valley; and, lo, they were very dry . . . ." Then, inspired by the Lord, Ezekiel prophesies the resurrection of "the whole House of Israel," whereby the bones come together, take on sinew and flesh, and finally have life breathed into them. For the archbishop it was a less than comforting interpretation, implying, as it seemed to, not a Christian resurrection but a Jewish one—and a political one at that, if one translated "the whole House" as the modern State of Israel.

He drifted into sleep. Significantly—as though exorcised by explanation—there was no flight of steps this time and no valley of bones. Instead, he was already beneath the cross looking up at the crucified skeleton. Calmly, he told himself that he was dreaming, and then in a continuous, fluid movement he rolled out of bed, across the floor, and onto the prie-dieu where he had earlier said his prayers. Whether now awake or still in the dream he wasn't sure—not until he looked up at the small crucifix on the wall and watched in awful fascination as Christ's flesh melted like wax to reveal the skeleton below.

THE FIRST DAY

W HERE TO?" asked the driver.

"EGHQ—north entrance," replied the Defense Minister, slipping into the back of the nondescript official car. Ten minutes later, Gideon Berman was in the center of West Jerusalem, walking up Teddy Kollek Mall, the pedestrianized part of Ben Yehuda Street. Two hundred yards up on the right, without looking round, he turned into the United Mizrahi Bank. The fact that neither the security guards, counter staff, nor any member of the public had ever seen him deposit or withdraw a single shekel was incidental. Anybody who spotted him—and with his face it was hard not to be spotted—would assume that such an important customer dealt directly with the manager in his office. Which also had to explain why he invariably used the elevator.

He inserted the strip of magnetized plastic into the unobtrusive slot beneath the row of buttons and after a two-second delay felt the elevator start downward. It continued dropping for seventy feet. At the same time—although an occupant was unaware of this—it would be corkscrewed through thirty degrees to confuse anyone minded to determine the precise location of the most secret command center in the Middle East, the Israeli Government's Emergency General Headquarters, or Begin's Bunker, as it was better known in recognition of the man who had conceived it. As an added precaution, both the elevator shaft and the hundred-yard tunnel leading underground from the elevator exit to the complex itself were sheathed in a mesh of wires carrying a low-voltage electrical current to ensure the malfunction of any compass, signal generator, or other directional device.

The elevator door hissed back to reveal a soldier in olive-drab fatigues with a .38 Webley in open holster at his waist. On recognizing the minister, he stepped back and saluted—a rare gesture in the Israeli army.

111

EGHQ was not designed for the claustrophobic. Built during the early 1980s, the subterranean honeycomb, consisting of more than fifty rooms protected by a bombproof ceiling of reinforced concrete five yards deep, was intended primarily as a replacement for "the Pit," the original emergency command center in Tel Aviv from which, in October 1973, the then Defense Minister Moshe Dayan had followed the progress of the Yom Kippur War. The siting of the new complex in Jerusalem was especially significant—as much psychologically as strategically. It was an affirmation of Israel's determination to defend her ancient capital at all costs. In no future war would ministers sit in the relative safety of Tel Aviv and direct battles from there. In future, Jerusalem would be both the front line—and the last ditch. As though the fact needed underlining, the Emergency Cabinet Room was dominated along its end wall—the one opposite the Prime Minister's chair—by the words, cast in bronze, of Psalm 137, the song of the exiled children of Israel by the waters of Babylon:

If I forget thee, O Jerusalem, let my right hand
forget her cunning.
If I do not remember thee, let my tongue cleave to the
roof of my mouth;
If I prefer not Jerusalem above my chief joy.

A few paces along the corridor was the Masada Room, a six-foot square cubicle, most of which was taken up by a console incorporating an array of numbered buttons which, when pressed in a predetermined sequence known only to the Prime Minister and the Defense Minister, would unleash Israel's nuclear arsenal on any enemies within a range of 1,700 miles. And here, directly above the console, another much shorter inscription. Just two words: *ein brera*—there is no alternative.

Berman continued to the end of the corridor and through the blast and bombproof automatic sliding doors into the Control Room, a large fan-shaped structure which, like a lecture theater, sloped down towards a well.

He took his seat high up at the back, from where it was possible to see everything without getting in the way of the operational personnel down in the well. Before him a double bank of television screens hung from gantries in the ceiling—

each one linked to a closed-circuit camera at a key city center intersection, ostensibly to enable the police to monitor peak-time traffic, but in reality to enable the Defense Minister in time of war to determine the progress of a very different traffic—Arab tanks, should they ever breach the city's outer defenses. Buried two yards beneath each intersection—unknown to the thousands of motorists and pedestrians who daily crossed them—were massive charges of explosive which, primed and detonated here in the Control Room, could transform the intersections into craters ten times more effective than any conventional tank trap.

Although there had been more than a dozen training sessions involving simulated attacks on both the capital and the country, this was to be the first time that the new EGHQ had been used as an actual mission control—having been chosen by Berman because of the unparalleled speed and security of its communications and the way, being so far below the noise and bustle of the real world, it seemed to concentrate minds wonderfully—his own not least.

Two things immediately struck him as familiar—the insistent chatter of signals equipment and, despite the ubiquitous NO SMOKING notices, the reek of tobacco. That, and the nervous static in the atmosphere, heightened by the absence of the usual small talk. There was an unmistakable eve-of-battle air about the place. He could feel the muscles tighten across his diaphragm and, as he looked round at the other thirty or so men and women sipping coffee, inhaling nicotine, and snatching glances at screens and maps, he knew he wasn't alone.

"The American inspection team is scheduled to land at Ben Gurion at 14:20, General."

The voice was that of the Defense Minister's personal assistant, Meir. Berman squinted at the row of clocks above the maps on the far side of the room. There were three hours still to go.

"And Major Hervitz is waiting in the briefing room. Oh, and there's this," handing him a tape. "It was picked up by one of our Hawkeyes."

Berman scanned the strip of paper and grimaced. The message, radioed in by a surveillance aircraft, reported that one of the Saudi AWACS was on its way north from the southern oil fields where it was normally on patrol. The

AWACS—airborne reconnaissance stations based on the Boeing 707 aircraft and supplied to the Saudis by the Americans as part of former President Reagan's "evenhanded" policy in the Middle East—had a phenomenal ability to track, in any weather, every aircraft and ship within a 230-mile radius by means of their computerized radar systems. Berman didn't need reminding that Dimona was just a hundred miles from Saudi Arabia's northern border with Israel.

"Jamming them shouldn't be any problem," remarked Meir.

Berman was tempted to reply that, as Minister of Defense, this fact was well enough known to him, but then reminded himself that his reason for appointing the outspoken young man in the first place had been his total disregard for rank coupled with an apparent ignorance of the sort of tact which on occasion meant keeping one's mouth shut. Every minister, he had observed at the time, needed just such a man at his elbow.

"True," he replied, "but if we jam them, we also have to jam ourselves. Since the Americans provided us with the jamming equipment, we can't afford to be selective in its use. We'll have to fog the entire area. You say Yossi is in the briefing room?"

A man rarely given to demonstrative acts, Berman clasped the young helicopter pilot to him and ruffled the wild tangle of hair.

"And your parents, how are they?" he asked.

"Mother is fine. I'm sure she'd have sent her love if she'd known we'd be meeting. Father of course is most of the time in the States on business—but, yes, he's well, too."

Berman was amused—partly by the younger man's efforts to negotiate the emotional minefield that the question had strewn in his path and partly by the recollection of the awkward youth barely out of adolescence who, eight years previously when Berman had been Head of the Paratroopers School, had walked into his office and announced that he wanted to train as a para and hoped the fact that he was the son of Berman's ex-wife wouldn't count against him—adding ruefully that his mother would be furious if she knew what he was doing. His chutzpah had been appropriately rewarded and at the age of twenty-six Major Yossi Hervitz was now rated as the finest combat helicopter pilot the IDF had ever produced—one of that rare breed to whom, whether dangling from a parachute or piloting an aircraft, the air is as natural as water to a fish.

Berman's expression tightened.

"Yossi, I think you have a right to know the risks involved. They are as great as any of the gunship missions you've flown into Syria. In some respects, greater. Not only will you be flying in radio silence but, from what I've learned in the last five minutes, you'll also be without radar. We won't even be able to track you."

"And the hardware?" asked Yossi.

"Standard issue Huey. I'd like to have given you a Cobra but, apart from the fact that we'd have had to sling the cargo between the skids, an attack chopper would only attract attention. I'll do what I can to keep your airspace clear, but again there's a danger of making it conspicuously so. There'll also be a decoy road convoy leaving Dimona shortly before you—not that I think anybody is going to be fooled by it."

"You think the Americans will try something then?"

Berman shrugged.

"I don't know, Yossi. Stewart Menzies, a former head of the British SIS, once said that if you credit your opponent with a mind so supreme that it thinks of everything, you are left with no choice but to do nothing." He laid a hand on the young man's shoulder. "That's precisely the dilemma we're in now and, although it is a gross breach of Cabinet rules, you're entitled to know that I personally voted against the use of a helicopter on this mission because of its vulnerability. If, knowing that, you want to pull out, I will understand."

The major gave a boyish grin.

"Planes were flying long before anyone thought of radio or radar. I'll risk it. What am I to tell my crew?"

"That the mission involves transporting a radioactive iso-tope from Dimona to a hand-over destination yet to be determined."

Berman read the expression on the younger man's face.

"I know. I don't like lying any more than you, but there is no alternative. I've already told you far more than I should." He looked into Yossi's eyes and clasped him by the forearm. "Look after yourself—and for God's sake don't put me in the position of having to break any unfortunate news to your mother. If you do, I swear I'll personally veto any posthumous medal!"

Alone in the briefing room, Berman sat down and pulled from his wallet a small passport-size photograph. The boy was his mother's son alright. The same generous mouth and slightly languorous eyes.

His action was prompted not by self-pity at the loss of the beautiful woman in the photograph to another man, nor by envy of that man's good fortune in having such a fine son by her. Certainly not the latter. On the infrequent occasions that Berman had seen Ariella over the years, it had been embarrassingly clear that Yossi and his father were at perpetual loggerheads and that the main reasons were the boy's idolizing of his mother's first husband and his unspoken wish that he had been *his* son, instead of the son of a man whose motivating force was commercial success and the accruing of wealth.

Rather, his action was a dispassionate attempt to analyze his own confused emotions; to explain the protective, almost paternal, feelings that his talk with Yossi had aroused in him. Why had he felt so like a latter-day Abraham binding his son's hands in preparation for sacrifice? It worried him; he thought he had learned never again to entrust emotional hostages to fortune. But there was no denying that over Yossi's shoulder he had seen the ghosts of other loved ones who had similarly left and never come back. For a brief, chill moment, he was once again the frightened eleven-year-old hiding in the cupboard in the house in Lodz, hearing his sister patiently explain to his mother that it was time to go.

The small Arab boy sped along the crowded pavement with the deftness of a shuttle on a loom. In one hand he clutched a parcel of food and from the other swung a tray of little glasses. Only once had the contents of the tray smashed to the ground and that had been ages ago—three months, to be exact, when he had still been six. He was tempted to make his usual stop at the charcoal maker's but the recorded voice of the muezzin over loudspeakers calling the faithful to their midday prayers reminded him of his father's injunction not to loiter.

Without warning, an Israeli army jeep came careering down the street. As everybody else leaped for the pavement, a blind man found himself helplessly marooned in the middle of the road. Bassem watched the driver swerve around him and carry on without even a backward glance. Another Arab took the man by the arm, shook his fist at the departing Israelis, and spat in the gutter.

Several things puzzled Bassem this morning. Not the Israelis. He had grown up with them and knew they were to be hated. They had taken away his grandfather's land—four thousand dunams of it—because they said it was of strategic importance. His grandfather still had the papers to prove he owned it; he kept them, faded and rust-stained, in a tin box. The Israelis had also sometimes shut down his father's printing shop because he had printed notices and posters they didn't like. Then one day—Land Day—they had forced him to open it, although he actually wanted to keep it shut like everybody else's.

But it was the three men that puzzled Bassem this morning— the men in the back of the shop. They hadn't been there the previous evening and certainly weren't from Hebron; they spoke with an accent that was quite different from the local one. When he had asked his father about them, he had been told only to mind his own business and, on pain of the most terrible thrashing, to tell nobody about them. Not even if he was asked. Even more curious was the fact that the men hadn't moved from the back room and, by the look of it, were also going to eat their lunch there.

As he walked in the door, he was immediately scolded by his father. Where had he been all this time? Had he been talking to anyone—been asked any questions? Bassem started to explain that he had had difficulty attracting the barman's attention because of the many customers, but his father snatched the parcel and tray from him before he could finish. It was unlike his father—normally a cheerful, easygoing man—to be so short-tempered. He was different and it was the men in the back room who had changed him. From being the proud man that he normally was with his customers, with these men he was servile and embarrassingly anxious to please. It upset Bassem to see his father like this.

★

After unwinding his black and white checked keffiyeh, the eldest of the three cradled the stuffed vine leaf in his hand and raised it to his mouth. He took a large bite and then a gulp of the green tea. His mouth still full, he wagged a finger at Bassem's father.

"The jeep, it is ready then?"

"It's just around the corner, in my brother's garage. A four-wheel drive Land-Rover—old but it goes well enough. It's being painted green—the correct shade—and will have the badge on the doors."

"And the back?"

"A removable canvas top, as you asked."

"What about uniforms?"

"They are not necessary. Most of the inspectors wear ordinary khaki shirts and trousers. You'd be more likely to arouse suspicion in a uniform. Believe me."

The Palestinian stared at Bassem's father over his stuffed vine leaf. It wasn't in the man's interest to deceive him, he decided.

"And documentation?" he asked.

Bassem's father produced a small plastic wallet and handed it over for examination.

"The Polaroid will be added after you have shaved off your moustache. And this," he added, passing over an official-looking document bearing the stylized Menorah of the State of Israel, "is just in case you have any difficulty."

The Palestinian glanced at it and frowned.

"An eviction order?"

"A genuine one. I got it from a lawyer friend. It was served on one of his Bedouin clients only last week. With this you'll be alright."

The Palestinian grunted and muttered an ironic, "Insh'-allah—God willing."

★

"The Americans have landed, General."

For a moment Meir thought Berman hadn't heard him and was about to repeat the message when he responded in a voice barely above a whisper:

"OK. Go ahead."

Meir shouted to the prettiest girl in the Control Room.

"Shoshana! Any number between one and six."

"Four," she replied with a look of bewilderment.

Berman consulted the list.

"Talmei Yosef . . . the moshav. Co-ordinates: 31:12 34:22 . . . Bearing: west-northwest . . . Distance: sixty-six kilometers . . .," and, scratching figures on a pad, he added: "Instruct Yossi to take off at 15:30, and the decoy convoy to leave a quarter of an hour earlier—not later than 15:15."

"And the decoy's destination?"

Beman consulted the list again.

"Site six."

Meir descended into the well to give the instructions. As he passed, Shoshana grabbed him by the arm.

"What was all that about?" she asked.

"Picking the number? Oh, just one of the general's ideas for passing the time. He's thinking of setting up a casino in the Cabinet Room . . . auditioning croupiers."

He carried on and then turned.

"*Mazel tov!* You got the job."

★

Six thousand miles away across a sea and an ocean, the telex and the Fotofax transmission machines in the CIA Langley Operations Center chattered away like hyperactive cicadas. Stan Harding watched as a cascade of tape spewed out of a telex marked NRO—National Reconnaissance Office, the government body responsible for the United States' satellite surveillance round the world.

Suddenly his myopic gaze sharpened.

"Chief," he said in an urgent whisper to Bob Spender, who was standing next to him, shirt-sleeves rolled up and very much the general amid his men in the thick of the action, "we're getting something. One of the Argus satellites has picked up activity around Dimona." He looked up and bellowed across the room, "Scotty, get the NRO to run its Middle East Argus pictures on Fotofax, will you?"

Seconds later the Fotofax twitched into life. Line-by-line and with eye-defying speed, there emerged first a time slug and grid reference and then a full color overhead view of the Dimona nuclear research establishment as though photographed—thanks to the Argus's telescopic computer-enhanced lenses—from no more than a few hundred feet up.

Harding ran his finger over the still-warm paper, tracing the outline of the images. There was no mistaking it: a convoy of troop-carrying trucks with a pair of armored cars front and back, and at the very center of the line, a single armored personnel vehicle. He did a rapid count.

". . . six, seven, eight troop carriers. Fully loaded, that's nearly two hundred men, not including the armored outriders."

Spender made a sound halfway between a grunt and a belch.

"Well, that's your happy band of warriors done for, Stan. There's no way three Palestinians can take on a bunch like that—rockets or no rockets. We'll have to tell Romford the only option now is the military one . . ."

"And another Middle East war?" queried Harding. "If we bring in Jordanian or Saudi jets to do the job, that's what it'll be. There's no way we could use our own aircraft against a friendly country and it's too late to start dressing them up in somebody else's colors."

Spender took a deep breath and tweaked his suspenders.

"Yea, well, that's their headache. There's nothing more we can do."

Harding detected the note of relief in his boss's voice and was angry. That the man was all flab and wind he had long known. Up to now, though it had worked to his advantage in that, knowing next to nothing about Middle Eastern affairs, Spender had been happy to leave it all to him and take the credit for any successes. But now the man was planning to pull the plug on an operation in which he, Harding, had invested not only considerable time and ingenuity, but also ambition, having already made up his mind that, if it came off, he would be rather less self-effacing than formerly. For all these reasons, he was determined to see it through—even if it meant bringing the whip hand into the open.

"Chief, I think you'd be better advised to wait," he declared curtly.

"Jesus, Stan, are you off your head? Do you think that convoy is a cardboard cutout or something?"

"It's an armed convoy alright, but I have yet to be convinced that it's escorting the bones. We haven't had the signal from the location generator yet, remember."

"Of course we haven't," squealed Spender. "The bones aren't at the fucking site yet and the generator is in *our* equipment, not theirs. Remember?"

"I remember," said Harding quietly. "And that's why I think we should at least wait for that signal before pulling out." He looked again at the Fotofax where by now the first photograph had been followed by another half dozen representing a sequence of ten-second time delays. "The convoy is coming out of the south entrance and heading southeast. If it is for real, then we can expect the signal to come from the same general direction. If not . . ."

Spender gave a contemptuous guffaw and reached for a telephone. Defiantly, Harding placed himself between the two and addressed his boss from less than a foot away and a similar advantage in height.

"Chief, let me ask you a question. Do you think the Israelis know we have reconnaissance satellites in permanent, fixed orbit over the Middle East? Do you think they know that, with their infrared facilities, those birds are capable of detecting a single puff of broken wind anywhere in the Negev—never mind an eleven-vehicle convoy?"

Spender displayed the first signs of anger. "What sort of a dumb question is that, for Christ's sake? Of course they know. Now, enough of this nonsense!"

Harding didn't move.

"So it follows that before they sent that convoy on its way they knew it would be spotted. The question is, therefore: Are they simply calling our bluff and challenging us to spark off another Middle East war or is this ostentatious little cavalcade of military transport something other than it seems? A decoy perhaps to sidetrack us from the real thing?"

Spender seemed to hesitate and Harding pressed his advantage.

"If we get this wrong, Chief, it'll rate as more than just an operations failure; it'll be an intelligence failure—a failure of interpretation. Without sparing you the verbal niceties, the Israelis will piss all over us. Everybody will know, and that'll reflect on the Agency and all its relevant personnel."

Spender stared up at Harding. He detected a thinly veiled threat in what the man was saying—that if the Israelis didn't leak the story of their successful duping then, sure as hell, *he* would. And of all the relevant personnel, who more vulnerable than the man at the top? He felt the sweat break through the back of his neck and, half-mesmerized by Harding's hugely magnified black eyeballs, thought for a moment that, like twin boulders, they would tumble from their sockets, smash through the pebble lenses and crush him.

"Well, it's against my better judgement," he murmured. "I only hope you realize the other side of this particular coin— that if you are wrong and that convoy really is carrying the bones, then by *not* informing the President right now we could be jeopardizing the success of any military option." He ran a damp finger round the inside of his collar. "Jesus, Stan, you'd better be right. That's all. You'd just better be right."

★

The only thing the four occupants of the transit van could tell for sure was that they had been on the road for more than an hour. There were no windows in the van; a steel divider separated the passenger compartment from the driver's cab; it was uncomfortably hot; and the only sound throughout the journey from the airport had been the whine of a faulty differential.

Without warning, the van bucked to a halt. A minute later, the twin rear doors sprang open to reveal a blinding expanse of pinkish sand and a cornflower blue sky washed back to white where it met the horizon. Only after a few more seconds did their artificially benighted eyes discern the rows of greenhouses and chalet-type bungalows.

"Welcome to the Negev!" said a cheery voice. "Dr. Schumacher?"

The last man to climb out of the van shielded his eyes and, without proffering a hand, announced:

"I am Schumacher."

The busy, bushy little man smiled nervously.

"Of course. I am Mordechai Ben Ami, Professor of Archaeology at the Hebrew University, and on this occasion your host." He noticed the hand, stiff and immobile, by the doctor's side and beckoned towards a cluster of modern grey and white concrete buildings, "If you will kindly follow me then, gentlemen."

As they set off across the sand, Schumacher asked testily:

"And are we to be 'kindly' told where we are?"

The professor waved his arm in an all-encompassing sweep.

"This? Oh, this is what's called a *moshav*—an agricultural cooperative."

"A sort of kibbutz?" asked another of the party.

"Not really. You're probably thinking of a *moshav shitufi*—a sharing moshav. This is a *moshav ovdim*. It's more independent. Every family here owns its own house and strip of land. But the fertilizer, the farming equipment, and such like is bought centrally, and the marketing of the produce—the flowers and vegetables—that too is done jointly. A good example of Jewish pragmatism, I think!"

Schumacher spotted a bright red tractor. An Arab was loading flowers onto its trailer.

"And you are fortunate in having a nearby reservoir of native labor," he remarked. "Another good example of Jewish pragmatism, no doubt."

The professor bit his tongue; he knew the dangers of sparring with a man like Schumacher. Later there might be a time and place, but now there was more pressing business. Reaching the moshav's administrative block, he ushered the physicist and his entourage past a pair of soldiers into the *moadon*, the members' club room-cum-assembly hall. It was only marginally cooler. If there was any air conditioning, it either wasn't working or had been deliberately turned off. Instead, a pair of fans at both ends of the hall ineffectually whisked the air, merely distributing the strata of heat more evenly.

Schumacher's eyes fell immediately on the large metal container and number of smaller cases piled up at the far end of the hall. He walked straight across and, disregarding the half-dozen armed guards, pointedly examined the seals on the catches and even the seams and rivets. It had been agreed during President McCrae's talks with Avraham Rubinger that any inspection of the team's equipment would be carried out in the presence of the Americans themselves.

Watching "Herr Doktor Schumacher," as he had already mentally dubbed him, the professor found it hard to disguise his dislike for the man. The tall, angular septuagenarian with his thin fingers and rimless glasses was too much the epitome of the German-born naturalized American nuclear physicist with an unsavory past rooted in the Hitler era. More telling, though, was the professor's own awareness of how closely, as Schumacher's physical antithesis, he conformed to the stereotype Jew that men like "Herr Doktor" so despised. He looked around the hall and, singling out a white-coated figure, beckoned to him. Cupping his elbow, he steered him towards the crates.

"Dr. Schumacher," he announced, "I'd like to introduce you to a professional colleague of mine from the Weizmann Institute at Rehovot. He is Israel's own resident expert in carbon-dating techniques, as well as in almost every other branch of dating technology."

Despite his studied indifference, Schumacher waited for one of the three names he had been given back in the States as likely candidates for the job of operation overseer and chief monitor. When none came, he gave a curt nod and resumed his examination of the crates.

"I imagine, Doctor," said the anonymous expert, "that you have brought one of your new compact particle accelerators with you. I look forward to seeing it, having read so much about its development." When Schumacher failed to respond, he added, "May I ask which particular model you have chosen to use on this occasion?"

Schumacher turned and with a gaze that seemed to be focused several feet behind the questioner's head, responded:

"A one-point-five megavolt Tandetron Tandem Analyzer with external ion source and ultrasensitive mass spectroscope—developed and manufactured by the General Ionex Corporation of Newburyport, Massachusetts. Does that answer your question?"

Before Schumacher's attention was lost again, the professor stepped in and handed him a typed sheet of paper.

"This afternoon's time schedule," he explained.

Schumacher gave it a supercilious glance and, handing it back, pronounced:

"Impossible. The preparation of the carbon-dating sample alone will take as long as you've allowed for the entire program."

"I hardly think so, Doctor," cut in the white coat. "If the accelerator is the latest Tandetron Analyzer you say it is, then the schedule will be quite adequate for your requirements, as well as those of your colleagues. Since, however, we are apparently agreed that time is limited, I trust you will have no objection if we proceed with the inspection of the equipment without further delay."

As he spoke, he pulled from his briefcase a sheaf of plans and specifications, making no attempt to conceal from the doctor the words *Tandetron Analyzer* on the front.

"I don't know what you've got there," remarked Schumacher icily, "but the technical details of this particular model have yet to be published."

The white coat smiled.

"So I gather, Doctor. As I am sure you know, however, the international scientific community is a very close one and I am fortunate in having several former members of my own Institute working in the United States. It goes without saying," he weighed the papers in his hand, "that we keep in touch over matters of mutual interest."

★

Painted in its desert mottle of brown, beige, and light blue, the Bell UH 1D helicopter—universally tagged the Huey—hovered, pitched forward, and assumed the dragonfly attitude that would take it up to its cruising speed of a little over a hundred miles an hour. Within seconds the Dimona complex below was a rapidly receding spot and, relaxing his grip on the collective lever by his left knee, Yossi settled back into his seat, the familiar rotor slap of the twin-bladed Huey forming a regular, comforting backdrop to his thoughts.

He was never happier than when cruising at between a thousand and fifteen hundred feet across the face of his beloved Israel—a lover caressing the cheek of his mistress. It went deeper than raw patriotism; it was a pride in what in just over forty years of statehood the Jewish people had accomplished in fulfillment of the Biblical prophecy, "The Lord thy God will gather thee from all the nations whither He hath scattered thee . . . and will bring thee into the land which thy fathers possessed, and thou shalt possess it." True, it had taken some nineteen hundred years for the Almighty to honor his word, but the prophecy had been fulfilled and lucky the Jew who was born to see it!—to see the forests of luxuriant pine and the field upon field of mangoes, avocadoes, cucumbers, tomatoes, citrus, and strawberries, where previously there had been only desert and dunes. The prophecy had been fulfilled. Vast tracts of desert remained to be cleared but within a decade the whole area from Beersheva to Yeruham would be one continuous carpet of cultivation. And who, watching the shadow of an Israeli military helicopter skim across such a landscape, could not be moved by the realization that all this had been accomplished by a people who for most of their two millennia exile had been barred from owning land or carrying arms?

Abruptly, the cultivated area gave way again to desert. Off to the left in the lee of a barren outcrop, Yossi spotted a Bedouin tent, voluminous and black, with scattered all around, as though flicked from an artist's brush, black specks which he assumed to be goats. Israel's smallness in relation to her hostile neighbors was a cliché of which every visitor was duly reminded the moment he stepped off the aircraft—even before if he happened to be sitting next to a returning Israeli—and yet from a quarter of a mile high there was plenty of land for everybody. Enough for Jew and Arab to live on and work side by side. Perspective was all. Why else had the Almighty chosen to give Moses his only sight of the Promised Land from the heights of Mount Nebo? Perhaps if every Jew and every Arab were to spend just twenty minutes in a helicopter, century-old attitudes would change and the dream of peace become a reality.

He smiled at the fanciful notion and glanced over his shoulder to check that the precious cargo hadn't shifted. The bright yellow oblong steel casket was still firmly in place, the webbing taut. The copilot, Zvika, followed Yossi's gaze and grinned at his exaggerated concern for the valuable load. Believing the casket to contain radioactive uranium or plutonium—high-grade bomb material of some sort—he wrongly attributed his commander's concern to a fear that, if something went wrong, they'd all become part of the Ultimate Sunset. He wondered whether the same thought had occurred to the third member of the crew, the flight engineer, Ehud. He doubted it, seeing him nonchalantly chewing gum, with one arm resting on the Huey's M-60 machine gun mount. An American girlfriend had once taught Ehud the expression "laid back," and ever since he had worked his hardest to become its most perfect living embodiment.

Yossi was pointing to a group of buildings below. Consulting the map, Zvika mouthed the words *He-vel Be-sor* and held up the splayed fingers of both hands to indicate the approximate number of nautical miles still to go to Moshav Talmei Yosef.

Five minutes later, laid out as neatly as a Monopoly board, a grid of red roofs appeared directly ahead. In the distance a double row of wire-fencing marking the 1982 Sinai border with Egypt shimmered in the heat haze. Zvika checked the compass bearings against the map reference and followed with his eye one of the bougainvillea-trimmed roads to a major intersection marked by the square of administrative buildings. According to the instructions, the landing site was alongside and next to an adventure playground. He spotted it, and gave the thumbs up sign to Yossi.

Yossi banked the Huey to the right and, reducing pitch on the main rotor, allowed the chopper to drift downwards.

"A chopper," murmured Harding staring at the Fotofax machine. "Now that's more like it."

Unwilling as he was to acknowledge that his Middle East adviser may have been right about the convoy, Spender found it impossible not to look at the pictures now spewing from the machine. It was a helicopter alright and taking off from Dimona. It was time, he decided, to reassert his authority and take personal control of the situation.

"Scotty," he called across in his most stentorian tones, "get the NRO to track that chopper, will you?"

The man's only reaction was a blank stare followed by a questioning look not at Spender but at Harding.

With a discreet lift of the hand Harding signaled to him to ignore what he had just heard and, turning to Spender, whispered:

"Chief, satellites in stationary orbits can't track; they can't follow a moving object. Their cameras can be tweaked in different directions, but basically all they can do is lock onto a predetermined area and then go in on it."

Spender blushed not just at the present embarrassment—although with an audience of sixty-odd people that was bad enough—but at the thought of the canteen tittle-tattle his gaffe would provoke: "And you know what he said, Art? He said, 'Track that chopper!' I kid you not!"

"You're saying we have no means of knowing where it's heading?" he asked, fighting to recover his composure.

Harding referred to the Fotofax.

"Not from this. The sequential photos show it heading in a

southwesterly direction before it disappears from frame, but that's certain to be the standard flight path out of Dimona. Tells us nothing."

"What about communications cross talk and, hell, what about radar?"

"There isn't any. On an operation like this they'll be flying in radio silence with possibly an open channel for emergencies. As for radar, we ensured that neither of us would be able to use it when we got the Saudis to bring their AWACS up from the Gulf. To jam us, they will have had to jam themselves."

Spender looked baffled.

"The idea, Chief, if you recall," explained Harding with the patience of one addressing a mentally defective five-year-old, "is that, although they will know the flight path of that chopper, at no point along the way—coming or going—will they now know precisely where it is, or what may have happened to it." His eyes flicked to the bank of clocks. "Anyway, it shouldn't be long now before we get the signal."

★

Two on either side, the soldiers lugged the steel casket to the center of the hall and laid it on a low angle-iron frame. Two then stepped back and took their place in the semicircle of guards already formed up, angling their Uzis at the same regulation forty-five degrees to the ground.

With the ceremonial gravity of a wreath-laying politician, the professor moved forward and gave a nod, indicating to the remaining pair of pallbearers to spring the catches on the lid.

It was heavier than either had imagined, being designed, like the casket itself, to survive not just burn and blast but, if necessary, a thousand foot fall in a crippled helicopter. As they slid it forward, a corner clipped the iron supporting frame and set every filling in every tooth in the room ringing at the same frequency. They laid it on the floor beside the casket and then similarly removed an inner lid of fiberglass, leaving only a protective layer of foam rubber, which the professor himself rolled back.

The Americans' surprise flashed across their faces. They had expected the skeleton to be displayed in roughly the same position it had assumed stacked in the ossuary—in accordance with normal archaeological practice. Instead, it had been laid out in lifelike fashion, the indented human form of the plastic sponge tray in which it rested serving only to heighten the beholder's sense of looking, not at a collection of bones, but at a once living, breathing, mortal being. The impact could hardly have been greater if the ankles had been crossed and the arms outstretched. What effect such a display might have if it were ever to go on public show was all too easy to imagine, and Schumacher for one made no attempt to hide his disgust.

"I hardly think such stage management is appropriate to our scientific endeavors, Professor."

Ben Ami determined to take the remark as a compliment and smiled.

"Gentlemen," he announced, "the remains are ready for your inspection. Perhaps if Dr. Schumacher would like to take his carbon-dating sample first, you other gentlemen will then be able to get on with your own examinations."

Schumacher crossed to the laboratory bench that had been set up along one wall and returned wearing surgical gloves and carrying on a tray a scalpel, miniature hacksaw, pair of tweezers, and petri dish.

"It is agreed, I believe, Doctor," said the professor, "that you will take no more than one gram of bone for your sample and . . ." He paused, uncomfortably aware of the Shakespearean parallels—"and that it will be from a part of the skeleton judged to be of least significance—the wrists, ankles, and skull being specifically excluded."

Making no response, Schumacher laid his instruments on a table alongside the open casket.

"I will take from the upper section of the left femur," he declared.

Ben Ami nodded his acquiescence and watched, the white coat by his side, as Schumacher meticulously sawed and cut away the fragment of bone, placed it in the glass dish, and carried it back to the bench to be purged of all extraneous substances likely to prejudice an accurate reading—before being converted into graphite and introduced into the accelerator.

With a clumsy attempt at casualness, Richard Klinger, the photographer of the team, turned back his cuff to look at his watch, which was still on U.S. Eastern Standard Time. There was a clock in the hall, but in the briefing before they had left America, the team had been specifically enjoined to ignore all Israeli clocks and watches in case of time tampering. Standing next to Klinger, the archaeologist McVaney noticed and read his colleague's anxiety.

"If you have no objection, Professor," said McVaney, "I think Mr. Klinger should go next, since he is responsible for all our photographic work and needs to be sure his negatives are of the necessary quality before the opportunity for a second attempt is lost."

The white coat was immediately alert. He had already singled out the twitchy young photographer as the most likely suspect for any underhand activity. For a start, he was the only member of the team without a professional pedigree or even—ironically—a published photograph for his identity to be checked against. More suspicious still was his equipment. Whereas Schumacher's Tandetron accelerator required only a tiny sample for its operation and could accordingly be kept at a safe distance from the bones behind a wall of lead bricks, Klinger's photographic gear had to be brought within a yard, where the potential for dirty tricks was unlimited. Uppermost among the white coat's fears was the possibility that any one of the three cameras—the X-ray, the ultraviolet, or even the ordinary photographic—might have been modified to bombard the bones with a massive dose of radiation, thereby rendering any future attempt at carbon dating impossible and so undermining the bones' claim to authenticity. With this danger in mind, every item of the photographer's equipment had been dismantled as far as was technically feasible, and had been tested under power while being simultaneously scanned by some of the Weizmann Institute's most sensitive monitors. Nothing had registered, but the white coat remained far from satisfied and, in a deliberate move to pressure the young photographer, now moved closer in—to a point where he could almost count the beads of sweat on the man's upper lip.

In a voice that kept breaking into a hoarse falsetto, the photographer first asked for the casket to be raised at one end. Mounting his camera on a high tripod he then checked his distances with a tape measure and placed the standard red and white measuring stick alongside the skeleton to enable anyone viewing the photographs to calculate dimensions against its calibrated scale. His hands were perceptibly shaking as he planted a lamp on either side of the casket and clipped the film-loaded back onto the Hasselblad. He flicked the switch on the light nearest him and, unable any longer to ignore the penetrating gaze, asked the white coat if he would oblige by switching on the other light to enable him to take a reading. Reaching into his breast pocket, he pulled out an exposure meter and directed it at the bones.

To his amazement, a white arm shot out and, instead of switching on the light, smashed into his wrist with a swipe that sent the light meter spinning through the air.

In the seconds that followed, the circlet of armed guards snapped shut around the casket, the photographer was thrown to the ground by an unidentified figure in civilian garb, and the white coat skated across the hall in pursuit of the object that had apparently and inexplicably given so much offense.

Recovering it, he proceeded to rip off the back and bang the contents out onto the table. Sorting through the fragments and failing to find whatever it was he was looking for, he then brandished the empty plastic case beneath the nose of the stupefied photographer, who was still picking himself up off the floor and nursing his bruised wrist.

"Why this one?" he yelled. "Tell me, why this one?"

The photographer was speechless but was saved from further interrogation or injury by Professor Ben Ami who—himself pursued by a furious Schumacher demanding an explanation for the white coat's behavior—took his colleague by the arm and led him, protesting in voluble Hebrew, from the hall.

Ten minutes later, the two returned. The professor addressed Schumacher.

"There has been a misunderstanding—for which I, as the one responsible for determining procedure, must take the blame. My colleague from the Weizmann Institute was momentarily disconcerted when he saw Mr. Klinger here take a light meter from his pocket, which he didn't know about and which had not been checked, instead of using the one in his equipment case which *had* been checked. He feared it might have been some sort of . . . device. In the circumstances, his action was regrettable but, I think, understandable."

Schumacher's lips were white with pent-up rage.

"Professor Ben Ami, there can be no excuse for such behavior in what is a scientific forum. This maniac has physically assaulted an individual for whose safety I am personally responsible. Since I am not prepared to have any other members of my team subjected to his arbitrary brutality, I must insist that this man whom you generously call a colleague leave. As for Mr. Klinger's choice of light meter, that is irrelevant; the object in question, like all the other items of our personal property, was thoroughly checked at the airport. If your colleague here didn't know that, he should have known. I repeat our scientific inspection of these remains is suspended until this man leaves."

The white coat started to object but was tactfully silenced by the professor.

"Dr. Schumacher," said the professor in a voice as quiet as a whisper, "I have to tell you that it is not in my power to comply with your demand, even if I agreed with it. Let me offer, however, a compromise. From now on, my colleague will observe from a distance, and any future intervention he deems necessary will be made by myself—and with appropriate warning."

Schumacher glowered at the white coat but, ever mindful of the clock, indicated by his silence that the compromise was acceptable.

Ben Ami gave a sigh of relief and waved the casket guards back to their original positions. Turning to the photographer, he said:

"Now, Mr. Klinger, if you would like to continue where you left off, using perhaps your *other* light meter."

Klinger looked to Schumacher and, getting the nod, removed his second meter from the camera box and rechecked the framing of his Hasselblad. A second time he switched on the lamp closest to him and, rather more hesitantly this time, pointed to the lamp next to the professor.

Anxious to promote at least a semblance of scientific cooperation, Ben Ami smiled and flicked the switch, unaware that, by so obliging, he was providing a surge of power sufficient to transform the eight-foot lampstand into a transmitter aerial capable of beaming its signal across land and sea to the American spy ship *Freedom IV*, moored in international waters thirty nautical miles off the Israeli coast. Thence, back to Washington.

★

The coordinates scrawled on his yellow jotter, Stan Harding turned to the map and ran his fingers along the lines of latitude and longitude to the point where they met.

"That settles it," he muttered, "definitely the helicopter."

"Why 'definitely'?" asked Spender at the risk of again parading his ignorance.

Harding marked the point with a felt-tip cross.

"Because to reach this place, Talmei Yosef, in the time it has taken, the convoy would have had to travel at speeds in excess of a hundred miles an hour. And that's without taking into account the state of the roads. If that convoy had been for real, our guys would be inspecting a pile of bonemeal now."

The beard parted to reveal a grin.

"Time to light the beacons, Chief," he said and picked up the phone. "Get me Dr. Talmahi's office in New York . . . yes, the Palestinian observer at the United Nations."

★

All eyes in the room were on Bassem's father as, cradling the telephone between chin and shoulder, he meticulously wrote down the seemingly innocuous order for headed stationery from the Namura Trading Company of Nablus, repeating each number aloud as it was given him. He rang off with a businesslike assurance that the order would be expedited within the week and—the others now pressing in on him— referred to a similar list of eight numbers on a piece of paper extracted from his back pocket. Placing the two columns side by side, he then added or subtracted according to the prearranged code to produce a third eight-figure column, which he handed to the leader of the three Palestinian guerrillas.

Having located the spot by its coordinates on the large-scale map spread out on the floor, the Palestinian stared at the name, mouthed it twice—the second time aloud for the benefit of his colleagues—and drew a straight line between it and Dimona.

Seven-year-old Bassem, whose presence had been overlooked, watched in wonderment, understanding only that— whatever this undertaking was—it was clearly of momentous importance to the grown men who were now scrambling around on the floor, tracing lines on the map, and slapping each other on the back. His only explanation for this curious display was that the men were looking for, and had apparently located, buried treasure. It was at this point, however, that he was spotted by his father who let forth an uncharacteristic flow of abuse, seized him by the neck, and propelled him from the room.

Several minutes later, from the upstairs bedroom that he shared with his older brothers, Bassem watched the three men leave by the back way and head in the direction of his uncle's garage. Alone, he mused on the significance of this place called Talmei Yosef that seemed to excite such strange emotions in grown-ups.

★

The air inside the hall was becoming intolerably hot and tempers correspondingly short. Even the fans seemed now to be grinding the air rather than circulating it, and there had been a second spat between the professor and Schumacher, with the Frankfurt-born American demanding that windows and doors be opened and the Israeli patiently explaining that in the Middle East one kept cool by keeping windows and doors *shut*. As a compromise, however, he had ordered a crate of chilled Maccabees from the moshav store.

The inspection was very nearly finished. Last in line, George McVaney, the team's archaeologist and the most imperturbably academic of the four, was strolling almost casually round the skeleton, viewing it from every angle and at the same time chatting in a confidential whisper into a miniature tape recorder. First impressions, he claimed, were often the most accurate, and by this means it would be possible to preserve them for later incorporation into his more reflective conclusions. Quite unfazed by the armed guards and the dozen other sets of eyes locked on him he circled the bones, back bent, like a vulture in search of a hitherto undetected scrap of flesh.

"General state of preservation: excellent . . . no evidence of arthritis . . . all teeth present; no caries . . . no apparent fractures of limbs, vertebrae, pelvis, ribs, or cranium . . . evidence of chipping and abrasion, though, on the inner surfaces of both the ulna and radius, on both forearms where they join the wrists . . . also extensive chafing of bone in second metatarsal area of right foot below the Lisfranc joint . . ."

He stopped the machine and turned to Ben Ami.

"And the ossuary that the remains were found in? Is it here too, Professor?"

"Unfortunately not," answered Ben Ami. "It is being stored separately—elsewhere." He handed McVaney a large envelope. "I have here, however, two sets of photographs of it—one black and white, one color—which you may take with you."

From the other side of the hall there were sounds of protest from Schumacher, but the archaeologist himself appeared unconcerned about the ossuary's absence.

"It doesn't matter, Doctor," he said, addressing Schumacher. "There are literally hundreds of first century Jewish ossuaries around and it would be impossible either to prove or disprove that these bones came out of this or any other of them." He slid the photos out of the envelope and shuffled through them. "The photographs are of the quality I would expect from Professor Ben Ami's department—and quite adequate for my purposes." He removed his half-frame glasses and poked them into his breast pocket, "I have seen all I need."

The professor was greatly relieved. It had been as trying an afternoon as he had ever experienced in his professional life. More to the point, the bones had now been out of Dimona more than two hours by his calculation; if they were to be back by sunset, as the Israelis had insisted—as much for reasons of security as the approaching Sabbath—then Yossi and his crew would have to move fast.

Ask an Israeli soldier what is the most boring but draining duty of all and the chances are he will reply, "manning a roadblock." It's the combination of repetition and responsibility—the occasional stomach-turning realization that, in retrospect, there *was* something suspicious about that truck you let through ten minutes ago. And the only training is experience; there's no manual, no study course—just antennae developed over months of doing the job. The old hands will say you can always smell something that isn't quite right. There are the telltale signs—the hand that shakes as it passes over the documents; the eye that doesn't meet yours when questions are asked. Which is probably true of most cases.

But does the hand of the *real* terrorist shake when it is on the trigger? Does the eye of the *real* terrorist veer away from its target? There's another dimension, too; for every security check represents to the Arab both a presumption of guilt—itself deeply offensive—and a reminder, if he needed it, that his land is no longer his. Nowhere are the reciprocal images of Arab and Jew more glaringly polarized than at the road-block—the Israeli, insensitive to the point of arrogance; the Arab, touchy to the point of paranoia.

After a morning and half an afternoon of alienating a good part of the local Arab population, it was with a sense of relief that the nineteen-year-old conscript watched the green Land-Rover with its distinctive ibex symbol pull up before him. The driver—by the look of him, a dark-skinned Oriental Jew like himself—leaned out of the window and flashed his identity wallet.

"Join the holiday special!" he joked. "A week in the desert—live like a nomad. All expenses paid!"

The conscript grinned.

"Where've you come from?" he asked.

"Beersheva."

"And going?"

"A couple of kilometers off the road to round up a few *arabushim*."

Perhaps after all, thought the conscript, there were worse jobs than manning a roadblock. The Green Patrol, as the Nature Reserves Authority inspectors were called, got it from both sides—from the Arabs because it was the patrol's job to stop the Bedouin squatting just wherever they felt like it, and from sections of the Israeli press and parliament who liked to compare their no-nonsense methods of eviction with the tactics of Hitler's storm troopers. It was a thankless task.

The Palestinian driver mistook the conscript's meditation for suspicion and produced the eviction order with which Bassem's father had furnished him.

"Members of the Azazma tribe, judging by the name," he remarked.

The conscript took in the official-looking court document and slapped the door panel.

"And good luck to you. *Shalom!*"

"*Toda*—thanks," responded the Palestinian and, slipping into first, swung the steering wheel to the left to avoid the row of viciously spiked teeth on the road ahead. His companions relaxed—the one beside him in the front passenger seat, the other in the back. Too soon. Without warning, the other soldier manning the checkpoint on the opposite side of the road twenty yards further on stepped out in front of the Land-Rover, hand raised.

The Palestinian did some lightning calculations. The choice was limited—either foot down and make a break for it, or stop and fight from within the confines of the Land-Rover. The first was already out; the 9-mm Uzi submachine gun can fire six hundred rounds a minute—enough to bring an unarmored vehicle to a halt within a few feet beneath the weight of lead alone!

He applied the brakes. Without a word passing between them, the other two reached for their Kalashnikovs, stowed beneath the front seat and a rug at the back respectively.

The Israeli soldier was smiling.

"You going in the direction of Yeruham, by any chance?" he asked genially, unaware of the devastating firepower aimed at his groin.

There was a moment's hesitation as the driver rapidly unscrambled his thoughts.

"Not . . . exactly. We're turning off into the desert a few kilometers down the road."

"Good enough! Anything to get away from this place . . ."

Beckoning to a relief to take over his duties, he clambered aboard, obliging the Palestinian in the passenger seat to move into the middle. It soon became evident that he was the talkative type.

"Not squashing you?"

The driver quickly intervened.

"He doesn't understand Hebrew. He's an Arab. They both are."

"Arabs?"

"Right. Trackers, to be exact, but they also help with the diplomatic niceties of the job. When you've got to move on Bedouin, it's better to have one of their own sort get rough with them. They're better at explaining."

The Israeli made no response.

Anxiously, the driver wondered what was going on in the man's head. He wasn't worried about his own command of the language; his Hebrew was a damned sight better than many Jews could manage, given the high proportion of immigrants who had to learn it at absorption centers. But he was none too sure that the Israeli had accepted the explanation about his Arab colleagues. Glancing in the rearview mirror, he caught the eye of his partner in the back, and prayed that he had the sense to keep the SAM-7 handheld missile launcher well covered.

"What's all the excitement about around here?" he asked, in an attempt to probe the Israeli's suspicions.

"We're the last to know," joked the soldier. "Our orders were simply to check everybody and turn back any blue number plates—West Bankers. Not even our commanding officer knew what it was about. Something to do with Dimona—that's all he'd been told—which could mean anything from a VIP trip to a full-scale nuclear war." As he talked, he inspected his surroundings. "Don't you have a two-way in this thing? I thought I saw a whip on the back."

"Being repaired," replied the driver flatly, convinced it couldn't be long now before the observant youngster noticed the Kalashnikov still lying on the floor at his feet. And if he didn't see it soon, he would be almost certain to spot it as he got out, by which time, if there were other traffic about, it would be too late to do anything about it. The decision was made.

He checked ahead and in the side mirror. A truck going the other way was nearly out of view; within five seconds the road would be clear. Out of the corner of his eye, he scrutinized the Uzi on the Israeli's knee. The clip was in, but the safety catch was on. He noticed too that—as though by telepathy—his colleague in the middle next to him had hooked his right arm over the back of the seat to brace himself. Another fleeting glance in the rearview mirror. The eyes met, held—and understood.

"So where do you come from?" asked the Israeli.

"Syria," replied the driver and in the same instant stamped on the brakes, pitching the Land-Rover violently forward and catapulting the Israeli headlong towards the dashboard, his mouth still gaping in astonishment.

As the Land-Rover slewed to a halt, the Arab next to him brought the full chopping force of his hand down on the back of the soldier's neck and then, yanking his head back by the hair, delivered a backhand scything swipe to the throat, crushing the larynx like a paper cup. There was a gurgle, followed by a convulsive spasm and, as life ebbed away, a gush of blood from the mouth and nose.

His assailant looked at his spattered trousers and swore.

"So what now?" he asked the driver, his commander.

"Stick him in the back or dump him?"

The other pointed to the sun, now close to the horizon.

"It's a risk either way." Then, after a moment's thought, "Dump him. It'll soon be too dark to find anything—him *or* the chopper."

★

With the departure of the bones, the atmosphere inside the hall had lost its emotional charge. Professor Ben Ami had turned his attention away from his American guests and was serving chilled beers to the soldiers who had acted as guards during the two-and-a-quarter-hour inspection. Only the white coat maintained his watching brief—from a distance.

At the other end of the hall, the Americans were packing away their equipment, except for Schumacher, whose radio carbon-dating hardware would still require another couple of hours on stream to give at least a provisional count. Even he, though, seemed to have unwound.

"So now you've seen the evidence, what do you think?" he asked the archaeologist McVaney.

"Certainly *looks* kosher," said the other, smiling. "I suspected before seeing it that we might be presented with a cleverly matched composite, using different bones from different skeletons—but that's not the case."

"How can you be sure?"

"Just by looking. The proportions are right; the surface texture and degree of calcification is absolutely consistent from head to foot; and, because there's no arthritis, it's easy to check that the ball joints match their sockets. Apart from that, they had no idea where you were going to take your sample from; so it would have been a risky game anyway."

"And a crucifixion victim, you think?"

"That would certainly be my assessment from what I've seen."

"The chipping of the forearm bones, you mean?"

"That's only part of it. It's been known for years that the conventional artistic representation of the crucifixion is wrong.

If you try to crucify a man by nailing through his palms, the flesh will tear and the body fall. In Paris back in the 1930s there was doctor called Barbet who spent a lot of time nailing freshly amputated arms and then weighting them. He came to the conclusion that you had either to hammer the nail between the ulna and radius, the bones of the forearm, or—and more difficult—drive right through the knot of bones in the wrist. That chipping I noted could have been made either by the nail or, equally, by the repeated seesaw motion of the victim shifting his weight from one area of pain to another. The clincher, though, is the scraping on the bones between the second and third toes of the right foot. If you didn't know what you were looking for, you could easily miss it." He held out his right hand to illustrate the point, jamming the index finger of his left up into the V between the second and third fingers. "Now, think of my hand as a foot, and this finger as the nail going through it. You can see that the entire weight of the body will be pressing down on it—and the nail, from what we know of Roman nails, would be square and sharp edged. Remember now that the victim will be continually swinging his weight from side to side, and this single nail becomes the fulcrum of the whole excruciating business, which in Christ's case we know went on for three hours. That's why you get the chafing. What about you? How's the dating progressing?

Schumacher glanced down the hall before replying.

"Too early to say yet, but everything so far is pointing to the first century. Within a couple of hours we should know the date of death to within a decade or two." He looked back down the hall. "Let's hope that by then it will be irrelevant."

Yossi glimpsed the setting sun over his shoulder; another half hour and the sky would be slashed with pink and purple. Apart from the rhythmic threshing of the fifty-foot rotor blades, it was quiet inside the Huey—each man alone with his thoughts and, for once, no radio chatter to interrupt them. Within twenty minutes they would be back at Dimona.

He checked the gyro: 104 degrees. Correct. They had now left the cultivated area around the moshav, and below and ahead as far as visibility allowed was all desert—not the rolling sand dunes of the Sinai but bare expanses of dust and

dirt, corrugated by a driving southeasterly wind and punctuated by the occasional stunted tree or Arab well. There was
sand in the air, though—Saudi sand, blown across by the
sharav which throughout the day had kept the air dry and the
temperature unseasonally high.

Ahead, there appeared a small Bedouin tent which, closer,
turned out to be a jeep with a canvas top. God alone knew
what it was doing in the middle of the desert in the middle of
a sandstorm. It looked military, and Yossi concluded it had to
be part of Berman's efforts to protect the chopper's flight path
on its way back from the inspection. The inspection. He
hoped that one day he'd be able to tell the other two what
was really in the yellow casket with its deliberately misleading radioactive symbol. Copilot Zvika would enjoy telling his
grandchildren how he had once acted as chauffeur to Jesus
Christ. By divine appointment!

His attention was caught by the temperature gauge indicating engine overheating. The Huey was fitted with the
usual screens on its air intakes, but there was no filter that
could be guaranteed clog-proof against the great curtains of
sand that were now drifting across the landscape, accentuated
by the sun's last slanting rays. He looked to the horizon for a
clue as to how the wind was gusting—whether to climb above
the curtains' invisible gantries or drop beneath them. Unable
to tell, he trusted to a mixture of instinct and experience and
pulled up on the collective lever to gain height.

By the time he recognized the thin trail of white smoke
arcing out of the dusk at twice the speed of sound, it was
already too late. He took the only action he could—back on
the cyclic stick and down on the collective—in the hope of
making the rocket overshoot. The effect was like reining in a
horse at full gallop and half a second earlier it might have
succeeded. As it was, the cabin and cockpit were momentarily filled with a blinding starburst as the heat-seeking SAM-7
ripped into the engine housing and turned everything into
color negative.

Stunned but conscious, Yossi could only watch as the horizon cartwheeled crazily around him. He waited for the inevitable impact, but after three or four somersaults through the
air the Huey seemed miraculously to regain her balance. The
explosion had deprived the chopper of power, but the main
rotor and shaft seemed to be intact, so that, although the

cyclic stick had taken on a life of its own, the Huey herself was autorotating groundward like a sycamore seed. They were going down alright—but floating rather than falling.

His first thought was of the high-frequency radio channel that had been kept open for emergencies. It was imperative now to raise the alarm, even at the risk of being detected by means of bearing triangulation. He shouted to Zvika, who was radio operator as well as copilot. When there was no response, he turned to see him slumped in his harness, apparently knocked out by the blast. The emergency microphone—deliberately independent of the crew headsets—had been dislodged from its cradle by the Huey's unscheduled aerobatics and was dangling by its cable well out of Yossi's reach. He tried gently releasing his hold on the cyclic stick but, as he did so, it started to vibrate and he could feel the chopper threatening to break loose again. Reasserting his grip, he swung round to find Ehud, the flight engineer/gunner, spread-eagled facedown on the cabin floor in a carpet of blood-flecked foam from the automatic extinguisher system which had been set off by the explosion. Desperately he looked again at the microphone bobbing tantalizingly on the other side of the cockpit, and cursed. Why in God's name hadn't they mounted an override switch on the panel as well as on the thing itself? At least then he could have left it to base to work out what was happening from the cabin noise.

The ground was coming up fast now and for the first time Yossi saw the agent of his destruction head-on. The Land-Rover, headlights blazing, was bucking towards him across the sand, a plume of dust in its wake. Indistinctly through the screen of dust, he could make out one man leaning out of the passenger window clutching what looked like a submachine gun, while another was standing up in the back, also apparently armed.

It occurred to him that a kamikaze attempt to crash the Huey into the Land-Rover might just be feasible if he could get it into the right attitude. But the cyclic stick and both rudder pedals were effectively dead; the only response was in the collective lever which still, but barely, controlled the rate of descent through the pitch of the free-spinning rotor blades. His only hope, he realized, lay in landing—or rather, grounding—the Huey as far away from the Land-Rover as possible and then keeping his assailants at bay with the chopper's M-60 machine gun long enough to flash back the emergency call signal.

Thanks to the skids, the impact was not as hard as he had feared, but the distance he had managed to put between himself and the guerrillas was considerably less than he had hoped. Three hundred feet at most, and they were already pouring rounds of automatic fire into the underside of the chopper where it had settled at an angle of forty-five degrees.

He had to make a snap decision. Which first? Microphone or machine gun? He made the wrong one. Clambering up the incline of the cabin floor, he lunged for the twin-grips of the M-60; glanced to check that the cartridge belt was free; and pressed the firing button, sending a stream of orange tracer bullets over the sill in the general direction of the Land-Rover. But the more he tried to get a grip on the sloping floor, the more his feet slid and slipped on the foam and blood. Not just trapped, he was unsighted as well.

The situation was hopeless. By now, the armed men would have left the Land-Rover and be fanning out around the Huey. He had only seconds. Half clambering, half tumbling, he clawed his way back to the cockpit—and the microphone. With just a few feet to go, he saw through the window one of the gunmen calmly lining him up in his sights. His last thought was how strange it was that the man's clothing should already be stained with his blood.

"As easy as harpooning a turtle," observed the guerrilla leader, surveying the wreckage of the fat-bodied chopper and its massacred crew. He turned his attention to the yellow casket strapped to the cabin floor.

"The fancy wrapping will have to be left behind," he said, loosening the webbing and releasing the catches. "Too heavy and too conspicuous. We'll have to empty it."

He scanned the cabin interior and, spotting a crew kit bag stuffed into a corner, shouted to one of the others to bring it to him and help with removing the casket lid. The other, however, failed to reckon on the weight and, standing at the top of the sloping floor, lost his footing, causing the rectangular steel lid to fall back across the casket and one corner to slice clean through the fiberglass inner shell. A stream of obscenities flowed from the leader's mouth, concerned more

with the possible damage to his own person than any actual
damage to the casket's contents. The lid finally extricated, he
enquired of his colleague whether he was at least capable of
holding open the mouth of the kit bag and, the bones transferred, checked his watch.

"Within five minutes they'll be starting to worry. Within
fifteen they'll put out an area alert . . . and within half an
hour a search party will be on its way. We've got to be back
through that checkpoint by then."

Outside again, it was very nearly dark. Lying on its side,
the Huey was silhouetted against the night sky—a broken
insect on the windowsill of the world. The wind had picked
up and was getting stronger. To speak in the open now was to
invite a mouthful of grit, and it wasn't until all three were
back in the Land-Rover with the kit bag and the copilot's
shirt and trousers that Yossi's killer produced a metal identity
tag on a leather thong.

"Our friend left this behind," he said sheepishly.

The leader turned over the engine and stamped the accelerator until it fired.

"What friend?"

"The one with the breathing problem, the hitchhiker. Want
me to throw it out?"

The leader was about to lecture his colleague, not for the
first time, on the danger of keeping incriminating souvenirs,
but suddenly reconsidered.

"No. Give it to me. And for God's sake change out of those
butcher's rags!"

Back in the Jerusalem bunker, Gideon Berman stared at
the clock. In any operation the waiting was the worst time.
Eliot had put it best: "Teach us to care and not to care. Teach
us to sit still." But it was doubly difficult when the operation
had to be carried out in radio silence—as had also the raid on
Entebbe. There was nothing like radio silence to induce a
state of retrospective anxiety—the stomach-contracting realization that something might *already* have happened even as
one worried that it might happen.

The trance was broken by the minister's assistant, Meir.

"There's a weather report in, General. The meteorological
people say a sandstorm is blowing up from the southeast.

They'd be heading right into it. They might have decided to ground the Huey till it blows over."

Berman drew a hand over his face. He didn't know what to think. He'd had virtually no sleep now for twenty-four hours. Crazy, but with the work to be done the previous night on selecting the half dozen possible sites and then tying up the myriad logistical permutations, there had been no choice. True, it was an essential qualification for the job of Defense Minister to be able to keep going for superhumanly long periods on little more than catnaps in the back of cars and helicopters, and Dayan, when he'd done it, had even carried around a pillow and rug everywhere like a security blanket. But Berman, for whom sleeping on demand had never been easy, had come to rely instead on sleep banks built up by retiring early to bed whenever the telephone permitted, and avoiding any social or diplomatic function that threatened to go on beyond midnight. His current account, he was aware, was running dangerously into the red. And yet, how could he turn in for an hour or two, at a time when the lives of Yossi and his crew could depend on the decisions he now took?

"If anything has happened," he said to himself as much as to Meir, "every minute that we delay is a minute lost in going to their help. But if you're right and they're simply taking shelter from the storm, then we could equally endanger their lives by pointing up their location." As though the clock held some intrinsically evil power, he unstrapped his watch and laid it on the desk before him, "They are now twelve minutes overdue. We'll give them another five. If we haven't heard from Dimona by then, we'll send a tone signal through the open emergency channel—nothing more. If they're safe, they'll follow instructions and respond with a triple click. If not . . .," he drew a deep breath, "we'll bottle up the area and send in a search team."

"And alert the ports and airports?" asked Meir.

"Not before we know what's happened to the bones. The one thing to avoid is having everybody shooting off in different directions without a clue what they're looking for. In the meantime, though, you could ask the ports and airports if they've anything suspicious to report—but make it sound like a routine enquiry."

★

The sand was lashing the metal cab like lead shot, the finer particles building up in mini-dunes against the wipers and around the spare wheel on the front. In some places, the driver noted anxiously, it was even stripping the Land-Rover's fresh coat of green paint. Visibility, meanwhile, was twenty feet at best and switching the headlamps to high beam only had the effect of reflecting the sand particles and reducing it still further. Their sole guide was the vehicle's compass and that was spinning wildly because of the terrain.

The leader glanced at the speedometer. Twenty miles an hour was about the maximum, which meant they'd be lucky to reach the road, let alone the checkpoint, by the half-hour deadline. Risking even more lost time, he pulled up to allow the compass to settle. It was reading east, 10 degrees north—a full 20 degrees out—confirming the fact known to professional trackers that a righthanded person deprived of all bearings will veer naturally to the right. It was no wonder they hadn't hit the road; at their present rate they'd soon be running parallel to it! He engaged four-wheel drive and, after an initial spin, gratefully felt the tires bite into the soft ground and nosed the Land-Rover back on course.

Ten minutes and two further course adjustments later, they were almost out of the storm area when they made out headlights progressing from left to right across their field of vision. They had reached the road—at a point the leader calculated to be three miles south of the checkpoint instead of the one he had planned. Twenty-five minutes of the half hour were already up, and he could only pray that his estimates of Israeli reaction time had been on the flattering side.

He saw the red-hand warning sign before he saw the soldiers. In the dark, there appeared to be no more of them than on the way in—one on each side of the road, and the commanding officer with a pair of reliefs in the shelter. The only difference was the flashlights.

Despite the open windows, the cab reeked of sweat and blood. Although Yossi's killer had changed into the copilot's clothes, the seat and floor were still sticky with the earlier spillage. This time there would be no margin for any inspection; at the first suggestion of trouble, there would have to be a shoot-out and, as the Land-Rover slowed to a halt, all three braced themselves for just such an eventuality.

The driver leaned out of the window, his outstretched arm dangling the metal identity tag on its length of leather thong.

"We gave a mate of yours a lift on our way down. He left this behind."

The soldier caught the tag and read the name.

"Karapov! Who else? That guy would lose his fucking prick if it weren't plumbed in. I'll see he gets it."

"Yea," responded the driver, "and you can tell him we're claiming a reward. Green Patrol, Beersheva office."

The soldier tossed the tag in his hand and laughed.

"I'll do that. *Shabbat Shalom!*"

"*Shalom Shabbat,*" responded the driver with a parting wave.

A hundred yards down the road his colleague turned to him.

"Risky, wasn't it? Now they're bound to remember us."

The leader gave a thin smile.

"Which is why they'll discount us. Nobody with anything to hide would go so far out of their way to make themselves conspicuous. That tag should guarantee our passage as far as the point where we hand the bones over, providing the Americans have been as good as their word."

The other gave a derisive snort at the mention of the Americans' "word" and then remembered that on this occasion the Americans were allies.

"I'll be in the Emergency Cabinet Room, Meir."

Berman pushed himself out of the chair, aware that all eyes in the Control Room were following him out of the double doors into the corridor. It was now obvious to everyone that there had been a mishap of some sort. The Huey was more than half an hour overdue; there had been no response to the tone signal sent over the emergency channel; and yet the meteorologists were reporting that the sandstorm had abated. With a heavy heart, Berman had finally given the order for the search party to be dispatched.

He sank into the chair at the top of the table—the Prime Minister's—and stared at the opposite wall.

"If I forget thee, O Jerusalem, let my right hand forget . . ."

The word stood out from the rest. Was there something he

should have done or should be doing, which in his exhausted state he had *forgotten* to do? Again he ran through the possibilities. The greatest temptation was to overreact and place the entire country on a full C alert, arguing that, if the Huey *had* been brought down and the bones taken, their chances of being smuggled out would diminish if every member of the armed forces—every regular, conscript, and reserve—were looking for them. But, apart from the enormous cost, such a move had two inherent dangers: First, it might force those responsible to destroy their plunder, and, second, it would be impossible to keep secret any longer the bones' very existence, upon which their value as a diplomatic bargaining chip depended. What, after all, could one tell the security forces to be on the lookout for? A box of bones? Whose bones? And why were these bones so important that they justified a national alert? Within hours the secret would be public knowledge.

Nonetheless, he wished Meir hadn't made such play of the sandstorm as a possible factor in the helicopter's lateness. It had given him reason to hope and that was always dangerous, because hope, in blinding one to the possibility of an unpalatable reality, dulled anticipatory reactions and clouded judgement. What had always distinguished Israel's political and military leaders from their foreign counterparts had been their refusal to hear only what they wanted to hear, to believe only what they wanted to believe. But now Berman wanted to believe that the chopper had been forced down by the sandstorm, because it would mean that not just the bones, but Yossi too was safe. He was alarmed at the extent to which his emotions had been tapped. It might have made him more human, but it had also made him more vulnerable.

The telephone at his right elbow buzzed into life. It was Meir in the Control Room.

"Nothing yet from the search party, General. But there's a report in from the checkpoint on the Beersheva-Yeruham road. It seems some members of the Green Patrol were in the area serving an eviction order on some Bedouin. I've left a message at their Beersheva office for them to report in the moment they get back, on the off-chance that they may have seen something."

"OK, Meir," replied Berman, his mind dominated by a picture of men in jeeps fanning out across the darkened

wastes of the Negev in search of . . . what? A helicopter crew
cursing as they attempted to top up a leaking hydraulic
system or unblock a clogged filter? Or a burntout shell?

He stopped himself and wrenched his mind back to what
Meir had just said. The Green Patrol. It was probably nothing but it was at least possible that they had sighted the
helicopter in flight and could give an approximate fix. Rather
than waiting for them to call in, their Beersheva base could
call *them*.

He picked up the phone but was preempted by the appearance of Meir in person. He could tell instantly that the
news was bad.

"Where?" he asked.

"About halfway, ten kilometers east of the Besor River. A
heat-seeking rocket by the look of it."

"And the bones?"

"Gone. They left the casket."

Berman held back a second. Then, cradling his head in his
hands:

"The crew?"

"Dead—all three."

Something inside him came close to breaking. His chest
contracted and he felt a burning behind the eyes.

"Do you want the next of kin informed immediately, or
. . ." Meir trailed off.

Berman seemed not to hear. Finally he answered.

"Yes, . . . except Yossi's. I'll see to that myself."

For a moment, he felt crushed beneath the sheer weight of
his responsibilities, aware that on what he did and decided in
the next hour or so, while still reeling beneath the shock of
his personal grief, hung not just his own future, but the
country's. It was time to be brutally honest with himself: Was
he up to the job, physically and mentally? In such a situation
the genuinely courageous act was *not* to fight on, but—even
if only temporarily—to hand over to someone else. It's what
Yitzhak Rabin, when Chief of Staff, had done on the eve of
the Six Day War. And what had been the public reaction?
Not praise, but insidious suggestions, which had followed
him right into the Prime Minister's office, to the effect that
his nerve had failed under pressure and that consequently he
would always be suspect in a crisis.

"Would you like me to leave you alone for a few minutes?" asked Meir.

Berman forced his eyes to focus through the curtain of crystal.

"No, Meir . . . but thank you. I'll come back to the Control Room with you. That Green Patrol—we must follow it up."

The Nature Reserves Authority at Beersheva wasn't answering; it was already Shabbat and the *shabbas goy* responsible for manning the switchboard had apparently converted.

"OK, Meir," said Berman wearily, "once again, take me through what the man who checked them through the roadblock remembered."

Meir referred to his clipboard.

"It was a Land-Rover—definitely Green Patrol—and there were three of them. The driver said they were on their way to evict some Bedouin squatters. That's all."

"And they were checked back through?"

"That was the impression I got."

Beman wondered whether his own zeal was perhaps misdirected—an overcompensation for the fatigue he felt. Since they now knew what had happened to the chopper and where it had been brought down, any sighting by the Green Patrol was really irrelevant. But he was still annoyed by the silence from the Beersheva office and his inability to contact the men.

"Keep trying Beersheva," he instructed Meir, "and get back to that checkpoint. Any other details they can recall."

★

The International Institute of Ecumenical Studies declared the blue and white sign surmounted by a plain, admirably nondenominational cross.

The driver dipped the Land-Rover's lights, dropped down into second, and, progressing slowly up the gradient to the institute proper, veered off to the left and round the back of the magnificent heap of masonry that under Turkish rule had been the regional administrative center. Standing inconspicuously in the farthest corner of the parking lot was the white Peugeot of the Apostolic Delegate with its diplomatic plates and, at the wheel, the grey-suited figure of the archbishop's Arab chauffeur.

"*Salaam, salaam,*" he croaked, extricating his considerable bulk from behind the wheel. "You are late. I thought something had gone wrong."

The Palestinian leader bristled at the chauffeur's accusatory manner.

"We had some difficulties, but it will be alright if you don't delay."

He looked up to the second-floor windows where lights shone through the slatted shutters.

"The archbishop?" he asked.

"He is up there now. He has been giving a talk to the students, but that finished nearly an hour ago. We expected you at least . . ."

Waving the protest aside, the Palestinian pointed to the Peugeot's back door. The chauffeur opened it and, lifting up the rear seat, revealed a space eighteen inches deep.

"It is enough?" he asked.

The Palestinian instructed one of his colleagues to bring the kit bag from the Land-Rover, prompting the chauffeur to exclaim at the smallness of the package.

"But were they not in a box—a stone burial chest?"

"Not when we found them. Our orders were to get the bones and that's what you've got."

The chauffeur started to protest but was cut short.

"By my watch," said the Palestinian, "you've got just fifty minutes to get to the Allenby Bridge crossing, and if you don't get moving, you'll find yourself with all the time in the world to discuss the ins and outs of Jewish burial practice—with the Israeli security forces."

The chauffeur was going to reply that, in asking, he too was only following orders, but the three Palestinians were already back in the Land-Rover, the driver swinging the wheel around again in the direction of the main road.

Meir read from the clipboard:

"They gave a lift to one of the conscripts manning the checkpoint. Uri Karapov, his name. He wanted to get home to Yeruham in time for Shabbat—seems he's Orthodox—and apparently they were going part of the way. Then on their way back they handed in his identity tag which he'd somehow left in the Land-Rover."

Berman's face registered more irritation than interest. "Seems," "apparently," "somehow" were not what he was looking for.

"That it?"

Meir hesitated.

"Well, one other thing. The man who checked the Land-Rover through on the way back remembers wishing the driver *Shabbat Shalom* and the driver, he says, responded with *Shalom Shabbat*."

Berman failed to see the significance. The driver had gotten his words the wrong way round—so? It was grammatically incorrect, but the poor bastard was probably tired.

"What is it you're trying to tell me, Meir?"

"Only this—that the Arabs reverse their greetings on many of the occasions that we do—*Salaam aleichum . . . Aleichum salaam*—and, whereas no Jew would ever reverse the Shabbat greeting, it's just the sort of mistake that might be made by an Arab masquerading as a Jew."

It was as though a bucket of ice water had been thrown in Berman's face. How could he have been so blind? The possibility of the Green Patrol vehicle itself having something to do with the downing of the chopper had never occurred to him. Blind, blind! It was a suddenly very different Gideon Berman who addressed his assistant.

"Get onto Karapov's home. If the family is Orthodox and not answering the phone, send someone round—in fact, do that anyway. I want to know from him everything he can remember—*any*thing."

He turned to one of the staff officers down in the well.

"Efraim! Put out a general alert for any Green Patrol vehicle trying to get through a checkpoint or border crossing to be held pending verification of identity."

"Do you want me to give a reason, General?"

"You can tell them we suspect the theft of a radioactive isotope from Dimona by terrorists who are believed to have hijacked one of the Green Patrol's vehicles."

A girl lieutenant approached with a tape torn from one of the machines. Seeing the minister occupied, she handed it to Meir. As he read it, he clutched Berman by the arm.

"This could be something, General. The Port Authority at

Ashdod report the unscheduled arrival of the USS *San Jose*, one of the supply ships for the American Sixth Fleet. The port superintendent reckons it's odd because the fleet normally does its victualing direct from the States or out of the NATO base at Naples. He says he hasn't seen a U.S. Navy supply vessel in months."

Berman was already scrutinizing the wall map. Ashdod, seventeen miles south of Tel Aviv, was the nearest major port to the Negev. Walking finger over thumb, he calculated that a Land-Rover could probably cover the fifty miles between it and the Beersheva-Yeruham roadblock in an hour and three-quarters. As he doublechecked the figures, the conviction grew that a getaway route was staring him in the face. *The* getaway route. He swung round.

"Meir, tell the port superintendent to stop all loading of that ship, to detain any of her crew who haven't returned on board, and on no account to allow her to sail. And get on to Security. I want the entire port area sealed off and anyone attempting to enter or leave to be detained until we get there."

"We?" repeated Meir quizzically.

Berman didn't reply immediately. He was torn between the feeling that, as overall commander of the operation, he should stay at the nerve center, and the need to get out of the place and *do* something instead of just reacting to the actions of others. He couldn't be everywhere at once, but it was a fact that everywhere he had *not* been so far there had been a mishap of one sort or another.

"Yes, *we*."

The chauffeur glanced in his rearview mirror and was surprised to see Archbishop Ramone sitting directly behind him instead of in his usual place diagonally behind, from where it was easier both to be seen and to talk. A second's thought suggested the reason, and with difficulty he stifled a smile. Nominally, Abu—or Michelin, as he was more unkindly known in some quarters—was a believer, but his was a belief born of the realization that if the Christian God was deemed to be one's ultimate employer, then it would be churlish not to believe in His existence and goodness. For this reason his relationship with Archbishop Ramone was careful rather than close. Vatican diplomats, he had always supposed, were chosen more for their worldliness than their godliness, but there were times when the archbishop aspired to mysticism. It could be singularly unnerving and Abu had come to dread those occasions on long journeys when he would find himself required to act as Ramone's unofficial confessor and still more when asked, "But, tell me, Abu, what do *you* think?" He suspected that, given half a chance, His Excellency would wash his feet for him. Working for a good man was much to be desired, but working for a holy man could, frankly, be a pain.

He adjusted the mirror. They were now speeding through the eastern suburbs of Jerusalem and by the street lighting he could see from the archbishop's expression that he had withdrawn into himself. Barely a word had passed between them since leaving the International Ecumenical Institute, and Abu's attempts at conversation had been met with responses of monosyllabic brevity. His Excellency, he assumed, was preoccupied with thoughts of the Allenby Bridge and the crossing into Jordan—with good reason. If the timetable was as tight as the young monsignor from Rome had indicated then five minutes either way could spell the difference between success and failure. That Ramone had grave reservations about the plan he knew for a fact, having been present at the final run-through when for the umpteenth time the red-faced young prelate had covered on the map every foot of the journey, down to the precise speed of the archbishop's car when approaching the Allenby Bridge checkpoint, apparently unaware that, as His Excellency's chauffeur, he made the crossing at least half a dozen times a year. He had been about to point this out but the conversation had suddenly lapsed into Italian and—as usual on such occasions—he had transferred his attention to the photograph of Pius XII striking a characteristically sanctimonious pose worthy of a handcream advertisement.

If Abu's present state of mind was less tense than the archbishop's, it was less because of any intrinsic reservoir of calm than because of the belief that he personally, despite his crucial involvement in the plan, was free of risk or potential blame. If something went wrong at the border, he was prepared to disclaim all knowledge of the package under the backseat; the sole culprit would be the one who was sitting on the thing or, more accurately, studiously *not* sitting on it. From the Arab's point of view, therefore, the escapade had all the vicarious excitement of flying an aircraft simulator.

So far the journey was going well. They were now heading out of Jerusalem towards Jericho past a succession of scruffy filling stations and, suddenly free of the built-up area, onto the new highway that carves through the soft Judean Hills, weaving between isolated Arab villages and the brash new Israeli settlements of the West Bank. From now on the going would be smooth, fast, and downhill all the way. He pushed himself back into the seat, rearranged the rolls of flesh under his thighs and, passing the turnoff to Ma'ale Adumin, noted with satisfaction that they were now only ten minutes behind schedule.

Taking advantage of the headlights of a vehicle coming the other way, he glanced again in the rearview mirror. The archbishop's head was bowed and at first he thought he was asleep. Then, from the feverish movement of his lips, he realized he was praying. As he watched, the head jerked up and the eyes opened.

"Stop! Abu, we must stop!"

Convinced that his charge had suffered a heart attack, the Arab wrenched the Peugeot over onto the hard shoulder, applying the brakes and reaching for the interior light switch as he did so.

"Excellency, you alright?" he asked and, swinging round, was surprised to find the archbishop half standing, his zucchetto down over one ear, and attempting to lift up the backseat.

"The bones are OK, Excellency," he said. "I check them myself at the institute. But we must keep going. To be late will be great danger."

To no avail. Ramone continued tugging at the unyielding seat.

"I must see them. I must!" he implored.

"Later, Excellency, please. Over the border. Then you look. Not now."

"No, now . . . now!"

The man had clearly gone mad. His voice sounded like that of an imprisoned demon. It only needed an Israeli patrol vehicle to spot the CD plates and witness the extraordinary scene and they'd be done for.

"Excellency," shouted the Arab in desperation, "here not good, I think. If you wish check bones yourself, better find another place—off road."

It seemed to work.

"Off road," repeated the archbishop mechanically and sank down again.

The small track led into the hills. It was rough, but for the first fifty yards or so was driveable. As soon as they were out of sight of the road, Abu stopped again and opened the door. With difficulty he persuaded the archbishop to get out of the car so the seat could be raised and the bones removed for his inspection.

He released the drawstring on the neck of the kit bag and coaxed, rather than shook, a couple of the bones only onto the velour upholstery, in the hope that this would be enough to satisfy His Excellency.

It wasn't. Having insisted that all of them be removed from the bag, the archbishop started picking them over like an Arab woman examining vegetables on a market stall. There appeared to be no rationale behind the exercise. Selecting the larger bones, he ran his finger along their lengths and, weeping copiously by now, held them against his cheek, one after another, as if blessing them or receiving a blessing from them. Finally, he took the skull in both hands and, quivering with emotion, kissed the top of the cranium.

Abu was exasperated. It was a clear case of religious hysteria, he decided. With difficulty he eased the skull from the archbishop's hands and replaced it and the rest of the bones in the kit bag, causing His Excellency to gibber like a child deprived of its rattle. With the bag stowed again in its hiding place, and the archbishop repositioned, he slammed the back door and climbed again into the driving seat.

The situation had changed. When a military commander goes insane, reflected Abu, it is the next in line of seniority who takes over—and that line was now the distance between the front and back seats. He considered. His instinct for self-preservation told him to head back to Jerusalem. But what if the archbishop had recovered by the time they got back? Whose story would be believed? On the other hand, the risks of carrying on were now immeasurably greater, in that he was now likely to be held a hundred percent accountable if the bones were discovered at the border checkpoint. If anybody were to end up in jail, it certainly wouldn't be His Excellency the Apostolic Delegate of the Holy See. By the same token, though, how great would be the commendation if he were to succeed, single-handedly and despite his master's raving incapacity! A shiver of excitement rippled through his flabby frame. Pushing down on the accelerator, he fancied he could feel the adrenaline squirting into his bloodstream.

★

The port superintendent at Ashdod was a sardonically efficient type who prided himself on having so well organized the running of the place that, in everything except the matter of his salary check, he had made himself redundant. He guided Berman to the window of his top-floor office and pointed out the USS *San Jose* moored up alongside the brightly floodlit quay.

"That's the one—in number three berth. A Mars Class combat supply ship, built late sixties or early seventies, I'd guess. Anyway, I've done as you asked and immobilized her."

Gideon Berman's expression sought an explanation, and the superintendent continued:

"Oh, it seems her screw somehow got fouled up—length of hawser or something similar. In a busy port such things are unavoidable from time to time. Our divers will be taking a look at it after Shabbat."

"What made you suspicious of her?"

"Primarily the fact of her being here. You asked if we had anything suspicious to report, and here she was—the first U.S. Navy ship in months. Then there were the supplies she wanted—a hundred and fifty tons of fresh oranges. You know how many oranges that is?"

Berman didn't.

"Near enough a million—a thousand *thousand*—and with a perishable life of about a month. I asked the captain if the Navy's buyers back home had heard of frozen or canned orange juice. His only response was that the refrigeration system on the aircraft carrier *Saratoga* had broken down and so they were having to take on fresh. Well, I don't know about you, but I can't see the American taxpayer forking out his hard-earned dollars so that the Navy can go into the bulk citrus business."

"Are they loaded yet?" Berman wondered.

"All done before sundown. Strictly kosher port this, Minister—unless we're talking about prawns or pigskin. She was scheduled to sail at six on the stroke; the captain was insistent."

Berman ran a finger along his lower lip. The timing fitted.

"What about the crew?" he asked.

"By the time your message came over, they were all back on board. About a dozen had passes to leave the dock area, but I can't tell you where they went." His tone grew confidential. "Look, I've been in this business long enough, Minister, to know not to ask what exactly it is you're looking for, but is it a person or a thing?"

"A thing."

"Big or small?"

"Small enough to fit into a suitcase."

It wasn't hard to see what was going through the man's mind: one thousand thousand oranges, and somewhere among them an object the size of a suitcase.

"What sort of mood is the captain in?" continued Berman.

The superintendent smiled.

"Litigious is the word I'd use. If he has his way, his government will be taking us to the International Court in the Hague to face a charge of maritime sabotage. I'll be interested to see how he takes to a suggestion that his ship be searched—assuming I'm allowed to be present?"

"It's your port," answered Berman. "Before we go, though, I want to check your regulations governing foreign vessels using the port."

"Piracy! That's what it is—goddam piracy!"

Berman and the superintendent watched in silence as the master of the USS *San Jose* paced the restricted length of his cabin, at every turn throwing out a declamatory finger.

". . . and now you say you're going to search my ship. Well, I tell you this, Minister: You can stick it. There's only one person in this whole world can give you permission for that—and that's the President of the United States—and I can tell you now, he ain't goin' to give it you! No way."

Berman remained silent, content to let the man talk himself out. When, by a process of verbal attrition, the "one person in the whole world" had been reduced to the Secretary of the Navy, Berman handed him a green carbon copy of the ship's pilotage authorization.

"Is this ship called the *San Jose*, Captain, and is this your signature as master, given on requesting entry to the port at 08:30 this morning?"

The captain gave the document a cursory glance.

"So?"

"So you have already agreed to submit your vessel to such searches as may be required by the Ashdod Port Authority. Paragraph 4 refers the signator to port regulation 23b which, if you care to read . . ."

He pushed the superintendent's copy of the regulations across the table.

"This is not a merchant vessel but a military vessel," protested the captain, "with, with some highly sensitive and classified equipment on board."

"On board a fleet supply vessel?" queried Berman.

"Communication equipment—codes and the like."

"In which we have no interest, and if you care to accompany us on our search—as is your right—you wil personally be able to verify that fact."

For the first time, the American seemed lost for words. Eventually:

"I will have to notify Admiral Dugan, my commanding officer, of your intended action."

Berman had anticipated the move and was determined to prevent it. He now had no doubt that the bones were on board. The captain's excessive show of outrage and his efforts to thwart a search were confirmation enough, but most significant was the fact that at no point had he asked what it was the Israelis expected to find, the implication being that he already knew. The danger was that the order would now go out to destroy the bones. Where that order might originate—whether with the President, the admiral, or even the captain himself acting on prearranged procedure—there was no knowing. It was essential, threfore, to isolate the captain from both the bones *and* the chain of command.

"That will not be possible," said Berman.

"Would you care to show me the regulations that prevent it, Minister?" retorted the captain, stressing "regulations" with a sneer.

Berman was looking through the cabin window at the security officers already lined up on the quayside, ready to board.

"This is not a question of regulations," he replied. "It is my own decision and I shall be answerable for it, should your government wish later to register an official protest. Now, Captain, if you will kindly order all your men to report to the mess hall."

Half an hour of watching crates being smashed open from the height of the superintendent's office brought home to Berman the enormity of the task before them. Less than a fifth of the crates had been checked and already the dockside resembled the upturned medicine chest of a hypochondriac giant. The search of the ship itself and the crew quarters, meanwhile, had yielded a total haul so far of just three hundred grams of hashish.

"And you're sure nothing has been thrown over the rails or out of the portholes?" he asked the security officer who broght the depressing news.

"Positive, sir. The ship has been under all-around surveillance from the moment we got your orders; that was the first thing we checked against."

Berman resumed his watch, by now feeling decidedly light-headed, not just from the lack of sleep but equally from an excess of coffee and cigarettes. He asked Meir to check again with the Jerusalem EGHQ for any news of Green Patrol sightings. The message came back that three vehicles had been apprehended, checked—and released.

One more crateload of oranges was sent rolling across the quay into the oily black water before he made the decision that had been forming at the back of his mind. Convinced though he still was that the bones were in the ship, he couldn't afford to wait another two or three hours to find out whether he was right or wrong.

"Meir!" he called, "get back on to the bunker. Give the order for every port, airport, and border crossing to be closed, and tell them to send a senior security officer to each to check that it's strictly observed."

"Closed until when?" asked the assistant.

A lone orange plopped into the water.

"Until we've had time to inspect our nets."

★

Framed in Abu's rearview mirror, Archbishop Ramone had all the animation of a ventriloquist's dummy. Sitting bolt upright, slack-jawed, he seemed to have lapsed into a catatonic state, which was infinitely preferable to his former nonsensical garrulity; at least, if asked any questions, he could be counted on to tell neither lies nor truth.

They were still behind schedule—a full quarter of an hour—but Jericho was behind them now and all that lay between them and the Allenby Bridge into Jordan was a seven-mile stretch of road, its running screen of eucalyptus growing more luxuriant as they neared the muddy trickle that passes for the river of Christ's baptism.

The road led only to the crossing, and Abu had noted the intermittent procession of coaches, buses, and trucks coming the other way. However, being increasingly concerned with his lateness and the condition of his passenger, he failed to note the sudden cessation of this flow about a mile from the bridge itself, indicating that the crossing had been abruptly closed.

The realization came too late. Rounding the final bend on the approach to the bridge, he nearly ran into the back of a huge air-conditioned coach advertising itself as "Another happy tour from Christian Tours International, Fort Lauderdale, Florida." He had made the trip too many times before to think that this was any normal queue. His mouth dried. Even without counting the string of red taillights, he knew there had to be a good two dozen vehicles for the line to stretch back this far.

It was then that he spotted the Uzi-toting Israeli soldier standing beside the coach talking to the driver. A second later, a large Arab truck loaded with lemons squealed to a halt behind him, its bumper and grille filling the Peugeot's rear window. He was boxed in. Any thoughts of doing a smart about-face were now out of the question. Even if there were the space, the soldier would be bound to stop him.

The coach driver had gotten down and, cigarette in hand, was ambling back towards the Peugeot. Abu lowered the window.

"What did he have to say?" he asked in reference to the driver's conversation with the soldier.

The Arab spread his hands.

"Security . . . security . . . He doesn't know what it's about any more than we do. They simply got an order five minutes ago to close the border. No explanation. Not even an indication of how long for. A bigwig from Security is on his way."

Abu felt his stomach flip. He too got out and readily accepted a cigarette from the coach driver. The soldier was now standing about twenty yards from them. He could hardly fail to have spotted the Peugeot's CD plates but, as far as Abu could judge, had made no effort to report the fact over his walkie-talkie. The coach driver made a joking reference to his wagonload of hot gospelers and Abu gave a hearty laugh, as much to banish his nerves as to dispel any suspicions the Israeli might have. It could be only a matter of minutes, he feared, before the bigwig from Security arrived—no doubt with orders to seize the occupants of CD 35004.

Looking up and down the line, he wondered about the chances of transferring the kit bag to another vehicle, the only feasible ones being the coach or the truck, front and back. But the Israelis were old hands at the game. All passengers and drivers were required to get out and have their baggage individually checked in the passenger terminal, while the vehicles themselves were screened by army mechanics who could spot the wrong make of distributor cap or a fresh weld on the chassis at ten paces. In addition, every one of the two-hundred-and-fifty-odd agricultural trucks licensed to crisscross between Jordan and the West Bank—dating back to Dayan's "open bridges" policy after the Six Day War—had to fulfill the most stringent specifications: no tubular or section metal; no padding on the seats; no dashboards; glass-ended fuel tanks; and lead seals on the wheels. The only vehicles traditionally excused from such microscopic scrutiny were the dozen cars on the VIP list, including that of the Apostolic Delegate who, CD plates apart, was permitted to cross not as a quasi-diplomat but as the head of a religious community.

Abu heard the siren before he saw the jeep speeding past the line of traffic on the wrong side of the road. His stomach went through a second revolution; the bigwig had arrived.

A minute later, a second soldier came up to the first and said a few inaudible words. But again no notice was paid to the Peugeot, its plates, or the waxwork figure in the back.

The coach driver was still bantering, but Abu had stopped listening. A desperate situation required desperate measures. Had he had the faith, he would have called on a higher power for inspiration but, with the sole available representative of that power in a state of trance, he knew he had only his own wits to draw on. Why was it, he wondered bitterly, that in their meticulous planning of the operation nobody back in the Vatican, or wherever it was conceived, had given any thought to such a contingency? He drew deep on his cigarette and cast his mind back over the previous occasions he had made the crossing in the hope that some bobbing cork in the sea of memory might mark the spot of a life raft.

The last occasion had been six weeks earlier when the archbishop had made one of his regular five-day visits to his Jordanian diocese. And the time before that, it had been at Christmas to collect a visiting cardinal who wished to participate in the celebrations at Bethle . . .

The idea hit him with the force of the divine revelation he had thought impossible. In an instant he had stubbed out his cigarette and was heading purposefully towards the two Israeli soldiers.

"Where I find the officer in charge?" he demanded in English.

Taken aback by the Arab's unexpectedly peremptory tone, one of them pointed to the passenger terminal building at the head of the line.

The inside of the terminal was stuffed with humanity—old Arabs with bulging suitcases strapped with string, clutching their *warkah*'s, their green travel permits; younger Arabs in cheap, ill-fitting Western suits; and in a far corner, a group of black American tourists looking sweaty beneath their red and white sunhats. Despite the numbered check-ins for baggage searches, nobody was standing in line and the customs officers stationed behind their low-level tables appeared at a loss as to whether they should impose order or provide diversionary entertainment.

It was just the chaos that Abu had hoped for. He singled out the commanding officer by his captain's insignia and watched for a carefully timed three minutes as the officer argued with the Security bigwig about whose responsibility it was to deal with the growing tide that at any moment threatened to spill over the barriers. Without a word to anyone, he then turned and walked out again.

He had only the outline of an idea as to how he would play the next scene; it would depend on what he found back at the car.

What he saw was promising. The coach driver had gotten back in his seat and the two soldiers were where he had left them within a few feet of the Peugeot—well within hearing.

Ignoring the soldiers, he went straight up to the car and opened the back door.

"Excellency, the captain says that if we come back in an hour he will see to it personally that His Eminence the cardinal he wait for us in the VIP lounge. It seem His Eminence is held up on the other side."

The glaze over the archbishop's eyes cracked momentarily, but betrayed no hint of surprise at what he had just heard. A trickle of blood ran down his wrist from where, in clutching the crucifix round his neck, he had pressed a sharp corner into his palm. Noticing it, Abu quickly slammed the car door and, for the benefit of his audience, stood back to examine the distance between the Peugeot and the two vehicles in front and behind.

"More room to turn," he said to the soldiers, inscribing a loop with his hand.

With a shrug, one of them shouted to the coach driver to move forward, simultaneously waving to the truck driver to reverse. The other, meanwhile, stood in the middle of the road and, as Abu swung the car back and forth through a three-point turn, gave a flick of his lethal hardware to indicate the road was clear. He watched the Peugeot disappear into the darkness and turned to his colleague.

"Patience doesn't seem to be among the Christian virtues," he quipped.

"They haven't had the practice we've had!" responded the other drily.

★

As soon as the subtropical heat of the Jordan Valley gave way to the relative cool of higher ground, Abu applied his mind to the job of unloading the bones. The safest place of all would be the Apostolic Delegation but, in view of the nation-wide search that he suspected to be in full swing, he reckoned his chances of being stopped at some point during the forty-minute journey back to Jerusalem were too great to risk. On the other hand, the area around Jericho was too built-up, and the plain between Jericho and the Judean Hills too open. Which left only the hills themselves.

The track was noticeable solely because of the break in the steel crash barrier where it joined the road, and Abu had already overshot it when he decided to back up and examine further.

It dropped down parallel to the road, which was an incline, and, although wide enough to take a car, was more likely used by goats and goat herders. As soon as they were below the level of the road, Abu pulled up, turned out the lights, and removed a flashlight from the glove compartment, half-inclined to take the pistol as well but finally rejecting the idea. It was pointless, as well as time consuming, to explain anything to the archbishop, and so, without a word, he forced him to lift his backside, raised the seat, and pulled out the kit bag. His last action before leaving the car was to activate the all-round locking system to ensure that the archbishop didn't go wandering off into the wilderness while he was gone.

For the first time, something akin to a supernatural terror gripped him. Before, when up against human antagonists, there had certainly been a good deal of stress and anxiety, but now it seemed the wretched bones were communicating to him the same disturbing power they had evidently had over his superior. They possessed an albatross quality, and he couldn't wait to get rid of them. Losing them, though, wouldn't be enough; they had to be carefully hidden in a place where it would be possible for someone else to find them, and that meant a recognizable landmark of some sort.

The track had turned into a gully and, by the light of the flashlight he could see that it led at the bottom to a wadi. The sensation was of walking through a scaled-down version of the Grand Canyon, the embankment of the road to the right being mirrored on the other side by a raw cliff face—a geologist's dream of convoluted layers of rock that twisted and swirled as though frozen in the very midst of molten motion. There were plenty of potential hiding places where the buckled rock had split, but none that was sufficiently identifiable to be communicated to another person, except perhaps by counting paces, which required more elaborate planning than there was time for.

Fear and fantasy were now flowing in equal measure through the Arab's veins. The Grand Canyon had become the Valley of Death and, hearing what he took to be a helicopter, he looked up to see a stork trail its ragged wings across the face of the moon. His ears deceived him in other ways too: The lower he got, the more he was aware of a hollow moaning, like the noise of somebody blowing across the top of an empty bottle. And yet the air was perfectly still. He turned and was suddenly seized by the quite irrational thought that the archbishop, panicking at finding himself locked in the car, would release the handbrake and send the unlikely instrument of God's vengeance plummeting down the gully to crush body and bones, chauffeur and Savior, against the bare rock.

With a supreme effort, he attempted to regain control. But the more he tried to still his errant limbs, the more wildly the beam of the flashlight danced against the cliff face. Then, inexplicably, it was as though another hand had grasped his wrist and held it firm, locked in midair. The beam had settled, steady as steel, on an outcrop that resembled nothing so much as a human skull. From beneath a beetling brow, a pair of oversized eye sockets stared vacantly back at him. He had seen the like only in one other place—Jerusalem, where behind the old Arab bus station was another similarly eroded rock formation, believed by some to be the original site of the Crucifixion: Golgotha, the place of the skull.

Whatever its associations, this new Golgotha was as good a landmark as he was likely to find. More desperate than ever to be rid of his load, he scrambled towards it with the intention of climbing up and pushing the kit bag into one of the sockets. But as he neared the foot of the cliff, a more suitable, less conspicuous hiding place suggested itself—an overhanging shelf of rock about a foot above the ground and directly beneath the outcrop. It was deeply undercut and, down on his knees, Abu found he could reach the entire length of his arm in and still not touch the back. And it was dry.

He pushed the kit bag as far in as possible and then banked up the loose shaley soil to hide it from view. Finally he did something he would never be able to explain: He crossed himself.

★

Meir was at a loss to know what best to do. While out on the quayside the search through the oranges had only just reached the halfway stage, Berman was enjoying his first real sleep in thirty hours on a sofa in the anteroom to the port superintendent's office. His face, normally so disjointed by the failure of the muscles to meet across the diagonal scar, had in repose regained its unity. It was the last sleep he was likely to get in many hours.

Meir looked down at his clipboard and the message he had just taken from Security via the Jerusalem EGHQ, and reluctantly put aside his feelings of almost parental protectiveness.

"General, news from Security," he said, gently rocking Berman awake.

In seconds Berman was aware of the whine of the cranes, the splintering of crates, and a headache that felt as if somebody was swinging a spiked ball inside his skull.

"They've found something?"

"No, but the senior officer sent to the Allenby Bridge to enforce the closure order reported back that a Vatican car with diplomatic plates had been at the bridge and had turned tail when . . ."

"Why in God's name didn't they stop it?"

"It seems he only found out about it much later when one of the soldiers mentioned that it was expected back to collect a cardinal coming from Amman. There was no cardinal and, by that time, no car."

"Do we know which of the Vatican cars?"

"Almost certainly Archbishop Ramone's. It was a white Peugeot with an Arab chauffeur and a man who 'looked like a bishop or something' in the back."

Berman groaned.

"Go on."

"Well, Jerusalem has pieced together Ramone's movements as far as possible. He gave a lecture at the International Ecumenical Institute—that's off the Jerusalem-Bethlehem road—between five and six o'clock. According to the director there, he left in his car around 6:40; the only thing that was unusual was that the lecture had been brought forward a week at the archbishop's insistence, and with only a day's notice. He must have gone straight from there to the bridge, because he was at the border certainly before eight."

"And where's the car now?"

"Back at the delegation on the Mount of Olives. As for Ramone, his secretary will say only that he is 'not to be disturbed.' It could all be a coincidence, of course."

Head in hands, Berman looked up from the sofa.

"Is that what *you* believe, Meir?"

Meir shook his head.

"So what *do* you believe?"

"That the ship was a deliberate diversionary tactic; that Ramone picked up the bones from the fake Green Patrol squad at the Ecumenical Institute, and then counted on getting them over the border while we were still busy counting Jaffas."

"Atalanta's apples!" remarked Berman bitterly.

"Sorry?" said Meir, mystified.

★

"I don't believe it. I just don't believe it!"

The monsignor was in full flight, scarlet with a rage that Abu suspected to be more histrionic than genuine, but impressive enough to make him realize that not speaking until asked a direct question was the best course to adopt.

"I knew the two of you weren't capable of seeing it through . . . just *knew* it. I told His Eminence the Secretary of State that you'd bungle it between you. And now what? Christendom's most holy relic stuffed in a foxhole somewhere between Jerusalem and Jericho, and the Apostolic Delegate of the Holy See wandering around the Old City half-crazed! I don't understand how it was possible for you to let him go, knowing the state he was in and knowing . . ."

"I not let him go," put in the chauffeur, breaking his vow of silence.

"You know what I mean."

Abu shrugged. "I tell you already what happen. I stop the car—two minutes, no more—enough time to telephone to here to be sure it is safe for us to return, to be sure place not surrounded by soldiers. But when I return to car, archbishop he is gone. I wait. I think perhaps he just go for a . . . make water. Then, when it become dangerous wait more, I come immediately here."

The monsignor's only response was a theatrical sigh. How in his right mind could the Secretary of State have entrusted such a vital mission to a pair of such incompetent *scemi*—a semiliterate Arab who could barely speak English let alone Italian and a saint *manqué* whose piety bordered on insanity. Worse still, in the absence of the archbishop, it would now be up to *him* to sort out the mess. Sobered by the thought, he adopted a suddenly different tone with the Arab.

"You must forgive me, Abu. It's just, just . . . well, I'm sure you can understand how difficult it is in my position. In part, I suppose, I blame myself for having been involved in the planning without fully appreciating all the . . . eventualities. Given those eventualities, you acted with commendable coolness. Now, you must tell me precisely where you hid the bones—while you can still remember."

Seating himself behind the archbishop's ornate inlaid desk, the monsignor took a clean sheet of paper from one of the drawers and placed it on the blotter before him. He waited, pen poised. The Arab said nothing, however, and it became clear that either he had already forgotten the details or, realizing the importance of the information, was holding back for more scurrilous reasons.

"I shall of course see to it," said the monsignor, "that Their Eminences in Rome hear of your great ingenuity and presence of mind in the service of our Mother Church, and the extent to which we all owe you a considerable debt."

The Arab drew up his chair, and began.

"You know the sign in the middle of the hills that says *sea level*?"

The monsignor wrote as fast as he could, fearful that at any moment the chauffeur's memory might fail. But Abu had been more conscientious than he had been given credit for and committed to memory every relevant detail and distance. When at last he finished, the monsignor was visibly relieved. Folding the paper, he leaned across the desk.

"Now, Abu, you must listen to me very carefully and do exactly as I say. On no account are you to leave the delegation building until you are instructed that it is safe for you to do so. You will be here for two days at least, and during that time you are to stay inside and not show yourself at any windows. It is for your own protection. Do you understand?"

He did, but he was under no illusions about the monsignor's concern for his safety. The monsignor's actual concern, he knew, was that he might be abducted, interrogated, and forced to reveal the whereabouts of the bones.

"You will be quite safe here," continued the other. "You are on inviolable territory. I shall instruct Sister Catherine to make up a bed for you in one of the guest rooms before I leave to look for His Excellency. In any event, I shall not be returning here nor shall I be in contact."

He was about to say more but, as a precaution, decided it was best not to entrust any more information about his intentions to the Arab. Instead, he concluded:

"Just show me on the map where you left His Excellency when you went to make the phone call."

Abu debated whether he should now reveal the *full* story of his parting with the archbishop. Given the monsignor's suddenly charitable disposition, he judged it better that he be found out now than later. He pointed on the map to a spot opposite the Rockefeller Museum and added:

"His Excellency, he also take my gun."

The monsignor mouthed an entire sentence before getting a word out.

"Your what?"

"I always keep a pistol in the glove compartment because I am His Excellency's bodyguard like also his driver. When I come back from telephone, archbishop is gone, gun is gone."

★

There were few people in the Old City to see the eccentric figure wandering along the Via Dolorosa, weeping and pressing to his chest a blood-smeared crucifix. Those who did see him took little notice; even this late at night, pilgrims in clerical garb exhibiting signs of religious fervor were a common enough sight in what for Christians is the most evocative street in the world.

But, instead of following the Stations of the Cross as far as the Holy Sepulchre, this pilgrim turned right at the Third Station where the Via Dolorosa makes a dogleg cut through El Wad, and headed north up El Wad towards the Damascus Gate. There, emerging through the walls, he carried on up

Nablus Road to a small turning a hundred yards along on the right.

He had been to the place before—every time conscious of the vaguely heretical nature of his visit, and on one occasion when he was recognized even feeling obliged to explain that his interest was archaeological rather than devotional. It was partly true, but truer still was the fact that the so-called Garden Tomb, although dismissed by the Roman Catholic Church as a Protestant ploy to undermine the claim of the Holy Sepulchre, nevertheless held for Archbishop Ramone far greater emotional appeal than the authorized location with its profusion of guttering candles and swinging brass. Landscaped like an English garden by the London-based association who owned it, the place had a beauty and tranquility that was unique in central Jerusalem, and which even the distant rumble of traffic couldn't diminish. Whether or not it really was the tomb of Our Lord, as the English scholar-soldier General Gordon had believed, neither the archbishop nor anyone else could say, but since his coming to Jerusalem, his most fruitful periods of prayer and contemplation had been spent sitting quietly on one of the slatted benches amid the wild cyclamen, the chirping of the blackbirds in the pines combining with the general ambience to produce an atmosphere more exquisitely Franciscan than that of Assisi itself.

Getting in was no problem. The custodian, a retired British Army colonel, had on an earlier occasion shown him where to find the key for the back entrance, indicating that His Excellency might care to use this facility out of hours for the purposes of what he tactfully left unspecified as "private study."

Ramone moved through the garden as a man walking beneath the waves. His body, no longer directed by thought but continuing to act as a vehicle for the senses, was drawn towards the semicircular terrace overlooking the tomb as if by a magnetic force. Coming up against a bench, he sat down and for more than a minute rocked back and forth, more in pain than prayer, mumbling and occasionally groaning in his effort to inject meaning into words and phrases that were now semantically bankrupt.

Exhausted, he stopped and stared at the tomb less than twenty yards away, trying instead to draw from the living rock of the dead the confidence in Christ's triumph over mortality which he had so often found here before.

The silence mocked him. His breathing now heavy and irregular, he looked up to the hard metallic sky hung around with stars and, desperate to the point of delirium, implored aloud in his native Italian:

"*Dio, un segno. Dammi un segno, Dio!*"

For a moment the stars seemed to respond, pulsating in time with the beating of his own heart. But it was merely a reflection of his own self-generating anxiety in the face of a vast, indifferent universe. Not only was nobody listening, there was nobody *to* listen.

The snout of the pistol tasted oily and, despite his two-handed grip, rattled against the teeth. He closed his eyes and in his mind repeated the only words that now had any relevance:

"*Eli, Eli, lama sabachthani?*—my God, my God, why hast thou forsaken me?"

A low-velocity bullet muffled by human cheeks makes comparatively little noise, and it would be seven hours before the archbishop's body was found by one of the Arab gardeners arriving for work.

A quarter of a mile away, the Vatican's special emissary incognito, Monsignor Giovanni, had come to the conclusion that continued search was futile. He had walked every street and alley in the Old City, had asked in bars and souvenir shops—even a pool hall—and had found not a trace of the archbishop. He never again wanted to hear another wail of Arab music or see another olivewood camel. The only places he hadn't checked were the dozens of religious institutions and hostels in the Christian Quarter, but there was no way, without drawing attention to himself, of enquiring whether the Apostolic Delegate had booked in for the night when it was well known that His Excellency had a perfectly good bed within walking distance.

Glancing at his watch, he was amazed to see that it was after midnight. Since he had already made up his mind not to return to the delegation for fear of being either arrested or, at best, bottled up without any secure means of communication with Rome, the most logical alternative was to book into the hotel reserved for him by the Vatican travel agent who had arranged the nuns' pilgrimage for which he was nominally the guide. He got a taxi without difficulty and within twenty minutes was standing beneath an ugly, modern, purpose-built hotel on the western outskirts of the city.

The front doors were locked and he had to ring for the night porter. The man had been in hotel service too many years to be surprised by the ruddy-faced cleric who carried only a briefcase and claimed to be with a party that had registered the previous evening. The room was paid for and, after asking the lost shepherd to fill in the usual form, he showed him up to his room on the sixth floor. He then returned to the reception desk and, little realizing the train of events he was setting off, penned a brief note explaining the circumstances of the new arrival's belated appearance, and clipped it to his registration slip.

THE SECOND DAY

THE Defense Minister ran through the catalogue of the previous day's events with the stoicism of one who knew that nobody else around the Cabinet table could judge his actions more critically than he himself. Even so, the Minister of the Interior was prepared to try.

"So we've lost the bones and, with them, the most valuable instrument of political and diplomatic leverage that has ever come our way."

Berman was too tired to react.

"Do we know where they are now?" asked the Interior Minister.

"Most likely in the Apostolic Delegation. We can't be sure, but, given that the archbishop's car tried but failed to cross the Allenby Bridge and that it is now visibly parked outside the delegation building, it seems highly probable."

"Then why don't we go in and get them? They're stolen property, aren't they?"

Berman looked to Foreign Minister Rosenstein to give the reply.

"It's not that straightforward," said Rosenstein. "Although the Apostolic Delegate does not formally have diplomatic status, he nonetheless enjoys it in practice. To this extent the delegation building is diplomatic territory and hence immune from entry or search without permission. We might be able to get over that if it weren't for the added religious dimension, for the building is the property of the Catholic Church— holy ground, in effect. To violate it would be to do incalculable damage to our argument that the holy places of Jerusalem are best defended by an Israeli government with sole control over an undivided city. The Vatican has always rejected that view and pressed instead for an 'internationalized' city; to invade the Apostolic Delegation would be to play into their hands. Besides . . . " He glanced back at the Defense Minister.

"Besides," Berman added, "any attempt at a forced entry would only drive them to destroy the bones—if they haven't done so already."

The Interior Minister raised his eyes to the ceiling in mock exasperation.

"What I find so incredible is that we fell for every trick they threw at us. We took their moving of the AWACS to the Saudi border as a sure indication of their intent to spy on us, when in fact it was designed to get us to deny ourselves our own radar; we were taken in by their phony Green Patrol vehicle not just on the way in but on the way *out* as well; and, even when we knew we had been duped, we then hightailed off after a decoy load of oranges while the bones were sitting within our grasp at the Allenby Bridge. And we still don't know how they discovered the exact location of the inspection site. If it weren't so serious, it would be laughable!"

Berman felt his anger rising. Instead, he said quietly: "Your memory, if you'll excuse me saying so, is rather selective."

He paused to give the Interior Minister a chance to respond, to defuse an atmosphere in which the mix of recrimination and personal animosity was about to go critical. When he didn't, Berman looked again to his only ally at the table, Foreign Minister Rosenstein, to act as intermediary. When, to his surprise, Rosenstein too remained silent, he was forced to say it himself.

"I refer to the other respects in which 'we' were duped—notably that we swallowed whole Dr. Schumacher and his supposed nuclear spying mission and so obligingly moved the bones out of the safety of Dimona—and then, to compound the error, we chose the most vulnerable possible form of transport, a helicopter which . . ."

He was cut off by Acting Prime Minister Reuven Shavit.

"This is old ground, Gideon, and is getting us nowhere. What we must concern ourselves with now is . . ."

"No!" retorted Berman, for the first time raising his voice. "I submit that this is an important matter of record, since it is the record with which the Interior Minister is apparently so concerned. I am quite prepared to concede serious errors of judgement on my own part, but the record will show that I was not alone and that the Cabinet as a whole bears at least equal responsibility for major errors made at the very outset of this operation. It will be recalled, I trust, that against your own wishes, Shavit, I demanded and got a vote on the advisability of moving the bones out of Dimona, arguing that if the proposed method of transport was to be a helicopter, then they should stay where they were. But," he glanced in the direction of the Cabinet Secretary, "and this is a matter of record, I was overruled by a majority, if I remember correctly, of fifteen to two."

The Cabinet Secretary refused to acknowledge his statement even with a nod and Berman accordingly looked beyond him to the stenographer sitting at his desk against the wall.

"Well, is that or is that not the case?" he demanded. "If there's any doubt about it, let's have it read out—the minutes for the last Cabinet meeting."

The same look of discomfiture came over the stenographer's face as Berman had detected on the Cabinet Secretary's, but before he could say more, Shavit had again intervened.

"I am sure we all appreciate that the Defense Minister has been under considerable strain these last twenty-four hours, quite apart from suffering the personal bereavement occasioned by the death of Major Hervitz. Faced with the decisions he had to take, I'm not sure that any of us could say he would have acted differently. Nor does it do any good at a time like this to start apportioning blame. I would sugg . . ."

Berman saw red.

"Shavit, I refuse to be patronized or slandered under the guise of commiseration. We are talking about a matter of simple, unequivocal record. I repeat, is it or is it not the . . ."

The Cabinet Secretary gave an apologetic cough.

"Perhaps the Minister should be appraised of the fact," he interrupted, "that emergency Cabinet meetings, like this one and the one to which he refers, are only recorded—that is, formally minuted—at the Prime Minister's discretion or, as in this case, the Acting Prime Minister's. Our last meeting was not so recorded."

For several seconds, Berman was struck dumb. Then:

"Am I to believe the evidence of my own ears?" he stammered. "Are you seriously telling me that everything we discussed at that last meeting, the vote included, has been conveniently struck from the record—that, like the Communists rewriting history, it simply didn't happen?" He pointed to the stenographer. "And what in God's name was he doing all that time—practicing?"

Only then did the wider implications dawn on him. He turned again to the Cabinet Secretary.

"When exactly did the Acting Prime Minister instruct you not to minute the meeting?"

"He doesn't have to answer that," cut in Shavit. "And, Gideon, I demand that you abide by the rules of this Cabinet and give way to the Chair . . ."

"You demand nothing!" Berman shouted, "Deception, distortion, deletion—is there no limit to how far you'd go to save your own skin?"

He felt Rosenstein's restraining hand on his arm.

"Gideon, this is not the way."

"Is *this* then?" demanded Berman, sweeping his hand around the Cabinet table. "You tell me, Ya'acov! Did you not vote with me against the helicopter plan, or am I just imagining the whole thing in my overemotional state of personal bereavement? Well? Everybody is listening."

"Gideon, Gideon," was the Foreign Minister's only reply, as he attempted to pull Berman back into his seat.

Contemptuously, Berman shook him off.

"I've misjudged you, Ya'acov. You're no better than this . . . rabble. You can stay if you want to, but I've got to go and tell a mother her son has been sent to his death by a bunch of yellow jobniks who haven't the guts to admit to their share of responsibility." He pushed back his chair, collected his papers, and, fixing his eye on the Acting Prime Minister, added: "Not until now, Shavit, did I fully understand the meaning of the expression 'beneath contempt.' "

Monsignor Giovanni was up early the next morning and, showered and shaved, was by seven-thirty eating his way through a prodigious Israeli breakfast of orange juice, grapefruit, hard-boiled eggs, cheese, cucumber, tomatoes, yoghurt, rolls, and butter. That the rolls were less fresh than they might have been, having been baked the previous day to comply with Sabbath regulations, escaped his notice, his mind being on the phone call he was going to have to make to Rome before eight o'clock—seven, Italian time.

Any reservations he had had about using the phone in his room had been dispelled by the discovery that it was possible to direct-dial foreign calls and so bypass the operator—*and* any bugging equipment. He dialled the number—Rome 6982—heard the familiar "*Vaticano*," and within five seconds was through to the Secretary of State.

The conversation was lengthy and punctuated by His Eminence's groans, first at the failure of the previous night's mission, and secondly at the inexplicable disappearance of Archbishop Ramone with a loaded pistol. The monsignor's boyish enthusiasm—his insistence that at least he knew where the bones were and, having escaped the delegation building, was still able to move and communicate freely—was but a small oasis of consolation in a desert of desolation.

Giovanni himself felt no such despair. Just the opposite. He relished the excitement of being involved in such an escapade, the prize for which was nothing less than the salvation of Christianity! And not just involved, but now one of the major protagonists—if not *the* major protagonist. It was the promise of intrigue and being privy to the secrets of Popes which, as a young seminarian, had first attracted him to a Vatican career; and, as he thought about it, he could even imagine himself retrieving the bones and smuggling them out; after all, he alone—apart from the Arab chauffeur who was confined to the delegation—knew where they were. To act on his own initiative, however, would be to exceed his present authority; instead, he made a mental note to suggest it to His Eminence when he phoned him again in exactly twelve hours' time.

Meanwhile, six floors below in the hotel's administrative office, the deputy manager was committing a technical infringement of the Sabbath by sorting and checking the guest registration slips for the previous twenty-four hours, prior to their collection by the local police. Every Israeli hotel of any size has its unpaid security officer—usually of the assistant or deputy manager level—whose job it is to liaise with the local police and notify them of any suspicious arrivals. Should it be necessary to bug a room or telephone, he is also the man who cooperates with the relevant government specialists to enable them to perform their task.

As usual, this morning's bundle of slips was the thickest of the week, with the regular influx of foreigners into the city to celebrate the respective Jewish and Christian Sabbaths. Package tour guests were generally of little interest to the deputy manager—bombers, assassins, spies, and fanatics tended to make their own travel arrangements—and he would have flicked past the monsignor's slip had it not been for the night porter's explanatory note. He was more intrigued than suspicious. To his knowledge, it was the first time the hotel had had anybody with a Vatican passport; such exalted visitors to Jerusalem were normally put up free of charge at any one of the many Catholic institutions in and around the Old City. Perhaps he just wished to be close to his flock. As to why he hadn't spent his first night in the bed he'd paid for, there were a number of perfectly innocent possible explanations, as well as quite a few more titillating ones. Whatever the reason, it was worth earmarking his slip for the police inspector's attention; if nothing else, it showed the hotel management's conscientious attitude towards security. The inspector could then follow it up if he wanted to, although on past experience it would be quite a few hours before anybody at the station even saw it; checking out suspicious visitors was one of the routine chores that attracted few volunteers at the best of times; fewer still on Shabbat.

The Sabbath traffic into Tel Aviv was light; Berman's mood anything but. The sense of loss and responsibility he felt at Yossi's death, so long pent up through the night, had been more heightened than dissipated by his exchanges in the Cabinet Room. How he was going to tell Ariella, he didn't know—still less, Nathan, Yossi's father, whom he barely knew—but he owed it to them to be the bearer of the news himself, and the more he thought about their loss compared with his, the more his own grief seemed selfish. Even so, as he took the turn off the Lod Road towards Savyon and Tel Aviv's "millionaire row," he felt his stomach muscles knot, and subconsciously hoped they would be away or out.

He had heard stories about the house but had never seen it. Not even the stories did justice to its opulence. He knew Nathan's electronics firm had done well—every week the papers carried reports of another big American deal—but this well? In his shabby fatigues, his body feeling only a little less crumpled, and driving his own battered, six-year-old compact, he felt like a pauper at the gate of Croesus.

The security system was commensurately formidable, rivaling that with which the Defense Minister himself was provided. He pushed a button on the six-foot-high gate and waited for a response from the black metallic grille. He gave his name and the voice answered, "Mrs. Hervitz is expecting you, Minister." The gate buzzed and he pushed it open.

He was halfway up the drive when the significance of the words hit him, but at that moment the front door opened and his ex-wife stood waiting in a simple shift that touched the floor.

He was taken aback. This was not the composed society beauty whose perfectly tricked-out face had stared at him from countless magazines and papers and—he could admit it—caused him a fleeting twinge of something like pain. There was not a trace of makeup on her face, and her sunbleached hair hung loosely around her shoulders instead of being gathered back to accentuate the high cheekbones. Save for the fine lines around the eyes, she could have passed for a woman in her twenties, not forties. The eyes had evidently been shedding tears.

"You know why I'm here then," he said, his expression betraying his confusion.

She nodded. "Ya'acov Rosenstein phoned an hour ago—just after you left the Cabinet meeting. He told me about Yossi. He said you were on your way. He, he thought . . ."

He caught her as she collapsed on his shoulder. The sandalwood smell of her hair and skin came back to him across a chasm of a quarter of a century and he was ashamed of the momentary sexual response it sparked in him.

She led the way into a spaciously cool drawing room built on three different levels and overlooking palm trees and the swimming pool. On the lawn a sprinkler was tossing graceful arabesques into the air. A maid, who had left through another door as they entered, had placed a tray of coffee on the table in front of the sofa. Beside it was a photograph of Yossi in his pilot's uniform.

He took the chair opposite and watched her trembling hands pour. What, he wondered, had induced Rosenstein to phone and tell her about Yossi? It was true that Ya'acov had known them both from the days of their marriage—had even been at the wedding—but it was unlike him to preempt what was after all one of the Defense Minister's duties. And he had known Berman was on his way.

"Do you see Ya'acov often?" he asked.

"We've kept in touch over the years," she replied. "He's been my best source of information about you—apart from the papers, which I take with a pinch of salt. He's very fond of you, Gideon. He thinks you should be the next Prime Minister."

Berman felt uncomfortable. Here they were discussing politics when nothing was further from both their minds. They couldn't even look at each other. Gently, he tried to bring the conversation round.

"Does Nathan know?"

She shook her head, bent over the cup; then tossed back her hair and Berman saw the tears start again. He wanted to put a protective arm round her but stayed where he was, waiting for her to regain her composure.

"He is in the States. I . . . I haven't seen him for six weeks."

"I could get our ambassador there to break the news to him, if you don't feel up to a phone call," Berman suggested.

Again she shook her head, this time biting her lower lip. Her body was shaking.

"Gideon, there's something you should know—something you should have known years ago,·but there's never been a right time to tell you, and now it's too late. Ya'acov is the only person I've ever talked to about it. That's why he phoned."

She picked up the photograph and passed it to him.

"Look at him, Gideon. Look at your son."

Berman showed no surprise. He had come across similar reactions before when required to tell mothers, fathers, brothers, sisters, wives, of the death of a loved one. Psychologists attributed it to a subconscious desire to inflict hurt on the individual ultimately responsible. Instead of looking at the photograph, he looked at her.

"Ariella, I have no son. If I had, though, I could wish for none better than Yossi. I loved him like a son."

"Gideon," she responded quietly, taking his hand. "Listen to me. I am still in a state of shock, but I am not delirious. It was Ya'acov who said you had the right to know. If it had been left to me, I would have chickened out." She paused, the grip of her hand on his tightening, "You remember after we split up and I met Nathan."

"Went off with Nathan. You met him before we split up," corrected Berman, but without edge.

She flushed.

"Yes, went off with Nathan. But you remember when I was going through a bad patch with him and couldn't decide whether to marry him—and you and I stayed the night in Tiberias?"

It came back across the years—a precious, painful memory that had been locked in his heart for fear of the emotional shrapnel it would wreak if ever let out. At the time and for a year after, the experience had gutted him. He had seen his wife, by then three months estranged and in all but name another man's, and had desired her as he never had in marriage. They had been like courting strangers again, excited, childish and inept. She had looked more beautiful—or perhaps just seemed to him so—than he could remember. They had eaten and danced, and his fingertips had tingled at the touch of her skin and the slimness of her waist.

In the morning they had parted—on his side with promises that he would quit the army, go into business or something, and they would start a family; and on hers, more circumspectly, with an assurance that she would put her thoughts about Nathan into order and would come to a conclusion which she would let him know within a week.

The letter had arrived exactly a week later. She had decided: Their marriage could never work. Whatever he might say about wanting to change himself, she had no right to make him change and it would only sow the seeds of resentment later. She was no more confident that she and Nathan would be happy in the long run, but she was going to take the chance. She wept, she said, for the hurt she knew it would cause him. For the one more bruise to a mind and body to which life had already dealt so many.

"I remember," he said softly.

"And the date—do you remember that?"

"Not precisely, except that it was summer."

"I do. Yossi was born nine months later, almost to the day."

He leaned forward to take her other hand.

"Ariella, this is fantasy. It proves nothing. You were living with Nathan at the time."

A sad smile came to her lips.

"No, Gideon . . . I didn't tell you then, but the reason I was able to see you at all was that Nathan was away for a fortnight on a business course. I didn't tell you because I didn't want you to think it was just that your company was preferable to no company. Nathan never knew that we met. When Yossi was born with such alarming precision, an obliging doctor at the hospital told him he was premature."

"Which he could have been," added Berman, on the defensive.

She let go his hands and crossed to a desk on the other side of the room. When she came back she was carrying a small, slightly ragged photo of Berman himself, taken at the time of their marriage when he was in his late twenties, many years before his facial injury.

"Gideon," she said, keeping the photo facedown, "I could tell you a lot of tales about a woman's intuition, about how a mother can recognize in her son a father's look, a mannerism, a way of speech, a way of just holding the head even—things that the father himself will never see. All these things I have seen in Yossi over the years. And there are some things that don't lie."

She handed him the photo, at the same time holding next to it the one of Yossi in his pilot's uniform. The similarity was undeniable, as though the one had been deliberately posed with the other in mind. Both were head and shoulder portrait shots and in both the subject was looking slightly to the left of the camera with the hint of a nervous, self-deprecating smile.

"Block out the hair, Gideon, and look at the eyes and mouth . . . and then tell me Yossi couldn't be your son."

It wasn't necessary.

He laid down the photos and walked to the window. As he looked beyond the palms, the sun momentarily caught the spray of the sprinkler and transformed it into a brief, dazzling rainbow. For a long while he couldn't speak, choked by a devastating and suddenly more poignant sense of loss, as if the dagger already in his chest had been given a second thrust into the heart. At length, without turning, he asked:

"Did Yossi know?"

She was standing behind him now, but as yet unsure of his response.

"I never told him, if that's what you mean. How could I? His relations with Nathan were never good; he despised everything Nathan stood for—his success, his wealth, his . . . flamboyance. There was only one father he ever wanted;

only one he ever modeled himself on. So many times I wanted to tell him the truth, knowing what it would mean to him, but there were always the consequences to think of. I was realistic enough to know it would have destroyed our marriage and, well, you once said it yourself—there's too much of the self-centered, pampered bitch in me . . ." She looked around the room. "I like to be comfortable, and being married to Nathan is comfortable. Perhaps too I wanted to protect Nathan. Whatever his failings, he has tried to be a good father. Then again, I suppose I wanted to protect you—from the publicity, the scandal, and, not least, the fierceness of Yossi's devotion. You've never been the most emotional man, Gideon, and neither Ya'acov nor I were sure how you'd react, how you'd deal with it."

"Did he never suspect—Yossi?"

"Perhaps, I don't know. He could work out for himself that he was conceived out of wedlock, but he never knew of our meeting in Tiberias and I never let him see the photograph. But that's by the way . . . How am I going to tell Nathan, Gideon?"

Berman turned, his face a mask of pain.

"You are not."

"But you cannot allow him to mourn an only son who in reality was another's."

Berman placed his hands on her shoulders and saw his tears reflected in hers.

"Would you rather then deprive him of that son at the moment of his loss? You cannot, Ariella. As Nathan was Yossi's father in life, so he must remain now Yossi is dead. I admit that my first reaction when you told me—convinced me—was one of anger at having been denied and cheated all these years, and I would give the world to take Yossi in my arms at this moment and call him 'son.' But, Ariella, I have to acknowledge that what you did was right—whatever your reasons. Neither you nor I will ever breathe a word of this to anyone, and I will instruct Ya'acov the same. Yossi will be my son *in pectore*. Isn't that how the Catholics describe it when the Pope creates a cardinal but doesn't publicize his iden . . ."

They broke down simultaneously, embracing with the desperation of survivors at sea with only each other to cling to.

"Can I ask a favor?" he said as he was preparing to leave. "The photo of Yossi, could I have it?"

She picked up the framed photograph from the coffee table and pressed it into his hands.

"He was your son, Gideon, and even without knowing it, he loved and worshiped you."

Her voice faltered and she shook her head in frustration. With a tenderness he thought he had forgotten he drew her to him, his fingers running through the soft hair at the nape of her neck. Through his own tears he tried to say "our son," but the words caught in his throat.

★

"I don't think we have a lot to say to each other, Ya'acov."

Berman busied himself with tidying his desktop and sorting through the drawers, taking pains to avoid the old man's gaze. He was annoyed and wanted to show it, and the Foreign Minister's walking into his office unannounced had only contributed to that annoyance.

"You think I betrayed you in Cabinet this morning," stated Rosenstein.

"Something like that."

"And my phoning Ariella—that, too?"

Berman didn't respond immediately. He was genuinely grateful for what Rosenstein had done with respect to Ariella and the support he had given her over the years. But he didn't want to be wrong-footed into softening his anger over the Foreign Minister's silence at the Cabinet table.

"That's different. There, you acted as the friend I always thought you were—which makes the other even harder to comprehend."

Without being invited, the old man pulled back the chair opposite Berman's desk and, with the help of his stick, eased himself down.

"In that case," he said, "you're likely to be more baffled still by my possession of this." He pulled an envelope from his inside pocket and tossed it onto the desk. It was addressed to Avraham Rubinger, Prime Minister of Israel, c/o The Israeli Embassy, Washington, United States of America. "One of the prerogatives of being Foreign Minister," he continued, "is the right to intercept mail going through the diplomatic pouches. This is yours, I think. I promise you I haven't opened it but I have a good idea what it contains—and I want you to tear it up."

Berman for the first time looked him in the eyes.

"You have a damned cheek, Ya'acov. Your support might not have made any difference this morning, but it would have been a welcome gesture."

"Gestures, Gideon! You talk about gestures. By their very definition, they are empty. There were good reasons why I kept my mouth shut this morning."

"And there were even better ones for opening it!" countered Berman. "You were the one man round that table who could have faced Shavit down; the one man who is close to Avram; the one man Shavit has reason not to cross. You had only to threaten to pick up the phone that instant and get through to Avram, but, no, you sat there like a deaf-mute contemplating his navel. Not so much as a peep! And it was you, Ya'acov, who warned me—remember?—about the dangers of being made a political scapegoat. What in God's name do you think Shavit was doing this morning?"

Rosenstein fingered the knob of his walking stick. As though confirming Berman's charge of deafness, he responded:

"Give me time, Gideon—just two hours, till midday. Shavit has called another Cabinet meeting for then, and I want you to be there . . . please. If you still feel then as you do now, you can announce your resignation and leave—and I will send this on to Avram personally. But just hold it till then. It is always a mistake to resign in pique—on principle, perhaps, but in pique, never."

There was an ironic ring to Berman's laugh.

"Ya'acov—friend?—at least do me the justice of imputing to my action some vestige of a higher motive! My mind was made up long before that charade this morning. Shavit may have pulled a shabby trick which I was dumb enough to fall for, but my resignation has nothing to do with hurt pride, pique, or whatever you want to call it. I'm resigning, Ya'acov, because quite simply I bungled the operation; I failed at my job. I have already been responsible for the death of four young men under my command—one of them, it now turns out, my own son—and I have therefore forfeited the right to demand the allegiance and confidence of all the others under me. I am taking, if you like, the honorable course, and you are no friend of mine, Ya'acov, if you now try to dissuade me."

The outburst from the other side of the desk was quite unsignaled.

"Gideon, I have never heard you talk such rubbish! Name me a single Israeli general who has seen active service and hasn't lost men under his command? How many generals— never mind Defense Ministers—do you think the country would be left with if they all took your attitude?"

"That doesn't alter the fact that I bungled the operation," retorted Berman. "I am no admirer of our Interior Minister, but what he said in Cabinet this morning was right: We—*I*— fell for every trick that was thrown at us."

"You didn't fall for every trick, Gideon. At the risk of getting back onto dangerous ground, let me remind you of what *you* reminded the Cabinet—about Schumacher and the helicopter. If you insist on the terminology, you bungled an operation that was already irretrievably bungled, and there was nothing that you, Shavit, or anyone else could have done to save it."

Berman was shaking his head.

"Wrong, Ya'acov. There was plenty I could have done— and *should* have done. Instead, I did what I despise: I played the politician. *Twice*. Having lost the battle to keep the bones in Dimona, I should have been as good as my principles and handed over command to someone else, but I feared the political repercussions if someone else pulled it off—I feared for my job. Then later, when my mind was failing to function properly because of exhaustion, when all it could do was pick at threads instead of analyze the overall pattern, I should again have handed it over—not necessarily to somebody more competent; just fresher. But I didn't; I thought of Rabin and the whispered innuendoes that years after the Six Day War he was never able to shake off, and I stayed. Now, do you understand?"

With evident pain, Rosenstein pushed himself up into a standing position and with his free hand grasped the lapel of his jacket. Berman recognized the stance; the old man was about to deliver a lecture.

"Gideon," he began in a tone that sought to combine intensity with great fatigue, "I ask you only to hear me out, if for no other reason than that age and experience deserve indulgence, if not respect. My generation is old and dying. Avram has a couple of months at most and, as I've told you before, my own time can only be a little way behind." He paused as though to underline the precariousness of his physical state. "I was at the birth of this country, Gideon. The likes of Avram and myself, we were its midwives. I have seen it grow and mature; survive attempted strangulation at birth; throw back seemingly insuperable enemies ranged on every side; fight and win six wars in a single generation—and until recently I really did believe that here was the biblical 'light unto the nations': a country founded by philosophers, blessed by God, and—most important in practical terms—with a capacity to produce an endless line of visionaries to keep the ideal alive. Remember how Ben-Gurion used always to hark back to the time of the First Temple—the nation living on its own soil, independent, working the land, defending itself by its own efforts, speaking its own language, and creating its own culture? Well, that's what I thought *we* had, except added to all that, we had democracy as well.

"I can remember the cynics in the early days saying democracy would never survive here because the external threat of a hundred million against fewer than four million would be too great for us to be able to afford such a luxury. But democracy *has* survived. What we cannot afford is politics— the politics of self-interest as practiced by Shavit and his batch of self-serving apparatchiks. Men like Shavit are dangerous not for the qualities they have, but for those they lack! I don't just mean honesty, integrity, leadership. I mean the quality that distinguishes the statesman from the politician: *vision*—the ability to think in decades, not days; to look beyond the cluttered foreground to the distant horizon, to the mountain peaks ahead, not the puddle at your feet.

"*You* have that quality, Gideon. On you and the handful of men like you will depend the survival of the Third Temple. I do not exaggerate. But if you bow out now and leave the field to Shavit, those few others like you will either be driven out by the party machine or will simply give up for want of an example."

He transferred his weight to the other leg and stared for a while at the corner of the desk.

"Do you remember, not so many years ago, coming to me and saying you had decided to go into politics? You asked my advice, but instead knowing how you despised politicians, I asked you why you had decided nonetheless to join them. Do you remember your reply?"

Berman was silent. He had more than an inkling of what was coming.

"You said that after you had lost all your family in Poland, you had been plagued by the question of why you alone had survived. And why *you*, when so many millions of other Jews had perished? You still didn't know the answer, you said, but you did know that in some way—in some positive way—your survival had to be justified. In your life you had somehow to attempt to accomplish what might have been accomplished by hundreds of thousands of others, had they lived . . ."

He rested his full weight on the stick and, leaning forward, asked:

"Was that the same man who now talks about 'taking the honorable course'? There is something more important than honor, Gideon, and that is duty. If you doubt me, go up to Yad Vashem and read the names aloud to yourself—Dachau, Bergen-Belsen, Mauthausen, Auschwitz, Treblinka, Chelmno, Drancy. Count the tiny black tiles on the floor and ask yourself, what chance did those millions have to exercise their honor? What would they not give to . . ."

He seemed momentarily to stumble and, looking up, Berman was surprised by the sudden pallor of his face. He was round the desk in an instant and helping him back into his seat, fearful that, for all the elements of theatricality in the old man's performance, the sheer strain of such a tour de force might induce another and possibly fatal heart attack.

"I will do as you ask," said Berman soberly, "until midday."

★

It was a very different Ya'acov Rosenstein who sat in the Prime Minister's office half an hour later—a model of self-control; jaunty even.

"I'm glad you dropped by, Ya'acov," said Shavit, getting up from behind Avraham Rubinger's stylish modern desk and, in deference to the Foreign Minister's leg, beckoning him towards the *arc* of easy chairs at the other end of the room. "It gives me a chance to thank you."

"Thank me?"

"This morning . . . for—how shall I put it?—not making matters more difficult than they already were."

Rosenstein gave a dismissive flick of the wrist.

"It was, I think," continued Shavit, proffering a cigarette

from the circular coffee table, "an embarrassing incident for us all, but for you, I imagine, more than most. I do feel that Gideon allows his heart to rule his head at times."

"Yes, not a political virtue, I think," observed Rosenstein, leaving Shavit to wonder how far the irony was intended.

"Anyway," Shavit resumed, "following our discussions in the Cabinet this morning, I have instructed a discreet surveillance to be maintained on the Apostolic Delegation to ensure, on the one hand, that the bones aren't smuggled out and, on the other, that those inside aren't panicked into destroying them. The matter is, however, rather complicated by this." He handed a flimsy sheet of paper across the table. "It came in only an hour ago. The police had no reason to appreciate its relevance."

The Foreign Minister read the brief account of the discovery of Archbishop Ramone's body in the grounds of the Garden Tomb and the police verdict of prima-facie suicide.

"Certainly backs up the theory that he was the carrier pigeon," remarked Shavit. "But what a price to pay for failure! I thought that was the sort of thing that went on in Hitler's bunker, not the Vatican. It's one of the matters we'll have to talk about at midday. That and Gideon's replacement."

The Foreign Minister feigned surprise.

"As far as I know, Gideon will be there himself. That's what he told me when I left him half an hour ago."

"But the man has resigned."

"Not officially, as far as I know."

"Well, if walking out in the middle of a Cabinet meeting and describing the Acting Prime Minister as 'beneath contempt' isn't resigning, I'd like to know what is."

Rosenstein smiled genially.

"Oh, that. You said yourself Gideon's heart at times gets the better of his head."

Shavit's manner underwent a sudden change as he started to suspect what lay beneath the old man's show of nonchalance. There was a crisp formality in his voice as he said:

"Ya'acov, I appreciate that Gideon is something of a political protégé of yours and that you personally have a claim to seniority in the Cabinet, but I trust you are not seriously suggesting that he should stay on as Defense Minister after last night's catalogue of mishaps, for want of a better word. It's inconceivable, quite inconceivable."

Rosenstein grunted. "Reuven, it was you who said in Cabinet that you didn't think any of us would have acted any differently in Gideon's position."

There was now no doubt in Shavit's mind why the Foreign Minister had come to see him. Rosenstein's reputation as a cunning old fox was justly deserved and Shavit—never one to underestimate an adversary—switched swiftly to the offensive.

"Ya'acov, I think I have a right to know, as Acting Prime Minister, what you will be proposing in Cabinet when we meet in an hour's time."

"Me? I'm proposing nothing," responded Rosenstein blandly. "Any proposing will be done by someone else, but I trust it will be to the effect that Gideon remain as Defense Minister and, in that capacity, in full operational control of our efforts to recover the bones."

Shavit's expression of disbelief gave way to derision.

"You're mad if you think that!"

"Then you're prepared to risk the alternative?"

"Are you threatening me, Ya'acov?"

"I'd call it blackmail, if you're asking."

Any pretense of bonhomie had now evaporated.

"Explain," said Shavit with a lift of the upper lip.

Rosenstein pushed himself into a more upright position and, taking his time, replied.

"The trick you played on Gideon this morning was one of the dirtiest I've seen in thirty years in and out of Cabinet— and that's saying something. What made it worse was that you resorted to it not to do another man down—which in politics passes for fair game—but to save your own despicable hide.

"Despite what you say, I don't believe in protégés—neither Gideon nor anyone else. I regard the practice as one of the many evils of our political system which threaten to drag us back to the ghetto politics of the centuries before we recovered our self-government. But I do believe in codes of conduct, if only because that is the only way the best and the most able will get to the top without dissipating their talents in scheming and infighting on the way up. In this respect, I do not hold with the philosophy of the survival of the fittest; it may work in the jungle, but in politics it merely creates a jungle. In an effort to keep that jungle back, I will do everything in my power to see that you don't get away with what happened this morning—even if it means bringing the matter to the attention of Avram."

Shavit relaxed.

"You may be a friend of Avram's, Ya'acov, but Avram has never gone in for confidants; it would be your word against the majority of the Cabinet's."

"No, Reuven," shot back Rosenstein, "it would be *your* word. Your recorded word, to be exact."

For a moment Shavit didn't react. Then a loud, contemptuous laugh escaped his throat as he threw back his perfectly groomed head.

"You're bluffing, Ya'acov. Nobody gets into the Cabinet Room without being both searched and electronically scanned. You should know that better than anyone after your 'thirty years in and out of Cabinet.' "

Rosenstein gave a smile of seraphic innocence and tapped his chest.

"Ah, blessed are the pacemakers, Reuven! You forget, I have special dispensation when it comes to going through those scanning systems—airports, shops, hotels, and, yes, even the Cabinet Room. Doctor's orders. A manual frisking, as the expression so indelicately goes, is all I get. Concealing one of those little Japanese tape recorders about my person— clipped inside the caliper of my injured leg, if you want the technical details—presents not the slightest problem."

The color drained from Shavit's face but his bravado was undiminished.

"It's an ingenious story, Ya'acov—I give you that much— but I don't buy it. Your days as an espionage agent finished with the disbanding of the Palmach, and anyway, you are betrayed by your own words: A man who talks about 'codes of conduct' with such moral enthusiasm doesn't conceal tape recorders beneath the Cabinet table. Apart from that, how would you have known in advance that the meeting you imply you recorded was going to have such significance later?"

"I didn't," answered Rosenstein, "but for the last eighteen months I've been recording *every* Cabinet meeting purely, and until now solely, for the benefit of my diary. Nothing more than an aide-mémoire, you understand. If, come the evening, I can't recall the precise wording of a motion or who said what, then I can just spin through and find it."

"A regular Richard Nixon in fact," sneered Shavit.

"Not really. There's no rack of tapes or transcripts secretly stored away, since I use the same couple of tapes all the time, recording new material over the old. I usually only have two, or at most three, Cabinet meetings on tape at any time. That way my conscience is clear—and still squares with all I said about codes of conduct. The diaries won't be published now till many years after my death and so anyone who objects will always be able to claim they were the muddled recollections of an old cripple already in his dotage. My concern is only that I should be sure of their accuracy and regrettably in the last eighteen months that has required some electronic assistance."

Shavit was silent, thinking, and for the first time visibly shaken. That the Foreign Minister kept a diary—had done since the day he entered the Knesset—was well known; a volume of his memoirs covering the period of Eshkol's premiership had already been published. That it was technically possible to record the Cabinet meetings he also had no doubt, nor, given Rosenstein's explanations, that it was also possible for him to evade detection. He remembered now all those occasions during Cabinet when the old man had clasped his knee to straighten his leg; he even fancied he could remember the tips of the fingers actually curling behind the knee.

The Foreign Minister sensed success.

"Are you calling me?" he asked, adopting the cardplayer's terminology.

Shavit regarded the fingers resting casually on the knee.

"What's the price of your silence?"

"Don't you mean *your* silence?" Rosenstein smiled.

The two cardinals sat at a table in front of the fashionable bars on the east side of the Piazza Navona, their scarlet sashes and skullcaps more in keeping with the Bernini fountains and neoclassical façade of Saint Agnes in Agony opposite than with the swarms of jeans-clad, pot-smoking dropouts all around.

Neither was moved to speak. As soon as the Curia Segreta had concluded its hastily convened morning session, they had been of one mind: to get as far away from the Vatican's oppressive sanctity as possible, preferably across the river where the all too conspicuous manifestations of sin at least attested to life and where, more practically, the constant hubbub guaranteed a confidentiality lacking in the pilgrim-and-prelate-packed bars around Saint Peter's.

Secretary of State Pellegrini had attempted to put a good face on matters, but there had been no disguising the fact that the operation had been a failure with potentially disastrous implications for the Church—the bones were still in Israel; a Roman Catholic archbishop had publicly damned his soul to perdition by an act of suicide; and the Israelis would have to be both blind and stupid not to link the activities of the Church with the death of at least three of their servicemen. As one of Their Eminences had asked—not entirely facetiously —How long before the headline, *Papal hit-squad downs Israeli chopper* appeared on the front page of every newspaper?

The midday cannon boomed out from the Janiculum Hill. It was time to take stock.

The stouter of the pair, whose round face and oversized ears made his zucchetto look more like a school cap, was the first to break the silence.

"*Tu pensi quello che penso io?*" he asked in his lyrical Venetian accent. "Are you thinking what I'm thinking?"

The other sighed.

"*Sí, ma è una cosa difficile—tanto difficile!*"

"But what is the alternative?" retorted the Venetian. "You saw Pellegrini this morning. Vatican Secretary of State? He couldn't organize a work roster in a monastery! My brother, the Curia Segreta is finished. We must face the reality that it can neither salvage the situation, nor even itself now."

He allowed the words to sink in and waited for his Florentine brother to respond before committing himself irrevocably. Not that he didn't trust him, but the other had a timorous nature, and lifelong experience inside the Church had taught the Venetian never to underestimate the frailty of his fellow men. With growing impatience he watched the Florentine twist the ring on his finger, until he was eventually obliged to prod him into a response.

"*Allora?*"

Staring at the fountains' gushing waters, the Florentine answered: "What about Sirelli? Shouldn't we bring him in on it? He's been the most insistent advocate of telling the Holy Father from the beginning."

"*Quello scemo!*" spluttered the Venetian. "That idiot! Never.

If he's felt so strongly about it all this time, why do you think he hasn't done it? Why do you think he didn't mention it this morning, when he's brought it up at every other meeting?"

"Perhaps he's been waiting for more support," shrugged the Florentine.

"Rubbish! The truth is that the old fool hates the Holy Father more than anyone—and with good reason for the way he has reduced the Holy Office to the level of a consumer council! I tell you, neither Sirelli's pride nor his age will permit him now to bend the knee and beg forgiveness. I can think of only one thing that might change his mind, and that is if he suspected that somebody else was going to get in first."

"So we go alone . . ."

"*D'accordo.*"

"And *our* motives. What are our motives in this?"

"How about salvation?" responded the Venetian with what in anyone other than a cardinal of the faith might have been mistaken for cynicism.

★

The first things Bob Spender saw on entering the Oval Office were the soles of the President's three-hundred-dollar Johnson and Murphy's propped up on the desk.

"So you blew it, Spender," said the voice from behind them.

"I'm sorry if that's the way it seems, Mr. President, but . . ."

"You blew it, Bob. No Monday morning quarterbacking. What I want to know is what in Christ's name you thought you were doing entrusting the most vital part of the operation to a suicidal priest! Had you taken leave of your senses?"

The Director of Central Intelligence gave a nervous, apologetic cough. There was an explanation and a damned good one, if McCrae was prepared to listen. But that was McCrae's game—give orders but never involve yourself in their execution. It was called delegating responsibility, although *avoiding* it was more accurate.

He looked to Secretary Romford standing behind the President. He had known about the Vatican's involvement and had even thought it a pretty sharp move. But Romford's only response was to make a face that said, "You know how he is; there's nothing *I* can say."

"Heads are going to roll on this one," declared McCrae.

"They will, Mr. President," replied Spender with a spontaneity that surprised McCrae as much as Spender himself, to the extent that the President found himself saying "See to it then," when his original intention had been to roll a head much closer to hand. Thinking about it later, he would ascribe his change of mind to an involuntary feeling of admiration for a man whose instinct for self-preservation was as quick as his own.

But Spender wasn't going to escape without at least one claw mark across his flabby face.

"So how do you intend to get us out of this mess?" asked McCrae.

Buoyed by his unexpected reprieve, Spender recovered some of his old bluster.

"Well, we've achieved our primary objective, Mr. President—we've deprived the Israelis of their bargaining chip. I wouldn't pretend that the present situation is as we would wish it, but the net effect is the same as if we'd managed to get the bones across the border into . . ."

McCrae shot him down before he could finish.

"The 'net effect,' Spender, is that you and your agency have delivered us a fucking time bomb! Are you going to guarantee me that the Israelis won't find that package? Can you even tell me for how long it's likely to remain undiscovered? The net effect of your bungling is that, until those bones are gotten out, I'm going to be sitting across the negotiating table from Rubinger and never know whether the pistol he's pointing at my balls is loaded or empty!"

Secretary Romford ventured to add a thought of his own.

"Joe, I know we considered and rejected it once before, but the destruction option could now be relevant. If we could just get somebody to the bones, it would certainly be safer and easier."

McCrae swung his feet off the desk.

"Are you seriously telling me, Carl, that the most technically advanced nation in the world—to say nothing of the wealthiest and most powerful—is incapable of lifting a sackful of old bones without getting caught? Are you telling me we have to resort to a second-best, fail-safe option because we're too scared or too incompetent to see through the original plan to its conclusion? Well, Carl, that was not the nation that elected me President, and I'm damned if I'm going to let that SOB Rubinger think it is. When I sit opposite him at ten o'clock Monday morning, I am going to have those bones sitting right there on the table beside me." He brought his hand down hard on the desk and turned again to Spender. "And if anybody here is thinking of the safe, easy option, they can forget it. We said we'd get those bones out, and get them out we will." He glanced at the grandfather clock to the right of the fireplace. Seven hours behind Israeli time, the small painted sun had barely emerged from its nightly journey through the cogs and ratchets. "And by my calculation you've got not much more than forty-eight hours to do it in."

Back in his Langley office, Spender surveyed the mess with the satisfying irritation of a man eager to find justification for an unpleasant act he had been called upon to perform. Every surface was covered with folders, sheets of paper, maps, overflowing ashtrays, and polystyrene cups of half-consumed, curdled coffee. The prime creator of this chaos was not to be seen, but a scribbled note taped to Spender's telephone indicated that he was in the canteen and could be beeped if needed.

Spender blew the cigarette ash from his desk and flicked the toggle on the intercom.

"Mr. Director?" cooed a voice from the outer office.

"Mary, will you beep Mr. Harding in the canteen, and instruct Services in the meantime to remove his desk."

★

Berman took his seat at the Cabinet table, aware of being the center of attention even though nobody was looking at him. At the far end Shavit sat hunched forward, cutting a smaller figure against the high back of the prime ministerial chair than on previous occasions.

"Gentlemen," Shavit began softly, "we have learned some important lessons from the events of the last twenty-four hours. There will be time enough for inquests later, but in the meantime we must avoid the recriminatory atmosphere that characterized this morning's meeting. The Defense Minister's emotional response was perhaps understandable in the light of his disappointments, but I trust it will not deflect him from seeing the operation through to a successful conclusion."

He looked to Berman for a confirmation, as did everyone else, baffled by the Acting Prime Minister's extraordinary about-face.

Berman stared at the cardboard folder before him, which he alone knew contained his letter of resignation. For all his confidence in Rosenstein's ability to turn black into white, he was still surprised.

But not unprepared.

"If it is the will of Cabinet, then I agree—subject of course to the usual expression of confidence."

Shavit shot a look at Rosenstein. A full-blown vote of confidence hadn't been part of the deal; at least it hadn't been specified. But the Foreign Minister's raised eyebrows suggested there had been no collusion, and if this was the price of satisfying Berman's pride, thought Shavit, then it was a small enough price to pay.

With a hint of impatience, the acting Prime Minister spelled out the wording of the motion "that Cabinet has full confidence in the ability of the Minister of Defense and in his command—continued command—of Operation Ezekiel," and put it to the vote.

Although suspecting the puppeteer of a brainstorm, the marionettes nevertheless obliged with a united show of hands.

"As recorded in the minutes," added Berman, looking to the stenographer.

Shavit turned again to Rosenstein. Whether by accident or design, the Foreign Minister's hand was resting lightly on his knee.

"As recorded in the minutes," he repeated tersely.

Wasting no time, Shavit then moved on to the details of the operation. After mentioning the guard he had already posted on the Apostolic Delegation and the report of Archbishop Ramone's suicide, he was about to launch into the possible steps that could be taken next.

"I don't think this is a matter for Cabinet debate."

The voice was Berman's. The air crackling with anticipation, he continued: "If we are talking about the important lessons learned from the events of the last twenty-four hours, surely the most important is the need for the planning of the operation to be in the hands of one person. No committee; no consensus. It is the function of Cabinet to define the end, not to determine the means. That end—the retrieval of the bones— has already been defined."

"What are you suggesting?" asked Shavit.

"That I assume control of the operation and every phase of its planning from this moment. Any advice that any Cabinet member wishes to offer will be welcome, but this time the final word will be mine. Cabinet has already voted and unanimously expressed its . . ." He referred to the scribbled notes on his pad, "full confidence in the ability of the Minister of Defense and in his continued command of Operation Ezekiel. I ask no more."

Shavit glared at Berman across the table but was otherwise lost for a reply. He had been outmaneuvered, but the injury was worse for having been publicly inflicted and, whether imagination or not, he sensed the balance of respect among his Cabinet colleagues tipping against him with their recognition of a superior tactician. It was the Minister of the Interior— until now, one of his most dependable supporters—who confirmed it.

"I have to say that I have some sympathy for the Defense Minister's point," he ventured, to Berman's amazement in view of their previous exchanges. "I think perhaps we have all been too eager to tell the Minister how to do his job."

The tide had turned and Shavit saw the futility of trying to stem it. To test his colleagues' loyalty by another vote would be disastrous if it went against him, and with the Cabinet already confused about his attitude to Berman there was no guaranteeing he could engineer another 180 degree turn. Outflanked, his only course of action was a tactical withdrawal.

"I am inclined to agree," he conceded, but adding in an attempt to salvage something from the wreckage. "Responsibility for the success of Operation Ezekiel will from now on rest entirely with the Ministry of Defense."

"No longer Operation Ezekiel," responded Berman. "As of this moment, it will be known as Operation Isaac."

"We'll make a politician of you yet!" joshed Rosenstein on their way out to the cars. "And I'm glad to see my talk had some effect."

"It was as much what you tactfully left unsaid as what you said," replied Berman.

"You mean Yossi?"

Rosenstein didn't wait for an answer. He could see he had hit the mark.

"What are you doing about lunch?" he asked.

Berman looked at his watch.

"A sandwich at my desk—if Eli Hausner hasn't eaten them all by now."

"That sounds like Eli," chuckled Rosenstein. "What was his excuse for not taking you out to lunch? That the head of the Mossad can't be seen in public talking to a government minister? That's his usual one."

They were already at the entrance, the official cars lined up outside to take the Cabinet members back to their respective departments.

"Before you go, just satisfy my curiosity, will you, Gideon?" said Rosenstein. "Why 'Operation Issac'? Was that too because of Yossi—the father called on to sacrifice the son?"

"Half-right—but only half," replied Berman cryptically, adding, "I'm not the only father who's lost his son. Anyway, on the subject of curiosity, how did you turn Shavit?"

The old man laughed.

"That's much easier to answer: It was a poker player against a chess player, and fortunately the poker player was calling the game." He was suddenly serious. "But don't underrate the man, Gideon. He may have retired injured, but he'll be back."

The reek of cheap tobacco in the corridor told Berman that the head of the Mossad Bitachon Leumi—the Institute for State Security, Israel's foreign intelligence agency, equivalent to the United States' CIA and Britain's MI6—had already arrived.

Cigarette in hand, Eli Hausner was scrutinizing Berman's framed color photograph of the late President Sadat's aircraft being escorted back to Egypt from Israel by four Kfir jets. He had also commandeered at least one of the Defense Minister's sandwiches, thoughtfully placed under plastic wrap by his secretary before going off to lunch. Counting the pile of butts in the ashtray, Berman calculated the intelligence chief had been waiting at least half an hour. Hausner was the only man he knew who could eat and smoke simultaneously.

"Sorry to have kept you waiting, Eli. You know how it is in Cabinet."

"It's a long time since I was asked to attend," remarked Hausner, reminding Berman of how little love was lost between the intelligence services and the present Government.

The differences went back fifteen years—to the report of the Agranat Commission into the reasons for what was popularly known as the *Mechdal*, the lack of preparation and foresight before and during the 1973 Yom Kippur War. Broadly speaking, the commission had absolved the politicians and put the blame on the intelligence bodies—especially military intelligence—for failing to appreciate that what looked like the Arabs' annual maneuvers were in fact the initial stages of a joint Egyptian-Syrian offensive.

And the man who was said to have most determined the balance of the final judgement—the man who, as some saw it, made the intelligence services the scapegoat—was commission member, now Prime Minister, Avraham Rubinger. Although in terms of prestige and authority Israel's other secret services—the Mossad and Shin Beth—had actually benefited from military intelligence's disgrace, there were those in the intelligence community who had neither forgiven Rubinger, nor forgotten. It was nonetheless a tribute to the Prime Minister's judgement that, despite their strained relations, he had never attempted to oust Hausner from his job, recognizing the irascible chain-smoker as Israel's most brilliant intelligence chief since the legendary Isser Harel.

To look at, he could be easily mistaken for a barman or taxi driver. Small-boned and birdlike, with a turkey neck and discolored teeth, he held himself in a perpetual stoop which, in his fifties, was already developing into a hump, while among his nonphysical attributes was a reputation for tightness that extended beyond national security into matters of personal finance.

But the key to the man was his eyes—eyes which sparkled like reflected sunlight at the bottom of a well.

Berman poured himself a coffee from the Cona machine in the corner and, his back to Hausner, said:

"This Nahalat Shim'on business . . . I need your help, Eli."

Hausner gave a cynical grunt. Of the present Cabinet, Berman was the only one with whom he had anything approaching a personal relationship—partly because they were both ex-generals (insofar as Israel's generals are ever "ex") and partly because Berman's political career postdated Yom Kippur. "The best of a bad bunch" was how the Mossad chief put it in his characteristically backhanded way.

"I thought the Cabinet had it all wrapped up," he responded, betraying his hurt at the extent to which the intelligence services had been kept out of the matter.

"*Screwed* up," said Berman, taking his seat. "They saw the operation as primarily a military exercise and largely ignored the intelligence aspects—with the result that we opted for the wrong tactics and were then stuck with them when we lost the initiative. I assume you know what happened."

Hausner busied himself with lighting another cigarette. He was in a potentially embarrassing situation. In his capacity both as head of the Mossad and as Chairman of the Intelligence (coordinating) Committee, he was personally answerable only to the Prime Minister—at least to the Prime Minister's Office. Having been snubbed by the Prime Minister, the Acting Prime Minister, and the Prime Minister's Office, however, he felt few reservations about talking to Berman. Besides, it was a source of some pleasure that he actually knew more about the operation and the reasons for its failure than the whole of the Cabinet put together, having regarded it as his business to know even if nobody else seemed to.

"I know you lost the bones but, more by luck than logic, then stopped them getting out of the country," he answered. "I'm even pretty sure I know *why* you lost them—despite the 'failproof' six-sites plan."

Berman's eyes widened.

"Go on."

"It could only have been one of two things—either the Americans have developed a surveillance satellite that is capable of tracking an object moving across the face of the earth at a hundred miles an hour, which I frankly doubt; or somewhere in that container-load of equipment they brought with them there was a signal generator which, unless you had taken a month to strip it down to the last nut, you had not a hope of finding. From what I hear, the examination that was carried out was on the same level as a security check at Lod Airport." He drew noisily on the cigarette. "I trust your plan for getting the bones back is better . . ."

"With your help it might be," responded Berman. "It's a variation of what the English call 'using a sprat to catch a mackerel.' "

"I'm not a fisherman."

"Using a small fish as bait for a larger one—the larger one being the bones," expanded Berman. "But whether or not it's feasible, I can't judge without additional information—and you're my only source."

"Ask away. That's what the Government pays me for— believe it or not."

Berman summoned up the mental checklist he had been working out.

"First, the extent of our infiltration within the CIA."

Hausner sucked in his lips before replying.

"In the field, excellent; at Langley, lousy. We know pretty well the identity of every CIA operator in the Middle East. We know the setup of stations and bases, and their methods of operating.

"Where we are weak is in our penetration of the nerve-center—Langley HQ. The politicians haven't made it any easier. The agreement with the Eisenhower administration back in the fifties to end covert operations against each other has meant we've always had to tread carefully. But the real problem has been the internal setup at Langley. From the moment the CIA moved into the new headquarters back in the mid sixties they were aware of the possibly divided loyalties of their Jewish employees. They could never ban Jews." For the first time the Mossad chief smiled. "Not without losing their best brains. So, instead, they screened every Berg and Stein out of the Israeli branch and then physically moved it out of the Near East Division where it belonged and tucked it away at the other end of the building within the Counterintelligence Section. Except for the odd snippet overheard in the halls or the canteen, hard information dried up overnight."

Berman was incredulous.

"Are you telling me we have not a single agent inside Langley?"

"Oh, we have agents. It's just that they're low-level and in the wrong places—a couple of GS-12 desk officers in the Near East branch, one on the Syrian desk and the other on the Jordanian desk; a cipher clerk in the cable room; and, on a much more casual basis, about half a dozen secretaries throughout the building. Ironically, our highest placed agent was a GS-14 in the Soviet Bloc Division until he was given one of Stansfield Turner's pink slips in '77—not because he was suspected but because he was regarded as dead wood!"

"What about the present director, Spender?"

Hausner looked pained.

"Well, it hasn't been for want of trying. We got him a lady friend as a sort of Camp David treat, hoping that he might be privy to some tittle-tattle in the Oval Office, and it all seemed to be going nicely. In the last two days, though, he seems to have spent his entire time in his office—even sleeps in the place. The last tab we had on him was a call he indiscreetly made on her phone early Thursday morning, when he was called to an emergency meeting of the National Security Council. Since then, nothing. His mind seems to be on other matters."

"What about gossip, then? The snippets from the halls and canteen that you were talking about?"

"Well, it's hearsay, but it's got the ring of truth. The story is that Spender is being kicked by McCrae all around the Oval Office to produce results and, because of this, has taken personal control of the operation. The brains behind the inspection ploy appears to have been a man called Stan Harding, his special adviser on Middle Eastern affairs. But he's now out. Spender decided to make a sacrificial lamb of him in the best American tradition of laying down one's friend to save one's life. To fill his place, Spender has now turned for help to the head of the Israeli branch, a more stolid, less imaginative type called Reynolds. He's one of Langley's great survivors and certainly far less impressive than Harding, who was probably the brightest brain in the building. Left to himself, Spender has trouble dialing a phone number."

"That's something," muttered Berman, swiveling in his chair. "What about the CIA setup *here*?"

Hausner's eyes twinkled.

"Ah, very interesting. Against all normal practice elsewhere in the world, the Agency station here is attached not to the Embassy but to a consulate—the East Jerusalem Consulate. The move from Tel Aviv was made a year ago, although of course still under cover of the political section. In a way it's a compliment—the nearest recognition we're likely to get from the Americans that Jerusalem is the capital of Israel."

"Why the East Jerusalem Consulate and not the West?"

"To do with the West Bank, I suspect. Almost all their informers and agents are Arabs. Their only Jewish agents are doubles planted by us—we hope. To encourage walkins, it makes sense to set up the main station on the most fertile recruiting ground. Their only other agents are Americans working here under commercial cover—managers of airlines, travel agencies, export firms, and the like."

"And the staffing of the East Jerusalem station?"

"As far as we can tell, it's the whole of the consulate's political section—a Chief of Station, a deputy COS, five operations officers, two communications officers, and three secretaries—plus the officers under nonofficial cover I've already mentioned, support agents renting safe houses and cars, and a couple of casual informers like your friend Kesler."

Berman raised a finger.

"It's Kesler I have in mind. He's the sprat."

He pulled back a drawer in the desk and took out a sheet of paper, which he pushed towards Hausner.

"What do you imagine would be the reaction," he asked, "if in the next couple of hours Kesler were to forward this request to his case officer at the consulate?"

Hausner's brow crumpled as he read the three lines of type.

"It's not possible to predict a reaction. All I can tell you is the procedure for dealing with such a request . . . such a request could only be granted by the head office, and, if his case officer here doesn't spot the relevance, there's a good chance the Israeli branch back at Langley will. Your biggest problem is likely to be one of time. Kesler's present case officer—a man called McKenzie—is not one of the brightest. The man who recruited him back in the mid-seventies was a razor-sharp black man by name of George Livingstone, but he was moved on after his statutory three-year tour of duty. The present character handling Kesler is a laid-back Californian who, when he isn't doing the social round in Herzliya and Ramat Hasharon, is to be found on the tennis court.

You'll have to inject more urgency into the cable to get him to move on it. You know how CIA cables are graded?"

"Remind me."

"It's a matter of what is termed 'perceived urgency.' There are five categories in all—ROUTINE, PRIORITY, IMMEDIATE, CRITIC, and FLASH, in ascending order of urgency. But the route is the same: from the station code room where they are encrypted—in this case, the basement of the East Jerusalem Consulate—via a radio relay across the Atlantic, probably bounced off a satellite, and into Langley, where they are decoded on the first floor and then pushed round to the appropriate division by pneumatic tubes, finally ending up on the right desk or branch within that division. In the case of the Israeli cables of course they go from the first floor direct to the Israeli branch, because of the segregation I mentioned earlier. What varies is the time all this takes—from twenty-four hours for a ROUTINE cable to precisely seven minutes for a FLASH, about the time it takes to draft the text."

Berman took back the sheet of paper.

"What would this rate, then?"

"In its present form, I'd say PRIORITY. That's about six hours. But if you were to beef it up by stressing that flights have to be booked and Israeli Government regulations complied with, you should get it upgraded to IMMEDIATE. That's delivery within two hours." He stopped. "You seriously think you can get Kesler to go along with this—*and* trust him into the bargain?"

Berman pushed back his chair.

"That's what I'm no going to find out—and thanks for the help."

"You mean you're not interested in our agents in the Vatican?"

Berman stopped in his tracks.

"Joking, Gideon . . . just joking."

★

The Supreme Pontiff of the Universal Church, representative of Jesus Christ on Earth, turned off the television and sat, head forward, fingertips together, on one of the red damask chairs in the otherwise plain, whitewashed suite of rooms. He was alone but, as always, not alone—the occa-

sional scrape or cough reminding him of the Dutch security
guards outside the door.

Having a healthy skepticism for journalism, His Holiness
wasn't normally moved by news bulletins, but this one had
made a greater impact on him than he cared to admit.

Inevitably, it had been dominated by his visit to Holland
and the reasons behind the specially convened synod of Dutch
bishops. "The Second Reformation" was how the television
reporter had just described it. The very structure of the
Roman Catholic Church, he had opined, was under threat of
a cataclysmic collapse. Holland was first, but Germany, France,
and Britain could not be far behind, waiting only to see how
the Dutch bishops fared with their Declaration of Utrecht
before coming out on their own accounts to challenge the
authority of the Vatican.

The reporter had gone on, almost gleefully, to point up the
many historical parallels and ironies of the present situation.
The last non-Italian pope, he reminded his audience, had
been a Dutchman—Adrian VI, former bishop of Utrecht,
elected in 1522—and it had fallen to him to try to bring the
Church to terms with Martin Luther's Reformation. So disastrous had been his attempt, effectively alienating still more of
the faithful, that the memory of his twenty-month reign had
been enough to ensure that it would be another four-and-a-
half centuries before the election of the next non-Italian
pope.

The world waited, concluded the reporter with sudden
solemnity, to see whether "the Dutch Curse" would repeat
itself—whether the Holy Father would compromise his stand
on contraception, married priests, internal democracy, and a
modern catechism, or would force the churches of northern
Europe once again into schism.

There was a second tentative rap before the Holy Father
was aware of someone at the door. He was surprised and
irritated. It was still what was euphemistically called "contemplation hour."

"Yes!" he bawled, hoping that his use of English would
intimidate any Vatican official who dared to disturb him with
a petty bureaucratic enquiry that could wait till the afternoon
session.

"*Siamo noi, Santità,*" came the reply. "It is us, Holiness."

The sight of the pair of cardinals shuffling towards him,

half-crouching like guilty children, would have been comic if it hadn't been so unexpected. They collapsed on the floor before him and, simultaneously attempting to kiss the ring on his right hand, succeeded only in kissing each other.

It was the large-eared Venetian who did the talking.

"Holy Father, we most earnestly seek Your Holiness's forgiveness. We have sinned most grievously."

" . . . most grievously," echoed the Florentine.

The Holy Father indicated a couple of chairs against the wall.

"*Si accomodatevi*—sit down. It must be grievous indeed for you to come all this way to report it—and *both* of you!"

"It is, Holy Father, it is. It concerns the activities of the Curia Segreta."

The Holy Father braced himself. Unlike his predecessors, he had never made any attempt to disband the secret council. His considerable insight into human nature told him that, whatever he did, it would only carry on under another name and that, apart from sacking every Italian cardinal in the Curia, there was nothing a non-Italian pope could do anyway. By far the best course, he reasoned, was to keep Their Curial Eminences occupied with so much administrative work that they would have no time for intrigue and would leave him free to pursue his own chosen role of international pastor. Accordingly, he had deemed it sufficient to make clear that, while playing at secret societies was one thing, undermining the ultimate authority of the successor of Peter was quite another. If necessary, he declared, he would not hesitate to call a General Synod of the Church's three thousand bishops in order to expose the secret council, trusting to the bishops to denounce it publicly.

But, as he now listened to the unfolding story of the bones and the Curia Segreta's disastrous liaison with the Americans and Palestinians, the enormity of his miscalculation was all too clear. An icy hand, reaching up from the bowels, snatched at his palpitating heart.

It was the hand of recollection.

"*Acceptasne electionem de te canonice factam in Summum Pontificem?*"

With the words still ringing in his ears on that day of his election many years earlier, he had accompanied his predecessor's—now his—secretary on an inspection tour of the

papal apartment in the Apostolic Palace. In the knowledge
that this would be his only home until the day he died, and
perhaps for him too the prison that it had become for so many
of those before him, he had followed the zealous monsignor
through the study, bedroom, private chapel, and dining room,
ending up on the trellised roof garden with its fountains and
shrubs where poor Pope Paul VI, that "walking question
mark," had paced out his troubled days fretting over the
responsibilities heaped on his frail frame. Back in the study,
the monsignor had taken his leave but, before going, had
indicated on the desk a discolored white envelope sealed with
the imprint of his former master. When asked what it contained, he had replied simply:

"Fatima."

His feelings, he recalled, had been a mixture of skepticism
and curiosity. The so-called Prophecy of Fatima had been a
source of controversy—even embarrassment—since 1917, when
three young shepherds, none of them over ten years old, in
the tiny Portuguese village of Fatima had claimed to have
seen the Blessed Virgin Mary on six separate occasions. The
apparition, seated on a lowland oak, had allegedly delivered
three prophecies. The first two—that the First World War
would end, and would be followed in 1939 by a Second—had
been borne out. But the third had been judged too alarming
to be published. Instead, years later, the only surviving member of the shepherd trio had vouchsafed it in writing, sealed
in an envelope, first to the Bishop of Leiria and, subsequently, to the Pope himself. Pius XII was said to have
fainted on reading it, and his successor, John XXIII, had
ordered its suppression in perpetuity.

In the meantime, speculation had run wild. Some claimed
that it foretold the reconversion of Russia; others that the
Devil would insinuate himself into the highest ranks of the
Church to bring about its destruction; and still others that a
Third World War would be unleashed in the second half of
the twentieth century, bringing about the extermination of
the human race.

The truth, the Holy Father now recalled, had been rather
more Delphic.

Before opening the envelope, he had waited till the early
hours of the morning when every light in the Apostolic Palace
had been extinguished and only the occasional squeal of a car

tire on the other side of the Ponte Sant'Angelo had disturbed
the night air. Then, by the light of a single candle guttering
across the white marble walls of the private chapel, he had
unfolded the slip of paper.

The words were easily remembered:

> As the Church of Jesus Christ is built on the body
> of Christ Crucified, so shall it be destroyed.

But not till now had he appreciated their significance.

"Fools!" he declared when the Venetian had finished. "Why
did you not destroy the bones when you had the chance?"

"At that p-point, Holy Father," stammered the Florentine,
"there was no guaranteeing that they were the right ones.
Even after the inspection, the Americans feared the Israelis
might switch them. So they had to be gotten out to check
that they were genuine."

The Holy Father was suddenly out of his chair.

"Genuine! How can they be genuine when we are told that
on the third day He rose again? Blasphemer, do you not
recognize the work of the Devil in this?"

"I only meant . . ." started the Florentine but was cut
short by the Venetian.

"We have indeed grievously sinned, Holy Father," he said,
dropping again to his knees. "We crave your forgiveness."

"Such forgiveness is not in my power," was the curt reply.
"That must come from a higher authority. Of far more immediate concern is what can now be done to prevent further
damage. You say we know where these bones are hidden?"

"We do, Holy Father," responded the Venetian with sup-
portive hen pecks from the Florentine. "Cardinal Pellegrini's
secretary, Monsignor Giovanni, took the details from the
Arab who hid them. The Americans are very keen to make
another attempt to get the bones out."

"And no doubt want us to tell them where they are,"
added the Holy Father.

"Exactly—but the Curia Segreta has taken no decision on
the request."

"Nor will they!" snapped the Holy Father, and, fixing the
two with a look that threatened instant excommunication,

continued: "From now on, you will take your orders from me—*only* me. It is my intention to fly back to Rome immediately, but you will contact Cardinal DeWohl in New York. You will make it clear to him that you are acting on my personal orders and will instruct him to tell the American President that we will give his people the details of the bones' present location on two conditions only—first, that any further attempt to get them out of Israel is coupled with the means of their instant and complete destruction if the plans go wrong a second time, and secondly, assuming the operation to be a success, that the bones are handed over to the Vatican for their eventual, verifiable destruction. *È chiaro?*"

Three hours later, as the sun dropped behind the cupola of St. Peter's, the Swiss Guard on duty at Saint Anna's Gate—the Vatican's nearest equivalent to a trade entrance—was amazed to see the unmistakable black Mercedes, registration number SCV 1, sweep past him at such speed that he didn't even have time to drop to one knee as required by Vatican protocol.

Within minutes the car's passenger, followed by his body-guard and private secretary, was striding across the austere courtyard of San Damaso to the elevator on the ground floor of the Apostolic Palace. Sucked noiselessly up to the third floor, the white-robed figure turned right, and then left in the direction of the offices of the Secretariat of State.

A pair of black-cassocked prelates chatting in the entrance hall sprang apart like reverse-pole magnets at the sight of the swinging pectoral cross and gawked as the double doors at the far end of the corridor yielded before the sudden, violent, two-handed, pressure.

It was a vignette neither of them would ever forget—the papal silhouette in the doorway, arms fully extended like Samson between the pillars of the Philistine temple, and beyond, the pinched face of the Secretary of State, pale even against the beige silk wall covering. They heard but one word before the doors swung to—a word seldom used in the Apostolic Palace, and never before by a Pope addressing his Secretary of State:

"Judas!"

★

It was an unlikely meeting place for two men so recently bereaved, but given the essential requirements of quiet and privacy and the fact that it was right next to the Hadassah Hospital where Kesler's wife was being treated, the British War Cemetery was in every other respect ideal. The only people who ever came here—increasingly few as time went on—were relations of the several hundred British soldiers killed overthrowing Turkish rule in the Holy Land during the 1914–18 War who had found their perpetual resting place in this "free gift of the people of Palestine."

The official car parked out of sight, Berman walked along the ranks of tombstones, noting ages and inscriptions and uncomfortably aware of inspecting the dead as on countless occasions he had the living. Mostly in their early twenties, they were tragically young, the pathos of their sacrifice heightened by the dogged Christian optimism of the epitaphs— *Until the day breaks*, *For ever with the Lord*, *He is not dead but sleepeth*.

He reached an incongruous Japanese-style gazebo on the far side and sat down in the barred shade of its concrete crossbeams, disturbing the siesta of a small green lizard which scuttled across the parapet and disappeared into a crack. He looked beyond the beds of mauve rosemary to the city laid out below, its buildings skeletal white in the shimmering heat haze. Jerusalem—*Ir Hashalom*, city of peace!—on all sides surrounded by the graves of those who had fought to possess it.

Two figures were walking slowly up the incline towards him.

He had never met Kesler face to face, although the American had no doubt been at press conferences he had given. Even at a distance, though, he appeared exhausted by his recent experience—a tall, stooping figure whose arms hung loosely by his sides in contrast to Meir's animated gesticulations. It was hard not to feel sympathy for the foolish American, but in Berman's mind sympathy was coupled with a hard professional realization that, one way or another, Kesler had to be persuaded, begged, or bullied into doing what was required.

Meir evidently hadn't told him who he was going to meet.

"You know the Minister of Defense, of course," he said casually.

The American's reddened eyes registered surprise. His hand was several seconds in meeting Berman's.

"Of course," he responded, taking in the familiar scarred face and the bizarre ambience of their rendezvous.

Berman nodded to Meir and waited till his assistant was on his way back to the car before saying:

"Sit down, Mr. Kesler. First, tell me the latest news of your wife."

"As well as can be expected," answered the American, "which is the doctors' way of saying not good. She's still on the critical list. They say the next twenty-four hours will be decisive."

"I'm sorry," said Berman, regretting the platitude. He felt awkward sitting alongside the man and suggested that they walk along the row of pines that separated the cemetery from the hospital grounds, tactfully screening the dead from the dying.

"Kesler," he began, all too aware how ill-equipped he was with the sort of persuasive subtlety that was now needed, "I have to ask you to do something which in normal circumstances I would be reluctant to ask of anybody, let alone somebody who has gone through what you have." He hesitated, undecided on the advisability of what he was going to say next. "And I must tell you—I *owe* it to you, although you can regard it as a measure of my desperation as much as my honesty—that I will use every means of coercion in my power to ensure your compliance, including, if I have to, the threat of your public trial as an agent of the CIA."

When there was no reaction from the American, he added simply:

"It concerns your son."

"My son is dead."

"But he may yet serve the country of his birth more than any living Israeli. I want you to put in a request to your CIA case officer at the consulate here to have his remains shipped to the United States for burial. You are to stress the urgency of a quick reply, giving as a reason the Israeli Government requirement that bodies have normally to be buried within forty-eight hours of death, and the fact that you have already been granted a maximum extension until 21:00 hours tomorrow night when there is a TWA flight from Lod to New York. Your case officer shouldn't need telling that TWA won't accept your booking without specific clearance from the U.S. Embassy in Tel Aviv; but, just in case, spell it out." He reached into his pocket. "Here is the letter from the Jerusalem Public Health Department agreeing to the extension. You will have to make the necessary reservation with TWA cargo division in person, and at the same time book yourself a seat on the same flight."

The American made no effort to take the letter.

"You don't know what you're asking, General," he said.

"I have an idea."

"Do you—really?"

Berman sensed that his strategy of blunt talking in the hope that it would appeal to the journalist in the American had backfired. It had antagonized him. Staring straight ahead, he forced himself to say:

"Perhaps not."

They were more than halfway along the row of pines and the American had lapsed into silence. Something told Berman that he had to be brought round before they reached the end of the path. By the time they had turned to come back, it would be too late; the momentum would be lost. The conversation *had* to be kept going.

"You already know enough about the goings-on at Nahalat Shim'on to make your own guess why we need your help. Having lost the bones but prevented them being taken out of the country, we have to persuade your colleagues back at Langley that there is still a way they can be smuggled out. If they take the bait, they will then, via you, deliver them straight into our hands before you get on the plane. That's the thinking, but only with your cooperation can it be put into operation."

"And my wife—what about my wife, General?"

"If the doctors are right and the next twenty-four hours are decisive, you will know her chances of recovery before you leave her bedside. Your departure time is thirty hours from now, but you'll in fact be away no more than a couple of hours—four hours at most."

"Don't you think my case officer would find my request a strange one—suspicious even?"

"No reason why he should. Your first reaction to the explosion was that it had to be *our* work. Continue to take that line and it makes sense that you should want your son buried anywhere other than the land of his murderers. Your own native land would seem a logical alternative."

They were near the end of the path, with no more than twenty paces to go, and still it was in the balance. There were no more questions and Berman had the feeling it was now a matter more of the heart than the mind. Putting the letter back in his pocket, he made a preemptive bid.

"Look, Kesler, by rights I should give you time to think about this, but I don't have time. To an extent, though, I can put myself in your shoes and, however presumptuously, perhaps do some of your thinking for you. You're an American but you're married to a Jew, and that makes your son a Jew. So, if we're talking about family allegiances, there should be no doubt where *they* lie. Your own national allegiances—to the country of your birth and upbringing—are, I concede, less clear-cut. Only you can say how much that country deserves your loyalty; how fairly it has dealt with you in the past. All I know is that your CIA activities here have represented a betrayal of the country that has hosted you—a betrayal therefore of your wife and son—and if you want to help to redress the balance, now is your opportunity. To put it bluntly, Kesler, you owe Israel something."

He stopped, angry with himself, frustrated by his inability to find the words of smoothness and seduction necessary. In trying to be blunt, he had succeeded only in being clumsy.

"And how," asked the American, "is my now betraying *two* countries going to help Israel, General? Answer me that."

It was the one question Berman had hoped wouldn't arise. And now he had brought it on himself. What government minister in his right mind would reveal to a man who was both a journalist and a CIA informer the details of a national strategy upon which depended the country's very survival? And yet not to do so now would be to jeopardize that strategy anyway. He looked across the cemetery and made out the top of the car, Meir pacing alongside. He had no earthly reason to trust the American—and no choice but to do so.

"You've asked and I will tell you," he sighed, bringing them both to a halt, "and in telling you I am putting my career, my reputation, and the safety of my people in your hands—something I have no right to do. I ask you to remember that, Kesler."

"I will remember," replied the American, tapping a pack of

cigarettes and offering Berman one before taking one himself.
The irony of the gesture wasn't lost on either.

"It helps my cover," remarked Kesler with a sad, wry
smile.

Berman accepted the light, and began.

"The reaffirmation of our hard line during the runup to
Camp David was, as most observers suspected, a negotiating
stance. What none of them has been able to determine—
fortunately—is what we would actually regard as an acceptable settlement.

"The truth is that we would be prepared to give up three-
quarters of the West Bank in return for a genuine, durable
peace with our Arab neighbors. The old Allon Plan, under
which, you remember, we indicated our readiness to give
back the entire central mass of the area so long as we could
maintain a fortified *cordon sanitaire*, never died—although
for political reasons it has often been necessary to imply that
it has long since been buried. Indeed, under Begin's premiership, it *was* buried.

"But two things we can never agree to—the creation of a
Palestinian state on the West Bank, and the redivision of
Jerusalem. The one for reasons of security; the other for
reasons of national identity. If McCrae had his way, we'd be
his South Vietnam. Within months of being forced to sign a
worthless peace treaty obliging us to give up every inch of
the occupied territories, we would have a de facto Palestinian
state in our midst, armed by the Russians and with most of
Israel in its rocket and artillery range. We would be naked.

"Certainly McCrae *talks* about Israel's need for defensible
borders, implying support for some version of the Allon Plan.
But there's a price—our relinquishing East Jerusalem to ap-
pease the Arabs. And that, he knows, is a trade-off we could
never make. Hence the bones. They are our only guarantee
of a durable peace, an undivided Jerusalem, *and* a worthwhile treaty to ensure the continuation of both."

"What do you call 'worthwhile'?"

"Something along the lines of the NATO agreement—
something backed up by men and machinery."

"You mean U.S. troops and U.S. weapons on Israeli soil?"

"Correct. There wouldn't have to be many, but enough to
let any prospective aggressor know that in aiming at an Israeli
he might hit an American, and that in taking on Israel he

would be taking on the United States. Is that not the principle that NATO works on, and hasn't Europe enjoyed forty-four years of peace because of it? If you can have a North Atlantic Treaty Organization, why not an East Mediterranean Treaty Organization?"

"Assuming the Arabs would buy it," observed Kesler skeptically.

The Defense Minister's expression hardened.

"They would have no choice. With the disintegration of OPEC and the glut of Mexican and South American oil, they have lost their former power of veto—and they know it. They'd be furious about Jerusalem, but if it could be seen that under American pressure we had been 'forced' to give up most of 'Judea and Samaria,' their faces would be sufficiently saved and the homeland requirements of the Palestinians sufficiently met to enable them to sign a mutual recognition treaty with us."

"Which would leave the problem of the Israeli settlements on the West Bank," added Kesler.

"There," admitted Berman, "there would be problems—but no more insuperable than we encountered in the Sinai after the last Camp David agreement with Egypt. Many of the settlements—certainly all the early ones—fall within the envisaged *cordon sanitaire* and so would stay anyway. So too would the new dormitory towns east of Jerusalem, which for defensive reasons we would insist be included in the cordon. For the rest, it would be a matter of negotiation and, if it comes to it, yes, they will have to be uprooted like Yamit. It is a price we are prepared to pay for a genuine, lasting peace. And, like Yamit, it has the political advantage of enabling us to be seen making sacrifices . . ."

He paused and, looking at his watch, said:

"I have answered your question. It is time now for you to answer mine. Will you help us?"

Kesler ground the cigarette stub into the grass and, head still bowed, said: "You're making a lot of assumptions, General, and I don't just mean my cooperation. For a start, you're assuming that my compatriots back in Langley will be quick enough to see my request as a heaven-sent opportunity to get the bones out of Israel, but *slow* enough not to suspect that you might have put me up to it. That's if I have understood the plan correctly—that you are banking on their swapping Beni's remains for the bones in the hope of getting them out of the country; so that, before they ever reach the airport, you can intercept the hearse and repossess the bones?"

"Correct. I don't deny that ultimately everything will depend upon your ability to act the part. In this you will be helped by the fact that they have no reason to suspect that you might have been turned."

For a moment Kesler seemed to waver.

"There is one thing you haven't taken into account in your elaborate scheme, General."

Berman prepared himself for the worst.

"You've forgotten that my cooperation doesn't depend upon me alone." He looked towards the hospital. "*That's* where the decision lies, and there's no threat you can devise to make me go against her wishes. It is the least I owe her."

Berman followed the gaze, feeling a sudden, unexpected admiration for the man who ten minutes earlier he had dismissed as "the foolish American."

"You appreciate that it will mean revealing your CIA connections."

"I realize that."

"Then I will see you up there in fifteen minutes."

He felt like a voyeur, standing at the back of the room and listening to Kesler's confessions. His eyes were not on Kesler but the figure in the bed who, surrounded by drips and tubes, listened impassively and at the end whispered only, "I understand." As a result of instinctively raising her hands at the moment of ignition, her face alone was unscathed by blast burns, but there was something about her expression that worried Berman. It had the serenity, the resignation, that he had seen on the faces of too many other casualties.

He moved forward, taking the chair on the other side of the bed and drawing to him the dark, cool eyes. Their blueness was freakish.

"Mrs. Kesler," he said, "what your husband has told you is only part of the story. From our own sources we know that the essence of his recruitment into the Agency was blackmail. He is not the first journalist it's happened to. Many others have innocently done work for the American Government without realizing the true identity of their employer—and have then been threatened with exposure as Agency informers if they don't continue to cooperate. In your husband's case, it's also clear that he was more concerned about your reaction than any public humiliation."

The eyes flicked back to her husband and smiled. Again Berman felt himself an intruder.

"Mrs. Kesler, the reason for my being here," he carried on, "has to do with your son—with the body of your son."

He noticed Kesler stiffen, but continued in sympathetic but unemotional language to explain what was required. As he did so, he was aware how much he dreaded her response. Kesler he would willingly bully and bludgeon into agreement, but, despite his professionalism and the knowledge that worthy ends could often only be accomplished by dirty deeds, he doubted that he would be capable of inflicting pain or pressure on the battered creature before him. He could do no more than appeal.

He finished and, listening to the pounding of his own heart, waited.

"How important is it, General?" she asked, every word an effort. "I don't want to know state secrets . . . just your own assessment.

"It could be our only chance for a genuine, lasting peace with the Arabs. I believe it is that important," answered Berman.

She looked to her husband.

"You must do it, Dani. Beni is dead . . . if it will help Israel, we cannot refuse."

Kesler bent over and kissed his wife's scorched fingertips. Berman saw the tears fall on the sheet and, with a muttered thank-you, left the pair alone.

He found the doctor in a small room at the end of the corridor.

"What's the prognosis?" he asked.

The doctor shrugged.

"Mrs. Kesler? When you bear in mind that she took the full impact of the explosion at thirty feet, it's amazing she's alive at all. Shock and shrapnel she seems to have survived, but the internal hemorrhaging is considerable. This time tomorrow I might be able to give you a better idea of her chances."

"And if there's been no deterioration in her condition by then?"

"Well, it's a medical truism that the longer you survive, the longer you *will* survive. In other words, the first days are the most dangerous; get over those and your chances of recovery improve all the time."

Berman looked back down the corridor and wondered how he was going to handle matters if the patient's condition started to deteriorate before Kesler was on his way.

He had always hated the smell of hospitals.

Few Mossad agents are lucky enough to be born with the first name Klaus; fewer still had Klaus Maegdefrau's good fortune in having a father who had been a member of the Hitler Youth before emigrating to America and was still known for his overtly anti-Semitic sentiments. That neither the CIA's regular screening of its employees nor even the lie-detector tests had been able to reveal the younger Maegdefrau's Zionist loyalties was a tribute to the ability he had developed in early childhood to mask his real feelings, when his father's oft-to-be-repeated words, "That is the case, is it *nicht*?" had first rung in his ears.

How ironic, therefore, that no one had been happier or prouder when Klaus had landed a job with the Agency than his father. And a cipher clerk!—with all the wartime connotations of espionage, Enigma machines, and code-cracking that the title conjured up. Maegdefrau Senior might have been less impressed if he had known the reality—that modern technology had reduced cipher clerks to glorified typists who spent the day sitting before a visual display unit, tapping in signals and watching the computer do the code-cracking in less time than it took the operator to press the keys. But, prosaic though the activity itself was, the access it offered to privileged information was vast, and when, in the winter of 1983, Klaus had gotten in touch with a member of the Israeli Embassy in Washington offering his services as "expiation for the collective guilt of the German people" the local Mossad chief had been moved to remark that perhaps after all he believed in Christmas.

The business of intelligence gathering and interpretation being no respecter of weekends, Saturday mornings in the cable room on the first floor of the CIA's Langley Headquarters were no different from any other. A conscientious timekeeper, Klaus had arrived to start his shift at nine o'clock sharp, just half an hour after being requested by his regular contact at the Israeli Embassy to undertake "a little monitoring exercise." So described, it sounded without risk. It wasn't.

The cable room worked like a sophisticated telephone exchange, handling cable traffic from Agency stations and bases— main offices and suboffices—all around the world. Since there were six operators per shift, and since each cable was deciphered by whoever was free at the time, Klaus's chances of receiving the Jerusalem cable in his booth were no better than six to one. Accordingly, he had to rely on the computer's log of incoming cables, which was updated instantaneously and which all operators were able to punch up on their own VDUs. The log wouldn't tell him what was in the cable, but at least it would notify him when it arrived. Finding out what it said would be more tricky, requiring a glimpse of the printed-out master copy lodged in the pigeonholes at the far end of the room, and made more difficult still on account of the hole for the Israeli branch's being conspicuously separated from the rest of the Middle East Division.

By eleven—two hours into his shift—Klaus had lost count of the number of times he had punched up the log. There had been no sign of the Jerusalem cable and he was beginning to think his embassy contact had gotten it wrong and that, instead of being slugged IMMEDIATE, it had been graded EYES ONLY or PROSCRIBED & LIMITED, in which case it would have come in on a separate circuit, bypassing the log altogether, and been handled personally by the duty officer. The possibility seemed a near-certainty when there was still no sign of any Jerusalem traffic another hour later.

Then he saw it, flicking to the log at the very moment that the computer was adding the Jerusalem cryptonym to the list. He also noticed that it was slugged merely PRIORITY, which in the hyperbolic language of Agency communications indicated to the average desk officer that he should take a look at it sometime before his next meal break.

He swung in his chair and, sipping a coffee, watched the

printer behind the glass partition chatter out the message. It was several more minutes before the print-out operator got round to tearing it off, putting it through the copier, dispatching the copies to their destinations around the building—one to the Director's office, one to the office of his now disgraced Special Assistant for Middle East Affairs, one to the Israeli branch itself—and finally stuffing the master into the Israeli branch pigeonhole.

The bold move, decided Klaus, was the best: Walk up, take out, walk back, and read in the screened-off privacy of the booth—certainly not standing next to the pigeonhole. Having a fair idea of its length from the time the printer had taken to spew it out, he reckoned it would take no more than two minutes to memorize. In that time nobody in the Israeli branch was likely to enquire about the master copy; with a PRIORITY slug, it could be at the bottom of the pile for hours yet.

He waited for the print-out operator to get tied up on what, despite the Draconian regulations forbidding it, was clearly a private call, and made his move.

Nobody took a scrap of notice. Sauntering across the room, he plucked the cable from its slot, adding it to the top of the pile of papers he was already carrying, and, without glancing left or right, turned to walk back to his booth.

He was halfway there when his name was called.

It was the duty officer. Would Klaus come into his office for a moment?

He felt the word "GUILTY" stamped on his forehead like a cattle brand. His first thought was to drop the incriminating cable and the rest of the bundle back in his booth, but there was always the chance, however remote, of somebody in the Israeli branch phoning down for clarification of a minor point and the master being discovered on his desk. So he took it with him.

To his considerable relief, the duty officer was so preoccupied with working out the shift roster for the next month that if Klaus had had the doomsday code scrawled in large red letters across his chest, the man would probably have mistaken it for an advertising slogan.

After twenty minutes of the duty officer stabbing the calendar with his pipe and bemoaning the seeming impossibility of getting eighteen men to fit into a straightforward three-shift

system, Klaus was getting anxious. Finally, in desperation, he
made the ultimate sacrifice and gave up three weekends in a
row to enable the man to plug the gaps in his confounded
roster.

Back in the deciphering room, nobody had noticed the
disappearance of the Jerusalem cable and, examining it in his
booth, he was heartened to see that the first word was Kesler's
agency cryptonym: ISCRIBE. It was the right cable—the one
he had been told to expect—and not for the first time he
smiled at the evident trouble taken by the girl who devised
and assigned the cryptonyms, managing in Kesler's case very
neatly to blend the two-letter digraph of the target country—IS
for Israel—with a hint of his journalistic occupation. He ran
through the message—quickly first, and then again slowly,
word by word, to memorize it:

> ISCRIBE REQUESTS PERMISSION BACKFREIGHT
> BODY SON STOP TWA DEPART SUNDAY 2100
> HOURS ISTIME STOP

Twenty minutes later, Klaus donned sneakers and tracksuit, and—as usual during his lunch hour—jogged out of the
back gate of the Langley HQ, down the George Washington
Parkway, and into Turkey Run Park.

Assiduously not looking behind him, he soon heard the
familiar padding and puffing, and glimpsed the green and
white tracksuit as the overweight Israeli came alongside.

"It arrived just after midday," said Klaus, lowering his
head, "but you won't like it."

"Like what?" wheezed the Israeli.

He repeated the message verbatim, adding, "No mention
of any urgency and the slug is only PRIORITY."

The Israeli struggled to catch his breath.

"Jerusalem . . . will like it . . . even less . . .," he panted.
"Keep your eyes . . . skinned for the . . . reply," and peeled
off in another direction.

★

In Jerusalem, seven hours ahead of Washington, it was
already eight o'clock in the evening and Monsignor Giovanni,
sitting in his hotel room on the western outskirts of the city,
was about to discover how rapidly events can change in the
space of twelve hours.

He dialed the Vatican number and, on giving his name and asking to be put through to the office of the Secretary of State, was inexplicably kept on hold and then, after a lengthy wait, switched to another extension altogether.

The speaker's drawn-out vowels and halting Italian were immediately familiar and within seconds Giovanni found himself instinctively adopting the *Voi* form of address and punctuating his every other word with *Vostra Santità*.

It was not the first time that he had spoken to His Holiness—he had been present at the occasional meeting between the Pope and the Secretary of State in his capacity as the latter's private secretary—but it was the first time he had had anything approaching a personal conversation with the man, and he was frankly awed to the marrow. He had always laughed at the stories of Vatican officials during Pius XII's time taking phone calls from His Holiness on their knees, but in future he would be less inclined to mock.

His awe was such that only later would he remember His Holiness's oblique reference to the Secretary of State's indisposition and only later appreciate the significance of the fact that he seemed to know everything about the bones and the Curia Segreta's ill-fated attempts to extradite them from Israel. He had even known something of which Giovanni himself, deprived of newspapers on account of the Jewish Sabbath, had been ignorant—the death of Archbishop Ramone.

His Holiness showed a surprising concern for the monsignor's safety and well-being, considering that Giovanni had been as much involved in the curial conspiracy as any of the other planners and participants. He even praised him for his alertness and presence of mind in taking the action he had, and trusted that he would continue to exercise extreme caution in what he throughout referred to as "this lamentable business." New arrangements had been made, however, and the most valuable service that Giovanni could now render the Church and the Christian community worldwide was to go along to the American Consulate in Nablus Road at precisely six o'clock Israeli time the next day, Sunday. There he was to ask to see a Mr. McKenzie in the consulate's political section—he spelled out the name—and was to divulge to him, and *only* to him, the information he had obtained from the archbishop's driver regarding the bones' hiding place. Under no circumstances was he to make contact with the consulate before then. Were the instructions clearly understood?

Yes, gagged Giovanni, they were. The part of a mere messenger boy, though, was not the role he had lately been envisaging for himself and, attempting to phrase it as a helpful suggestion, he intimated that he might perhaps *himself* retrieve the bones. After all, he was free to move and knew where they were.

His Holiness was not to be persuaded. Thanking him for the idea, he declared that Giovanni had already done more than enough and would not be required to take any more risks. Had the monsignor been able to see His Holiness's expression, he might have glimpsed something of the horror with which he viewed the prospect of a second ingenuous cleric being infected by the bones' diabolical powers; better by far to leave the job to confirmed atheists who could be counted on to be indifferent to God and the Devil alike.

The inspector arrived at the hotel shortly after nine to find the deputy manager sorting out a demarcation dispute in the kitchens. On a Saturday night there was never any shortage of less-than-honest-to-goodness police work, and normally he would have left a routine security follow-up till the next morning—except that only that afternoon his chief at headquarters had received a "Mark One bollocking" from the Acting Prime Minister for not notifying the P.M.'s Office of the discovery of Archbishop Ramone's body in the grounds of the Garden Tomb. As a result, anything connected with the Catholic Church now rang alarm bells of deafening volume. For his own part, the inspector couldn't understand the fuss; there was not a shadow of doubt that His Excellency had blown his own head off and not a shred of forensic evidence to suggest otherwise. True, he had chosen a rather emotive place to do it, but persons contemplating such a supremely dramatic gesture often chose their locations accordingly.

"This Catholic priest you've got . . ." he began, with difficulty attracting the deputy manager's attention, "does he strike you as the nervous type?"

The deputy manager suddenly appreciated the reason for the inspector's presence and, with a parting injunction to his still feuding staff, led the policeman out of the kitchen.

"The priest, you were saying . . . the nervous type? Can't honestly tell you; I haven't talked to him. All I know is what I put on the note—the Vatican passport and his appearance a day late. I just thought it might interest you."

"What's he doing here—a pilgrimage?" asked the inspector.

"Of sorts. He's with a party of fifteen nuns. It's one of the standard Holy Land Tours packages. He's supposedly their guide."

"Why 'supposedly'?"

"Just that he doesn't seem to have much to do with them. He ate breakfast alone this morning and has spent the day in his room while they've been out sightseeing."

"Is he in his room now?"

The deputy manager walked over to the reception desk, checked the key racks, and had a brief word with the receptionist.

"Went out half an hour ago," he said. "Asked if there was a good Arab restaurant within walking distance."

"Tactful bastard!" grunted the inspector. He glanced at the elevators. "Anybody checked his room?"

"Only the chambermaid—to clean it," replied the deputy manager, pulling his master key from his pocket.

It was as bare as a monastic cell. Indeed, the only immediate indication of habitation was a zipped-up toilet bag hanging from one of the taps of the washbasin and a small brass crucifix propped against the headboard of the bed.

Pulling back the shower curtain, however, revealed a pair of blue underpants draped over the shower head to dry and, for the same purpose, a pair of thin black socks knotted into the emergency cord like flags of mourning. The inspector examined the items for labels and name tags and, finding only an Italian manufacturer's label in the underpants, made a predictable reference to the relationship between cleanliness and godliness, and turned his attention to the wardrobe.

It was empty—as were all its drawers.

"How long's he booked in for?" he asked.

"Ten days. That's what the block booking is for, at least."

The inspector made a clicking sound with his tongue and started rummaging through the tour brochures on the coffee table, the wastepaper basket, and the cupboard in the bedside table.

Nothing.

Finally, he turned to the small, square notepad provided by the hotel next to the telephone. He carefully peeled off the top sheet and, holding it edge-on, level with his eyes, examined it for imprinted traces of any message that might have been scribbled on the sheet above.

He sniffed.

"Could be something . . . see what the lab boys make of it."

Slipping the square of paper into an envelope, he nodded towards the phone.

"Do you have a record of his calls?"

"We're direct-dial here," responded the deputy manager, more in pride than regret.

"Bane of my life, that!"

"But at least the number of his dialed units will tell you how active he's been."

The inspector didn't reply. He was pulling back the bed covers and lifting the pillow.

"Not even pajamas!" he remarked. "Do you think he carries them around with him in case he gets lucky?"

He laughed at his own joke and in rearranging the pillow knocked the crucifix off the headboard. He picked it up and in similar jocular vein addressed the small brass figure:

"And what's a nice Jewish boy like you doing in a place like this, eh?"

His grin froze.

"What's this fellow's name again?" he asked.

Thinking it was all part of the joke, the deputy manager was going to reply "Jesus something-or-other." Then he realized. "The priest? Ciampolini, Mauro Ciampolini."

"Then why," the inspector wondered aloud, "do you suppose his own mother calls him 'Giovanni?' "

In response to the other's obvious puzzlement, he indicated the inscription on the back of the cross: *Al mio caro figlio, Giovanni. Ordinato prete, 16 Settembre 1979. Mamma.*

"Now," he continued, "my Italian may be limited to ordering spaghetti bolognese, but I'd stake my pension on it that this was a present to young Giovanni from his mother on the occasion of his ordination." He pulled the hotel registration slip from his pocket and quoted: "Date of birth: 17.5.54 . . . and this is dated the sixteenth of September '79. So he was made a priest at twenty-five; sounds about right."

"Do you think the difference in names could be significant, then?" asked the deputy manager.

The inspector repositioned the crucifix on the headboard with a care that could have been mistaken for reverence by anyone ignorant of his profession.

"Can't tell for sure . . . It could be a middle name or a pet name . . . even possible that the cross belonged to someone else originally. Did you see the passport for yourself?"

"No. Do you want me to ask him for it?"

The inspector nearly choked.

"Don't you dare! Not unless you want to tip him off. No, we'll keep him under surveillance for a couple of days and see what that produces."

A mile away in downtown Jerusalem, the Saturday night revelers were out in Ben Yehuda Street to mark the end of Shabbat—singing, shouting, shrieking, and at the junction with Jaffa Road attracting the usual wrath of traffic-stalled motorists by their hood-vaulting antics.

By contrast, seventy feet below these exuberant street scenes, Gideon Berman was sitting once again in the Defense Minister's chair at the back of the fan-shaped control room of the Emergency General Headquarters, and staring grimly at the slip of paper the Mossad chief had just handed him.

"I warned you about Kesler's case officer being more of a playboy than a company man," said Hausner.

Berman leaned back, crumpling the note in his fist.

"You did, Eli, you did. But to tag it merely PRIORITY and not to inject even a hint of urgency into it . . ." He stared at the clocks on the opposite wall. "Is there *nothing* we can do to speed it along?"

Hausner wagged a finger.

"You know what I've always said: God save the intelligence services from men of action! Be glad that they've taken the bait. You can't make them swallow it by pushing it down their throats. Anyway, if the Agency's Jerusalem station is as slow on the uptake as this suggests, there isn't going to be much cable traffic coming out of the place on a Saturday night, and whoever's sitting on the Israeli desk at the other end isn't going to have a lot to distract him." He noted the dark, puffy pouches beneath Berman's eyes. "The best thing you can do is go home and get some sleep, because if you're needing it now, you're going to need it even more by this time tomorrow."

Berman was about to wave the advice aside but Hausner carried on.

"Gideon, I've spent a lifetime in the intelligence game. I've seen our so-called decision makers at closer quarters than you, and I swear to you that, nine times out of ten, errors of judgement are the result not of great strain but of simple dog-tiredness. Get out of this claustrophobic rat hole and clear your mind. Your plan is a good one; it has the hallmark of some of the best intelligence operations; but from now on you've got to let the other side make the running. Meir and I will alternate shifts through the night here, and I promise we'll let you know the moment anything comes through from Washington. Now, go."

Berman was touched by the Mossad chief's solicitude, in such contrast to the image of gruff taciturnity that he normally presented to the world. And a moment's consideration of the events of the previous night told him Hausner was right. He pulled his jacket off the back of the chair.

"OK, Eli, you win—but you pick up that phone the moment anything comes in."

"So help me God," declared Hausner, his hand raised in parody of the countless American courtroom dramas he had seen on television.

Berman was back in Ramban in fifteen minutes, his ministry residence distinguished from the other houses in the street by its illuminated pillbox outside.

He had never liked the place and would have far preferred to stay in the flat he had owned previously. But security considerations ruled it out, and it had to be admitted that official entertaining was easier here, even if the daytime housekeeper's attempts to devise homely touches—like filling with flowers the 105mm shellcase he had kept as a memento of the Yom Kippur War—were more often an annoyance than a comfort.

He got out of the car, arranged for the driver to pick him up again at seven the next morning, and headed for the front door, acknowledging the guard in his pillbox on the way.

"You have a visitor, General," said the soldier coming out to meet him.

Berman's heart sank. In the back of the car he had fantasized—not too strong a word—about a long drink, a deep bath, a soft bed, and delicious oblivion. And now a visitor.

The soldier read his expression.

"I told her there was no guaranteeing you'd be back tonight, but she insisted on waiting just in case." He pointed to a black sedan on the other side of the road.

Berman looked and instantly recognized the occupant sitting impassively in the driver's seat. He walked over. The window was down.

"Ariella?"

She didn't raise her head.

"Gideon, I'm sorry. I shouldn't be here, I know; it's not fair on you, and you've got other things on your mind. It's just . . . just that I didn't know who else to go to. I don't want to be alone, Gideon."

He opened the door and helped her out.

Inside the house, he guided her to a sofa where she sat, huddled in a ball. He poured a large brandy and eased it between her clenched hands; then poured himself an equally generous measure and sat opposite. It was several sips before she unwound.

"I've told him," she said starkly. "Nathan . . . the truth about Yossi."

Berman frowned.

"But we agreed."

"We did," she broke in, "but I couldn't *not* tell him. It was bad enough on the telephone, but when he arrived back at Lod, I knew . . . Gideon, I couldn't see him mourn a lie, I just couldn't."

Berman looked away.

"And his reaction?"

"Anger, hurt. That's why I'm here. He's flying back to Chicago."

"Before the funeral?"

"Tonight. He said he couldn't go through with it—not with you there as well, reading the eulogy. Gideon, I'm sorry, but I just couldn't stay on in that house on my own—not tonight. And there was nobody else to turn to, nobody else who knows the truth."

He came towards her and kissed her forehead, smelling again the forgotten fragrance of her hair.

"I understand," he said, and more formally, "Is there anything I can get you to eat?"

She shook her head and a strand of the neatly pinned-back hair fell forwards over her face.

"I'm going to have a bath," he added. "Help yourself to whatever you want."

He checked her glass, saw it was already empty, and replenished it.

Lying stretched out in the bath, he felt the aches and stresses of the last forty-eight hours ebb from his body. His limbs floated effortlessly in the water and his brain too seemed suddenly lighter in his skull, buoyed by the alcohol. He was aware of Ariella next door and of the bizarreness of having an emotionally distraught ex-wife clearly intent on staying the night, but his mind, in conspiracy with his body, refused to focus on the implications.

He lost track of time. Only when the water started to feel cold did he realize how long and dangerously he had been half-slumbering.

He got out, dried himself off and, towel round his waist, walked back into the hall.

The only illumination in the house came from the small table lamp in the living room. She wasn't to be seen. He wondered whether she had left, but found the front door still locked from the inside. Bemused, he pushed open the bedroom door and saw the dark blue dress draped over a chair, the shoes kicked off beside the bed, and a patch of white sheet where the counterpane had been turned back. The atmosphere was warm with the smell of fresh linen, silk, and femininity.

He slipped in beside her and, lying on his back, felt the crisp sheets cool against his shoulders and buttocks. The street light from below, strained through the curtains, threw a pattern on the ceiling. Concentrating on it, he tried to make sense of what was happening, but the lines and intersections dissolved into each other. He was a body out of time, suspended in space, the only reality the reality of the senses. Right, wrong, guilt, decorum—all seemed supremely irrelevant. To be aware without being conscious. That was the important thing.

"Gideon?"

"Yes."

"Should I feel ashamed for wanting you to make love to me?"

"Because of Nathan?"

"Not Nathan, no. Things haven't been right between us now for years. I don't deceive myself about his social activities in the States."

"Yossi, then?"

To his surprise, she laughed.

"He of all people wouldn't disapprove! If he had any wish how we should spend tonight, it would be like this. The idea of our being brought together by his death—that would appeal to him. He hated the very idea of sitting shivah." She turned. "You know, before he went on those operations into Syria he always made me promise that, if anything happened, I wouldn't sit around for a week wailing on a stool. That was the way he put it. Then he would do this ridiculous mime down on his haunches which usually ended up with both of us rolling around on the floor in hysterics."

She laughed at the recollection, but this time, Berman noticed, she was wrapping her own hysteria up with the memory of Yossi's. He put out a hand and, finding hers, held it tight. Deep sobs shook her body and he felt the wetness on his chest as she nestled into him.

He lay still in the dark, savoring the contact and closeness, the weightless weight of her body against his, and the slow fire kindling in his groin. He turned to face her and felt his penis swell and harden against the soft, yielding skin of her abdomen. In response she arched her back into him, and bringing her lips against his, filled his mouth with the tang of her tears and the heady, lingering aroma of brandy. Slowly, with a hungry but measured urgency, she drew him into her, clasping her hands behind his buttocks, forcing him deeper and higher, and letting out a low cry in which pleasure became pain and the pain pleasure again. There was no exertion, no sudden release—just an act of sublime exorcism as, with exquisite slowness, she drew him off into her.

That night, he was to sleep a sleep deeper than he had in months, the two of them lying entwined on a shore light-years distant from the cruel reality of the world beyond the curtains.

★

America's Director of Central Intelligence was neither looking nor feeling well. Installed in the office of Tom Reynolds,
the head of the CIA's Israeli branch, Spender was suffering
from self-imposed temperance, while the purely physical need
to reenergize his flagging system gradually assumed more
urgency than the requirement to maintain a clear head.

And still they had no plan.

Belatedly, Spender now realized that his dumping of Stan
Harding had been a mistake, though it had seemed an inspired act of self-preservation at the time. Harding's replacement, the "durable" Reynolds, was incapable of coming up
with a single original, let alone imaginative, idea. His guiding
philosophy being to avoid any initiative that might later re-
bound and be laid at his door, he had two stock responses to
any suggestion: "Seems like a possible" and "Could be developed," invariably accompanied by the infuriating twitch of
the head of an anxious-to-please poodle.

So it was that after several hours' brainstorming and the
accumulation of an abundance of maps and charts, Bob Spender
was again feeling the familiar stirrings of panic in his bowels.

A young desk officer knocked at the open door of Reynolds's
office and apologized for interrupting.

"Yes, what is it, Walter?" sighed Reynolds, as if to indicate
that his already stretched cerebral powers might just be
tipped over the edge by this latest intrusion.

"A cable from the Jerusalem station, sir," replied the desk
officer hesitantly. "ISCRIBE wants to freight back the body
of his son for burial over here . . . wants to clear it with us
before he . . ."

"For Christ's sake!" snapped Reynolds. "Can't you see
we've got enough on our minds without that sort of crap?
What's the urgency? Haven't they got ice in Israel?"

"Seems he's trying to get booked on a flight at 2100 hours
tomorrow night Israeli time, sir, and he needs . . ."

"OK, OK, I hear you," cut in Reynolds. "That's a whole
twenty-four hours away. We can deal with it later—not now
while the director is here. Just shut the door, will you."

"Wait," croaked Spender from the other side of the room,
holding out a fat, twitching hand. "Bring that cable here . . ."

Mystified, the young man handed it over and watched as

Spender read and, as though by levitation, rose slowly from
his seat.

"Who here knows the procedure for doing this sort of
thing?" he asked of the desk officer, ignoring his superior.

"Well, it's actually my specialty, Mr. Director. That's why
I'm handling it," answered the young man, looking to Reynolds for a clue to the sudden importance of what a few
seconds before had been dismissed as of total irrelevance.

"Then explain it to me, stage by stage," ordered Spender,
spraying him with the full blast of his stale breath.

"Well, Mr. Director, the remains for export are normally
stored temporarily in the mortuary of the Hadassah Hospital
in Jerusalem. Embalming isn't customary in Israel—it's against
Jewish religious law—but, purely for the purpose of shipping
bodies, the hospital's forensic department operates a rudimentary embalming service. Then, as soon as the paperwork
is completed—death certificate, government clearance, customs, etc.—our own consular officials formally assume responsibility for the disposal of the body and can pick it up from
the hospital mortuary on the understanding that it will be out
of the country within the time specified by the authorities."

Sweat was beading on Spender's brow.

"And the customs, what about them? What sort of checks
do they make?"

The desk officer spread his hands nervously.

"Well, just the normal, Mr. Director."

"But what is normal for a corpse? That's what I'm asking,
man. Do they open the goddam box or what?"

"Oh, no, no. That wouldn't be allowed for health reasons.
The coffin has to be hermetically sealed at the hospital, but
the authorities do insist that it will permit X-ray inspection,
which obviously rules out lead. The coffins used by the
Hadassah are usually made of plastic or fiberglass. And there's
another security measure they insist on: Either the deceased's
next of kin or a consular official has to accompany the body if
it's going by air." He paused and added with a timid smile,
"Just be on the same flight is what I mean."

The comic implications of whether the next of kin was
expected to sit next to the coffin in the cargo hold or have the
coffin beside him in the passenger compartment hadn't occurred to Spender. His mind was already way ahead.

"So under no circumstances," he continued, stabbing at

the cable, "at no point after it has left the hospital will this coffin containing Kesler's son be opened up. Is that what you're telling me?"

The young man glanced at his boss for support, but Reynolds was looking elsewhere.

"Well, obviously, Mr. Director, it would depend on whether they have any reason to be suspicious. I couldn't be one hundred percent categorical on it, but, in view of the circumstances of the boy's death, I can't imagine any customs or security officer insisting on any inspection other than the normal X-ray. I would certainly be . . ."

Spender slammed the desk.

"That's it!" he whooped. "That's the way we do it." He turned to Reynolds. "What do you say, Tom?"

"Certainly seems like a possible, Mr. Director," responded the other on cue.

Two hours later, sitting before his visual display unit in the cable room on the first floor, Klaus Maegdefrau noted the arrival from the Israeli branch upstairs of a FLASH cable for transmission to the Agency's Jerusalem station. It was impossible to miss it, since all other cable traffic was automatically suspended, even in mid-message, for the sending of FLASH cables.

It was long—too long for even Klaus to memorize—but its gist was clear, and within the hour another message would be flashed from Washington to Jerusalem—but this time from the Israeli Embassy to the Mossad Headquarters. It would contain just three words: OPERATION ISAAC GO.

★

THE THIRD DAY

$\mathbf{D}$O YOU WANT the good news or the not-so-good?" asked Eli Hausner dourly as Berman entered the underground control room just before half-past seven on the Sunday morning.

"I have a choice?" queried Berman, more rested and refreshed than he had looked in weeks.

"I'll give you the good news first," said the Mossad chief by way of reply. "They've swallowed the bait. We're just waiting for Kesler's case officer at the consulate to contact him. You'd have known at two-thirty this morning if we'd been able to wake you."

"And the not-so-good?"

Casting around for an ashtray and not finding it, Hausner tapped his ash onto the floor.

"That came in later when we finally got a full version of Langley's cable to the Jerusalem Consulate. It seems His Holiness the Pope is now in on the act. He's furious over the mess-up at the Allenby Bridge and wants the bones destroyed at the first possible opportunity—right here in situ, and preferably the moment they're picked up. Fortunately, however . . ."

He waited to see Berman's reaction and, after drawing out the suspense to the limit of Berman's patience, continued:

"McCrae is acting true to form and regarding the whole exercise as some sort of virility test, insisting the bones be got out as a matter of national honor, although it seems he's been forced to agree to a destruction option if things look as if they're going wrong a second time."

Berman was puzzled.

"Eli, I don't understand. If the Pope wants them destroyed, why doesn't he just order his people at the Apostolic Delegation to go ahead and do it?"

Hausner snorted a double stream of grey smoke.

241

"That's just the point—they're not there. *Can't* be. As you say, he wouldn't have to worry about McCrae if they were."

"Then where in God's name are they?"

Hausner's expression indicated that the Chief of Intelligence was the last person to ask.

"According to the cable, it's one of the divine mysteries of the Catholic faith, and will remain so until the last minute when the Holy Father will impart the information to the Americans. How, we don't know. It seems pretty certain though, that, by the time we do, the destruction option will already have been primed."

Berman leaned forward on his desk, his head hanging between his arms. "And we have no idea where they might be in the meantime?" he asked.

Hausner pointed to the map beneath the glass of Berman's desk and inscribed a rough triangle that embraced the entire country.

"Somewhere within this area, I should guess." Then, more seriously, "They could be anywhere, Gideon. They could have been dropped off somewhere along the road between the Allenby Bridge and Jerusalem, but it's just as likely that the mad archbishop wandered off into the night with them and hid them somewhere, or entrusted them to somebody, before he shot himself. Personally, I'm inclined to the latter possibility. Whoever he gave them to would logically be the person to tip off the Americans. Perhaps he'll even hand them over personally. It would make sense."

"Are you saying then there's nothing we can do—that we shouldn't even bother looking for them, even though we now know they're not in the delegation building?"

"There's plenty we *could* do. We could have every man and dog out scouring the country. But our chances of success would be so small as not to justify the risk of pushing whoever may be holding the bones or knows where they are into destroying them."

Berman sighed and ran a hand through his hair.

"What about at least monitoring Kesler's progress when he makes his rendezvous to switch the bodies? I wasn't thinking of anything as obvious as a tail, but I reckoned we might bug him some way."

"Too risky. For a start, he's unlikely to be alone, and secondly, you can bet that whoever is sent to hold his hand will be wise to all the tricks. If he finds Kesler has been bugged, he'll know the whole thing is a setup. To extend your fishing analogy about the sprat and the . . . whatever the bigger fish was called . . ."

"Mackerel."

"Right. Well, to extend the analogy, we've got no choice but to play the line out and wait till the airport before hauling the big fish in. Wasn't that always the essence of the ploy anyway?"

Berman nodded reluctantly, and was aware of Meir standing at his shoulder. He had just been on the telephone to the Hadassah Hospital about the condition of Kesler's wife.

"And?" Berman enquired.

"It's bad. Her condition has deteriorated during the night and is, quote, 'giving cause for concern.' "

"Does Kesler know this?"

He's been at the bedside all night, but he's been told only that she's holding her own—as per your instructions."

Berman and Hausner stared at each other grimly. Each read the other's thoughts perfectly.

★

"There's a call for you, Mr. Kesler."

The words were spoken with the forced cheeriness of all nurses in the presence of the seriously ill.

He looked at Aya. With the oxygen mask on, it was hard to tell but she appeared to be still sleeping. Gently he released her hand. The nurse indicated a phone at the end of the corridor.

"Dan Kesler," he announced, shaking off the drowsiness induced by a night of fitful dozing in a hospital chair.

"The U.S. Consulate, Nablus Road, here, Mr. Kesler," said a strident female voice. "It's about the shipment of your son's body. Mr. Crawford, who normally deals with these matters, would appreciate it if you could bring over the death certificate and any other relevant documentation so we can expedite the necessary arrangements for transshipment."

"I'll be there within the hour," replied Kesler and put the phone down.

Hands on hips, he drew in a deep draft of air. His role as a double agent was about to begin. He had never felt less up to such a challenge in his life.

★

He hadn't been near the consulate in years—in the mistaken belief that by scrupulously avoiding the place he might keep his CIA connections secret from the Israeli security services who were known to maintain a watch on such premises.

It hadn't changed. Hidden behind a high stone wall and additionally screened by tall cypresses, it was in the middle of a large triangular traffic island at the point where Pikud Hamerkaz forked off Nablus Road—just inside the area of East Jerusalem which until 1967 had been part of Jordan. Apart from the usual crested roundel, the only external adornment was an aluminum sentry box to the left of the main gate—the gate itself continuously monitored by a closed-circuit camera mounted above for all to see, and be seen by. Even the flag was inside the compound and half-hidden by the trees.

The fortress aspect of the place was further enhanced by the three security air locks that had to be negotiated to get inside, manned respectively by a civilian bag-checker, a Marine guard, and an Arab deskman.

Kesler announced his arrival at the enquiries desk in the large rectangular reception hall and within minutes found himself holed up with the courteously correct Crawford in his office on the ground floor. Since he was now safely on American ground, he expected the man at least to give a hint that he knew the extent of his Agency involvement, even if he, Crawford, wasn't personally on the consulate's CIA staff. But there was none and, as Kesler watched him start on the fourth page of the State Department's Human Remains Reentry Form, he began to wonder whether Berman's elaborate plan had backfired. Having no desire in reality to ship Beni's body back and even less to be away from Aya at such a time—not even for "four hours at most" as Berman had promised—he could see himself being committed to an absurd and pointless exercise because of an Israeli miscalculation.

At the end of forty minutes, which had included a call to the hospital forensic department to check on the progress of the embalming, he was beginning to think that, rather, he was the victim of a practical joke devised by the Israelis to punish him for his CIA involvement. Then, everything apparently to his satisfaction, Crawford laid down his pen, gave a fleetingly apologetic smile, and picked up the telephone.

"I have finished with Mr. Kesler now—if you would like to see him," he said matter-of-factly to whoever was on the other end. "I shall send him along."

Another brief smile, followed by the appearance of a secretary.

"The young lady will take you along to the Political Section, Mr. Kesler. If there are any problems, I trust you will contact me . . . and thank you."

Art McKenzie, Kesler's Agency case officer, was filling himself a paper cone of ice water from the dispenser as Kesler was ushered in. Disorientated by his experience with the inscrutable Crawford, and by now suspecting that he was in some way being tested, Kesler had decided that the best way to cover his collusion with the Israelis was to adopt the persona of a man broken by grief—which wasn't difficult.

"All OK with Crawford?" asked McKenzie.

"Seems so."

"Good—I'll be coming with you tonight—at least, as far as the airport."

Should he show surprise? Kesler wondered. Not yet. After all, the request to ship Beni's body had, as Berman had specified, gone through McKenzie himself, and, besides, consular accompaniment on such occasions was, he gathered, required by Israeli law.

"Thanks," he said lamely.

McKenzie picked up a tennis racket leaning against the filing cabinet and carved an imaginary forehand through the air.

"There's a bit more to it than that, Buddy Boy," he added with the patronizing style that had so infuriated Kesler on the three occasions that they had previously met in safe houses. "It concerns this business with the bones you turned up at Nahalat Shim'on, property of one J. Christ. Langley wants to take advantage of your trip back home."

"I don't follow," responded Kesler with as little theatricality as possible in the circumstances.

Still wielding the racket, McKenzie explained the outline of the operation but, Kesler noted, held back on the details. Either he didn't know them, which was unlikely, or he didn't fully trust his forcibly enlisted accomplice.

Kesler affected anger. "McKenzie, I don't care a fuck about your Boy Scout pranks. My only concern is to get my son's body out of this place, and I resent the implied blackmail."

"Blackmail?"

"That if I don't cooperate with you, Beni's body won't get out."

McKenzie gripped his shoulder in a gesture of camaraderie.

"Hey, Buddy Boy, you've got it all wrong. Your son's body will get back OK, don't you worry; only it won't be on the flight the Israelis think. But we'll find a way, and on that I give you my word."

"And in the meantime?"

"In the meantime, it will be stored—temporarily stored—in a suitable . . . resting place."

"Like?"

"Like somewhere suitable."

Kesler remained silent, sullen. The grip on his shoulder suddenly tightened.

"Look, Buddy Boy, just quit giving me a hard time. This is a mission we're talking about and I'm your case officer. Don't forget that. There's a hundred ways I can screw you and, if you start fucking me around, I will. I don't want to because, well, you've got your feelings and I can appreciate them, but this thing is bigger than any feelings—yours, mine, or anybody's."

Kesler unlocked the hand from his shoulder.

"Thanks for spelling it out so . . . sensitively."

McKenzie was about to grin but stopped himself. Instead, he took another swing—this time a backhand—noting with satisfaction the clean line of his follow-through. He sensed that Kesler's resistance was broken and returned to his old expansive self.

"I knew I could count on you, Buddy Boy, and I meant what I said about your feelings. I *can* understand them."

Kesler stifled an instinctive "bullshit," and reminded himself that what he was doing was for Aya and the memory of Beni. Later there would be time enough to relish the grim irony of the present situation; satisfaction would not be long delayed. One day soon, "Buddy Boy" McKenzie would recall this conversation and would blanch at the realization that the roles of puppet and puppetmaster had been precisely the opposite of what he, in his racket-swinging complacency, was now imagining.

"So that's fixed," McKenzie declared. "I'll meet you at the hospital morgue at 18:45 tonight. I'll have a consular limo and we can set off from there."

"To the airport?" Kesler couldn't resist asking.

McKenzie smiled.

"After a little detour . . . to the airport."

By way of afterthought, he added: "Say, your wife, how is she?"

Kesler repeated the well-worn formula.

"Yea, well, good. Nasty business, but don't worry, Buddy Boy, Langley won't forget what you're doing for them."

Kesler permitted himself a grim smile. No, Langley wouldn't forget.

★

The inspector was about to go to lunch when his attention was drawn by a tapping on the glass partition. It was one of the forensic staff, waving a yellow envelope.

"The stuff you dropped in last night," he announced, "the slip of paper from the hotel telephone pad. Remember?"

The inspector's mind was more on his empty stomach, but, yes, he remembered.

"Anything worth looking at?" he asked indifferently.

The man from forensic pulled a photograph from the envelope and presented it to him like a schoolboy with his homework.

"We used ultraviolet on it. See what you make of it. We think it's come out rather well."

The inspector looked and saw nothing. Then he thought he could discern what was possibly a single word, the number of straight strokes suggesting it was in capital letters. The most prominent looked like an "M" followed by a "K," which to the inspector's mind suggested the English abbreviation for "Member of the Knesset." The word that followed, he assumed, would be the name of the parliamentarian. And, now that he looked more closely, there did indeed appear to be a punctuation point between the two letters. Perhaps, he speculated, the Italians used the same abbreviation: "M.K. —*Membro di Knesseto*." Possible.

He was about to voice his thoughts but was aware of a

barely contained smugness about the man from forensic which suggested that he had already worked it out.

"What do *you* think it is, then?" he asked.

"Well," burst forth the other, prodding the photo with a chemical-stained finger, "I'd say it was the Scottish name *McKenzie*, if you want my opinion."

He traced the letters and, having it pointed out, the inspector could clearly see it for himself. He was glad he had so narrowly escaped providing material for stories about his incompetence back in the labs, and gave a noncommittal sniff.

He scribbled the name on a sheet of paper and called to a young officer who was eating his snack lunch at his desk and reading a newspaper.

"Moshe, check this out, will you!"

Moshe wiped his lips, strolled across, and with a marked lack of interest took the sheet of paper.

"It's Scottish in origin," added the inspector. "The only other clue is that there may be a Catholic connection. Go through the phone directory and ring up every McKenzie in it. I want to know if any of them know, or have recently had any contact with . . ." He checked the hotel registration slip, "a Monsignor Mauro Ciampolini—C-I-A-M-P-O-L-I-N-I—who might also be using the first name Giovanni. When you've done that, ring round the Catholic establishments and, if you come across any more McKenzies, ask them the same question. Finally, run the name through the immigration computer. It might throw up something."

Moshe's expression needed no interpreting: "And *this* is what I joined the police for?" was written all over his large, ugly, pockmarked face.

By the time the inspector returned from lunch, the resentment was almost tangible.

"Anything?" he enquired, masking a belch.

Moshe gave an insolent shrug.

"The computer was a waste of time. All it could come up with was a Canadian couple who entered the country last Wednesday, giving their address in Israel as the Hotel Kinneret, Galilee—both in their sixties and anyway they spell their name 'MacKenzie.' The phone book wasn't much better—a Dr. McKenzie who is the director of a British-Israeli cultural exchange organization here in Jerusalem and has never heard of anybody with a name remotely like the one you gave me."

"And the Catholic establishments?"

"So far, only a Father Michael McKenzie at the Pontifical Mission in the Christian Quarter of the Old City—and he's Irish."

"Irish?" queried the inspector. "I thought all 'Macs' were Scottish."

"Quite a few Catholic ones went to Ireland during the seventeenth century to avoid Protestant persecution," piped up a voice from the other end of the office.

Another smart bugger, thought the inspector. How come the place was so full of them today?

Bob Spender was pleased with his presentation. It had obviously impressed. Romford was nodding genially and—surest sign of all—McCrae was silent.

"Sounds like a winner, Joe," prompted the Secretary of State.

The President gave a grudging grunt.

"So long as there are no fuck-ups along the way this time." He turned to Spender.

"You're saying those bones will get through Israeli airport security without detection. Absolutely sure of it?"

Spender 'took the plunge.

"Absolutely, Mr. President. Not even the Israelis open coffins, and their X-rays will show exactly what they are expecting to see in exactly the right . . ."

"They're expecting to see the skeleton of a goddam eight-year-old child," broke in McCrae, "not the skeleton of a fully grown man in his mid-thirties."

Spender was unfazed; he had already been fully primed on the point by the Agency's technical services division.

"With respect, Mr. President, age aside, the contents of the coffin are supposed, first and foremost, to be the remains of the victim of a bomb blast at point-blank range. Recognizable skeletons don't survive that sort of impact. Such remains as there are have usually to be *packed* into the coffin rather than laid in it. In addition, the Nahalat Shim'on bones will be suitably padded out with latex rubber to simulate flesh or, more accurately, the way flesh would separate the bones from each other. What will appear on the airport X-ray will be not a skeleton but a mere jumble of bones, and I am assured by our experts that it would take a trained anthropologist to spot the age discrepancy."

McCrae shot a cynical glance at Romford.

"Better be right—that's all."

"I am confident, Mr. President," reaffirmed Spender. "All our Jerusalem station needs is the details of the bones' present location."

"Which they'll get at six o'clock Israeli time precisely," replied McCrae. "I talked to the Pope an hour ago; he assures me that one of his men in Jerusalem will present himself to your McKenzie at the Nablus Road consulate with all the relevant information. I don't pretend to be happy about the arrangements but that's the way he insists it has to be done."

"Couldn't they let us know before?" asked Spender. "The flight is at nine . . ."

"I know when the fucking flight is!" retorted McCrae. "And if it had been possible to persuade his almighty Holiness to let us know earlier, I would have done it. He's adamant, and that's it. If you want to know the truth, he doesn't trust you bastards not to screw it up a second time—and with that I can sympathize!"

★

By pressing the tip of his middle finger against the underside of Aya's wrist, Kesler had found he was able to monitor her pulse at the same time as holding her hand. He was alarmed. It was now so weak that its strength and regularity no longer seemed to have any connection with her alternating periods of sleep and consciousness. He had mentioned it to the doctor but had been assured that the nurse was keeping a constant eye on his wife's electronic cardiac monitor down the corridor. He was not to worry; intensive care meant what it said.

In an attempt at self-induced optimism, he forced himself to think beyond his present anxieties. When all this was over—when the wretched bones were safely back in Israeli hands; when Aya was out of hospital and recovering—he would become the Israeli she had always wanted, but never forced, him to be. He would probably have to renounce his American citizenship anyway and, after what he had done for Berman, there could be no bar to his taking out Israeli nationality. It would be a relief after the years of leading a schizophrenic half-life; a measure of self-respect would be restored. God willing, they would have other children—children who would never have to sense their father's embarrassment at wearing a *kipa* or saying the blessing at the Sabbath meal. Their father would be, like them, a Jew—and proud to own to the fact.

As though in response to his thoughts, he felt Aya's pulse rally. Despite the oxygen mask, he could discern the smile in her eyes and gave her hand a gentle squeeze. She struggled to mouth something but, raising a finger to his lips, he stopped her. She had to conserve her strength; there was more to live for than she knew. He would tell her when she was better—God willing.

At first he took the figure in the white coat to be one of the medical staff but, looking up, he recognized the man who had taken him to meet Berman in the military cemetery the previous afternoon.

"I must have a word with you outside," whispered Meir.

They walked out onto the long veranda-cum-terrace-cum-parking lot that stretched the length of the hospital's modern façade and, leaning on the railings, overlooked the raised rectangular lawn with its impressionistic bronze representing the "Tree of Life."

"The Minister asked me to have a word with you about tonight," said Meir, adjusting his dark glasses, as much against the glare of the concrete as to preserve his anonymity. "I assume everything went well at the consulate?"

Kesler confirmed.

"McKenzie is picking me up here at six-forty-five—down in the morgue. He's bringing one of the consulate's official cars."

"Did he say what else he'd be bringing?"

"How do you mean?"

Meir explained about the Pope's destruction option, taking note of Kesler's reaction from behind the glasses. To his surprise, in view of Kesler's recent experience with explosives, he seemed quite unconcerned about the possibility of being a passenger in a traveling bomb.

"It's going to complicate our interception plans of course," continued Meir. "McKenzie will be that much jumpier. One precipitate move could blow the bones *and* you sky high . . . literally."

"Of course," repeated Kesler. He too was surprised by the calmness of his own reaction, but in the wake of Beni's death and Aya's mutilation, his capacity for all feeling—fear included—seemed to have been dulled. No longer was he moved by emotions; only by events.

"Anyway, what you need to know," Meir said, "is that we plan to make the interception on the main Jerusalem-Tel Aviv highway shortly after kilometer marker 15—that's the last before the Lod Junction and the turnoff for the airport. So, as soon as you see the number 15 on that little roadside post, be ready."

"For what?"

"Hasn't been decided exactly yet. It could be an ordinary security check, road crew, a broken-down truck, or perhaps even a staged accident. But you'll know when you see it, and the moment you do it'll be up to you to get out of the line of fire—down behind the dash. The only target will be the guy behind the wheel."

"And you're going to hit him before he can get a finger to the button. Is that the idea?"

The Israeli was hard put to mask his own skepticism.

"That's the idea. Remember that McKenzie's mind will be on the driving and, with the element of surprise in our favor, the odds are good that we'll be able to take him out before he realizes what's happening."

"And my odds?"

"I was including yours," answered the Israeli without conviction.

Watching from outside, Berman waited for Meir and Kesler to appear on the terrace before taking the elevator up to the third floor—and a confrontation that was not unexpected.

The doctor was in no mood for pleasantries.

"What you are doing, General," he spat out, "no, what you are asking *others* to do for you . . . is by any standards of medical practice or normal decency immoral! And I tell you, neither I nor my staff are any longer prepared to keep Mrs.

Kesler's husband in ignorance of her true condition. The man has a right to know."

Berman surveyed the contorted face. On another occasion he might have taken the doctor aside and attempted to reason with him. Now there wasn't the time for anything other than a blunt instrument. He focused on the bulging eyes.

"Doctor, I cannot force you to go against your conscience and, since we are on your territory here, I doubt whether I can even order you to comply with my instructions." His voice dropped to a confidential whisper. "But I promise you this: that if you or any of your staff say one word to Kesler which might jeopardize this operation—an operation for which four men have already given their lives and of which you understand not one-hundredth part—I shall personally ensure that you are held accountable at any subsequent enquiry. Translated into biological, if not exactly medical, terms, I shall screw you, Doctor."

He walked away, sufficiently confident of the effect not to worry how the good doctor would react if he knew what he was about to do next.

As he entered the room, the nurse glared at him with the same pop-eyed resentment he had just witnessed in her colleague, and with a curt "General," pushed past, as though to stay would be to risk infection.

He pulled a chair up to the bedside.

"Mrs. Kesler," he said with a gentleness that anybody hearing him a few seconds earlier would have thought impossible.

The eyes that had so haunted him on the previous occasion opened. There was a smile of recognition. Pain, too. It was evident that every movement involved effort.

"Please," he urged, "don't try to talk."

Then, the words that he had thought a thousand times how best to phrase:

"Mrs. Kesler, I have come to ask you to tell your husband a deliberate lie."

Monsignor Giovanni checked his watch against the clock in the hotel lobby and calculated that, if he walked, he could be at the Nablus Road consulate in forty minutes. Given a stop of about fifteen minutes along the way to effect the necessary change in his appearance, an hour would be more than adequate.

The possibility of somebody following him didn't arise. He had done nothing yet to excite suspicion, having taken care to leave the Apostolic Delegation two nights previously under cover of darkness. Admittedly, once he was in the immediate area of the consulate, it might be different, but that was why he had decided on a change of clothing; his clerical suit, black shirt, and cutaway collar were all too conspicuous, even in a city teeming with Christian clerics of all denominations.

He had noted the shop the previous evening during his vain attempt to find an Arab restaurant in Jewish West Jerusalem. It specialized in cheap American-style menswear— denims and garish check shirts calculated to make every construction worker feel like an all-American cowboy.

The proprietor made no attempt to conceal his amusement at a man of the cloth asking to try on a pair of jeans and rodeo shirt. With a broad grin, he suggested that the total effect might be further enhanced if the gentleman were also to change his lace-up shoes for a pair of thick-soled sneakers. Looking at himself in the mirror, Giovanni could see what he meant and readily agreed, enquiring with an unseemly prurience whether these were what were known as "brothel creepers." After a lifetime in clerical garb, he was feeling an elation which, if the exercise had not been undeniably in the interests of Mother Church, might well have been a source of transvestite guilt. As it was, the circumstances allowed total dispensation and, pulling the cubicle curtain across, he couldn't resist striking a couple of gun-slinging poses for the benefit of the mirror.

A glance at his watch brought him back to reality. Carefully folding his trousers, he packed them with his black shirt and clerical collar into his briefcase. The shoes and jacket were too bulky and would have to go into a carrier bag. There was just one more task to perform—the jettisoning of the incriminating sheet of paper on which two nights previously in Archbishop Ramone's office he had written down the Arab driver's instructions for finding the bones. It was fortunate that the sight of it sticking out of an inside pocket of his jacket had reminded him; having already committed it to memory, he should have disposed of it before.

He examined the cubicle. There was a small ashtray screwed

to the wall but he could hardly start burning paper in such a confined space and besides, not being a smoker, he had no matches. An alternative, however, presented itself. There was a slight gap between the wall and the mirror, and with a little dexterity it was just possible to push the folded sheet out of sight behind the glass. Ten, twenty years from now, he speculated, someone would take down the mirror and discover the faded scrap of paper with its meaningless Italian scrawl—and not have the slightest intimation of its unique historical importance!

Back outside and heading east along the Street of the Prophets, Giovanni himself had even less intimation of the consternation his quick-change act had wrought in the plainclothes policeman trailing him, who couldn't have been more surprised if he had emerged in high heels and a sequined leotard.

After satisfying himself that this really was the sober-suited prelate he had watched enter the shop, the Israeli was now convinced that such a master of disguise must be a top enemy agent, and tagged along behind at a more respectful distance as Giovanni continued on his way past a succession of schools, convents, and hospitals.

Two hundred yards before the Damascus Gate, he saw the "monsignor" cut through to Nablus Road and, turning left, head north. For the first time he had an idea where the trail was leading. Five minutes later, his suspicions were confirmed as the "monsignor" glanced nervously up at the security camera and pushed the iron door in response to the buzz of the automatic lock release.

"Gone *where*?"

The inspector's voice was incredulously shrill.

"Into the American Consulate on Nablus Road," repeated the crackly voice on the two-way from little more than half a mile away.

The inspector stared at the microphone, his mind working feverishly to find a common link between the Vatican passport, the brass crucifix, the name on the notepad, and now the American Consulate. A fragment of thought from earlier in the day came to him: Ireland wasn't the only place that persecuted Scots had fled to . . .

"Moshe," he said, his arm outstretched, "give me the list of diplomatic personnel."

The officer passed over a loose-leaf binder and watched as his superior flicked to the page he wanted, ran his finger down it, and let out an uncharacteristic cry of triumph.

"McKenzie, Arthur J. McKenzie," he quoted, "member of the political section of the East Jerusalem Consulate of the United States of America," and tossed the binder back at the startled Moshe with the observation that if one believed *that*, one might also believe that Hitler had a Magen David tattooed on the end of his penis.

He grabbed the microphone.

"Zev, stay where you are. I'm sending a van down to bring this character in the moment he comes out of there."

"Do you want me to alert the Chief, so he can pass it on to the P.M.'s Office?" asked Moshe with, for him, uncommon foresight.

The inspector thought. A wrong move either way at this stage could affect his chances of promotion for life. A compromise suggested itself.

"Alert him, but suggest he doesn't talk to the Acting P.M. personally until we've had a chance to question our friend. We'll know soon enough, once we've got him in here."

Monsignor Giovanni was frankly disappointed. He hadn't expected a reception committee, but McKenzie's offhand treatment had bordered on the offensive. Understandably the man's mind had been on other matters, but there was no excuse for his contemptuous rejection of the offer of further assistance. Apart from which, one did not address the personal representative of His Holiness the Pope as "Buddy Boy," no matter what his apparel. Whatever their technological achievements, concluded Giovanni, they were a singularly uncivilized race, the Americans.

The iron door clanked behind him and he was left to ponder his next move, now that he was clearly to be barred from the climax of this historic operation. It was a terrible letdown. In his wilder fantasies he had pictured himself getting off the plane at Fiumicino, still in cowboy garb but with the possible addition of a pair of stylish dark glasses, the bones in a holdall casually slung over one shoulder, to be met by a small party of curial cardinals and thence driven straight to a private audience with the Holy Father in his third-floor study. Instead, he found himself marooned on a dusty, noisy, traffic island, opposite a rundown filling station and surrounded by wretched Arabs.

In a mood of the deepest despondency, he decided to return to the hotel, little realizing that within seconds of passing out of sight of the consulate, his hopes for an exciting, eventful afternoon would be more than fulfilled.

★

It was six-thirty. In fifteen minutes Kesler was due to meet McKenzie in the morgue. More than ever he was reluctant to leave Aya's bedside, knowing that it would be four hours at least before he would be able to get back, whatever Berman's assertion of "four hours at most." Fearing, too. The doctors had retreated into jargon. "As well as can be expected" and "holding her own" had now been modified, he noticed, to "still critical but stable," which—given its least favorable interpretation—was the equivalent of standing still on a moving walkway that was running backwards.

The only positive indications had come from Aya herself. She hadn't spoken, but by squeezing his hand in response to his questions had assured him she was feeling stronger. Self-deception or not, he had in turn comforted himself with the knowledge that, having trained as a physiotherapist and worked in hospitals with hundreds of patients, she was well qualified to judge her own condition.

Her eyes flicked to the clock and back to him.

Letting go her hand, he took a last look. The lustrous black hair, olive skin, and lapis lazuli eyes combined to remind him of a Pharaoh's daughter. The sort depicted on funeral caskets.

The associations troubled him and, on his feet now, he bent to kiss her forehead.

"You won't go away, will you?" and, stroking back the hair, ". . . love you."

Her eyes narrowed into a smile and held back the tears till he was out of the room.

★

"You speak English?" asked the inspector, examining the first page of the Vatican passport.

"Sí," replied the priest perversely.

"Then we speak in English, OK?"

"OK."

"Your name is Mauro Agostino Ciampolini; you were born in Bologna on the seventeenth of April, 1954; and it says here that your . . ."

"May . . . the seventeenth of May, 1954," corrected Monsignor Giovanni.

"May," repeated the inspector, annoyed with himself for trying a stupid trick. On reflection, the one thing *least* likely to be fabricated on a false passport was the date of birth.

"First," he resumed testily, "what was your purpose in visiting the American Consulate?"

"I wished to enquire about visa requirements."

"For what? Where?"

"For getting into America—on a Vatican passport."

"Why?"

"Because I wish to visit there on my holiday in the summer."

"Why make enquiries here? Why not wait till you get back to Rome?"

"I was told there was a consulate here in Jerusalem, and I had the time."

"And what about your flock—the party of nuns you're meant to be showing around our country? You don't seem to be spending a lot of time with them."

The priest smiled.

"They don't really need me. I just have to be around in case of difficulties. You see, I speak English and they speak only Italian."

The inspector picked up the passport again, flipped it over, and turned to an inside page.

"Your passport, it is new, brand new. It appears to have been issued only a day before you arrived here."

Another smile.

"My normal passport is an Italian one but it expired without my realizing it. To have gotten it renewed would have taken weeks and for this trip I needed one immediately. The Vatican passport office was very understanding. Sometimes an old bureaucracy can move faster than a young one."

The inspector was tempted to pursue the point. Why was it that, apart from his Alitalia return ticket and a letter of credit issued by the Istituto per le Opere di Religione—the Vatican bank—through the Banca di Roma, the priest had no documentation other than his shiny new passport to substantiate his identity as Mauro Ciampolini? And how would he explain the apparently contradictory inscription on the back of the brass crucifix? Having seen the passport, it was now clear that Giovanni was not merely a preferred middle name. But to ask so much at this stage would be to reveal the extent of investigations already made and perhaps frighten him into silence. The matter of the crucifix could wait.

For a further twenty minutes, therefore, the inspector worked through a succession of routine, predictable questions. To each the priest had an answer, and yet, far from themselves being predictable, they bore the marks of inspired improvisation.

QUESTION: Why had he felt it necessary to change his clerical clothes?
ANSWER: He had always wanted to break the sartorial mold imposed on him by his vocation. Just for once. Now had seemed the ideal opportunity.
QUESTION: Why had he not booked into his hotel till halfway through the second night?
ANSWER: He had been reliving the hours leading up to Christ's crucifixion—from His prayers in Gethsemane, His arrest shortly before midnight, His trial in the Old City, right up to His death and burial in what was now the Church of the Holy Sepulchre.

The inspector had been unable to fault him. He had listened as the priest had displayed his intimate knowledge of all the appropriate locations—the Mount of Olives, the Via Dolorosa, the streets of the Old City—not realizing that the knowledge had been gained following the footsteps of a lesser Christian personage.

At the end of it all, the inspector wondered whether he had misjudged his man. Perhaps he *was* just a religious nutter. A harmless one at that—hardly the sort who would go off and desecrate a synagogue or burn down a mosque.

And yet, and yet . . .

One thing remained quite inexplicable: Why had he shown such little surprise at being taken in? An innocent man would have demanded to know why he was being treated in this way; what he was meant to have done. An innocent man would have insisted that his embassy, consulate—in the priest's case, the Apostolic Delegation—be informed of his detention. But this character had neither demanded nor insisted on a single thing during the three-quarters of an hour that he had now been held. Not so much as a glass of water.

Frustrated and baffled, the inspector retired to his office. Interviewing foreigners was always an exasperating business. When a suspect was speaking a language other than his own, it was virtually impossible to detect a lie; the hiccup, the hesitation, the search for the right word were the perfect cover for the man boxing his way round the truth. Added to that, the infuriating cleric seemed to be atually enjoying the experience, as though it were some sort of childish word game!

More than anything at this moment, the inspector needed a sounding board, but, looking through the glass partition, he saw only the disconsolate Moshe, still bashing the telephone. Reluctantly, he called him in.

Had anything come up? he asked. Nothing had. He offered him a coffee—from his *own* machine—and, as he poured it, went over the sequence of questioning he had just conducted with the priest. At first surprised by this unexpected display of confederacy, the young officer gradually warmed to the unstated invitation to contribute his own thoughts.

"Well, this quick-change act would fit the spy hypothesis," he remarked.

"How?"

"Oh, you know the sort of thing. Drops. Every spy novel has a drop in it—a lavatory, a phone booth, a hollowed-out tree—anywhere where a secret message can be hidden by one agent to be picked up later by another. A men's changing cubicle would be ideal for the purpose. And of course, to avoid suspicion, he would have to buy something."

The inspector wasn't convinced. The transformation from cleric to cowboy had hardly been the act of someone anxious to avoid suspicion. Not that he could pretend to know the mind of a spy. Spies were more the concern of Shin Beth, the counterintelligence service. Terrorists, nutters, and plain old-fashioned criminals were the daily fare of the police. As for reading spy novels, any time the inspector had for reading was spent on files, statements, and charge sheets.

All in all, it seemed a pretty farfetched idea. Still, there was the McKenzie tie-up, and, if that was more than just coincidence, what *was* the priest doing parleying with a likely agent of the CIA? The political section of an American consulate—which was what McKenzie was listed under—didn't waste its time sorting out visa problems.

There was also a purely negative consideration to be taken into account. The risk of doing nothing and then, after the priest had indeed been exposed as a spy, having the pock-marked pipsqueak opposite go around telling everybody how *he* had suggested searching the cubicle in the first place, was greater than the effort of following up what in all probability was a false lead.

"OK," he decided, swinging round in his chair, "get Silver and Meisels to go down there and check the cubicle. We know which shop it was?"

"Herut Square—on the same side as the Davidka Memorial. There's only the one menswear shop," replied Moshe, suddenly fired by a more professional approach to the job than he had displayed in months.

"And as soon as you've done that," added the inspector, holding out the English edition of the Jerusalem Post, "pass by the interrogation room and throw our dog a bone—something to help him while away the time. Say I am tied up on some other business at the moment."

Moshe's eyebrows arched.

"I'll be in the observation chamber next door," explained the inspector. "I just want to test his reactions."

Along the corridor, Giovanni was experiencing something similar to the elation he had felt when he had doffed his ecclesiastical garb. The interrogation had been a stimulating reverse of the confessional—a license to lie, which had permitted his imagination full fantastic rein. Not that he hadn't often been required to lie in his capacity as a Vatican official, but those lies had been more in the nature of half-truths, requiring selection rather than invention. This was altogether different, and he was amazed at how easily—and well—he did it.

Initially, he had been too excited to read the newspaper that had been tossed in, but as the minutes wore on and his fantasies about enduring modern martyrdom at the hands of his Jewish captors gave way to sheer boredom, his attention drifted towards it.

The front page and most of the second were devoted to Camp David and, in the absence of facts, the usual reams of speculation. He moved on to the third page.

The headline halfway down knocked him not so much sideways as forwards. Bringing his face to within a couple of inches of it, he read: *Apostolic Delegate's Death—Suicide Theory*.

It was riveting stuff. He knew Ramone had killed himself—he had been so informed over the telephone by His Holiness—and had assumed that he had used the gun taken from the car. Here, though, was the titillating detail—the fact that it had all happened in front of the Garden Tomb, of all places; that the Arab gardener who had found the body had at first thought that the blood trickling down from the parapet and congealed between the paving stones in the form of a cross was either a divine revelation or a practical joke; and that, despite diplomatic representations at the highest level, the Holy See had refused the Israeli authorities permission to speak to anybody in the Apostolic Delegation about the incident. In the meantime, concluded the article, the Anglican owners of the Garden Tomb were planning to hold a special service for the soul of their Roman Catholic brother in Christ. A wry smile crept across Giovanni's face. Was there no limit to religious opportunism?

Watching through the one-way glass from the dimly-lit cubbyhole next door, the inspector was similarly intrigued, but less by the article than by its reader. *Any* Catholic priest would have been interested in such a story but this one's repertoire of facial expressions pointed to a personal involvement. It was still a hunch, but it would now be easier to put to the test.

Almost graciously, the inspector apologized for having kept him waiting so long. There were, though, a couple of formalities still to be tied up before he could be allowed to go and, since this might require holding him for a further hour or so, the Apostolic Delegation would of course be notified . . .

No, no, the priest assured him, that really wasn't necessary.

Necessary or not, replied the inspector, it was standard procedure when detaining a foreigner for any length of time—as much to protect the authorities as the detainee.

For the first time, the priest seemed agitated. The Apostolic Delegation, he declared, represented the Holy See and, although the Holy See also issued passports, his was actually issued by the Vatican City State; the two entities were in this respect quite different. So—since the Vatican itself had no representation in Israel—the best people to inform, if anybody, would probably be the Italian embassy. He was, after all, also an Italian national.

The inspector pushed back his chair and laughed.

"Oh, come now, Giovanni, this really is splitting hairs!"

"Not at all," responded the priest. "There is a very strict division between . . ." and, realizing too late the trap he had fallen into, stopped.

The inspector, suddenly serious, leaned forward.

"Yes, Giovanni, you were saying?"

The moment of satisfaction was interrupted by the buzz of the telephone at his right elbow.

It was Moshe reporting back on the inspection of the cubicle in the menswear shop. His tone suggested that he too had reason to be pleased with himself.

The coffin was small, pitifully small.

White, clinical. Less a coffin than a capsule. Plastic. Roughly tubular with rounded ends. A flange and seam around the edge, studded at intervals with chromed screw heads. Hermetically sealed. No symbols, no lettering. A nondenominational, all-purpose, body box.

Kesler watched impassively as the two mortuary attendants loaded it into the back of the big, black Plymouth station wagon, secured it with straps, and closed the tailgate. He was asked to sign a release form; was given a copy, and with it a small polyethylene bag. The attendant said something about personal effects and, looking more closely, Kesler saw the bag contained Beni's watch—the one he had bought him for his last birthday. "Commando style" was how it had been described on the box, meaning it was made of chunky, olive-drab plastic with a strap of army-type webbing. The glass wasn't broken but the cheap clockwork movement had stopped at twelve minutes past nine. *Been* stopped. He slipped it into his pocket and climbed into the passenger seat.

McKenzie, who had been subdued during the pickup at

the hospital, was soon back to his "Buddy Boy" self as they
descended the slope of Mount Scopus, not that Kesler had
ever had any illusions about the suitability of his temperament for hearse driving.

Dusk was falling fast now. The lights were on in the old
Augusta Victoria Hospital and, glancing back, all that could
be seen of the Hebrew University was the red aircraft-warning
light on its familiar conning tower.

As they carried on along the upper ridge of the Mount of
Olives, past the right-hand turn that would have taken them
down to the Apostolic Delegation, and on through the scruffy
little Arab town of A-Tur, it became clear to Kesler that
wherever they were heading, it was not in the direction of
the airport. A few minutes later, when they hit the main
highway and turned left for Jericho, he knew it was exactly
the opposite direction.

"Why this way?" he asked.

"You'll find out soon enough, Buddy Boy," smirked Mc-
Kenzie, checking the side mirror, "but, first, a little service
stop . . ."

As he spoke, he yanked the big Plymouth over onto the
hard shoulder and slewed it to an untidy halt. Without explanation he leaned across and pulled from the glove compartment a contraption that looked like a flashlight but with a
built-in meter.

"OK, Buddy Boy, spread your legs and lift your ass off the
seat," he ordered, and, like an over-zealous valet, scanned
him all over. Apparently satisfied, he started going through
the pockets of Kesler's jacket.

"What's this?" he demanded, seizing on the plastic bag.

"My son's watch. They gave it to me at the mortuary."

"*They* gave it to you? The Israeli attendant you mean—*he*
gave it you?"

Before Kesler could reply, McKenzie had the watch out of
the bag and was scanning it too, back and front. Not satisfied,
he eased a penknife under the backplate and twisted it off
with a ping. The innards seemed to engross him and, pushing
the reset button, he again scanned it. But, instead of then
handing it back, he lowered the car window and threw it as
far as he could into the scrub. When Kesler protested angrily, he turned on him.

"Look, Buddy Boy, you'd better get one thing straight

before we go any further on this little jaunt. You're not playing the journalist-mailboy now. This is hardball, kid, and that means no fooling around taking chances. And you wanna know why?" His eyes flicked to the back of the car. "That oversized shoebox there is sitting on one hundred pounds of C-4 plastic explosive—on the express orders of His Holiness the Popeship." He pulled from his breast pocket what looked like a transistor radio. Extending the aerial, he flicked a switch that caused a tiny red light to wink into life. "And, as of now, Buddy Boy, it is primed. If this baby goes up, you, me, the bones, and any Israeli who cares to join us will be swimming round the firmament for the rest of fucking eternity!"

He smiled—an evil smile—and recited: "Twinkle, twinkle, little car. How I wonder where you are . . ."—followed by his muffled imitation of an explosion as he slowly widened his hands.

Kesler could have done without the demonstration. Knowing that his own car had been blown up by just ten pounds of ordinary commercial gelignite, he could imagine well enough what ten times that amount of plastic explosive packed beneath the floor of the station wagon would do.

McKenzie, meanwhile, was out of the car and, scanner again in hand, was going over the casket in the back and checking the wheel arches and the entire underside in case a bug had been placed at the hospital morgue.

"Wouldn't put anything past those bastards," he remarked, getting back behind the wheel. He started the engine again and at the same time handed Kesler a typed sheet.

"The directions," he grunted, "and you're the navigator, Buddy Boy."

★

Berman was astonished.

"Down here? . . . Why?"

Meir repeated that the Acting Prime Minister was waiting in the Emergency Cabinet Room and *demanded*—his word—to see the Defense Minister urgently on a matter directly related to the present operation.

The Mossad chief, Eli Hausner, was sitting a few feet away.

"I couldn't help hearing; I was listening," he remarked drily. "Do you want an independent witness with you?"

Berman nodded and got up. The last person he needed putting his oar in right now was Shavit. He recalled Ya'acov Rosenstein's warning after the last Cabinet meeting—that Shavit's seeming capitulation wasn't to be taken at face value—and, angry and worried, led the way down the corridor to the Emergency Cabinet Room.

The self-assured smile told him he was right to be suspicious.

Immaculately groomed as ever, Shavit was sitting in the Prime Minister's chair, predictably exploiting the full theatricality of the situation. His gaze, though, quickly passed from Berman to Hausner.

"I asked for a personal meeting, Gideon—alone."

Berman pulled out a chair and motioned to Hausner to sit down.

"I am sure," he said, "that the head of the country's intelligence services can be trusted to keep a personal conversation secret."

Shavit was evidently not in the mood for mere point-scoring, which struck Berman as ominous.

"I'm not going to argue with you, Gideon. There isn't time. We know where the bones are."

"We?" enquired Berman, with difficulty masking his surprise.

For a second Shavit relished the suspense. The pleasure of what he was about to disclose was not to be wasted.

"The Prime Minister's Office," he elaborated, "was notified twenty minutes ago of the arrest of a Catholic priest by the police. He has admitted to being Monsignor Giovanni Corvo, the personal secretary of the Vatican Secretary of State, Cardinal Pellegrini. He's been under suspicion for a couple of days—since the death of Archbishop Ramone, in fact—and this afternoon was seen entering the American Consulate on Nablus Road. Subsequent investigations have brought to light the details—*written* details—of the precise hiding place of the bones. Since Cabinet voted you control of the operation, I am passing on this information for you to act upon without delay."

Berman caught the look in Hausner's eye: "Proceed with extreme caution!" it said. He turned back to Shavit.

"I am grateful for the information, Reuven, but I have to tell you that the extent to which we'll be able to act on it may be limited by other developments."

"In God's name," retorted Shavit, "I'm telling you where

the damned things are. All you have to do is go and get them!"

Again Berman was aware of the restraining figure on his left; again his reply was measured.

"It's unfortunately not as straightforward as that. If the bones haven't already been collected by somebody else, they are likely to be very shortly—and before we could get anybody there."

Shavit leaned back in the chair.

"Ah, so you know where they are," he taunted.

"No, we do not . . . although we do know that they are not in the Apostolic Delegation, as was at first . . ."

He stopped. There was no time for childish guessing games. The only way to avoid a shouting match was to present Shavit with the full facts and trust that, for once, his reason would get the better of his ambition.

"Reuven," he said calmly, "let me explain to you why we can't just go in and grab them . . ."

He ran through every stage of the operation, starting with the recruiting of Kesler in the Military Cemetery and ending with the hoped-for repossession of the bones at the airport. Although concise, no relevant detail was omitted.

"Do you see now?" he concluded.

But Shavit wasn't to be persuaded. He was arguing from a position of strength and was determined to exploit it—for if Berman did as he suggested, he, Shavit, would be credited with providing the information that got the bones back, but if Berman stuck to Operation Isaac and it went wrong, then equally Shavit would be able to claim that Berman's pride had compromised his judgement.

"So where is this consular car now?" he asked.

"We don't know. It left the Hadassah just after seven. Our next fix, as I've explained, will not be till the airport."

"You mean you haven't tried to bug it or anything?"

"No—deliberately not. Bugs can be detected, and if this man McKenzie were to find out that the car, the coffin, or Kesler had been bugged, he would know that the entire operation was a put-up job to get him to lead us to the bones. The same would go for any attempt to tail the car."

Shavit shook his head in feigned disbelief.

"So you're going to sit here for the next hour and a half and just *hope* that the bones are going to present themselves at the airport, without the slightest notion—not even interest apparently—where they may be in the meantime?"

Hausner sensed that Berman was close to losing his temper and answered for him.

"That has been the thinking behind this operation from the start—which is not to say it wouldn't be of help to have any information you may care to give us."

With a flourish Shavit pulled a map from an inside pocket and pushed it down the table.

"My pleasure! You can see where it's marked—less than a kilometer beyond the sea level marker on the Jericho road. There's a track that runs off to the right down to a wadi. Some hundred meters down on the left is an outcrop of rock that looks like a skull. They're in a hole directly beneath it. It's all written down. Here." He tossed across a sheet of paper. "This is the translation of the priest's directions. And if you're not going to do anything about it, I will."

Berman pointedly ignored the remark and studied the map. It was less than twenty miles from the Hadassah Hospital to the spot on the map—half an hour's traveling time at most. The nearest Army patrol was based on the southern outskirts of Jericho. By the time messages had been passed, the patrol briefed, and the extreme—not to say explosive— delicacy of the situation explained, it could be twenty minutes before they got there. If McKenzie and Kesler had stopped for any length of time or had had difficulty following the instructions, then it might just be possible to cut them off before the turnoff, but the odds were overwhelmingly against it. Much more likely was a bungled shoot-out with the bones being blown sky high. The decision was made.

"I'm not prepared to order an intervention at this stage. The operation will continue as planned."

Shavit stood up, his features sharpened by the overhead lighting.

"I don't think you heard what I said, Berman. I am assuming command of this operation."

Berman looked down again at the map and asked quietly, "By what authority?"

"By the authority vested in me as Prime Minister!"

"Acting Prime Minister."

"Same thing."

"Wrong—and, as a politician, you should know." Looking

to Hausner for confirmation, Berman continued, "Decisions collectively agreed in Cabinet cannot be overruled by an Acting Prime Minister *except* with the specific authority of the Prime Minister. My command of this operation was granted me by a unanimous vote of the Cabinet. I am grateful, though, for your information."

Hausner inclined his head as though to confirm, while Shavit gave a passable imitation of a man who had belatedly realized his legs had been cut off.

For several seconds nobody said a word, each of the three frozen in an attitude of waxen immobility.

Shavit was the first to bring the tableau to life.

"My God, Berman, I hope you know what you are doing," he spluttered; "I just hope you know the risk you are taking. That's all," and stalked out of the room.

As the footsteps receded down the corridor, Hausner turned to Berman.

"I had no idea you were such a keen constitutionalist."

"Nor I," responded Berman. "I made it all up. But by the time he discovers the truth, it'll be too late for him to do anything about it. Even Shavit wouldn't risk blowing the operation by ringing up Avram at Camp David and discussing such a matter over the phone. Remind me to thank Rosenstein."

"Why?"

"It was he who told me Shavit was no cardplayer."

★

Kesler no longer had any doubts about the mental state of his driving companion. With the road now dropping away at an average 160 feet per mile, the normally cumbersome Plymouth seemed largely to be determining its own speed and direction, barreling though the Judean Hills with the gathering, terrifying momentum of a four-man bobsled on the Cresta Run—while the mad McKenzie behind the wheel spouted a stream of inconsequential babble to maintain his own highly charged ego.

From repeated firsthand experience, Kesler was sufficiently familiar with the road to know at roughly what point to expect the sea level marker. The white triangular slab was the height of a man and, even at night, was impossible to miss. Normally. At the speed they were hurtling, it was upon them before they realized.

"Slow—that's it!" he yelled, fearful that any overreaction by McKenzie might secure them their allotted place in the firmament even without the assistance of the remote detonator.

Tires screeching, the Plymouth shuddered to a sufficiently sedate pace to allow Kesler to crane his neck out of the window in search of the turning.

According to the directions, it was on the right, and less than a mile beyond the marker. It was—but only if you knew what you were looking for and when.

In response to a second yell, McKenzie threw the station wagon through a 160 degree hairpin turn, winding the wheel like a stopcock as the spongy suspension tried to absorb the rutted terrain. A cloud of red dust thrown up by the rear wheels enveloped them, finally settling to reveal a deep, narrow gorge that fell away into a darkness which even the Plymouth's powerful lights couldn't penetrate.

"Jesus! You sure this is it?" muttered McKenzie, easing the lumbering beast forward in a series of jerks.

"Sure," replied Kesler, noting that even the swaggering McKenzie seemed susceptible to the Dantesque atmosphere of the place.

They drove no more than fifty yards into the mouth of the gorge, at which point it contracted into a throat, forcing them to abandon the Plymouth and, as the directions had indicated, go the rest of the way on foot.

It was eerily quiet. Even the gentle click of the car door seemed to ricochet off the opposing rock faces with pinball clarity, while the carpet of wild thorn crackled beneath their feet like glass.

Flashlight in hand, McKenzie led the way downwards, allowing the beam to trace the curves of the convulsed rock in search of the skull-like outcrop. Nothing even remotely like a skull was to be seen, and by the time they had reached the wadi at the bottom of the gorge McKenzie's impatience was outrunning his nervousness.

"It *can't* be this far down," he said in an urgent whisper. "We must have missed it."

Recalling the precision of the directions, Kesler was inclined to agree.

"Could be it's higher up than we've been looking. It's described as an outcrop."

He took the flashlight from McKenzie and, retracing his steps up the incline, directed the beam along a line about ten yards up.

It was hard to be sure. If somebody had told you the bulging ball of rock looked like a skull, then out of politeness you might have agreed. The two holes, side by side, naturally suggested eyes, but it required some imagination to paint in the forehead and jawline.

"*Must* be it," he declared, "and if it is, the bones will be directly beneath it under a shelf of rock just above ground . . ."

McKenzie was already there, scooping out handfuls of the loose earth and cursing the ants, beetles, and spiders that swarmed over his hands. He called for the flashlight and, lying flat on his stomach, shone it inside.

"Yes, sir, that's my baby!" he exclaimed, and reached the full length of his arm into the gap.

Whatever it was either of them expected to find, it wasn't an Israeli Army kit bag.

"And no extra charge for the dandy packaging!" McKenzie joked, releasing the drawstrings. He shone the flashlight inside and, beaming like a Halloween pumpkin in the reflected light, stood up.

"OK, Buddy Boy, let's get back to the car. This place is giving me the heebie-jeebies."

Despite his passion for tennis, McKenzie's physical condition appeared to be no better than his mental condition. Puffing from the exertion of the uphill hike, he rested a few seconds against the side of the station wagon before opening the tailgate. Brandishing a screwdriver, he then released the retaining straps on the coffin, evidently with every intention of transferring the contents there and then. Kesler was appalled, and showed it.

"Well, do *you* want to do it?" asked McKenzie contemptuously, proffering the screwdriver.

Kesler turned away. The thought of handling Beni's mangled remains horrified him—but, on consideration, not as much as the thought of McKenzie handling them and, with a cheery quip or two, irreverently stuffing them into the foxhole.

"Well, it's got to be done, Buddy Boy, and, if you're not going to do it . . ."

Kesler turned back to face him.

"Give me the screwdriver," he said. "Help me carry the coffin down to the hole and leave me there with the flashlight. You can get on with packing the latex round the bones. The interior light should be enough to work by."

McKenzie gave a grunt of surprise.

"If that's what you want, I'm more than happy to oblige. But no dawdling . . ."

Back beneath the outcrop, with the coffin laid beside the hole, he pulled a pair of surgical rubber gloves from his pocket and handed them to Kesler.

"You might need these," he said.

Kesler took them and watched as the figure puffed off again into the darkness.

Suppressing his natural revulsion for the act he was to perform, he palmed the screwdriver and inserted the point into the first screwhead. Then the second, followed by the third. On undoing the fourth, there was an audible hiss as the hermetic seal broke, releasing a strong smell of what he recognized from his schooldays as formaldehyde.

All the screws extracted, it remained only to lift the lid. Not knowing what he was likely to find, his imagination had already filled the void, making him wonder whether to switch off the flashlight and do it by feel alone.

But Beni deserved better. He rolled on the gloves and, his hands white and sepulchral in the beam, lifted the lid just enough to clear the lip and slide it slowly to one side.

To his relief, the body was wrapped and taped in heavy-duty black plastic sheeting. Body? Half a dozen separate packages. Fight the thought as he did, it was impossible not to be reminded of a jointed carcass bought at the butcher's for the deep freeze.

And yet it had to be done.

One by one, maintaining the tightest bridle on his imagination, he lifted the packages and placed them in the space formerly occupied by the kit bag. The coffin now empty, he heaped the loose earth back to fill the entrance to the hole and, in an attitude of Christian humility—on his knees, hands clasped—recited Kaddish, the Jewish prayer for the dead:

"*Yisgaddal v'yiskaddash shmey rabboh*—May His great name be magnified and sanctified . . ."

The guttural cadences of the pure Aramaic had a therapeutic power of their own that went beyond the bald exhortation to reconcile oneself to the will of God and, as the words were swallowed up by the gorge, he found himself picturing Beni as he had been in life—the huge brown eyes, prominent ears, and impish grin that on the instant could dissolve into an expression of pure wonderment.

He smiled at the recollection. Beni was dead but would always live in his memory. And perhaps in another, more substantial way. They would have another son and he too would be called Beni—a literal reincarnation in which memory would become flesh, the same spark of conception kindling again the same birth, growth, and development. In every respect he would be Beni so that, eventually, there would be no need for memories, except in the sense that one remembers what day of the week or month of the year it is. Less a memory than an awareness.

A more immediate awareness bore in on him—the need to return to the car.

Putting one half of the coffin shell inside the other, he took a last look at what he trusted would be only a temporary resting place for Beni's remains, and started back.

McKenzie was wrapping the last of the bones in what looked like the sort of lagging they used in Baltimore to stop the pipes freezing. He was cursing under his breath at their refusal to stay inside the jackets and, seeing Kesler, snatched the empty coffin halves with a gruff rebuke that was lost on the air.

Only after several more minutes of struggle and bad temper did he succeed in getting the piled-up bones and latex to stay in place long enough to clamp on the lid and screw it down. Finally, with a check of the seal to ensure it was properly bedded all round, he strapped the casket back into its original position and—only just remembering not to slam it—closed the tailgate.

Kesler stood on the other side of the car waiting to get back into the passenger seat. He was about to climb in when something small and metallic slid across the roof towards him—something that struck more terror into his heart than anything he had experienced or imagined in the depths of the gorge. The keys.

With every mile the Plymouth consumed, he heard the words of Berman's assistant louder and more urgent: "It'll be up to you to get out of the line of fire. The only target will be the guy behind the wheel." If previously he had worried about being hit by a stray bullet, that now seemed nothing compared to his present situation, perched on the cross hairs.

Keeping his hands on the wheel, he attempted to scrutinize McKenzie out of the corner of his eye. The man was sitting awkwardly, wedged against the door, his left arm slung over the back of the seat and his right resting on the sill of the open window, detonator in hand. Every now and again, his head would jerk to the back of the car—a nervous gesture usually accompanied by a flick of the priming switch and a brief twinkle of the tiny red light. His changes of temperament were alarmingly unpredictable, ranging from a sudden flow of manic verbiage, through impatience and anger, to the present twitchy silence which, in view of the destructive power at his fingertips, was potentially the most dangerous of all. Kesler swallowed hard; there was not the slightest doubt in his mind that the man was capable of pushing the button at the first sign of trouble.

It was only when they had climbed the two and a half thousand feet back into the relative cool of Jerusalem that Kesler noticed a curious omission. There had been no checkpoint at Ma'ale Adumin—despite the fact that he could not remember when there had *not* been one on this, the eastern gateway into the capital and hence one of the strategically most important strips of road in the whole of Israel. There could be only one explanation—that Berman was taking no chances of an accidental armed encounter before the final shoot-out at Kilometer 15. And yet it was unreal to be the carrier of a cargo so vital to the country's future and at the same time be so totally ignored.

Fortunately McKenzie seemed not to have noticed the absence, as they now sped within sight of the long, straight, crenellated wall of the Temple Mount and followed the contours of the Kidron Valley past the bricked-up Golden Gate of the Old City, through which it was said the Messiah would enter on the Day of Judgement.

But not tonight. Tonight He was going straight on to the Rockefeller building and thence west along Paratroopers Road, past the Damascus Gate, up Jaffa Road out of the city again.

The traffic lights were with them and, all too soon for Kesler, they were hurtling downhill towards Tel Aviv, past shadowy cypresses and the familiar rusting relics of the War of Independence. With just forty minutes to go, the trigger-happy maniac in the passenger seat was psyching himself up for his starring role in the airport customs shed.

"Once we get there you leave everything to me—right?" he said, breaking a half-hour silence. "You just stay back and let me do all the talking. I've done this trip a dozen times. I know these guys and by now they know me. It's always the same: The car is backed up into the bay, the coffin lifted out, through the X-ray, back into the car, and then driven at walking pace across the tarmac to the aircraft. Never varies . . . and the beauty of it is that at no point will it be more than a couple of yards from the car; so if anything goes wrong, no matter how late in the game, it'll be twinkle-twinkle time all around . . ." He tossed the detonator in his hand. "Just warning you, Buddy Boy—'cause if you don't get your head down, you'll be picking it up from the other end of the fucking runway!"

He laughed at Kesler's obvious unease, not appreciating how little interest the minutiae of airport procedure were to him. They would never get that far.

The grim realization was underlined by the appearance of the first of the kilometer markers. The countdown had begun, and, with the desperation of a man who knew the rest of his life was measured out in neat black numbers on small blue signs, Kesler ran through the chances of avoiding what all reason told him was now inevitable.

Every option seemed hopelessly flawed—to contrive an accident deliberately before Kilometer 15 would be to risk an explosion, irrespective of the detonator; to try to alert Berman's men to the changed identity of the driver by sounding the horn or flashing the lights would be to alert McKenzie likewise; and even to ease his foot off the accelerator just to give himself more time to think would be to arouse the man's suspicion.

Kilometer 20 flashed past and without difficulty Kesler was imagining the Israeli marksmen taking up their positions three miles—less than three minutes—away.

By Kilometer 19, they had released the safety catches.

At Kilometer 18, Kesler decided there was nothing to be lost by sheer audacity, and, transferring his foot from accelerator to brake, he pulled over onto the hard shoulder.

"You'd better take over from here," he remarked to a puzzled McKenzie. "The airport turnoff is coming up . . ."

For a moment he thought he had pulled it off. Had it not been for a large, swaying moving van which prevented him getting out immediately and so forcing the issue, he might have done. But the extra seconds gave McKenzie time to consider.

"No, you carry on . . . it's better that I look after the baby," he smirked, indicating the detonator.

"But this is a consular car; it's got diplomatic plates," countered Kesler with an inventiveness born of necessity, "They'll be expecting a consular official at the wheel."

It was no good.

"Expecting maybe, but they know me well enough to recognize me wherever I'm sitting. Now cut the cackle and get this crate back on the road. And step on it."

Kesler's body obeyed, but not his mind. Refusing to proceed to its own destruction, it turned the windshield into a movie screen—projecting upon it the events formerly seen through it; transforming the threatening world of reality into a plush chair and a canvas sheet; and, most treacherously, persuading the brain that Kilometer 15 would be, at worst, a signal for the lights to go on.

Or out.

Within the still deeper recesses of Kesler's subconscious, a reckless instinct suddenly asserted itself, informed by an animal sense of survival that predated the human mind's delusory mechanisms by several million millennia.

Anything was suddenly worth trying. When the alternative was extinction, it *had* to be.

A variation of the idea which he had earlier rejected—the contrived accident—acquired a desperate feasibility. At the first sign of Berman's diversion, whatever it was, he would ask McKenzie for a cigarette and a light, which—if only for a moment—would require him to release the detonator. In that same moment he, Kesler, would throw the car into a controlled skid, sufficient to disorientate McKenzie, separate him from the button, and give Berman's sharpshooters time to work out where the real target was sitting. There would be no margin for error; the pinprick of red light, he noticed, was now permanently on. And they would have to be going faster—much faster. The road was too dry and the Plymouth too heavy to break away at anything less than eighty miles per hour, he reckoned.

Kilometer 16—the penultimate.

He kicked down on the accelerator and felt the great gas-guzzler surge forward. McKenzie showed only passing surprise, apparently satisfied that they were at last getting the move on that had been ordered.

Kesler glanced at the speedometer to see the needle clipping ninety and, his right foot now flat on the floor and his left hovering over the brake, waited for the signal.

Nothing. No checkpoint, no road crews, no flashing lights. And yet it could be only seconds before Kilometer 15 would be hurtling towards them, followed by the lethal cross fire. He could wait no longer.

"Light me a cigarette, will you?"

The response seemed an eternity in coming, during which—immediately beyond the fifteenth marker and assuming infinitely more importance—there appeared an aluminum hut of the sort used by road workers. His imagination stripped away the cladding to reveal two, maybe three, men kneeling and squinting through infrared telescopic sights, waiting only for the word from their commander to . . .

"You'll have to wait, Buddy Boy. It's the surest sign of nerves and every security man knows it."

There was a moment of numbness before the realization hit him that the workmen's hut was already behind them and there had been no attempt to stop them. Incredibly they were still moving—fast, straight, and inexplicably unscathed.

"Hey, dummy, the turnof! Ease off for Christ's sake before we miss it!"

They already had—by about fifty yards. Raising a plume of blue smoke from the scorching tires, Kesler pulled the Plymouth over, stopped, and reversed raggedly back to the turnoff. Still he waited for the crack of a rifle or the rattle of an automatic—if ever they were a sitting target, it was now—but the only sound was a single, prolonged blast on the horn from the motorist he had just cut off immediately behind him.

He couldn't understand it. Berman's assistant had been quite specific: The interception would be just after Kilometer 15—and yet here they were off the main highway, rolling down the access road towards the airport compound. There could be only one explanation: Somebody had spotted him in the driver's seat—perhaps Berman had posted a lookout at Kilometer 18 where he had stopped the car in his attempt to get McKenzie to take over—and the order had been given to abort the ambush. But why then not simply shift the aim from the driver to the passenger?—unless they had calculated that McKenzie, without his mind on the driving and his hands on the wheel, would be that much quicker on the button.

The car was at the entrance to the airport. McKenzie, fulfilling his self-appointed role of spokesman, was leaning out the window to attract the attention of the green-bereted soldier who was heading round to the driver's side.

"Cadaver for the 21:00 flight to New York," he announced with a formality which contrasted oddly with his customary flipness.

More impressed by the coffin than the vocabulary, the soldier stood back and raised the barrier, allowing them into the strangely two-dimensional movie-set world created by the airport's harsh artificial lighting.

Following McKenzie's directions, Kesler took a side road off towards the cargo sheds, but carried on past the TWA shed to a building on its own beyond the end of the row—a low, flat-roofed structure with the architectural individuality of a public lavatory. This, explained McKenzie, was where—irrespective of the carrier—all incoming and outgoing human remains were handled for transfer and customs purposes.

Still following instructions, Kesler backed the Plymouth into the reception bay until the tailgate came up level against the raised roller conveyor that fed the coffins into the X-ray scanner.

The detonator now in his pocket, McKenzie greeted the customs officials with a forced familiarity and singled Kesler out as the bereaved parent. He added a remark concerning the incident that had occasioned the bereavement, which he was sure they had read about in the papers.

One of the officials gave a perfunctory nod and, noting that Kesler himself was booked on the same flight, requested his passport, ticket, and the Israeli Ministry of Health release-permit for his son's remains, while a colleague frisked him and went through his luggage. McKenzie, meanwhile, right hand tucked casually into his pocket, was keeping a discreet distance from everybody, aware how easy it would be in such a confined space for him to be overpowered or felled by a single well-aimed shot. The same thought had occurred to Kesler. Why in heaven's name, he wondered, hadn't Berman planned the ambush for here, instead of on a crazy stretch of open highway?

"If we could take a look at the coffin now . . .?" suggested the senior official, pointing to the tailgate.

"Sure thing. Help yourselves," responded McKenzie, deliberately leaving it to the Israelis to lift it out and shunt it into the grey metal housing of the X-ray scanner.

The crucial moment. Feigning indifference, McKenzie was monitoring every muscle in the operator's face as the man pushed a button and studied the screen.

The operator's expression changed. Shaking his head, he muttered something in Hebrew that neither McKenzie nor Kesler caught. In the same instant, Kesler saw McKenzie's right arm stiffen, and instinctively drew back from the open tailgate, even though he knew it could not make a scrap of difference with such a quantity of explosives in such a confined space.

The operator repeated the words and this time they both understood. He was merely expressing his shock at the butchery indicated by the image on the screen. Still shaking his head, he pushed another button and the coffin rattled out the other side to be loaded back into the Plymouth.

"*Beseder*—OK," said the senior official. He closed the tailgate and, turning to Kesler, added, "*Shalom!*"

Shakily, Kesler climbed back into the driving seat, drove forward out of the bay, waited for McKenzie to get in, and followed the revolving orange light of the airport tractor sent to shepherd them out to the waiting 747 in its red and white TWA livery.

The air was filled with the impatient whine of the giant Pratt and Whitney engines, but still Kesler half-expected a devastating burst of cross fire. At least now there would be no

confusion over the target and, given the time they'd spent in
the customs building, Berman would have had plenty of
opportunity to regroup his ambush team.

But apparently not the inclination.

The tractor stopped beneath the belly of the jumbo jet and
a loader dropped out of the hold. Together, the tractor driver
and the loader then came round to the back of the Plymouth,
slid out the coffin, and hoisted it up into the waiting hands of
a second loader still inside the aircraft.

Kesler watched, mesmerized and uncomprehending, while
the revolving light threw flickering shadows across the underside of the wing. Suddenly he was aware of his right hand
being grasped. It was McKenzie. Masking his satisfaction
beneath a facial veneer of condolence made grotesque by the
alternating flashes of orange, he was mouthing a singularly
inappropriate "bon voyage" and pointing him in the direction
of the steps up to the passenger compartment.

Twenty minutes later, out of Israeli airspace and climbing
to thirty thousand feet, Kesler was still trying to make sense
of the events of the last two hours. Operationally, something
had clearly gone badly wrong for the Israelis and, the more
he thought it through, the more he convinced himself that
the fault was his. It had been up to *him* to ensure that
McKenzie would be driving, and he had failed. Tried his
best, but ultimately failed—and from that failure had sprung
every subsequently missed opportunity.

He felt sick and shivery. Not just a double traitor, he was a
double traitor who had failed *both* countries. Worse still, he
had failed Aya and Beni. In his own estimation he could sink
no lower. The most wretched of all wretches.

"There is a seat reserved for you in the VIP Lounge upstairs, Mr. Kesler," said a voice at his right shoulder, "on the
orders of the White House."

With doglike obedience he followed the chief steward up
the twisting stairway, to find not just a reserved seat but an
opened bottle of champagne in an ice bucket and a small
envelope bearing his name.

It contained the transcription of a radio signal received
minutes earlier in the cockpit:

"On behalf of the American People," it read, "the President of the United States proudly salutes you and congratulates you on your magnificent services to your country."

Never had champagne tasted so sour.

COVENANTS

LIKE A KID on Christmas Eve, the President had been up all night—first, just waiting; then, at 1:00 in the morning when the bones had been flown by helicopter direct from New York's Kennedy Airport to Camp David, delighting in their possession; and now, just before 10:00, reveling in the anticipated pleasure of parading that possession before the disbelieving eyes of Israeli Premier Avraham Rubinger.

Not that they would be placed physically on the negotiating table, as McCrae had threatened. At least not immediately. Showing uncharacteristic restraint, the President had agreed with Secretary Romford that it would be sufficient to hold them under Marine guard in the next room, to be brought out only if the Israeli P.M. demanded visual proof, which privately McCrae hoped he would.

There was a sound of voices outside, and McCrae and Romford composed their expressions for what, it had been agreed, would be a brief preliminary session with the Israelis alone to fix the agenda for the week's talks.

Rubinger entered, his two principal aides in tow, and greeted McCrae with a chirpy "Good morning, Mr. President. I trust you had a good night?"

"Indeed so, and you too I trust," responded McCrae, suppressing a grin.

They took their seats at the massive circular table which, at the start of the talks a week earlier, had been brought in as a diplomatic replacement for the Conference Room's resident rectangular one. Observing the five of them lost at the perimeter, the Israeli P.M. joked about flies around a soup bowl, more seriously aware that McCrae had deliberately chosen the most intimidatory setting he could devise for their premeeting.

"We have drawn up what we think will be an acceptable agenda for the week, Mr. Prime Minister," remarked Secretary Romford, indicating the sheet of paper on Rubinger's blotter.

The Israeli extracted from his breast pocket a pair of ludicrously old-fashioned black plastic spectacles, worthy of a 1950s Sears catalogue, and, squeezing them onto the bulb of his nose, perused the document.

There were no surprises. It fairly bristled with emotive headings:

UN Resolution 242—Israeli return to pre-1967 borders
The West Bank—Palestinian autonomy
Jewish settlements—dismantling/compensation
Jerusalem—international status of

In short, it displayed all the tact of the presidential hand that had clearly drafted it.

Rubinger replaced his glasses carefully in his breast pocket.

"You do not think, Mr. President," he said, "that it might be advisable to discuss the other matter first?"

An ingenuous smile came to McCrae's lips.

"Other matter?"

Rubinger glanced at Secretary Romford before expanding: "I may talk freely about the arrangements you and I discussed alone last Thursday evening in your study in Aspen Lodge—the 'verification' arrangements?"

"But naturally," replied McCrae, "although I would hardly have thought they are any longer relevant, now that the issue has been resolved."

"You were satisfied with your inspection then?"

"Quite satisfied—but, as I say, that is not now a matter that need bother us. Not that I would deny its purely archaeological interest, you understand."

The Israeli P.M. appeared puzzled. "I don't see how the position is altered—except insofar as you are now surer than you were of the wider *political* interest of this archaeological matter. As I indicated at the time, we are prepared within reason to accommodate you on the exact timing of the press announcement and the public display—and have already done so—but these matters cannot be delayed indefinitely," he paused and added quietly, "nor will they be, Mr. President."

McCrae leaned forward. "The announcement and the display of *what*, Mr. Prime Minister? I am not aware that you any longer have anything to announce or display."

"Then you have been ill-informed by your advisers, I fear,

Mr. President. Only an hour ago, I received confirmation from Jerusalem that the archaeological remains to which we refer are safely back under guard."

The moment could not be delayed.

"They are indeed," chuckled McCrae, and nodded to Secretary Romford to instruct the Marine guard to bring in their precious charge.

A minute later, the small cylindrical white casket was trooped in and placed on the table. At a sign from the President, one of the two Marines, a sergeant, raised the lid to display the contents.

To McCrae's disappointment, Rubinger's face underwent no perceptible change. There was even the suggestion of a quizzical smile.

"Well, Mr. Prime Minister," demanded McCrae, "what do you say now?"

"I say they look like bones," answered the Israeli.

"Exactly so, which is wh . . ."

"Look like," repeated the Israeli and, stretching out a hand, asked, "If perhaps I may be permitted to inspect one of them?"

McCrae gave a curt nod to the sergeant, who, cradling it in his white gloved hand, passed one of the slender ribs to the Prime Minister.

"I don't pretend to be an archaeologist," said the Israeli, holding the precious relic at each end, elbows on the table as if about to gnaw it, "but even without my glasses I can spot a . . ." snapping it in two, "plaster cast when I see one." He turned the broken ends towards the dumbfounded Americans, exposing the powdery white interior.

"The casket, on the other hand," he continued, "that is authentic. It's the sort we use for shipping more recently deceased humans out of the country. The Hadassah Hospital in Jerusalem has many such, although *that* one, I would guess, probably originated at Ben-Gurion Airport."

Sensing that he was never again in his life likely to have such an eminent and captive audience, he added, "I could be even more specific. It emanated from the X-ray scanner in the airport customs building. It's a bulky old machine, but it does its job well enough."

He looked down and, clearing his throat, pulled a sheet of typed paper from his folder.

"But, as you say, Mr. President, these are matters of purely archaeological interest. We were talking about the agenda—so perhaps you would like to see what *we* have in mind . . ."

★

For a man who hated social occasions of all sorts but Saturday night get-togethers in particular, the Minister of Defense was concealing his antipathy remarkably well. Some suspected him of even enjoying himself.

More than a hundred people were crammed into the Rosensteins' spacious ground-floor flat in the Rehavia district of Jerusalem. Among them, almost the entire Cabinet. There were only two notable absentees—the Prime Minister, who was still at Camp David negotiating the small print of what was already being unofficially called the East Mediterranean Treaty, and the Acting Prime Minister, who claimed to be engaged on "party business" which, considering most of the party was *at* the party, was strange.

A pillar of smoke coming his way across the room indicated to Berman the approach of Eli Hausner, the Mossad chief.

"You were the last person I expected to see here," said Berman, adding mischievously, "You must let me introduce you to the Cabinet."

Hausner covered his discomfort with a cough.

"I thought," he recovered, "you'd like to know the latest news about our mutual acquaintance, Robert K. Spender."

"Director Spender?"

"*Ex*-director. Gone the way of all flab, I'm afraid. He was fired the day before yesterday, although the announcement won't be made till after Camp David. It seems he was given a choice—early retirement, or his remaining years spent filing blotting paper." A twinkle came to Hausner's eye. "And there's an intriguing footnote . . ."

"Go on."

"The internal CIA postmortem apparently came to the conclusion that 'our man' was not Kesler but the Catholic priest, the monsignor fellow. Knowing that he was picked up immediately after passing on the directions to McKenzie in the consulate, they assumed he broke under questioning and told all."

"But he didn't know all."

"Perhaps not—but enough. His knowledge of the bones' whereabouts and his visit to McKenzie would have been sufficient to make us follow McKenzie to the hospital morgue and there make the connection between the agency, Kesler, his son's body—and ultimately the bones. They weren't to know that the priest didn't break until McKenzie and Kesler were already on their way."

Berman felt a hand on his shoulder. It was Ya'acov Rosenstein.

"Gideon, a word with you."

He led Berman out into the corridor where, apart from the clatter in the kitchen, it was possible to hear and be heard.

"I had a call from Avram earlier this evening," said the Foreign Minister. "He wants you to fly to Washington first thing tomorrow morning—officially, to advise on the drafting of the agreement relating to the defensive *cordon sanitaire;* unofficially, to be at the signing ceremony in the White House. He thinks it important you be there." He winked, and without another word hurried back to his guests.

Only then did Berman suspect a secondary reason for his being brought out into the corridor. Looking through the half-open door to the kitchen, he was surprised to see a figure he had last seen at Yossi's funeral four days earlier, when they had maintained an overdiscreet distance from each other.

She laid down the knife, dried her hands, and came towards him.

"I have a habit of being in places I shouldn't, don't I?" she said with a smile, resting a hand lightly on his forearm. "Hanna Rosenstein insisted I come tonight. I told her I couldn't so soon after the funeral, but she said I had to get out of that big empty house and mix with people. As a compromise, I agreed to come if I could help her in the kitchen. But, anyway, I hear congratulations are in order. *Mazel tov!*"

"You hear more than I do," hedged Berman.

"That I doubt! Are you telling me you *haven't* been summoned to Washington?"

"As a map-bearer, yes. It's more reliable than sending them by mail."

"In which case Ya'acov has got it wrong. He's under the impression Avram wants his successor to be seen by his side at the signing ceremony."

"That's one interpretation."

She lowered her head and, wrapping her hands tightly around his forearm, said: "Gideon, we haven't really spoken since we last . . . met . . . except for the funeral which I suspect was a hundred times worse for you than me; I at least could show my emotion. But I want you to know my feelings because, being how you are, you'd probably regard it as an intrusion into my privacy to ask about them yourself." She paused, her grip tightening. "For me, the other night was Tiberias again. We were the same people with the same feelings, despite the intervening years, but with this difference—that the unknown future of those days of our youth had become the known past. This time I felt no need to test my feelings against experience; I felt a total confidence in my emotions. Do you understand what I am saying?"

He placed a protective arm around her shoulders.

"I think so."

"Then, having come this far, let me go on. A Prime Minister needs experts and advisers, and a large part of a Prime Minister's life, however much you may despise it, is purely social. Now, I may be a spoiled bitch who likes her creature comforts, but you'd have to go a long way to find a better-qualified adviser on the art of socializing."

"Are you proposing to me?" laughed Berman.

She looked him in the face.

"It's my turn, isn't it?"

★

He stood waiting in the VIP lounge—the same one into which he would be ushered the next morning for his flight to Washington, but now, at close on midnight, with very different emotions.

There was a brief shriek of rubber as the 350 tons of aircraft bounced onto the tarmac, followed a couple of seconds later by the roar of the reverse thrust, itself then drowned by the loudspeaker announcement of the arrival of the TWA flight from New York. Ten minutes later, a drawn, unshaven individual was shown into the VIP lounge. The eyes registered no surprise; only exhaustion.

"*Shalom*," said Berman, indicating a low chair and offering a cigarette, "they held you all this time?"

The cigarette shook between Kesler's fingers.

"You think I would have stayed there voluntarily, with my wife critically ill and when I wasn't even expecting to go in the first place?"

"No," said Berman, adding apologetically, "you are owed some explanations."

"Too damned right! You can start by telling me how my wife is, since all I could ever get out of the hospital was that she was sleeping or not to be disturbed."

"That was not their fault," said Berman. "They were acting on my orders."

Kesler's face suddenly assumed the expression of a man who feared his own powers of comprehension.

"What do you mean 'on your orders'?"

Berman watched the pale grey eyes recede into their sockets as he continued:

"Your wife died at 7:00 Monday morning—about the time you would have been landing at Kennedy Airport."

There was a long silence, interrupted by the loudspeaker requesting the owner of a badly parked car to come and move it. Awkwardly, absurdly, they both waited for the announcement to finish.

"I don't believe you, Berman," said Kesler at last. "This is another of your psychological games to test my loyalty. You just want to see how I'm going to react. Besides, she couldn't have died when you say—not so soon after I left her. She was feeling better, and she would have known if she was dying. You forget, she's worked in hospitals . . . she knew what drugs she was on and how much . . . I tell you she would have known she was dying . . ."

"She did know."

"What! And still let me go?" he mocked. "You expect me to believe *that*?"

"She let you go because I asked her to let you go. I asked her to lie to you."

Like an unstrung puppet, the lanky frame seemed suddenly to give way. With a clinical remorselessness Berman carried on.

"I asked her to convince you that she was better, because I knew you wouldn't believe it coming from the doctors or myself. She knew, as you say, precisely how long she had to live . . . knew that patients with a chance of recovery weren't given morphine in lethal doses. But it was vital that *you* didn't."

Kesler was shaking his head from side to side as though the words were too painful to hear.

"You're not making sense, Berman. She expected me back within a few hours—as soon as I could get back from the Kilometer 15 business. There would have been no need for her to lie to me because she would still have been alive if she didn't die till seven in the morning."

Berman steeled himself to deliver the second blow.

"She knew the truth about Kilometer 15—that nothing would happen there, that you'd be getting on the plane and couldn't be back for twenty-four hours at least. I told her . . ."

"Told her what, for Christ's sake?"

"That the plan was to switch the caskets in the X-ray machine, but that, for security reasons, it was necessary that you believed otherwise."

"You mean you didn't trust me. You thought I'd revert to type . . . Trusted me enough to let me risk my fucking neck for you but not enough to tell me the simple truth. The fact that I sweated blood on that freeway wondering which was going to get me first—a high-velocity bullet or a hundred pounds of explosive—*that* was of no relevance in your Grand Design, I suppose?"

"It was necessary," repeated Berman. "A man who has crossed the line once is always capable of crossing again. What we couldn't risk . . ."

Again the loudspeaker filled the room. Berman lit another cigarette, but this time it was refused.

"Kesler," Berman resumed, "your wife was an exceptional woman . . ."

"Who died alone," added Kesler bitterly.

The words hung in the air—half statement, half question. Berman hesitated and then said: "No, I stayed with her till the end. Before she lost consciousness, she made me promise to tell you that she loved you . . . and to tell you whatever was needed to help you understand her action."

He expected a violent reaction, a justified resentment that another man had taken his place at his dying wife's bedside, but grief had flooded in to quench Kesler's anger.

"Thank you," he said simply with what sounded like genuine gratitude, and helped himself to the cigarette he had previously refused.

"Do you think you'll stay here or go back to the States?" asked Berman.

"Don't know—haven't thought it through."

"If you decide to stay, you'll be granted Israeli nationality and . . . well, I might be in a position to push your way a job that would make good use of your writing talent and your knowledge of both the American and Israeli political scenes."

"A position of trust?" remarked Kesler, a glint of the old anger sparking in his eyes.

Berman looked away.

"The offer stands if you're ever int . . ."

"And what'll you do with the bones now?" cut in Kesler, catching him off balance.

"They'll . . . They'll be reburied—as required by Jewish Law. Probably within the compound at Dimona. There's a certain strategic and symbolic neatness in keeping the two deterrents—the ultimate and the penultimate—together. Also, the fact that we still have the bones is itself a more feasible and useful deterrent than any number of nuclear warheads."

"As you've demonstrated," observed Kesler coolly. Suddenly he was on his feet.

"If there's nothing more, there are things I have to do."

This much at least Berman had anticipated.

"Your son's remains have been collected and taken back to the Hadassah Hospital. There is an official car waiting to take you there."

Berman led the way in silence round the back of the airport building to the Authorized Personnel Only parking lot, the air heavy with the smell of burnt aircraft fuel. An official driver was leaning up against the car, arms crossed, a thin trail of cigarette smoke rising straight up into the night air.

"You were lucky," said Kesler apropos of nothing as they crossed the tarmac.

"In what way?"

"Chancing on the bones just when you needed them most."

Berman's pace slackened.

"That's not exactly how it was. They were actually found fifteen years ago—shortly after the Yom Kippur War, when the major building program started north and east of Jer . . ."

Kesler stopped and turned.

"Are you telling me you've been sitting on them ever since?"

"Well, the United Nations helped us without knowing it. Their protests about our violation of the old no-man's-land gave us the excuse we needed to stop the building work and cover up the tomb. It's one of the few occasions that we've given way to international pressure. I wouldn't say that we've been 'sitting on them' since then; rather that the discovery itself has taken time to come to light."

★

It was after two in the morning when a lone figure left the Hadassah Hospital, walked the length of its curving drive, over the highway at the bottom, and on down the slope of Mount Scopus to one of the few remaining patches of scrub not consumed by the sprawling complex of the Hebrew University.

He would sit there till dawn—knees drawn up, back arched, and head buried in his arms. Occasionally, he would look up to take in the Old City below or to follow the Valley of Kidron past the illuminated "onions" of St. Mary Magdalen, and up as far as the twinkling arches of the Intercontinental atop the Mount of Olives. But mostly he would keep his head bowed and his eyes shut. He would not sleep—not until the sun rose again over the Mountains of Moab to proclaim the Christian Sabbath, when he would return home to the house in Bnei Brit, to the upstairs bedroom with its long windows that opened onto the veranda.

Acknowledgments

The Institute of Archaeology, The Hebrew University of Jerusalem
The Rockefeller Museum, Jerusalem
The Government of Israel Press Office, Jerusalem
The Israel Defense Forces Press Office, Jerusalem
The Apostolic Delegation, Mount of Olives, Jerusalem
The Jerusalem Post
Moshav Talmei Yosef, the Negev
Harwell Nuclear Research Establishment (Carbon-14 Dating Dept.), U.K.

The above have all generously provided information which I have used in different ways. Mostly—in the case of locations, protocol, weaponry, etc.—I have incorporated it straight into the text. Since, however, this is a work of fiction set in the future, I have on occasions embroidered the known truth. To take two examples: The principles of carbon-14 dating and the procedures as described are accurate in themselves, but I have anticipated likely developments in speed and portability of equipment over the next five years; likewise, although the Israeli Government does have an Emergency General Headquarters, the detailed location of my Begin's Bunker is an invention.

For the record, the following references are factual insofar as they are drawn from academic works, nonfiction periodicals, news agency reports, and other such source material:

The discovery of the crucified man at Giv'at ha-Mivtar in 1968
The Pope *v.* Curia power struggles
The Nazarene/Nazirite controversy
The 1930 Sukenik lecture
The murder of Richard S. Welch in 1975

The Israelis' downing of both their own fighter and a Libyan airliner

The wartime history of the Lodz Ghetto

The activities, arrest, and release of Archbishop Capucci

Dr. Barbet's work on crucifixion

The findings of the Agranat Commission

Pope Adrian VI and the "Dutch Curse"

The Prophecy of Fatima—although the third remains a mystery

Where I have quoted the Bible, I have used the American Revised Standard Version, Catholic Edition, for the New Testament, and the English Authorized King James Version for the Old Testament. The "Burial Vault of a Nazirite" diagram is a concoction of my own, modeled on drawings and photographs that have appeared in the *Israel Exploration Journal*.

Finally, my thanks to a number of individuals for whose help I am especially grateful: Rabbi Henry Skirball of Jerusalem for checking my Hebrew; Signora Marcella Bonsanti of Florence for checking my Italian; Captain Peter Saxton of the International Federation of Airline Pilots' Associations for the benefit of his experience flying helicopters; and Peter Hebblethwaite, the writer on Catholic affairs, for his valued observations—not least, that "in fiction anything is possible."